STATESIDE

A ROBERT HOON THRILLER

#5

JD KIRK

CRIME

STATESIDE

ISBN: 978-1-912767-86-1

Published worldwide by Zertex Media Ltd.
This edition published in 2024.

2

www.jdkirk.com
www.zertexmedia.com

CHAPTER ONE

SO, this was it, then. This, after everything, was how it ended.

Not under fire in the western deserts of Iraq. Not at the hands of some sinister criminal cabal, or gun-wielding terrorist cell. Not in battle, or in glory.

But here, in his own bed, of a heart attack.

Fuck sake.

He could feel it, the tightness radiating through his chest, pressing down. Squeezing the breath and the life out of him. How long did he have left? A few seconds? A few minutes? An hour?

He didn't think he could lie here for an hour. His bladder wasn't what it used to be. Its capacity and the strength of the seal were both still decent enough, just as long as you added the proviso 'for a man of his age' at the end of that statement.

He needed to add that caveat to a lot of things these days.

There was a definite tingling in his left arm, he thought. The pain in his chest radiated down through him, making it hard to breathe.

He should probably shout his sister, but he had no idea what time it was, and she didn't take well to being woken up, even for matters of life and death.

And really, was that the last thing he wanted to see before he shuffled off this mortal coil? The skelped-arse, scowling face of Roberta Hoon? Was that the image he wanted imprinted on his mind as he slipped peacefully into the void?

No. Bollocks to that. If he was dying, he'd do it on his own.

Bob Hoon had just resigned himself to his peaceful passing when his heart attack stuck a finger up his nose.

"The fuck?!"

Hoon flicked open his eyes and came face to face with the grinning, semi-naked toddler who was sitting on his chest. He barely had time to register the fact that he wasn't dying when a hairbrush swung down and clonked him on the bridge of the nose, and made him wish that he was.

"Ow, ya little shite!"

Hoon covered his face with his hands, stemming the blood flowing from his nose, and shielding it from further attacks.

It was then, just thirty short seconds after waking up thinking he was at death's door, that Hoon felt a warmth cascading across his bare chest and into the hair of his armpits.

It took him a moment to identify the sensation, and a half second longer to recognise the smell.

"You pissing wee bastard!" he roared.

Grabbing the boy, he leaped from the bed, and thrust him out at arm's length. The movement was impressively fluid for a man of any age, although not as fluid as the stream of urine that continued to flow, uninterrupted, from the grinning child.

Cal Neish, the son of two detective constables Hoon had the misfortune of knowing, looked entirely too fucking pleased with himself as Hoon stumbled around the untidy bedroom in his threadbare boxers, trying to figure out where to put him.

"Fuck me, how are you still going?! What did you drink, the fucking Lake District?"

Cal continued to hold eye contact while Hoon zig-zagged around the room, leaving a dark trail on the carpet, strewn shoes, and discarded clothes that marked the route.

"Berta!" Bob roared. "He's pissing everywhere!"

A shout from downstairs suggested that Berta currently had problems of her own. Cal's twin, Lauren, wasn't quite the wee bastard that her brother was, but she still found ways of getting into trouble whenever the Hoons were called on for babysitting duties.

Berta's reply had been a bit muffled, but Hoon was fairly certain she'd used the phrase, "up the fucking chimney," which didn't bode well for anyone. It also meant that he was probably on his own.

Cal, somehow, was still in full flow. The spray was hitting Hoon on the tops of his bare feet, and his arms couldn't stretch any further.

Hoon's gaze fell on the window, and a decision was very quickly made.

The curtains were soaked by the time Bob managed to wrestle the window open, and the chest of drawers beside it would never be the same again.

Finally, though, with a roar of triumph, he thrust the boy out into the fresh air, and took great pleasure in the feeling of no longer being directly urinated upon.

A third of a second later, the pissing stopped.

Hoon ground his teeth together. "You little..."

As a matter of principle—and because he didn't trust the obnoxious little shit—Hoon continued to hold Cal out the window. His hands gripped the boy around the ribs and under the arms to minimise, although admittedly not completely eliminate, the chances of dropping him.

Cal hung there, gazing back at him. He was smiling like he knew a secret, but he wasn't peeing.

Hoon gave him a jiggle to see if that started things up again. It would be just like the boy to hold it in until he was back inside. That was the sort of thing he did. That was the little shitebag all over.

"Come on then. Let's be fucking having it," Hoon urged. The child's legs dangled limply, bare feet pointing down at the driveway below, swinging left and right in the breeze. "Out with the rest of it. I know you're fucking keeping it in there."

It was then, while holding a baby at arm's length out of an upstairs window, that Hoon noted the blue hatchback car in the drive, and the person in the front seat, looking up.

The reflection on the glass made it impossible to see who they were, but the concern on their face was unmistakable.

"Fuck!"

Hoon hurriedly pulled Cal back into the room, slid the window down, and closed the piss-soaked curtains.

"Shite! This is your fucking fault!" he hissed at the child, then he grimaced in pain when Cal slapped a hand down on the rapidly swelling bridge of his nose. "Ow! Jesus! Fucking quit that!"

Though he looked around for somewhere dry to set Cal down, Hoon drew a blank. The room wasn't particularly large, and any solid surfaces were littered with crushed beer cans, empty takeaway boxes, and discarded whisky bottles.

Cal, somehow, seemed to have been specifically targeting the room's soft furnishings, so the bed, pillows, and even the carpet were all too wet to dump him on.

From outside, Hoon heard the sound of a car door opening and slamming closed, and the crunching of footsteps on gravel.

He ejected another few obscenities, juggled the child as he pulled on a pair of creased and dirty—but miraculously un-pissed upon—combat trousers, then raced out of the room and took the stairs two at a time.

At the bottom, he met his sister coming out of the living room.

At least, he assumed it was his sister. The inch-thick layer of soot covering her face made it hard to be sure.

"For fuck's sake, Berta! You know the fucking Black & White Minstrel Show's been cancelled, aye? They're no' holding fucking auditions."

Berta scowled at him. He could only tell because her eyes changed shape, and he could see more of her teeth.

"What the fuck are you...?" she began, then she stopped when she clocked herself in the hall mirror. "Oh, Christ!" She reached a dirty hand up to touch her cheek, then thought better of it. "Is that me?"

Hoon's response was practically a squeal. "What the fuck do you mean? Of course it's you! Who the fuck else would it be?" He caught his own reflection, all grey buzzcut and wrinkles, then pointed past his sister to the living room door. "Did you get her?"

Berta jerked her head left and right, like she still wasn't convinced the reflection was hers, and was testing to make sure it was keeping up.

"Who?" she muttered.

"What d'you mean, 'who?' The fucking child you said was up the chimney!"

"Eh? Oh. No. The little madam was behind the fucking couch, killing herself laughing." She hissed a breath in through her teeth, still staring at her reflection. "They're going to be the fucking death of us, Bobby. And I'm no' convinced it'll no' be fucking premeditated."

The sound of approaching footsteps drew closer. Hoon thrust Cal in Berta's direction. "Here, take him. There's someone coming to the house."

Berta shot a look at the door that was soaked with contempt. "So?"

"So, I'm dripping with pish and you're doing fucking black-face! It's hardly a good first impression!"

Berta sneered. Again, it was all in the teeth. "Since when did you give a flying fuck about first impressions?"

Hoon opened his mouth to bite back at her, but then stopped. She had a point there, right enough. The events of the morning had knocked him off balance a bit. He'd only been awake about three minutes, but it had already been a roller coaster.

But, his sister was right. Since when did Bob Hoon give a damn about what some random stranger thought of him? He was in his own house. He could do what he liked.

The doorbell rang. Berta folded her arms and narrowed her eyes, like she was issuing some sort of challenge. Nestled in his arms, Cal stuck a cold, wet finger in Hoon's ear.

"Fucking quit that!" Hoon spat, jerking his head away and drawing a giggle of delight from the child.

He looked at the door, and the silhouette blurred behind the frosted glass.

"Ah, fuck it."

Whoever it was could take them as they were, or they could take themselves elsewhere.

He opened the door.

His breath caught at the back of his throat.

There, on the front step, was a woman he'd loved, and who he'd once thought could love him back.

A woman he'd thought he'd never see again.

The wife of his best friend.

The wife of the man he had murdered.

"Gabriella?"

Her name was sweet and sour on his tongue. She regarded him in silence as he stood there, half-undressed and piss-soaked, with a semi-naked child in his arms, and a female Al Jolson peering over his shoulder.

"Honestly," he said, and his voice became a croak. "Not one bit of this is what it fucking looks like."

CHAPTER TWO

SHE WAS SITTING at the kitchen table when Hoon returned, cleaner, drier, and more fully dressed. Her hands were wrapped around the chipped mug of the coffee he'd told her to make herself, right before he'd ushered Berta into the living room and warned her to stay out of their way.

The sight of Gabriella sitting there, surrounded by the humdrum every day of his kitchen, made him hesitate.

How long had it been since he'd last seen her? Two years? Three? Not since the funeral. He'd kept out of her way since then, for both their sakes.

She'd changed a little. Her hair was shorter, cut into a bob that curved down to her chin. Her skin still had the same hint of burnished copper to it, but her crow's feet were a little more pronounced than when he'd last seen her.

That said, she looked ten years younger than her fifty years suggested, and a century less than Hoon felt most days.

Although, despite the shock of it, seeing her on the step had instantly shaved a few years off his age.

Her fingernails were short, like she'd been biting them. She still wore her wedding ring, he noted, and the memories it triggered forced him to take a breath before he spoke.

"Sorry about all that," he said, quickly closing the door behind him to prevent his sister lugging in. "I was soaked in piss," he added, before coming to the conclusion that this detail may have been better left unsaid.

Gabriella smiled awkwardly, nodded, then looked past him to the door. "Yours?"

Hoon shook his head. "Naw, the wee one's."

"I meant, is *he* yours?"

"Oh! Right. Aye, that makes more sense!" Hoon cried. "I thought you were asking if I'd pissed all over myself. I mean, my aim might not be great sometimes, but I'd have to fucking go some to coat myself from head to toe."

He could hear his own voice like he was an outside observer. There was a desperate edge to it, and after listening to himself babbling on for a few more seconds, he bit his tongue to put a stop to it.

"We're babysitting," he explained, after pulling himself together. "We look after them for a couple we know."

"Ah. Right," Gabriella nodded like this made more sense. "You and your...?"

"Sister," Hoon said, rushing to nip any confusion in the bud. "She's no' normally that colour, I should stress. She's no' some sort of 1930s dancehall act. She just thought one of the kids had climbed up the chimney."

The lines on Gabriella's forehead deepened for a moment, but she decided not to question the remark any further, which Hoon was immensely grateful for.

He crossed to the sink, took a mug from the drying rack, then filled it with water from the tap. He tried very hard to ignore the slight tremble in his hand as he took a big swig.

"You're, eh, you're looking well," he said, wiping his mouth on his arm and turning to face her.

"You're limping," Gabriella pointed out.

Hoon seemed momentarily confused by this, then looked down at his lower limbs.

"What? Oh. Aye. A bit. Broke my leg a few months back. It's fine."

"Sorry to hear that."

"Aye. Cheers. Fine, though, like I say. It's pretty much good as new."

He bent and rapped his knuckles against his shin, then straightened up and nodded as if all this had proved something.

"Aye. Good as new," he confirmed.

A silence lingered in the kitchen. It was awkward and full of questions, like it didn't quite know what it was doing there, but didn't have the brass neck just to come out and ask.

"Have you—"

"Bob, I—"

They both smiled. They both laughed.

It was excruciating.

"Sorry, on you go," Gabriella said.

"No, no, after you," Hoon urged. "You've, eh, come a long way. I mean, I'm guessing. Obviously, I don't actually know where you're... And I don't want to. It's best I don't. Safest that way."

That was true. The less he knew about Gabriella's new life and new identity, the better it was for everyone.

After all, it was thanks to him she'd been torn from her old life.

Thanks to him that her husband was in the ground.

He didn't need to know where she'd been. He didn't deserve to know.

But there was one thing he had to ask.

"Are you OK, though? Wherever you are? Are you, you know, happy?"

Gabriella's mouth moved. Her tongue shifted around inside it like she was chewing over her answer.

"I'm not here to talk about me," she finally said.

"No." Hoon shook his head. "Course not." He crossed his arms, leaned against the sink, then crossed them the other way and straightened up again. "So, why are you here?"

Gabriella took a long, slow breath in through her nose. "It's about Miles."

Hoon's forehead furrowed in confusion at the mention of the name. Miles Crabtree was the MI5 agent who had first recruited Hoon to help investigate an international criminal cabal known as the Loop. Nice guy, largely useless, but his heart was in the right place, and he had the good sense to dislike most of the same people that Hoon did.

If the wind was blowing in the right direction, Hoon might even describe him as a friend. He'd never say that to his face, of course, because he didn't want the bastard getting too chummy-chummy.

But there were only a handful of people on Earth that Hoon trusted, and Miles, despite being a drone on the payroll of the UK Government, was one of them.

"Crabtree? Should have known. What the fuck's he after now?" Hoon asked. He necked his cup of water, lamented the lack of burning in his throat or buzzing in his head, then returned it to the draining board. "He too scared to come ask me for something himself, is he? No wonder. Do you know I ended up getting talked about on *Loose* fucking *Women* because of that arsehole? He's lucky I'm still fucking talking to him."

"He's dead."

Hoon felt the water turning sour in his stomach.

"Dead?" The word was flat. Heavy. It barely made it across the gulf that lay between them. He gripped the edge of the kitchen worktop behind him. "The fuck do you mean?"

Gabriella's long, curved eyelashes lowered. She stared into the mug she was clutching, saying nothing.

"What are you talking about?" Hoon prompted. "What the fuck happened?"

"He was in America," Gabriella began, after another few seconds' pause. "For... work. But, I don't know, off the record, I suppose. He had a lead on something. Wouldn't tell me what other than that it was connected to the Loop. Or, I don't know, someone in it. He said it was something big, but..." She sighed. "You know what he got like."

Hoon nodded. Miles had suffered more than most at the hands of the criminal network. It had cost him the lives of his wife and child, and almost destroyed him.

"And then what?" Bob urged. "What happened to him?"

Gabriella shrugged. "I don't know. He was keeping in touch, said he was starting to get somewhere, then nothing. He just stopped contacting me. Four days ago. He's not opening texts, not answering his phone. There's nothing."

Hoon felt the hairs on his neck pricking up, but for all the wrong reasons.

He tried, but failed, to stop himself from asking the question.

"You're in contact a lot, are you? You two?"

Gabriella studied her reflection in her coffee for a moment, then looked up at him. "Yes," she said, and she left it there. "I've got some details for people he works with, but they're refusing to tell me anything. They've made it clear, though, that if anything did happen to Miles, then there would be nothing they could do about it."

"Because he's not meant to be there," Hoon realised. "They'll deny all knowledge of him."

"How is that right?" Gabriella asked, and anger flashed behind her big brown eyes. "After everything he's done for them?"

Hoon felt an urge to point out that he was the one who'd done most of the things Miles had been given credit for, *thank you very fucking much*, but decided that now probably wasn't the right time.

"So, you don't actually know that he's dead?" he asked. "Nobody's told you that for sure?"

"No, but I—I don't know—feel it, I suppose," Gabriella said. She considered her mug again, then shrugged. "But I don't know for sure, no. Even if he is alive, though, he must be in trouble, or I'd have heard from him. Something's happened to him, I'm sure of it. Something's not right."

"He could just be having a lovely fucking time to himself on holiday," Hoon reasoned, but the look on Gabriella's face made him regret it.

Whether or not it was the case, she was fully convinced that something terrible had happened to the MI5 man.

A list of questions lined themselves up in Hoon's head. When had she last heard from Miles? Where had he been? Where was he going?

Did she love him?

"I don't blame you, Bob."

Hoon blinked, caught off guard by this sudden subject shift. "Eh?"

"For what happened. For"—Gabriella seemed to struggle with her dead husband's name, like it was fighting back against her—"Gwynn. For Welshy. I just... I want you to know that I don't blame you for what you did."

Hoon sniffed, shrugged, and shoved his hands deep into the pockets of his combat trousers.

"Right," he said, because he had no idea how else to respond.

"I did. For a long time, I did. I was angry," she continued. "But, I eventually came to realise that it wasn't you I was angry with. It was me. I was angry that I didn't have the guts to do it myself. That I couldn't be there for him the way that you were, and do what he wanted me to do. What he needed me to do."

Her fingers kneaded the outside of the mug she continued to cling to. When she looked up at him, there was a misty haze across her eyes.

"You were a good friend to him. Maybe his only true friend, at the end."

Hoon still hadn't come up with the right response. His head, for the first time in as far back as he could remember, was empty.

He was so busy trying to think of something to say that the next words out of her mouth blindsided him.

"You're Miles's friend, too. Aren't you?"

Hoon frowned. "What? I mean, aye, I suppose—"

"He was in Florida. Last I heard from him. He was headed for a town called Muckwater."

Hoon suddenly got a sense of where all this was going. He held his hands up like he was simultaneously surrendering to her and trying to ward her off.

"Now, hang on a fucking minute," he began, then the details of what she'd said filtered through. "Wait. Go back. What kind of fucking name's Muckwater for a place? That can't be a fucking real town. Where's it twinned with, fucking Stool Sample, Idaho?"

Gabriella didn't laugh. She barely seemed to notice that he'd spoken.

"It's a little place at the edge of the Everglades. I looked it up. It's on Google Maps, but you can't do the street view thing, so you can't really see it."

"No fucking wonder. The guy driving the camera car probably saw the name and gave it a fucking wide berth," Hoon replied. "He probably assumed that nobody on the face of the fucking planet would be bothered enough about a place called Muckwater to check. I mean, fucking *Muckwater*? What were they thinking there? Just go the whole fucking hog and call it 'Toxic Arse Spray,' and be done with it."

She did smile then, but it was slow and half-hearted, and it just made her look tired.

"He's got nobody else, Bob. Nobody else will help him. Nobody else can."

"I thought you reckoned he was dead?"

Gabriella's smile became thinner. Suddenly, she looked her age. Older, even.

"Then, he's got nobody else to make them pay."

She rose from her chair, leaving her coffee untouched. The scent of her swirled around the kitchen, sweet and delicate, but with an underlying kick of something sharper.

There was a time when Bob Hoon would have done anything for that woman.

Aye, he thought. *There was a time.*

"I'm sorry, Gabriella," he told her. "I really am. But, I can't help. Miles is a big boy. He can look after himself."

He wasn't, of course.

He couldn't.

Hoon pushed those thoughts away, boxed them up alongside the daft notion he'd once had that he and this woman in his kitchen might someday have a life together.

Some ideas just shouldn't be entertained.

"It was lovely to see you," he told her, not giving her a chance to reply. If she kept talking, he might buckle.

If she kept talking, he'd end up risking everything.

He picked up her mug, tipped it into the sink, then stood with his back to her, hoping she got the hint.

"Sorry it was a wasted journey," he said. "And I really do hope that Crabtree's OK."

HE WATCHED the shape of her through the frosted glass of the door, a slow blur of colour and movement that faded with the crunch of her footsteps.

She hadn't argued. She hadn't begged, or twisted his arm, or tried to convince him to help.

She'd just looked disappointed. And then, she was gone.

"Who the fuck was that?"

Berta's voice was a low rumble behind him. Hoon kept watching the door until he heard the *beep-beep* of a car being unlocked, then turned to face his sister.

She'd had a go at getting the soot off, with limited success. While she no longer looked like she was doing blackface, she did give the impression she was due to storm an enemy camp under the cover of nightfall. The solid coating of black had become a camouflage of greys and char-coals, with patches of blotchy red skin shining through the gaps.

"No one," Hoon told her. Outside, an engine came to life, and tyres crawled across loose gravel. "Doesn't matter."

Berta regarded her younger brother like a hawk watching a mouse scurrying through the fields below. Bob's jaw tensed as he tried to anticipate all the things she might say, then decided that he couldn't be arsed with any of them.

"Don't," he warned. "I'm not in the mood."

His sister sniffed, and crossed her arms beneath the heaving weight of her bosom.

"If you think I give a flying fuck, you've another thing coming," she told him.

She drew herself up to her full height, as if to hammer the point home, then stared expectantly at him, waiting for some foul-mouthed retort that didn't come.

"You OK?" she asked. The question, and the softness of it, surprised them both.

"Aye. Fine," Hoon told her. "Kids alright?"

Berta recognised the sudden change of subject, but didn't pick him up on it. "They're in their cage," she told him. "Though, the little fuckers'll no doubt find their way out again before I know what's happening. Here."

She thrust a large tartan flask so violently against his chest that it likely qualified as aggravated assault. He scrambled to catch it before she let it fall to the floor.

"I was going to bring that up earlier, but now you're here, you can shift your arse and do it yourself," she told him. Her eyes darted upwards, like she was shooting a dirty look at God Himself. "And this whole thing up there is still bloody weird, by the way."

"Aye," Hoon conceded, heading for the stairs. "You're fucking telling me."

CHAPTER THREE

HOON DIDN'T BOTHER with the special knock. He knew the rhythm of it off by heart now—the three, then the five, then the two, then the one.

Then the pause.

Then the two, then the four, then the other four, then the six.

Then the five, really quickly, and the final two.

Then a last follow-up knock, six seconds later.

He knew how to do it. He just could not bring himself to be arsed with it.

That was why the one-eyed Scouser living in his loft let out a panicky squeal when the hatch was shoved open, and tried to bury himself under a roll of what may very well have been asbestos.

"Fuck sake, Iris, calm down," Hoon said, creaking his way up the ladder and into the dimly lit attic. "It's just me."

"You didn't do the knock, Boggle," the Liverpudlian replied. The insulation dampened his volume, but not his accent. "How am I meant to know it's you?"

"Because I've got my fucking face," Hoon shot back.

He tutted, annoyed at himself as much as he was at the other man. It wasn't a stretch to say that Iris wasn't exactly stable. He'd never been the most well-adjusted person in the world, even back in their special forces days, when lives had depended on his knowledge of explosives and weaponry.

Back then, his tendency to get into trouble had earned him his nickname, which stood for 'I Require Intense Supervision,' and he'd gone by that for so long that Hoon couldn't remember his real name.

Nor, he insisted, could Iris.

A decade or more of living alone in a bunker on the Isle of Skye had turned Iris into a paranoid wreck, convinced that the government, 'the man,' or—depending on how far gone he was that week—aliens, were coming to take him away.

Hoon had repeatedly tried to persuade him that none of those groups would have the slightest bit of interest in a cycloptic Liverpudlian conspiracy theorist. But then, a few months back, a planning team from the Highland Council had declared the homemade bunker an unlawful construction, and had the whole thing bulldozed to the ground.

This, as far as Iris was concerned, had proved that dark government forces were out to get him. Despite the perfectly good spare bedroom just a ladder's length away, he'd been hiding out in Hoon's loft ever since.

"They can change people's faces, Boggle," Iris said, his voice still muffled by the roll of insulating material he was lying under.

Hoon sighed, squeezed the bridge of his nose between finger and thumb, then rapped out the pattern of knocks on one of the beams that held up the roof.

After the final knock, Iris sat upright like a vampire in his coffin, and let the wad of insulation flop to the side. His good eye looked over at Hoon, while the glass one, which had a life of its own, seemed to be studying the tip of his nose.

"There. You happy?" Hoon asked.

"Cheers, Boggle!" Iris held up two raised thumbs. "You can't be too careful."

"Well, clearly, you fucking can," Hoon muttered. He shook his head at the much smaller man in his ex-army camouflage gear, and at the sleeping bag rolled up in the corner of the loft.

Prior to Iris's arrival, Hoon had rarely ventured up here, other than to shove the occasional box of odds and sods into a corner and out of the way. It was now a mausoleum of old junk and spiderwebs, but Iris had made himself right at home.

"Here."

Hoon tossed him the flask. Iris caught it in both hands, raised it to his ear and listened like he was expecting to hear it ticking, then twisted off the lid and sniffed the contents.

"Is that vegetable again?" he asked, unable to hide his disappointment. "Doesn't she know how to make any other soups?"

"No. Does she fuck. She just makes that one," Hoon told him. "And if you know what's fucking good for you, you'll keep your mouth shut, because if she hears you fucking moaning, it won't just be aliens you have to worry about knocking you out and shoving stuff up your arse."

Iris winced, as if recalling some painful memory, then dribbled some thick, lumpy soup into the lid of the flask and set about it with the same battered metal spork he used for everything.

"Tastes different," he said, slittering half a mouthful down the front of his camo jacket. "You sure it's the same recipe?"

Hoon wiped the dust off the top of a box of Christmas decorations and took a seat. "There's no recipe. She just makes it up as she goes along," he mumbled, taking his phone from his pocket and thumbing the screen awake.

Iris slurped and watched him for a few seconds.

"Who was that woman?" he eventually asked.

"No one," Hoon replied on autopilot, then he looked up and narrowed his eyes. "Hang on, how the fuck do you know there was a woman?"

Iris's eyes both widened, though they still weren't pointing in the same direction. He swallowed down a mouthful of soup with a gulp. "Women intuition," he said.

Hoon's brow furrowed. "What? The fuck do you mean?"

"You know, women intuition, Boggle. When you can just sense women, like."

"It's fucking *women's intuition,* not women intuition!"

Iris's expression was a blank and vacant thing. "You're just saying the same thing, Boggle."

"Jesus fuck. No! I'm not!" Hoon sighed with exasperation. "Women's intuition is an intuition that women have, while, and I'm fucking guessing here, you seem to think that *women intuition* is an intuition about where women are at any fucking given time!"

"Oh. Right." Iris stared back at him, his lips moving like he was doing some mental maths. "Which one's the real one?"

"None of them! So, it doesn't fucking matter!"

Iris nodded, which jiggled his glass eye around in the socket. "It's probably the second one," he reasoned.

Hoon gripped his forehead, finger and thumb massaging his temples. He counted to ten in his head.

Then, when that wasn't enough, he counted to thirty.

"Forget it," he finally said, then he raised a warning finger. "But, if I find out you've bugged my fucking house..."

Iris laughed. A little too keenly, and a little too quickly, for Bob's liking.

"Don't you worry about that, Boggle. The only bugs I've got are body lice."

Hoon regarded him in silence for a few moments.

"Christ," he said, after some thought. "I don't know whether to be relieved or fucking horrified."

He turned his attention back to his phone. Iris continued to work his way through the soup. It was clear, though, that there was something on his mind.

"Are you going to go?"

Hoon didn't look up. "Well pardon fucking me for trying to give you a bit of company."

"I meant to America, like," Iris clarified. He was already wincing when Hoon slowly raised his head. "OK, there's *one* bug. Just one. Kitchen light shade. That's it, I promise!"

"You're a fucking..." Hoon began, but he didn't have the energy to finish the insult. "And, no. I'm not."

"Right. Good. That's great, Boggle," Iris said. The sound of soup slurping filled the loft space. The Scouser nodded at the phone in Hoon's hand. "But, if you're not going, like, how come you're looking at a map on your phone?"

Hoon frowned. His gaze crept down to the phone he'd been tapping away at. A small red dot in the Florida Everglades sat in the centre of the screen like a bite from a body louse.

"Fuck," he muttered, then he pressed the button that put the phone to sleep and returned it to his pocket.

"It's best you don't go, Boggle. Sounded dangerous. And, like you said, I'm sure your man, Miles, can look after himself, like."

"Right. Aye. Exactly."

"And, I mean, it's not like you owe the guy anything. He owes you, if anything. If it wasn't for him, you wouldn't have been saddled with your sister. You wouldn't have me living in your loft."

"I wouldn't have been on Loose fucking Women," Hoon added, but there was a distant, faraway note to his voice.

"Exactly! There you go. You'd have just been on your own, like you always wanted. Just you, with this big house all to yourself. No babies pissing on you to wake you up. No one coming round. Just nothing but free time on your own."

He brought the cup of soup to his mouth, and let the steam warm his lips.

"I mean, like, it's a miracle you didn't kill the guy yourself."

Had Iris been a different man, Hoon might have considered

the possibility that he was being played. But, the Liverpudlian wasn't smart enough, or maybe just not sly enough, to work that way. He meant every word.

And he was right, of course. All that stuff—solitude, peace and quiet, the place to himself—was what Bob wanted. He'd been the terrifying, no-bullshit boss for years, and nobody had dared come near him.

Now, he spent half his day pulling funny faces at toddlers, and sorting out the problems of half-wit policemen.

OK, mostly just the one half-wit policeman, but the point still stood.

He'd never needed friends beyond out on the front lines. He'd never quite known what to do with them, or where to fit them into his life.

Aye, he should be on his own. He was meant to be alone. But Miles Crabtree, whether by accident or design, had come along and fucked all that up.

"Aw... Shite!" Hoon ran a hand down his face and stood up. "Have you got a passport?"

Iris snorted. "What, with the photo and the microchip, Boggle? Course I don't. Why, do you, like?"

"Yes. Course I've got a passport."

"With a photo?!" Iris cried.

"No, with a portrait painted in the fucking Renaissance style. Aye, with a fucking photo."

Iris stared at Hoon. And, at the same time, at a box of old vinyl records in the far corner of the loft. Both looks were filled with horror.

"Aren't you worried they'll recognise you?"

"That's the whole fucking point!" Hoon ejected, then he pinched the bridge of his nose and did some more counting.

Once he'd reached a suitably high number, he exhaled and looked down at the Scouser huddled in his nest of insulation.

"Right. Well. Looks like I'm on my own, then."

"Just the way you like it, Boggle," Iris replied. And, for the first time ever, Hoon wondered if he'd underestimated the man.

"Aye. Just the way I like it," he said.

He rose to his feet.

He stoated his head off a low wooden beam.

He muttered a "Fuck!"

And then, to a soundtrack of a one-eyed Liverpudlian slurping hot soup, Bob Hoon went to find his passport.

CHAPTER FOUR

THE JOURNEY TOOK TWENTY-ONE HOURS, not including the bus to the airport.

The first bit, down to London, was fine. Just a quick jaunt in an aisle seat, with a young lassie reading quietly beside him, minding her own business.

The wait at Heathrow hadn't been too bad, either. He'd had a couple of drinks, almost got into a fight over the bill, then made his way to the boarding gate, thirty-seven pounds poorer.

It was the ten-hour grind across the Atlantic Ocean that had been the main problem. The direct flight from London to Miami had been cancelled at the last minute, and he'd been bundled on a flight to Houston, Texas, instead.

Because of this, he'd ended up in the middle seat in a row of five, jammed between a wheezing, red-faced man who'd never heard of deodorant, and a four-year-old American girl who'd never heard of shutting the fuck up.

After politely asking her to stop, he'd tolerated being hit on the kneecap by a semi-naked Barbie almost eight more times before he'd torn the doll's head off and launched it the full length of the economy cabin.

The girl's father, a boorish and loud Texan with a stupid hat, had tried to order Hoon to go and bring it back, and the foul-mouth outburst that had followed had almost resulted in the plane being diverted to Iceland.

The queue at US Immigration in Houston had taken almost as long as the flight itself, though it felt longer thanks to a five-foot tall, blonde-haired harridan screeching at people every thirty seconds that taking photographs wasn't allowed. Even though, as far as Hoon could tell, nobody had been.

And why would they? Unless they were planning an exhibition on the bleakest, most depressing sights in the world, why would anyone want to take a picture of this huddled mass of tired, smelly, irritable people?

Or, for that matter, of the line of passengers queuing to be vetted by them?

After eight more hours of delays spent in various airport bars, he'd boarded the final flight to Fort Myers Airport in southwest Florida, and had slept for around half of the three-hour flight time, albeit in thirty-second intervals.

When he'd left the airport, he'd immediately felt that something had gone terribly, terribly wrong. Either some cosmic heater had been left on a high setting for far too long, or he was having a stroke.

There was no air outside the airport. Instead, he was breathing in a sort of sticky moisture that coated the inside of his lungs and made his whole body feel like it had been sculpted from a wet sponge.

He'd been in heat before—the Iraqi deserts had been known to spike the Mercury—but this was something else. This was like someone had taken the concept of heat and boiled it until there was nothing left but the steam.

By the time he had stumbled his way to the car hire place, his shirt was stuck to him with sweat, and rivers of it were being diverted down the backs of his legs via the crack of his arse.

The building's aircon hit him like a tundra wind, instantly chilling the sweat to just above freezing point.

He'd been in Florida for less than twenty minutes, and already he despised the place.

Dishevelled, exhausted, and shivering, Hoon now stood before the car he'd booked from his phone while he had been kicking around the airport in Dallas.

Although, calling the armoured tank in front of him a car felt like doing it a disservice. Two people could have comfortably lived in the thing without necessarily ever meeting.

"Jesus Christ. Who did you think was going to be driving? The fucking Bigfoot?"

The young man smiled. He'd smiled a lot since Hoon had first walked in, though it was becoming less convincing by the second. He was hanging onto it valiantly, though.

Hoon had disliked him at once. He was somewhere between his early twenties and mid-thirties, and had so few remarkable features about him that he could only really be described as 'a human male.'

Everything about him seemed to have been designed to be as bland as possible, like he'd been stamped out of dough with a man-shaped cookie cutter, then dipped in a vat of wholesome sincerity.

He was so boring to look at that when Hoon closed his eyes, he essentially ceased to exist. He'd left so little of an imprint, that even when he tried, Bob was unable to recall a single defining characteristic about him.

He was also, it was safe to say, struggling a bit with Hoon's accent.

"I'm sorry, sir, did you say you'd like a bigger one? That won't be a problem. This is one of our standard-size SUV models, but if you'd like to upgrade to something from our luxury range—"

Hoon sighed. "No. I don't want anything bigger, son. I'll no' be running the London Philharmonic Orchestra to the fucking shops. I'm saying this is stupidly huge. My car'd fit in the fucking boot."

The smile lost a little more lustre. The young man's lips twitched like he was trying to replicate the series of low, guttural-sounding noises that Hoon had just made.

"You want to wear your boots in the vehicle? Sure, sir. Of course! We wouldn't have any kind of problem with that."

"Fuck sake. No, that's not remotely what I'm saying, son. Do you need your fucking ears cleaned or something?"

The car hire assistant's smile took another dunt. He glanced around the showroom to where other members of staff were ushering their customers out of earshot.

"I'm sorry, sir," he said, lowering his voice a little. "Could you please refrain from using curse words?"

"Curse words? These aren't fucking curse words," Hoon told him. "This is just adding fucking flavour. Trust me, you'll fucking know when I'm using curse words, son. How? Because your fucking nose'll start bleeding and you'll shit your guts all down the back of your legs. Now"—he clicked his fingers and made a beckoning motion—"keys."

The assistant rocked on his heels as if Hoon's outburst had almost knocked him off his feet. Then he produced a remote key fob from his pocket and handed it over.

"Don't forget, sir, over here we drive on the right side of the road!" he trilled, his smile rallying a little.

Hoon unlocked the door of the enormous SUV and began the ascent to the driver's seat.

"No, son. You drive on the *wrong* fucking side of the road," he said. "And don't *you* fucking forget it."

TWO HOURS LATER, Hoon was lost. He blamed the American woman on the SatNav, who'd managed to sound relentlessly confident while directing him along a series of long, uneven roads that had all ended at different swamps. Or, quite possibly, different parts of the same swamp.

He had ignored her repeated instructions to keep going, as he was fairly certain that driving underwater would invalidate the car rental insurance he'd been forced to take as a non-American driver.

Eventually, when she hadn't acknowledged his counter-suggestion that she should fuck off, he'd deactivated the whole system and decided he would find the place himself.

That had been an hour ago, and he was no closer to finding Muckwater than he had been when he'd started.

It wasn't like he could ask anyone for directions, either. He'd passed less than half a dozen other vehicles, and neither they nor the black bear he'd had to swerve to avoid, had been forthcoming with help.

And, of course, asking directions was not Hoon's style, bear or no bear.

Night was starting to draw in, and Hoon found himself yawning every hundred yards or so. The roads through this stretch of the Everglades seemed to run straight on forever, turning driving into a tediously monotonous affair.

The only thing that took the edge off the boredom was the occasional skoosh of the windscreen washers, as he tried to clear off the smear left by the latest giant bug to splatter itself across the windscreen.

If his sense of direction was to be trusted, he had taken a right off the Tamiami Trail a few miles back, and was now somewhere in the Big Cypress National Preserve.

A canopy of bald cypresses, slash pines, and the fan-shaped fronds of Sabal palms hung over the road, the last remnants of the day's sunshine flitting through gaps in the foliage. A kaleidoscope of reds and oranges danced across Hoon's eyes, forcing him to narrow them.

To close them, just for a moment.

He yawned again.

Just for a while.

A horn blared. High-beams forced his eyes open. Hoon gripped the wheel and wrenched it to the right, swinging himself back to the correct side of the carriageway just as a rust bucket pickup truck went thundering past, the driver communicating his anger through a series of elongated horn blasts.

"Aye, aye. Fuck off," Hoon hissed, watching the retreating tail lights in the SUV's rearview mirror.

He rubbed at his eyes, then opened a window to let some fresh air in. The humidity hit him like a punch to the face, and he wound the window closed again.

Through gaps in the trees, the SUV's headlights reflected off the surface of a murky, rippling water. More swamp.

The bloody thing was everywhere.

Up ahead, the road curved slightly to the left. Hoon slowed for the bend, and had just started to accelerate out of it when he spotted a shape lying across the cracked and weed-strewn asphalt.

He hissed and kicked his foot against the brake pedal, left hand instinctively grabbing for a gearstick that wasn't where it should have been, left foot seeking out the missing clutch.

Tyres squealed, black rubber staining the road surface behind him. The whole back end of the SUV started to skid, but he managed to wrestle it back under control.

The imposing front grille of the vehicle stopped just an inch or two short of impact. The car's shed-sized bonnet now blocked Hoon's view of the road directly in front of it, but for a moment he'd been sure he'd seen someone lying there, their edges picked out by the car's blazing headlights.

"Fuck it," he muttered, looking around to make sure it wasn't some sort of ambush. Who'd be ambushing him way out here, he had no idea, but old habits died hard.

He opened the door and made the descent back down to sea

level. As he did, the stench of the outside world assaulted him. The air was thick and heavy, laden with the earthy, organic scent of the swamp. It was a smell that seemed to cling to the back of his throat, a mix of damp vegetation, stagnant water, and the faint, musky odour of unfamiliar wildlife.

The sounds around him were equally overwhelming. A constant buzz of insects filled the air, punctuated by the occasional sudden splash of water, and the rustling of leaves.

Somewhere in the distance, a bird let out a cry like a widow in mourning, its echoes bouncing around off the dense foliage so it was impossible to tell which direction it had come from.

A little closer by, the gentle lapping of waves against the shore created a rhythmic backdrop to the other noises, like the swamp was a living, breathing thing.

Though the sun was more or less completely gone now, its heat lingered, and the five steps from the driver's door to the front of the car were among the most arduous and challenging of Bob's life.

By the time he made it around to the front, there was nothing on the ground, and no sign that there ever had been.

Bugs fluttered and danced in the beams of the headlights as he squatted to check under the vehicle. Given the tank-like construction of the SUV, it was possible that he had braked just a little too late, but there was nothing under there, and the wheels were notably lacking in gristle or gore.

He had almost convinced himself that he'd imagined seeing something there, when he heard a rustling from the trees lining the road on the left. Movement.

Staying low, he peered into the forest, scanning the deep dark folds of its shadows. He immediately got the feeling that they were staring right back at him.

Or that something else was.

The rumbling of the SUV's engine right beside him made

listening difficult, but he was sure he heard footsteps among the foliage. Running. Racing towards him.

He opened his mouth to bark out a warning, then stopped when he spotted the shape lurking in the undergrowth at the side of the road.

A cold, unblinking eye watched him from above a row of prehistoric-looking teeth. A tail as long as he was tall twitched menacingly in the long grass.

Down among the grass and reeds, the primordial behemoth hissed.

"Aye. Course," Hoon muttered. "Should've guessed. Eaten by a fucking alligator on day one. Classic. Wait till Berta fucking hears about this. Oh, she'll fucking love it."

Further out beyond the trees, something bellowed. It was a low, mournful sound that he could've sworn he felt resonating through his bones.

"The hell was that?" he wondered aloud. But, if the alligator knew the answer, it was remaining tight-lipped.

Hoon could only hope that this state of affairs continued.

The tail gave another twitch. Another hiss of air rushed from the animal's flared nostrils.

"Right, ya fucking walking handbag, cool the fucking beans," Hoon urged. The SUV was right beside him, but its ludicrous size meant he had a short sprint to get to the wide-open driver's side door.

The alligator was level with the door, but across the other side of the road. Distance-wise, they were pretty evenly matched. Hoon quite fancied his chances, but he had no idea how fast an alligator could run. He vaguely remembered hearing on a nature documentary that they could go like the clappers.

Or were they painfully slow? It was one or the other.

He kind of wished he'd paid more attention to the documentary now. As nuggets of general knowledge went, it would be quite a useful one.

"Hang on!"

He remembered that his phone was in his pocket. Staying low, he took it out, typed 'How fast can an alligator run?' into Google, then waited for the results to load.

They didn't. The network display at the top told him he had no connection.

"So much for that, then."

The alligator hissed at him again as he returned the phone to his pocket. It was starting to feel a bit like a bluff. This, Hoon reckoned, was one of those 'it's more scared of you than you are of it' moments.

He had half a mind to march over there and kick the thing right up the arse. Assuming, of course, that it had an arse.

Again, he should've listened more carefully to that documentary.

"Right, fuck it," he decided, then he stood upright, his gaze locked on the gator in the grass.

The animal hissed. The bulbous eye watched him. Sized him up.

And then, with a thrashing of its tail, it whipped itself around and shot back through the trees towards the water.

"Aye! I should fucking think so, too!" Hoon called after it. "Close call for you there, son!"

He was so busy being pleased with himself that he failed to notice the sound of footsteps rushing up behind him until they were almost upon him.

Spinning, he caught a glimpse of a fully naked adult man flying through the air towards him, balls first and legs akimbo.

He had just enough time to eject the first syllable of a questioning expletive before impact. They both went down in a flailing tangle of arms, legs, and genitals, then Hoon's head cracked hard against the ruined asphalt. He tasted blood, heard a high-pitched ringing sound, then the ground beneath him became a soft and squidgy, putty-like substance that sucked him down into it.

Far overhead, the canopy of trees spun like a centrifuge, and Hoon spent a nauseating few seconds trying to blink the world back under control.

By the time things had stopped spinning, he no longer had a naked man squirming on top of him.

That was something, at least.

He sat up, and caught an eyeful of a hairy arse crack as his attacker scrambled up into the SUV and slammed the door closed.

"Don't! Don't you fucking dare, ye scuddy wee bastard!" Hoon bellowed. He tried to get to his feet, but his legs felt too long, and he had more knees than he'd been anticipating.

He fell backwards onto the cracked and weed-strewn road, and barely had time to throw himself into a clumsy sideways roll before the tractor-sized tyres of the rented vehicle squealed through the spot where he'd been lying.

Sprawled on the ground, he watched the red taillights of the SUV go speeding off into the distance.

A few feet away on his left, something hissed at him from the undergrowth.

"Jesus Christ." He groaned. "I fucking hate Florida."

CHAPTER FIVE

"WELL, now, y'all lucky them gators ain't done made a meal of ya, roaming around out here this time of night."

The old man stood at the back of his ancient, rust bucket flatbed truck, one arm leaning on the drop gate like he didn't have a care in the world.

He was a tall, portly man, wearing a checked shirt and denim dungarees with a bulldog clip where one of the buttons should've been. The top of his head was bald, but long locks of silver hair hung down from the back and sides. Paired with his grey handlebar moustache, he could almost pass for a long-past-his-best Hulk Hogan.

"Aye, I saw a few of them, right enough," Hoon said. "And believe me, I wasn't out here by choice."

He had walked for a good three or four miles, limped for another two, then had practically thrown himself in front of the first vehicle he'd come across.

It had blasted its horn and sped up, and he'd barely managed to avoid being impaled on the jagged deer antlers mounted to the front grille. He hadn't been so lucky with the half-empty beer can that had been hurled from the driver's window as the pickup had passed, which had cracked him a belter on the side of the head.

Had he been in better shape, Hoon would've run after the gaggle of cackling bastards in the truck, like the big shiny robot bastard from *Terminator 2*, and torn them, one by one, through the back window.

Instead, he just gave them the finger, said some deeply uncomplimentary things about both their parentage and genitalia, then was almost knocked down by the out-of-nowhere arrival of the second pickup truck, which he was talking to the driver of now.

"Ya saw a few of them? Sure thing. But you can bet them boots o' yours that a lot more of them saw you." Laughter bubbled up inside him and emerged through the sides of his mouth as a series of hisses, like his body was performing an emergency jettisoning of air. "Guessin' they reckoned you was just too tough an' stringy lookin' to be appetising!"

"Ha. Aye. Maybe," Hoon said. It wasn't what he wanted to say, but this man was possibly his only chance of making it to civilisation. Assuming, of course, that civilisation even existed out here. "So, eh, I'm looking for a place called Muckwater. You heard of it?"

"Oh, I heard of a lotta places," the old man replied.

Hoon's nostrils flared. He did a quick internal five count, then continued. "Right. Aye. But have you heard of that place specifically?"

"Yessir, I have. Matter of fact, I'm heading that way right now. Taking my best girl drinkin' and dancin'."

Hoon glanced into the front of the pickup, but saw no one. Still, he felt a surge of relief rushing through him. Maybe, just maybe, he wouldn't end the night by being eaten alive in a swamp.

"Fuck, seriously? Can you give me a lift?"

The old man looked suddenly wary, like the request had triggered some sort of internal alarm.

"How come y'all're out here all alone, anyhow? It's a long, windin' road from nowhere."

"I had a car," Hoon explained. "It was nicked. Some fucking naked guy jumped me out of nowhere."

"Naked guy, huh?" The old man rubbed his moustache, trailing his fingers down the length of it like he was Ming the Merciless about to call for the head of Flash Gordon. "Dark hair? Face tattoo? Missing an ear?"

Hoon shrugged. "No idea. I mostly just saw cock and balls flying at me out of the fucking darkness. I didn't exactly have time to ask him for a mugshot."

The old timer chuckled. "Most likely Brett Goggins. He's been known to do that kinda thing. Brain's a little scrambled from all them bath salts. Nice boy. Good kid. But you's lucky he wasn't fixin' to eat no one's face off."

Hoon blinked. "That was quite a fucking juxtaposition of information in that sentence there," he said. He glanced deliberately at the cab of the pickup. "So, eh, any chance of that lift?"

There was another moment or two of hesitation from the old man, then he spat a wet wad of black onto his hand, thrust it out, and grinned a largely toothless grin.

"Welcome aboard the good ship Betsy-Mae, son. I'll have you in Muckwater before you can say gator stew."

Hoon didn't really want to shake the hand, but felt obliged to. As soon as they'd finished, he wiped his palm on the arse of his dirty grey combat trousers, where it joined all the other stains they'd picked up that evening.

"Name's Tobias. But most folks call me Humperdinck."

"Humperdinck?"

The old man's face fell. "But I don't appreciate it when they do."

"Then why the fuck did you even mention—?" Hoon blew out his cheeks, then forced a smile. "Tobias it is, then."

Tobias's toothless grin returned. "Hop on in up front, son!"

He started shuffling for the driver's side, and Hoon hurried around to the passenger door, not wanting to be left behind. When he pulled it open, a pair of big, watery eyes looked back at him.

"The fuck?" he ejected, still holding the handle of the door.

Across the other side of the cab, Tobias creaked into the driver's seat. "Now, don't you mind Betsy-Mae none. She'll just squish right on up. If you's lucky, she might even whisper sweet nothin's in your ear."

"Betsy-Mae?" Hoon looked from the old man to the passenger and back again. "It's a fucking pig."

"Incorrect. *She* is a prize-winning Florida Cracker pig, and the best darn co-pilot a man could ask for. Now come on. Want a ride, or don't ya?"

Tobias turned the ignition, firing up the truck. Betsy-Mae's big, wet eyes regarded Hoon curiously, like she was waiting to see what he would do. A frilly bonnet had been tied onto her head, the ribbons fastened in a bow beneath her hairy chin.

The pickup wasn't small, but then neither was the pig. At best, Hoon reckoned he had about half an arse width of room before he was encroaching on Betsy-Mae's personal space. Either he was sitting on the pig, or pig was sitting on him. Neither one was a hugely appealing prospect.

"How about I just get in the back?" he suggested, indicating the flatbed. It was rusted, and though there were a few bundles of rags scattered around the floor of it, it wasn't the most comfortable looking.

But, in the pro column, it didn't contain a full-grown adult pig in a fancy hat.

Tobias turned and looked back through the grimy strip of

glass at the back of the cab. Dirt and dead insects were crusted to it, making it almost impossible for light to pass through.

A smile tugged at one corner of the old man's mouth. "Sure thing, son. If you wants to take your chances back there, then I ain't gonna be the one to stop ya."

"FUCK. OW. JESUS."

Driving in a brand new, state-of-the-art, ludicrously oversized SUV, Hoon hadn't really noticed all the potholes pockmarking the road surface.

Now, though, in the back of a forty-year-old pickup with a suspension apparently made of concrete blocks, they jarred up his spine and rattled his bones.

It didn't help that Tobias was driving like a mad bastard. He had accelerated away before Hoon was even sitting down, resulting in a frantic scramble to stay in the back of the truck. He swerved and weaved from one side of the road to the other. At first, Hoon had assumed he was trying to avoid the potholes, but was now fully of the belief that the old codger was aiming for them.

"Jesus fuck!" Hoon ejected, as the front left and back right wheels hit two different ditches at the same time, almost catapulting him into the air.

Shouting was pointless. The engine was roaring like a Spitfire coming in for a crash landing, and some sort of star-spangled country music was blasting from the truck's ancient stereo system.

Add to the fact that Tobias's hearing likely wasn't great at the best of times, and Hoon had come to accept the fact that this was just yet another ordeal for him to tolerate.

And to think, he could've stayed at home.

Another spine-shunting jerk hammered him from below, the

cold metal of the flatbed floor bouncing him up, then slapping his arse as he landed.

"Right, fuck this," Hoon muttered. He grabbed one of the piles of rags. They turned out to be grubby, oily sacks. Hoon wasn't sure that he wanted to know what they'd been used to carry, but he hoped that, if he stuffed enough of them under his arse, they'd at least cushion him from the most jarring impacts.

That was when he saw it.

That was when he saw the snake.

Or rather, when he saw part of the snake, which had been covered by the sacks he was now hanging onto.

It wasn't one of the more interesting parts, like the tail or the head. Instead, it was a three-feet-long curved section of the animal's body, roughly the thickness of Hoon's thigh.

Its scales were a light, tawny brown, but with a complex pattern of earthier tones. Dark, almost black patches ran down the centre of its back, each one outlined in a thin ribbon of pale cream.

Between these dark islands were continents of reddish-brown, scattered across the python's body like an ancient, inscrutable map of a place Hoon had no desire whatsoever to visit.

Along the side that Hoon could see, black spots with pale centres seemed to stare out like unblinking eyes, watching his every move.

Quietly, without uttering a single one of the many, *many* obscenities that popped into his head, Hoon placed the bundle of rags back in the same spot he'd lifted them from.

He sat in silence, hoping for the best.

A moment later, down by his feet, another stack of dirty fabric rose from the rusty floor.

A diamond-shaped head appeared. Two beady eyes regarded him with slow, considered disdain. A forked tongue flicked out, hungrily tasting the air.

"Aw, for fu—"

A densely packed coil of muscle twitched, launching several feet of angry snake towards him. Hoon caught a glimpse of a dark, gaping maw, and sharp, backward-curved teeth, then he flung himself sideways and heard the *clang* of the snake's head striking the metal he'd been resting against.

It turned before he did, but a sharp, sudden boot to the side of its head was enough to buy Hoon half a second. He grabbed for one of the oily rag bundles, then the pickup swerved to hit another pothole, and he was tossed headfirst into the back corner of the flatbed with a grunted, "Ya bastard!"

By the time he'd flipped onto his back, the snake was above him, jaws unhinging, beady eyes staring down.

"Oh no you fucking don't!" Hoon yelped, snatching up one of the oily cloth bags. He dodged another strike, then pulled the bag down over the snake's head, and drew it tight around its... what? Neck? Throat? Upper body?

He really should've paid more attention to those nature programmes.

Twisting the neck of the bag to tighten it, he delivered a couple of right hooks to the snake's head, which did precisely fuck all to deter it.

The coil of its tail slipped around his ankles, pulling them together. Another loop of scaly flesh wrapped itself around his wrist, and he suddenly got a sense of the strength of it. It was like an iron rod had become liquid, but retained all its original core strength. It was already twisting itself around his arm. If it managed to tie itself in a knot around him, he was a dead man.

Only one thing for it, then.

With a sharp, violent jerk on the bag, he smashed the snake's head off the tailgate of the truck. Once. Twice. Again. Again.

"Fuck off, you big wriggly bastard!"

On the fourth impact, it seemed to get the hint. The grip on Hoon's legs loosened just enough for him to frantically kick his way free. It was still holding onto his arm, but with his legs back in play, he could turn himself around and get enough leverage to do what he needed to do.

With a roar of effort, he hoisted the snake above his head, exposing the full, terrifying length of it.

Then, still twisting on the bag that covered the creature's head, and bracing himself against the back tailgate, he launched all twelve writhing, wriggling feet of the thing into the darkness behind them.

For a moment, he saw the red glow of the tail lights reflected in the snake's glistening scales, but then they were too far away, and the shadows raced up to claim it.

Hoon sagged down, breathing heavily, his heart pounding in his chest. He rubbed his ankles and rotated his wrist, then shot a foul-tempered look back along the road.

"And good fucking riddance."

HOON COULDN'T REMEMBER a time when he'd been more grateful to arrive at a destination, even one as relentlessly grim-looking as Muckwater, Florida.

His first impression was that this was a place where all hope came to die. And, chances were, it would be a lingering, awful death, too.

It sat right at the edge of the swamp, which seemed to be encroaching upon the town, like it was trying to do the world a favour by wiping the place off the map.

Foot-high weeds sprouted through cracks in the road, like even they were trying to uproot themselves and get away. The pavements, what there were of them, were broken and full of gaps, like a meth-head's smile.

The whole place had a damp and decaying feel to it, like a cancerous lung filled with mould spores. Half the buildings were boarded up, their paint peeling and flat roofs sagging sadly. The other half looked like they were one stiff breeze away from collapsing into piles of soggy timber.

One of the more intact buildings was a general store that looked like it hadn't seen a customer since the Reagan administration. Through the grimy windows, Hoon could see that the shelves were half-empty. The only things it seemed to have in plentiful supply were booze, cigarettes, and despair.

If the Everglades in general was the devil's own arsecrack, then Muckwater was a festering boil upon it.

Tobias hit the anchors as the pickup pulled into a cracked and uneven car park, and the back of Hoon's head dunted off the filthy back window.

"Last stop! All ashore what's goin' ashore!" the old man hollered, then he let out another hiss of laughter before clambering out of the driver's door with his pig hot on his heels.

He was cackling gleefully when Hoon vaulted the tailgate and landed, ankle-deep, in something brown and swampy.

"How'd you like the trip back there? Have fun?" Tobias asked, and his eyes sparkled beneath the jagged electrical bolts of his eyebrows.

"No' really, no," Hoon said, which only made Tobias laugh harder.

"Peggy keep you company?"

Hoon frowned.

Somewhere, at the back of his brain, a tiny voice let out an even tinier groan.

"Peggy?"

"Burmese Python! Mighty fine specimen, too. She's friendly enough, but she sure can get a little frisky!" He winked theatrically, then put his calloused hands on the hips of his denim dungarees.

"Right. Aye. A Burmese... Right. Like a snake? That's a snake?"

"A constrictor! She ain't venomous, but she sure likes to give hugs to gentlemen callers!"

He laughed at his own joke, then his gaze went past Hoon to the scattered rags in the back of the truck.

"Guessin' ya got a real fright!" the old man continued, as his faded, milky eyes scanned the rusted flatbed. "Where's she at?" He pursed his lips together and made a sound like he was calling for a cat. "Peggy? Come on out, little missy. Come to papa."

Down at Tobias's heel, the pig fixed Hoon with an accusing look, as if it knew full fucking well where Peggy was.

"I, eh, I can't say I saw a snake," Hoon said. He wasn't proud of it. "Although, now you mention it, I might've seen something. Is she sort of twelve-foot long and scaly?"

Tobias's eyes widened hopefully. "That's her! That's my Peggy, alright!"

"Right. Aye." Hoon nodded. "She fell out."

The hope became confusion as the old man frowned. "Fell out?"

"Aye. I think so. When you were swerving to hit every fucking pothole. I mean, I only got a glimpse..."

"Oh, Lord," Tobias turned and looked back the way they'd come. The pig, on the other hand, remained fixated on Hoon, condemning him with its stare. "Shoot, Peggy! Not again!"

The old man began the frantic hobble back to the driver's door, whistling for the pig as he ran.

"Betsy-Mae, get your bacon-tastin' ass in that seat right now. We gotta go find your sister!"

With a single snort of indignation, the pig trotted past Hoon, hopped into the truck, then took her seat just as Tobias hit the gas pedal and went racing out of the car park, pulling the door closed as he went.

Hoon watched the pickup speeding off in a cloud of dust and petrol fumes.

"This place is fucking mental," he concluded, then he turned towards the only building in town that still had its lights on.

Or had some of them on, at least. A neon sign flickered above the entrance to what could well have been a long, low-roofed shed. A few of the letters had burned out, and it took Hoon a moment or two to figure out the establishment's name.

"The Gator's Hole," he read, then he tutted and sighed. "They're really fucking leaning into it, aren't they?"

The sign darkened for a moment, like even the ripples of air from his voice were enough to trigger a short in the wiring. With a *pop*, the lights returned, coating the peeling door below with a wash of red and blue neon.

It had windows, which was something of a surprise, but they were all boarded up, which wasn't. He'd seen his share of shite pubs in his time, but this one looked like it was going to take things to a whole new level.

The only way the place could've been more of a dive was if Jacques Cousteau had been circling it in a wetsuit and an aqualung.

It was just the sort of place Hoon had hoped to find. If anyone in this shithole town knew anything about Miles Crabtree, he was sure he'd find them in there.

He was halfway to the front door when he spotted the shiny black jeep with the antlers mounted on the grille. Stopping to place a hand on the bonnet, he felt heat still radiating from the cooling engine.

Through the passenger-side window, he saw a stramash of empty *Bud Light* beer cans.

For the first time since he'd left home, a smile crept across Bob Hoon's face.

"Well, would you look at that?" he muttered. He flexed his fingers and gave his knuckles a *crack*. "It must be my lucky night, after all."

CHAPTER SIX

THE FIRST THING that hit Hoon when he walked into the Gator's Hole was the stench of cheap whisky and poor sanitation.

The second thing that hit him was a pool ball. It came ricocheting off the cushion of an old pool table with a patchwork-quilt surface made up of various shades of green.

It bounced across the sawdust-covered floor like a stone skipping across a lake, then came to a sudden stop when it clonked against his shin.

Over by the pool table, a roar of drunken, boorish laughter rang out. Hoon glanced over, sizing up the four men making the racket.

A Bud Light-branded hanging light illuminated the table, making it the brightest spot in the place by quite some distance. The four men, all wearing torn-sleeved T-shirts and a range of redneck head gear, hung just at the edge of the shadow, beer bottles in hand, grins contorting the shapes of their awful moustaches.

Hoon bent and picked up the ball. It was a solid purple colour, with a number four printed in a small white circle on the side. He tossed it into the air and caught it a couple of times, then placed it very deliberately in one of his pockets and proceeded, without a word, to the bar.

As he walked, he sized the place up, and tried to rank it against all of the other shithole bars he'd ever been in. The only way to do that, though, would be by redesigning his entire rating system from the ground up.

Everything—literally everything in the place—was coated with a layer of thick brown grime. It clung to the ancient jukebox with its broken glass. It coated the wire mesh that surrounded a tiny stage in the back corner. The stage was big enough for two singers at a push, and even then, only if they knew each other well.

The same scum of brown muck crept up the walls and gathered in the corners by the ceiling. The walls themselves, Hoon realised, were leaning at a twenty-degree angle, like the whole place was slowly trying to throw itself into the swamp outside.

The opening chords of a Hank Williams tune began to crackle out of the jukebox. The twangy, melancholic sound seemed to fit the Gator's Hole like a well-worn glove, the perfect soundtrack for a place where broken dreams and broken teeth were almost certainly the norm.

There were three patrons slouched in mismatched stools at the bar, nursing their drinks and smoking tightly rolled cigarettes. Judging by the state of them, their hangovers seemed to have kicked in early. One of the three was asleep. The other two were wincing in the glow of the neon Budweiser sign above the bar's cracked and grimy mirror, their eyes bloodshot, their chins rough with days-old stubble.

To be fair to her, the only woman in the group carried the look off far better than either of the men sitting beside her.

"Hey. Give us the fucking ball back, buddy."

Hoon ignored the request from behind him and picked a spot at the bar. He leaned both hands on the countertop and felt his fingertips sticking to it.

The barman, a heavy-set older guy with cheese-grater skin and a rapidly retreating hairline, seemed utterly nonplussed by Hoon's arrival. He stood at the opposite end of the bar with a dirty cloth draped over the shoulder of his ill-fitting Black Sabbath T-shirt, and a bottle of Old Crow whisky in his hand.

"I'll have one of them, pal," Hoon said, pointing to the bottle, then to the bar in front of him.

The barman continued to stare at him like he was a ghost. The woman sitting at the bar puffed on her cigarette and squinted at him through the smoke.

Her hair was dyed red, just a shade or two darker than the lipstick she had smudged across her cracked lips. Too much sun had dried her out and shrivelled her up, giving her the colour and texture of a withered old orange peel.

"The hell kinda accent's that supposed to be?" she asked. Her voice was like two bricks being scraped together, and at least one of them was probably riddled with cancer. "You Scotch or something?"

"Or something."

"You sound Scotch to me."

"It's Scottish. Scotch is a drink," Hoon corrected. He whistled through his teeth and beckoned the barman over. "Speaking of which, come on, chop-fucking-chop, pal. It's been a long fucking day."

"You deaf there, buddy?" one of the men by the pool table hollered. "I told you to give us the fucking ball back."

"No' deaf, son, just no' fucking listening," Hoon said, not taking his eyes off the barman. "You'll get your ball back when I'm good and fucking ready."

An excited, "Whoa!" rose from the guy's gaggle of pals. Backs were slapped and pool cues were grabbed, like they were readying to enjoy a good ruckus.

"I'd just give them their ball back," the woman with the five o'clock shadow rasped. "Or'n they's gonna take it."

Hoon gave a noncommittal tilt of his head. "Aye, well. Good fucking luck to them on that." He stabbed a finger at the bottle that the still stationary barman was clutching. "Do you need me to come over there and work your fucking hands for you? Are you fucking coin-operated or something? Is there a big fucking handle on your back somewhere that I need to crank?"

This, finally, jerked the bartender into life. He picked up a glass as he shuffled up to Hoon's end of the bar, clunked it down in front of him, then poured in a finger of cheap firewater.

"You want Coke in that?"

Hoon's nostrils flared. "Oh aye, and how about a wee fucking daud of ice cream and jelly on the side?"

He put a hand on top of the glass before the barman could skoosh in a jet of syrupy cola.

"No," he said, flatly. "I don't want fucking Coke. Put it on my tab."

"You don't got a tab."

"Aye, well." Hoon raised the glass in toast. "I fucking do now."

As he brought the drink to his lips, a hand shoved him in the back. Laughter exploded behind him as a big glug of the whisky became just another sticky stain on the bar top.

"I want my ball." The voice was a low, menacing drawl, just a pace or two away.

"Aye, well, keep fucking going the way you are, and you'll lose at least another two," Hoon said.

He tried again with the glass. Another shove jarred him, but this time he was ready for it and managed not to spill any.

The chipped tumbler *clunked* as he set it down.

He turned and found himself looking up at two tiny versions of himself reflected in a pair of aviator sunglasses. The guy was a big bastard, with a Stars and Stripes bandana knotted around his watermelon-sized head, and a moustache so thick and bushy that he must've been cultivating it for all of his thirty or so years on the planet.

"This ball?" Hoon asked, fishing it from his pocket. "This what you're after?"

The bandana man held his hand out, but Hoon didn't pass the ball over. Instead, he tossed it from hand to hand, and scoped out the guy's pals.

All three of them were standing midway between the bar and the pool table. They were all holding pool cues, but with the heavy ends pointed towards the grubby, graffiti-stained beams of the bar's oppressively low roof.

"That your car out front?" Hoon asked. It sounded casual and offhand, like he was making small talk. "The one with Rudolph the fucking Red-Nosed Reindeer's forehead mounted on the front?"

A grin twisted across bandana man's face, revealing teeth the colour of old ivory.

"Holy fucking shit! Look here, boys. It's that hitchhiker guy!"

A burst of laughter rang out, making one of the old-timers at the bar momentarily jump awake.

"Oh, man!"

"That's too fucking perfect!"

Bandana man snorted like he was clearing his sinuses. "Sorry, we couldn't stop to pick you up. We had kinda a full house. No hard feelings, I hope?"

He sniggered, like he'd said something funny.

Reflected in the mirrored lenses, Hoon saw the barman take a few steps back.

"Now, are you going to give me the ball?" Bandana man asked, his smile losing some of its lustre. "Or do I gotta fucking take it from you?"

Hoon considered the much larger man looming over him, and his squad of sidekicks waiting in the wings. They had pool cues.

More than likely, at least one of them had a knife. Or even, given where they were, a gun.

Finally, he sighed. "Fine. I'll give you it," he said.

"Good boy."

"But I want you to do something for me," Hoon continued.

Bandana man's grin returned. "Oh, yeah?"

"Aye."

"And what might that be?"

Hoon held the ball out, like he was presenting it. "I want you to eat it."

The men laughed. The barman, who clearly had a sense of where this was all headed, retreated another few steps.

"The fuck'd you just say?" Bandana man asked.

"I know it might seem challenging at first," Hoon said. "Eating a whole fucking pool ball in one go. But if you get stuck, maybe your wee coven of inbred yokels over there can stop tugging on them pool cues like their fucking pimp's watching them, and help you out."

"Haha! You're a funny guy, stranger!" Bandana man declared. His hand slammed into Hoon's chest. His fingers tightened, bunching up Bob's shirt. "But, see, we don't much like funny guys around—"

Hoon snatched the guy's sunglasses from his face, snapped the plastic end off one of the legs, then buried the metal part in the side of his thigh.

That was why, rather than ending on the word "here," Bandana man's sentence instead became a high-pitched scream of shock and pain.

Hoon slammed the pool ball into the man's open mouth. It fit perfectly, give or take a few flying teeth, and the redneck stumbled back, gasping and choking as he frantically tried to cough it back up.

"See?" Hoon said. "Wasn't so fucking difficult, was it?"

And with that, the whole damn place erupted into chaos.

CHAPTER SEVEN

HOON WAS GETTING RUSTY. A big swing from a pool cue had nearly taken his head off, and he'd barely had time to pull Bandana man into the path of it before it had made contact.

The wood hadn't shattered into splinters like it would've in the movies. Instead, there was just a stomach-turning *thunk* as it connected with the back of Bandana man's skull, and a gasp of horror from the man wielding it.

On the plus side, it had at least dislodged the pool ball. Bandana man watched it bounce twice on the scuffed floor, before toppling like a tree and falling on top of it.

A bottle shattered at Hoon's back. He half-turned, but was too late to stop the bearded woman launching herself onto his back, the broken bottle neck clutched in her hand like a dagger.

She screeched like she'd been demonically possessed, which couldn't have done her nicotine-ravaged throat any favours. Hoon caught her by the wrist before she could landscape his face with jagged shards of glass.

Pirouetting, he launched himself backwards towards the bar, slamming her lower back against the coarse, sticky wood, and huffing all the fight out of her in one sharp, sudden blow.

She dropped the bottle. He grabbed her hair. With a duck and a pull, he flipped her over his head and launched her at the pool cue-wielding fuckwit who had KO'd his bandana-wearing mate.

They both went down together, and the cue rattled across the floor. As Hoon bent to snatch it up, the knee of one of the other men—a toothless wonder who was mostly beard and baseball cap —caught him across the jaw, sending him staggering into a free-standing ATM.

It was bolted to the floor, but the weight of a stumbling Bob Hoon was enough to rip the rusted bolts from their moorings. An alarm squealed, drowning out the insipidly sincere country song that had started crackling from the jukebox just as the first punch was thrown.

Hoon heard a racing footstep, and caught a glimpse of a fast-approaching cowboy boot. He blocked it, tore the metal spur from the back, then buried it in the kicker's kneecap.

A quick follow-up punch to the bollocks put paid to the beardy bastard, and Hoon shot to his feet just in time for a folding metal chair to hit him across the back.

Thrown off balance, he went careening across the bar until he hit the pool table. Grabbing a ball, he turned and launched it at the man with the chair. It missed, and smashed a row of spirit bottles at the back of the bar, spraying cheap booze and glass in all directions.

"Fuck sake. Now look what you made me do!"

Chair guy charged, his weapon of choice raised above his head. Hoon went for his middle, rugby-tackling him and driving him backwards into his pal with the pool cue. They all went down together, punching, and kicking, and hissing, and cursing.

BOOM!

The sound of the shotgun firing was like a dragon's roar in the confined space of the bar. It rattled the remaining bottles on the shelves and tipped the building's walls another degree or two closer to the swamp.

The noise was all-consuming, drowning out every other sound. It was as if the world had suddenly contracted, narrowing down to nothing but the shattering, ear-splitting report of the gun. A pressure wave followed that compressed Hoon's chest and struck his sinuses.

"Everybody just *calm the fuck down!*" the barman screeched, bubbles of snot and spit bursting on his lips.

A haze of smoke hung in the air, barely visible in the dim light of the room. Remnants of the shot lingered in the smoke, tiny particles of gunpowder and metal that swirled and danced before settling on the sticky bar top.

The acrid scent of gunpowder lingered, too—a harsh, bitter, burnt-metal smell that filled the nostrils and clung to the back of the throat.

The final echoes of the gunshot faded. Now, the only sound was an unholy, ear-splitting mix of the ATM's alarm, and Lynyrd Skynyrd's *Sweet Home Alabama* that stuttered from the old jukebox.

The barman snapped down the lever of the shotgun, ejecting a shell high into the air. Hoon realised that the gun was trained on him now, and slowly raised both hands above his head.

"Alright, keep your fucking hair on, pal," he urged. "No need to go all Dirty fucking Harry on us."

"Stand up," the barman ordered. "Up! Up!" His hands were trembling, making the barrel of the gun sway back and forth. At that range, though, with that weapon, there was no way he could miss.

Granted, he'd probably hit half of the other people in the place, too, but Hoon would take the brunt of it.

Hoon complied and slowly got to his feet, keeping his hands in full view.

"Here, these fuckers were the ones who attacked me, remember?" he pointed out. "I was just minding my own fucking business."

"You shoulda just given them the ball, like Krystal-Lynn told you to!"

"Who the fuck's Krystal-Lynn when she's at home?" Hoon asked, then he pointed down to the wheezing, semi-conscious woman on the floor. "Wait. Is that her?"

"I don't know who the hell you think you are, mister, but I'm giving you a count-a-five to get the hell out of my bar."

"Can't do that, pal," Hoon told him. "I'm here looking for a friend of mine."

"One."

"Can't leave here until I know what happened to him." He gave the man at his feet a kick. "Thought this gaggle of fucks might know a thing or—"

"Two."

Hoon sighed and let his arms flop down to his sides. "Aye, look, your counting skills are very fucking impressive, pal, but like I said—"

"Three! I ain't messing!"

"You'd best do what he says, son," one of the old timers sitting at the bar told him. "He'd be well within his rights. Legal-like."

"Who the fuck are you, his lawyer?"

The bum raised a shot glass in salute, knocked it back, then slammed it, upside-down, onto the bar.

"Yup."

"Four! I mean it! I swear to God, I'll shoot!"

Hoon suddenly got the sense that the barman wasn't messing around. He saw a finger tightening on a trigger, a gun butt pressing hard against a shoulder.

An eye was closed and an aim was taken.

"Aw," Hoon muttered. There was nowhere for him to go. No way to dodge. "Shite."

"Five!"

"Fuck. Wait!"

An eye closed.

A trigger was pulled.

And the roar of thunder filled the Gator's Hole.

CHAPTER EIGHT

DARKNESS.

The absolute absence of everything.

But only for a moment.

Hoon opened an eye just as the big dirty mirror behind the bar fell to the floor as big jagged shards.

"Drop it, Harlan. One and only warning."

A man in a wide-brimmed hat stood in the doorway, his double-barrelled shotgun trained on the barman.

He wore a khaki uniform that had seen better days, with frayed cuffs and a shirt pocket that was partially torn at the seam. A shiny gold star, tarnished and scratched, was pinned crookedly to his chest.

He looked to be in his late fifties, with a weathered, sun-beaten face that told a story of a life spent in the great outdoors. Tall and broad-shouldered, he had a slight paunch that hinted at too many meals eaten on the go, and too many nights spent drinking at the Gator's Hole after his shift had ended.

Even if the man hadn't been wearing the uniform, Hoon would have pegged him as a copper right away.

His accent was a deep, Southern drawl, as thick as the Florida humidity. The gun in his hand was locked tight and rock solid. Neither it nor his piercing blue eyes had yet deviated from the barman.

Standing behind the sheriff, pistols drawn, were two less impressive-looking deputies.

The first was a much younger man, maybe in his early thirties, with a lean, wiry build that could've done with a good feed. He had a mop of unruly dark hair that seemed to be damp with sweat, and a thin moustache that looked like it was still trying to decide whether it wanted to fully commit to living full time on his face.

His uniform was slightly newer than the sheriff's, but it was already starting to show signs of wear and tear. His badge was so straight it could've been measured with a spirit level, and was polished to a high shine, as if he was still trying to prove himself worthy of it.

The other deputy, not to put too fine a point on it, looked like a half-wit.

He was a large, lumbering forty-something, standing at about six-foot and weighing in at a good twenty-five stone. His face was round, doughy and flushed red, either from exertion or from spending too much time in the Florida sun. Or maybe, he was just embarrassed by this whole situation.

His uniform was stretched tight across his ample belly, the buttons straining to contain his girth. One half of his shirt was untucked, and his trousers rode low on his hips, held up by a worn leather belt that looked to be stretched close to breaking point.

His feet shuffled slowly on the spot, like it was taking a lot of effort just to stand still. Hoon got the impression that he wasn't a quick man, either physically or mentally. He stared blankly around at the bar, like he was trying to figure out where he was, and how he'd got there.

Hoon hoped, for all their sakes, that the gun he was holding wasn't loaded. He wouldn't trust that guy with a water pistol, let alone a firearm.

"They was fighting, Sheriff! This one done started it!"

"Did I fuck," Hoon objected. "Your fucking home-brew Village People here were the ones who kicked off. I was just fucking defending myself. Is self-defence no' allowed over here? So much for the land of the fucking free."

"I ain't asking, Harlan," the sheriff said. "Drop that weapon, or I *will* shoot. I don't want to, but you know I will."

The barman was still staring at Hoon, the gun shaking in his grip.

"Here, come on now, Thundertits," Bob urged, which earned a little snigger from the slow-witted deputy. "You seen the fucking hat he's wearing? A hat like that tells me he's a no-fucking-nonsense guy. I'd do as you're fucking told, and be quick about it."

For a moment, it looked like the barman might be about to open fire and plaster the walls with little bits of Bob's face and torso.

But then, with a little hiss of frustration and disappointment, he placed the shotgun on the bar top. The sheriff kept his gun trained, but gestured with an elbow for the brighter of his two deputies to go and retrieve the weapon.

Once the deputy had picked up the shotgun and safely ejected the remaining shells, the sheriff stopped pointing the gun at the barman.

And pointed it at Hoon, instead.

"Oi, the fuck's this now? I'm a fucking law-abiding citizen," Hoon protested, despite the pile of groaning, whimpering, bleeding bodies scattered on the floor around him. "You should be giving me a fucking medal for sorting this lot out!"

"Sir, I don't know who you are, or where you've come from," the sheriff intoned. "But I regret to inform you that you are under arrest."

THEY WALKED Hoon the hundred or so yards to the Muckwater sheriff's office with his hands cuffed behind him, and the shotgun trained on the centre of his back.

None of the men, despite Hoon's many and varied attempts to engage them in conversation, uttered a word as they plodded along the cracked, dried-out pavement towards a low, squat, cinder-block structure with bars on the windows.

As they approached, Hoon noted that the concrete walls were stained with water marks and mildew.

"That fucking swamp gets everywhere, eh?" he remarked, but nobody responded.

The building's flat roof was dotted with rusty air conditioning units that rattled and wheezed in the sticky, humid evening air.

"Does it ever fucking cool down here?" Hoon asked.

Again, nothing.

At the front of the building, just by the door, a faded sign bearing the sheriff's star logo was propped up against a wall. Two prongs of the star were stuck into a patchy lawn that was more sand and weeds than grass.

A few battered police cars were parked haphazardly around the building, their paint chipped and their hubcaps missing. They looked like they'd all been abandoned in a hurry, many years before.

As they approached, the quicker-thinking deputy jogged ahead to open the door, and Hoon was marched through into a bout of depression so acute it had taken on an actual physical form.

The sheriff's office was one of the dingiest, bleakest spaces Hoon had ever been in. And he'd been in Dundee. Twice.

Its stark fluorescent lights flickered across an ancient, yellowing linoleum floor. The walls had been painted, apparently decades ago, in a dull, institutional green. They were decorated, if you wanted to be very loose with that description, with faded posters warning about the dangers of crystal meth, and reminding citizens to buckle up while driving.

The main room was dominated by a large, battered metal desk, behind which sat a surly-looking middle-aged woman with a beehive hairdo and a cigarette hanging straight down from her bottom lip like she was doing a magic trick. She eyed Hoon suspiciously as he was led inside, her hand resting lightly on the butt of the revolver holstered at her hip.

"I love what you've done with the place," Hoon said. "Who'd you get in for it, Laurence Llewelyn-Bowen? He can turn his fucking hand to anything that man, can't he?"

The shotgun shoved him forward. He muttered a protest, then shuffled onward.

The air in the office was thick and stale. It tasted of sweat, cigarette smoke, and the faint, underlying funk of mould and decay. An ancient ceiling fan turned lazily overhead, doing little to dispel the oppressive heat.

For the effort those air conditioning units on the roof were putting in, they didn't seem to be doing much.

Over on Hoon's left, a row of old-fashioned cell blocks lined the wall, their bars rusty and their cots sagging. Most of the cells were empty, with the exception of the last one along, which held a small, scrawny wee guy with a missing ear and a face tattoo.

"Here! Is that fucking Brett Goggins?" Hoon demanded, indicating the lad with a nod. "I think he nicked my fucking car!"

"Mr Goggins has been here since the early hours of this morning," the sheriff replied.

"Fuck. Seriously?" Hoon muttered. He tried to look back over his shoulder. "I'd still like to report a stolen vehicle, though. Don't worry, it's fucking enormous, you won't be able to miss it. I'm sure if you call NASA they'll be able to spot the bastarding thing from space."

There was a giggle from the larger of the two deputies. Hoon didn't see the dirty look this must've earned him from the sheriff, but heard the deputy's response.

"Sorry. He's funny, Uncle Buck."

It was Hoon's turn to eject a burst of laughter. "Uncle Buck? What, like the fucking John Candy film?"

"I suggest you keep walking, and quit talking," the sheriff told him. "Else you wanna see a very different side of me."

"Well, I mean, considering this side's got a fucking gun to my back, that might not be such a bad thing," Hoon said, but he shuffled on towards a frosted glass door at the back of the room, where the lawmen seemed to be leading him.

The word 'Sheriff' was emblazoned across the glass in a shiny gold sticker that had seen better days. It clearly wasn't designed to stick to all the bumps and distortions on the glass, so a few of the letters were peeling away, and strips of masking tape had been used to hold them in place.

Just as he had outside, the more fleet-footed deputy darted ahead and opened the door, just in time for Hoon to be ushered into the sheriff's inner sanctum.

The room was a cramped, cluttered space that seemed to serve as equal parts office, break room, and storage cupboard. It was dimly lit by a bare light bulb that dangled precariously from a wire that trailed across the ceiling.

A single dusty window looked out onto the car park, the view obscured by yet another decrepit air conditioning unit that rattled and wheezed like a lifelong chain smoker in the grip of an asthma attack.

A scuffed wooden desk took pride of place in the centre of the room, its surface barely visible beneath a jumble of paperwork, empty beer cans, and greasy fast food wrappers. A grimy, ancient-looking computer monitor perched precariously on one corner, its screen flickering with a screensaver that showed the Windows 95 logo hurtling through space.

The walls were a dingy, nicotine-stained beige, adorned with a haphazard collection of faded wanted posters, outdated calendars, and a few framed photographs of the sheriff posing with an assortment of dead animals. Trophies from past hunting trips, presumably. A bulletin board hung crookedly on one wall, its surface obscured by a tangle of yellowing memos and Post-it Notes, the writing on all of them long since faded away.

In the corner, a sagging couch that might once have been brown but was now a mottled grey sat beneath a precarious stack of cardboard boxes, their sides stamped with labels like 'Evidence' and 'Cold Cases.' A small refrigerator buzzed intrusively beside the couch, its door plastered with stickers advertising various brands of cheap beer.

Though they weren't all that similar, something about the office reminded Hoon of his old one back in Burnett Road Police Station in Inverness. Probably just the lingering whiff of stale beer and bad food choices, he reckoned.

His old office had at least maintained a veneer of professionalism, even when he himself couldn't be arsed. This room, though, felt like it had thrown in the towel a long time ago, and was now just waiting for someone to notice.

"Sit," the sheriff urged, placing a hand on Hoon's shoulder and manhandling him into a hard plastic chair on the wrong side of the desk.

Sitting brought Bob down to desk level, and his face lit up when he saw the brass nameplate propped up among the paperwork and food debris.

"Buck Eisenhower? Is that your name?" he cried, unable to hide his glee.

"That's *Sheriff* Eisenhower to you."

"Fuck me. Buck Eisenhower. That's the most American fucking name I've ever heard! Although, I suppose this is when you tell me your two wee pals there are called Randy Eagleflag and fucking"—he gestured vaguely with his head at the larger deputy—"Teddy Constitution."

At the mention of the word 'constitution,' the larger, more intellectually challenged of the deputies practically stood to attention. Hoon was sure he saw his arm twitching as he physically resisted the urge to salute.

He considered humming the start of the American national anthem to see if he could break him, but it felt like it would be too easy.

And besides, he couldn't remember what the American national anthem actually sounded like, and if he accidentally slipped into a few bars of 'God Save the King,' he'd never fucking forgive himself.

The sheriff ignored Hoon's remarks, and nodded at both deputies in turn.

"Thank you for your service again, gentlemen," he told them. "That will be all. Y'all have a good night."

"Thank you, Sheriff."

"Night, Uncle Buck!"

"Arthur, you be back here first light."

"Sure thing, Sheriff."

"And Cletus, you tell your momma you did good today."

"Thank you, Uncle Buck!"

The deputies left. The door was closed. The floorboards creaked as the man with the shotgun stalked slowly around to the other side of the desk.

He set the weapon down next to a filing cabinet so full that none of the drawers shut properly, then removed his hat and hung it from a hook on the wall.

His hair was a crop of silver, cut into no discernible shape or style, with a few darker strands woven through it like undercover agents preparing to mount a coup.

It was a good head of hair, Hoon thought.

For a man of his age.

Sheriff Eisenhower let out a little grunt as he lowered himself into his chair, and despite the handcuffs and the perp walk, Hoon felt a certain sense of kinship with the guy.

"Long day?" he asked.

"Every damn one of them. And you ain't making it any shorter."

"I didn't start that. The Fucklebrothers were the ones that kicked off. After nearly fucking running me down, too."

The sheriff shrugged, and took a cigar from the top drawer of his desk. "Sticks and stones," he said, very deliberately snipping the cigar's end off with a little guillotine device.

"No, I don't mean they lowered my fucking self-esteem. I mean they literally tried to hit me with their fucking car."

"Ah. Yeah, sounds like them. Those boys've been pains in my rump since they was hanging off their mother's titties. They like to rile folks up. Usually get away with it, too."

He lit his cigar and the end flared red as he puffed on it. His blue eyes glinted behind the veil of grey smoke.

"Looks like they finally picked the wrong guy to mess with."

"Wrong guy, wrong fucking night."

A smirk curved up one corner of the sheriff's mouth. "Long day?"

Hoon grunted. "Every damn one of them."

"Well, then, I guess we got that in common."

"We've probably got a lot more in common than you realise," Hoon said.

"That a fact?" The sheriff set his cigar down in a Jack Daniels ashtray, then loosened his tie. "Difference being, couple of hours from now, I get to go home. You, sir, do not." He pointed to the door. "You'll be languishing right out there in one of them cells, with just that idiot fucking Goggins boy for company. And that boy, well, let's just say he sure likes to holler all night long."

His chair groaned as he sat forward and leaned his elbows on the desk, his fingers interlocking.

"Tell me, stranger, d'you like the sound of that?"

"Nope. Do I fuck."

"I thought not. You strike me as a sharp-witted kinda fella. You also seem like a man who knows how to handle himself. Am I correct in that assumption?"

"Maybe," Hoon said.

The sheriff's smile widened, showing his cream-coloured teeth.

"Modest, too. I like that."

He picked up his cigar again, then sat back until he was almost reclining. One foot, then the other, was placed on his desk.

"Because you strike me as a sharp-witted guy, and because I believe you know how to handle yourself, it's your lucky night, stranger."

"Oh, aye?" Hoon asked. "And how the fuck do you work that out?"

"Because I'm about to make you an offer that you ain't gonna be able to refuse."

CHAPTER NINE

BERTA HOON WAS FUCKING RAGING.

The first morning in days when she had the whole house to herself—with the exception of the one-eyed cretin in the loft—and a real possibility of a lie in, and some arsehole was hammering on the door at half-six in the bloody morning.

She had a good mind to go down there and cut their hands off for them. And, indeed, she might.

Wrapping her dressing gown around her like she was a boxer getting ready for a ring walk, she looked out of her bedroom window at the driveway, and saw three black SUVs parked out there with the headlights blazing in the darkness.

She would've found the sight alarming, had it not been for one important factor.

She was Roberta Hoon. She didn't do 'alarmed.'

She did angry, and all the various flavours thereof.

"Alright, alright, hold your fucking horses!" she bellowed at the window.

Then, pulling her dressing gown cord so tightly it would've cut less sturdy women in two, she charged out of the room and descended the stairs like a vengeful god.

"Are you getting fucking sponsored for every knock?" she barked, pulling open the door before the man in the dark suit and mirrored glasses could make contact with it again. "And what in the name of Christ are you wearing sunglasses for? It's the middle of the fucking night. Who do you think are? Tom fucking Cruise? Where have you parked your fighter jet? Because I know where I'd like to park the fucking thing."

The man on the doorstep seemed remarkably unfazed by this greeting.

"Roberta Ho—?"

"Up your arse," Berta said, for the sake of clarity. "That's where I'd like to park it. Sideways, with its fucking engine running."

"Roberta Hoon?" the man finished.

He was in his mid-forties, with dark hair that was starting to whiten at the temples. He wasn't tall, or particularly well built, but he gave the impression that he could not only handle himself, but would take great pleasure in doing so.

When he spoke, it was with the upper-class lilt of an English toff.

That was his second mistake of the day.

"Who's asking?" Berta demanded.

"The British Government," the man replied. He nodded past her into the house. "Would you mind awfully if I came in?"

"I'd very fucking much mind," Berta shot back.

She squinted out into the darkness, trying to get a sense of how many people were out there, but the headlights of the vehicles were trained on the door, presumably in a deliberate attempt to dazzle her.

"Have you got a warrant?" she asked.

"No," the man admitted. "However, in my capacity, I don't need one. You see, I'm not law enforcement, Miss Hoon. Please, don't let me give you that impression."

He clasped his hands together, as if pleading with her, and Berta noted his black leather gloves.

"I work for the security services."

"Oh, aye? And what one are you? Double-O fuck all?"

The man didn't smile. The precise, particular way in which he didn't smile made Berta pull her dressing gown even tighter around herself.

"There are a couple of ways this can play out, Miss Hoon. You can invite me in. We can have a conversation. I can leave." He held up a gloved finger. "That's option one. Option two involves handcuffs, and interview rooms, and a cell from which, depending on my feelings on the matter, you may or may not return."

He left that hanging there between them for a moment, giving it a chance to sink in.

"I have no real preference for either option, but I suspect you might. Most people in your position do. So, how about we go inside, and you put the kettle on?"

He clicked his finger and held out a hand. A figure Berta hadn't even noticed emerged from the darkness and passed him a paper bag.

"You make the coffee," the man said, holding up the bag. "And I'll supply the pastries."

HE INTRODUCED himself as Agent Fotheringham. Presumably, he had a first name, but he was in no hurry to share it.

He had given quite precise instructions for how he took his coffee—black, strong, one sugar—but had remained impressively unperturbed when Berta presented him with a mug of milky tea, instead.

Much to her disappointment.

The 'pastries' he had produced from his bag had turned out to be muffins, which he had offered quite a sincere-sounding apology for. It was the first thing that seemed to have dented his confidence since he'd first arrived on the front step.

Berta had assured him that she didn't mind, then had picked up both muffins, stuck her thumb all the way inside each of them in turn, then set them back on top of the bag he'd laid out like a plate on the table.

He picked up the closest one—a plump blueberry with, as Berta's thumb had discovered, a cream cheese frosting—and took a sizeable bite.

"Hmm," he mumbled, pointing to his mouth and twirling his finger as he chewed. "Tasty."

His point apparently proven, he returned the rest of the muffin to the table, dusted the crumbs from his hands, then finally removed his sunglasses.

The eyes that were revealed were dark and cruel. They were the kind of eyes that had watched flies wriggling around without their wings, and fireworks exploding up the arses of unsuspecting cats.

And they were fixed, like a missile lock, on Berta.

"So? What the fuck do you want?" she asked. "And why couldn't it wait until a reasonable fucking hour?"

"I know. I apologise for the early wake-up call, Miss Hoon," Fotheringham said. "But, unfortunately, terrorists don't work office hours."

"Bit fucking inconsiderate of them."

"Yes. Well, that's certainly one of their less appealing qualities, their lack of consideration for others."

He picked up his mug of tea, gave it a swirl, then took a gulp. There was, Berta thought, just the faintest implication of a grimace.

It wasn't the result she'd been hoping for, but it would have to do.

"A woman came here. Day before yesterday. I'd like to know why."

"What woman?" Berta shrugged. "I don't know what the fuck you're on about."

Fotheringham winced. This wasn't what he'd been hoping to hear.

"Remember what I said, Miss Hoon, about the two ways this can go? Option two is still very much in play. A woman came here. She pulled into that driveway, she came into this house, she spent thirty-seven minutes here, and then she left. I would like to know why."

"I'm sure you fucking would, but I don't know what you're talking about," Berta insisted. "Maybe she was a friend of my brother's."

"Robert. Yes. She was," the agent confirmed. "Unfortunately, he appears to have left the country. Dashed inconvenient. What that means, Miss Hoon, is that all this is left to fall upon your shoulders. It's very unfair, but there we go."

He removed his leather gloves, tugging on each finger until they slid off. His fingers were adorned by a variety of tiny, inexpertly done tattoos. Berta didn't recognise any of the symbols, though one could've been Christ on the cross if you used a bit of imagination, and if the artist had sneezed midway through.

"I'm going to ask you the same question nicely two more times, Miss Hoon," he said, holding up the corresponding number of fingers. "If I have to ask a third time, then my demeanour will change."

"Oh? Will you stop being an arsehole?"

Fotheringham smiled. Every angle of his lips, every curve of every tooth, set an alarm bell ringing in some deep, primal part of Berta's brain.

He held up a finger. One.

"What did Gabriella Evans say to Robert?"

"Fucked if I know," Berta said. "I wasn't listening."

That was true. Granted, Bob had filled her in on most of it before he'd left, but there was no way she was telling this toffee-nosed bastard that.

Fotheringham raised a second finger. Two.

"What did Gabriella Evans say to Robert?"

Berta sighed and raised both hands in surrender. "Fine. Fine. OK." She chewed on her bottom lip as she thought. "I'm pretty sure she said, 'Away and fuck yourself, you Tory-voting, mirror-eyed, flag-shagging, muffin-munching, horrible wee fucking goblin that you are.'" Berta sniffed and shrugged. "Or, you know. Words to that effect."

Fotheringham stared at her across the table. His dark, ruthless eyes didn't flicker, but Berta was sure she saw just the slightest flaring of his nostrils, and a downward twitching of one eyebrow.

Even years of secret service training weren't enough to keep Berta Hoon from getting under the skin.

He exhaled slowly. Steadily. "Oh, Miss Hoon, Miss Hoon, Miss Hoon," he said, and the words were a mournful whisper, like he was already grieving the loss of her.

He leaned his head back and looked up, as if seeking forgiveness from on high for what he was about to do.

Berta eyed up the range of weapons available to her. The knife block was a good bet, but there was a cast iron frying pan sitting on top of the cooker that was within easy-grabbing reach.

Panning in the skull of a secret service agent probably qualified as treason or something, but by fuck, it would be fun while it lasted.

Before she could grab for it, though, Fotheringham let out a little throaty gasp of surprise.

"Well, now," he said, peering into the light fitting that hung above the kitchen table. "What *do* we have here?"

BERTA CLAMBERED UP THE LADDER, her weight, and the force with which she applied it, drawing squeals of protest from each metal rung.

She didn't do the special knock, because she hadn't bothered her arse to learn it. Even if she had, she'd have refused out of principle. The last thing their unwelcome houseguest needed was more encouragement.

Bobby had always been too quick to indulge the bugger's deranged, half-baked fantasies. Given half a chance, Berta would've slapped the gibberish out of him months ago.

But Bobby wasn't here now. And Iris was more in need of a slap than ever.

"Right, you monocular liability, what in shit's name is all this about a fucking listening device in my kitchen light?" she demanded, shoving the loft hatch so hard it was catapulted into a full flip in mid-air.

She caught it one-handed, then continued up the ladder until her whole upper half was in the loft.

"Don't you fucking play dumb," she warned, squinting into the darkness. "Or even dumber than usual, I suppose. You've got a lot to fucking answer for, you earwigging, skelly-eyed, fuck-brained pile of..."

The lack of response brought her up short. That wasn't like him. Usually, Iris would be protesting his innocence by this point, or shouting for Bobby to come help.

Today, though, he wasn't making a sound.

Berta shifted her weight to one side, allowing light from the upstairs landing to squeeze past her not-inconsiderable bulk.

It pushed back the shadows, revealing the remnants of a makeshift campsite. Iris's lantern was there. Iris's sleeping bag lay unfurled on a bed of insulation.

But Iris himself was nowhere to be seen.

CHAPTER TEN

HOON BLINKED in the harsh white glow of the flashbulb, then thumbed at his eyes, trying to clear away the little circles of light imprinted there.

"Maude'll get that printed up for us," Eisenhower said. "Won't ya, Maudy?"

Maude, the surly-looking woman who'd eyed Hoon up from the front desk when he'd been led into the station, glowered at him like he was a smear of shit on her new carpet.

"Yup," she said. After some prolonged glaring, she plodded through to the back office with her ancient-looking camera in hand.

"She's a barrel of laughs," Hoon remarked when the door was slammed behind her. "Although, I'm thinking there might be a big fucking hole in the bottom where it's all leaked out."

"Maudy don't say much, but she's a fine worker," the sheriff replied. "She'll get that photo whipped up for us in the next five minutes."

"That'll be a lovely memento of my trip to Florida. Never mind the Mickey Mouse ears, here, stick this fucking mugshot on your fridge."

"Oh, no. That picture ain't for your mugshot," Eisenhower said, leading the way back to his office. He held the door open for Hoon to lead the way, and winked at him as he passed. "It's for your passport."

After returning Bob to the uncomfortable plastic chair, Eisenhower relit his cigar and pulled the cord that shut the blinds over the grubby window.

"Tell me, Mr...?"

"Hoon."

"You know anything about the drug trade?"

"Bits and bobs," Hoon said, not giving anything away.

"Well, round here, we got a problem with it. Manufacturing and using." He turned his back on the window, the smoke from his cigar circling his head like a halo. "You ever see anyone on bath salts?"

"Not that I know of," Hoon admitted. The cheap to produce crystalline drug had almost certainly made it to the UK, but that sort of thing hadn't been his problem in a while now.

"You're lucky," Eisenhower told him. "Couple of towns up from here, we had a father-of-two drown his three little ones in the swamp. Said they had the devil in them."

"Jesus," Hoon muttered.

Eisenhower's eyes flitted accusingly towards the ceiling. "No. Guessing He had other things to do that day." He puffed on the cigar again, then sniffed. "Out west, a sixteen-year-old girl got it into her head that there were wires running through her body. Through her bones. Cut herself open to get them out. Bled to death right there on the kitchen floor. Her four-year-old sister found her like that when she came in from playing in the yard."

The sheriff all but fell into his chair, like his legs had lost their strength. He considered the cigar for a few seconds, then stubbed it out in the ashtray.

"And that ain't the half of it. Meth. Cocaine. Some new designer bullshit they say's worse than all of them. Folks are either making it here or they are taking it here. That second group, I have some sympathy for. The first, I do not."

"Sounds rough. But what the fuck's it got to do with me?"

Eisenhower rolled his tongue around inside his mouth like he was searching for the right words. He steepled his fingers together, took a breath, then came out with it.

"I find myself in a predicament, Mr Hoon. See, just before first light tomorrow, I had something of an undercover operation due to take place. A gentleman—sharp and capable, like yourself —was going to pose as a buyer in a transaction taking place out on the swamp a few miles from here.

"We'd given him a convincing backstory. Made it look to anyone searching his details that he was a millionaire businessman from out of the country. He was going to hand over a briefcase full of cash, he was going to accept a case of narcotics in return, and then he was going to bring that evidence straight back here to me."

"Right," Hoon said, sensing where this was going. "But?"

The sheriff shifted a little uncomfortably in his chair. "But, let's just say, he went and got himself eaten."

If that was some sort of euphemism, it was a new one on Hoon.

"Like, is that code for something, or...?"

"No, sir. Went swimming where he shouldn't. Literally got himself eaten alive. Couple of big gators tore him apart."

"Fuck me," Hoon muttered. "I thought you said he was sharp?"

"He was." Eisenhower shrugged. "Guess the gators' teeth were sharper."

"Who was he? Police?"

"No. Well, once, but he retired. Investigator for hire these days. Or, he was. Fine man. Wanted to help fight the good fight."

"So, let me get this all fucking straight in my head here, Bucky boy," Hoon said, sitting forward.

Despite the turn the conversation had taken, and the potential thawing of relations, his hands were still firmly cuffed behind his back.

"You want me to pretend to be some semi-digested fucker, pretending to be a middle-man, pretending to buy a fuckload of drugs from who the fuck knows who?"

"That's about the size of it," Eisenhower confirmed, after some consideration. "But maybe we could do it with a little less of the cussin'."

"Fuck that."

"To the cutting back on the cussin'?"

"To the whole fucking shebang! How are they going to fucking believe me as their guy? I'll walk in there, open my mouth, and immediately get fucking machine-gunned to death. Thanks, but no fucking thanks. I'll take my chances with that spangle-eyed prick in the cell. Just bring me a fucking roll and square sausage in the morning, and keep the coffee coming."

One of the sheriff's silver eyebrows raised. "A *square* sausage? How would that work? You mean like—?"

"Don't fucking start," Hoon warned. "I'm no' going through all that again. My point is, I'm no' interested."

"You'll pass for my guy because they only have a name and a few basic details. They don't know what he looked like. They ain't even talked to him, so they don't know his voice," Eisenhower said. He sat forward, his fingers interlocked like he was praying. "These guys? They're amateurs, nothing more, nothing less. Uppity young bucks looking to make a name for themselves. Right here in my territory. But, truth is, I could move in and take 'em out right now, if I so chose to."

"Well, good. There we go. Just fucking go ahead and do that, then. Problem solved."

"Except, I want to know where they're manufacturing. If they got a factory hidden somewhere in my swamp, I want to know where so I can shut that shit down."

"Fuck sake. So, what's your plan? Tracking device in with the cash or something?"

It was probably what Hoon would have done.

The sheriff pointed across the desk at him, then brought his thumb down like it was the hammer of a gun. "Like I said, Mr Hoon. You're a sharp man. All I need is for you to keep your cool, make the swap, then turn around and come back here with the narcotics. Couple of hours later, I'll have all I need to make my move."

Hoon sniffed. "Is this no' a fucking DEA thing?"

"Down here, we prefer to keep the Federal government out of our business," Eisenhower said. "We deal with our own problems when we can."

"Aye, or rope some other poor bastard into dealing with them for you, you mean?"

The sheriff smiled. It was the first time he'd looked genuinely amused all night. And, quite possibly, ever.

"Needs must sometimes. I ain't happy about it, but I'm afraid that's where we find ourselves."

"And what's in it for me?" Hoon asked.

"You get to walk out of here a free man."

"Fuck that. You can't fucking hold me for long, anyway. I'll be out by tomorrow without the risk of dying in a hail of fucking drug lord bullets and being dumped in a fucking swamp."

Eisenhower used the nail of his little finger to pick at something stuck between his teeth. "OK. I hear you. What do you want?"

"Miles Crabtree," Hoon said. He watched the sheriff's face closely, but not a muscle moved. Not a hair twitched.

His poker face was too good, if anything. Too realistic to be all the way convincing.

"Can't say I know the name."

"He's a friend of mine. No, wait. Fucking scratch that. He's a useless bastard I know. Gone missing. Last heard of round this neck of the woods. I'm trying to find him."

Eisenhower's eyes narrowed. "English fella? Like you?"

The temperature in the room seemed to drop a degree or two. The atmosphere, which had already been stifling, became thick enough to choke a horse.

"I'm going to let that slide this one time," Hoon warned. "But, call me English again, and that shiny wee star of yours'll be so far up your arse, they'll need to install the Hubble fucking telescope in your lower intestine just to try and find it."

He let the threat linger there for a moment, then nodded.

"But, aye. *He's* English. Why? You know him?"

"Maybe," Eisenhower conceded. "I might have some information I would be willing to share." He picked up his cigar again, then lit it with a flick of his Zippo lighter. "But, if I'm gonna be scratching your back, Mr Hoon, then it's only right that I get to feel your nails on mine."

He reached into his shirt pocket, took out the keys to the handcuffs, and slapped them onto the desk.

"So, Mr Hoon. What's it gonna be?"

CHAPTER ELEVEN

THIS WAS NOT A REAL VEHICLE. It couldn't be. No civilised society would stick an enormous fucking fan on the back of a raft and call it a boat. It was ludicrous. It was nonsense.

It was also the only thing currently keeping Hoon from swimming with hungry alligators.

It had taken a bit of instruction before he could get the airboat to go in a straight line, and half an hour of practice before he learned how to turn it around.

There hadn't been time to rehearse all the steps involved in stopping the fucking thing, so he could only hope that friction and drag would handle most of the heavy lifting.

The training had been an hour ago, under the cover of darkness. Now, the sun had just begun to peek over the horizon, painting the sky in soft hues of pink and orange.

Were he a different man on another day, he might have stopped to admire it. Instead, he adjusted himself in the seat at the back of the airboat, the worn leather creaking slightly under his weight, and edged the throttle handle forward a notch or two.

The roar of the propeller shattered the tranquil silence of the Everglades, sending a flock of startled ibises flying from the nearby saw-grass, their big wings beating frantically against the warm air, their long, spindly legs trailing across the surface of the swamp.

The airboat glided across the still, dark water, leaving a trail of ripples in its wake. The air was even thicker with humidity than it had been the night before, and the pungent smell of decaying vegetation permeated it. Hoon had no choice but to breathe it in, and the earthy scent was a reminder of the wild, untamed nature of his surroundings.

He was, he realised, a long way from Inverness.

Taking his phone from his pocket—carefully, so as not to drop the thing into a fucking hippo, or whatever the hell might be swimming around down there—he checked the Google Maps app. A red pin marked the spot where the exchange was supposed to be happening.

Unfortunately, it was located slap bang in the middle of a big section of the swamp that, as far as Hoon could tell, was indistinguishable from all the other bits.

All he could do was rely on the GPS to keep tracking him. As long as the little blue dot was headed towards the big red pin, he should be fine.

Although, how long that state of affairs would last after he arrived remained the big question.

As the route led him deeper into the swamp, the vegetation grew denser. Towering cypress trees emerged from the water, their trunks adorned with shaggy, green Spanish moss. The leaves of pond apple trees rustled in the gentle breeze, their glossy green surfaces catching the first rays of sunlight. A few palm trees dotted the banks, their sharp, serrated fronds a stark contrast to the smooth, dark water below.

The buzz of insects filled the air, a constant hum that seemed to emanate from every direction. Dragonflies darted across the water's surface, their iridescent wings glinting in the morning light.

Mosquitoes swarmed around Hoon's head, their high-pitched whine like a bad backing vocal. He swatted at them absently, called them bastards and told them in no uncertain terms to fuck off, then fixed his eyes on the glossy, sun-dappled water ahead.

As the airboat rounded a bend, Hoon caught a glimpse of movement in the water. A pair of alligators, their scaly backs barely breaking the surface, glided silently through the swamp. Their eyes, dark and unblinking, followed the boat's progress. Neither animal reacted when Hoon gave them the finger and went gliding on by.

Hoon checked his phone again. The red pin on the map was closer now, the blue dot tracking towards it like a slow-moving homing missile.

The sun was already climbing higher in the sky, its warmth burning away the last traces of the morning mist. Beads of sweat formed on Hoon's brow. He wiped them away with the back of his hand, but not before the salt had a chance to sting his eyes, momentarily blinding him.

God. He fucking hated Florida.

Up ahead, half-hidden by the last dregs of morning mist, a platform about half the size of a tennis court bobbed up and down slap bang in the centre of the swamp's dark surface.

Hoon felt down around the side of his seat, and eased the throttle back a couple of clicks. The airboat slowed, the propeller's roar fading to a dull hum.

There was nobody waiting on the floating dock, and no sign of any other boats in the immediate vicinity. Hoon glanced down at the briefcase chained to the chair beneath him. It contained several impressive-looking stacks of hundred-dollar bills. Quarter of a million, he'd been told. A temporary loan from the evidence room, apparently, though Hoon had some niggling doubts about that.

Just not niggling enough for him to bother asking questions. If making the drop meant finding out what had happened to Miles, then make the drop he would.

Assuming, of course, that the suppliers actually showed up.

The first attempt at stopping by the dock resulted in Hoon overshooting it and having to loop back around. On the second try, he decided to just ram nose-first into it, which proved to be a far more effective way of bringing the airboat to a halt.

Grabbing the railing that ran around two edges of the platform, Hoon held the boat close long enough to tie it in place. Then, after unlocking the briefcase and fastening the chain around his wrist, he took a wobbly step onto the floating dock, and felt it bounce sea-sickeningly beneath him.

With the sun continuing to rise, and without movement and a giant fan providing a cooling breeze, the heat was already starting to become unbearable.

The cloud of insects that had chased him the whole way all caught up with him at once, and he slapped and scratched at himself to drive them away.

"Fuck. Off!"

He checked his watch, then the map on his phone. Right time. Right place. But a scan of the swamp in every direction showed no sign of anyone else approaching.

Hoon cursed below his breath. And then, for the hell of it, he cursed out loud.

The buzzing of the mosquitos grew louder and more insistent. He swatted them away, then realised that the sound was actually coming from elsewhere.

In the shadows beneath the overhanging palm tree fronds, an airboat had detached itself from the shore and started crossing the swamp towards him.

While he had made the trip on his own, there were three men aboard the other boat. Two of them were dressed in white suits with the sleeves rolled up, while the third—a sizeable older black man who sat working the controls—looked like he was pretending not to be with them.

The white suits were a bold move, given the amount of general muck that seemed to coat everything that came within five hundred feet of the swamp. As they got closer, though, he realised that both men looked young, which explained a lot.

Young people, in his experience, were fucking idiots.

While he waited for the boat to arrive, Hoon quickly ran over his cover story, rehearsing the name that was printed on the passport in his back pocket.

Maude, sure enough, had turned out to be a whizz, not just at taking photos, but at inserting them into the travel documents of men who had recently and unexpectedly been eaten alive.

As the airboat drew closer, the lads in the white suits pulled open their matching jackets to reveal handguns stuffed into their waistbands.

Hoon tried not to react. He hated guns. Specifically, he hated guns that he wasn't holding. Any in his possession were all well and good.

Unfortunately, the sheriff had refused to arm him, insisting it would be more dangerous that way.

Now, standing alone on a man-made plastic island, about to pull a sting on a gang of armed drug dealers, Hoon begged to differ.

There was a suitcase, also white, sitting on the deck of the approaching raft. It wasn't particularly big—a little larger than aeroplane overhead locker size, maybe—but it was the only place he could see where they might have stashed the drugs.

The puttering of the engine slowed, and so did the boat. One of the men in white leaned forward, like the extra few inches would make all the difference when it came to his voice carrying across the gap.

"Mr Mohammed?"

Hoon successfully stifled a grimace. When he'd seen the passport of the man he was supposed to be replacing, he'd almost called the whole thing off. Going undercover had never been his strong suit. But even if it had been, convincingly portraying Jamal Mohammed, an agricultural exports magnate from South Sudan, was always going to be something of a stretch.

"Yep," he said, and the word sounded hollow, even to him.

Both younger men regarded him in confusion. The older man at the boat's controls just looked bored, like all this was the absolute last thing he needed today.

Some mumbled conversation went on between the guys in the white suits, who he instinctively dubbed 'Tacos' and 'Clunge.' Even if pressed, he wouldn't quite be able to explain why the names fit. They just did.

"You don't sound like you're from Sudan," Clunge reasoned. He was stacked like an athlete and looked to have barely scraped in at the bottom end of his twenties. His deep, orange-brown tan was of the sort that would turn his skin to beef jerky by the time he hit the top end.

"Aye, I do," Hoon said. "This is what we all talk like."

It was a gamble, but he'd long-heard the stories of Americans and foreign travel. He had no idea what the fuck someone from Sudan sounded like, and was betting that these bastards didn't, either.

There was some more murmured conversation between the two young men. They tried to get their companion involved in the chat, too, but he was having none of it.

"What's the codeword?" asked Tacos. He was less rugged than his friend, and most likely the brains of the outfit. Although, that wasn't exactly saying much. The sun had reddened his skin, rather than tanning it, and he had quite a bit of white flaking going on around his neck and forehead.

"Hindenburg," Hoon said.

On the other boat, eyes narrowed. Hands reached for firearms.

"Wait. No. The other one." Hoon clicked his fingers a few times, making a show of trying to recall. "Heisenberg."

The other men relaxed. Clunge broke into a broad, slightly oafish smile. "Breaking Bad, baby!"

Tacos gave the pilot a nod, and the airboat crept on until it was close enough for the white-suited imbeciles to hop onto the platform.

"You seen that? You get that over there?" Clunge asked. "Breaking Bad? You seen it?"

Hoon shook his head. "No."

"Fuck! It's amazing. You gotta see it. You know Malcolm in the Middle?"

"No," Hoon said again, then he held up a hand before Clunge could continue. "I don't care."

The bulky black man in the boat was looking Hoon up and down. He was getting the measure of him, and going by the look on his face, the numbers weren't adding up.

Time to go on the offensive, then.

"Actually, sorry, lads, I've changed my mind," he said. He shook his head. "Something about this doesn't feel right."

Taco's eyes widened. "What?"

"I don't know. Maybe it's you two being dressed like you're time-travelling background artists from an episode of Miami Vice, but I don't like it. I don't trust you. No offence." He jabbed a thumb back over his shoulder. "So, how about I just jump on my fucking floating hair dryer there, and be on my way? No hard feelings. Better luck next time."

"Hey, fuck that!" Clunge snapped, scrabbling inexpertly for his gun. Tacos quickly stepped in front of him, though, hands raised to try and calm the situation.

"Whoa, whoa, everyone just cool down," he instructed. "Everyone just calm down and listen to me."

"Nah, bro. It's all gone to shit. Let me shoot him," Clunge insisted.

"Nothing has gone to shit. Nothing is fucked here," Tacos said. He nodded encouragingly at Hoon. "Right, Mr Mohammed? We all just want the same thing. A smooth deal. That's all we want."

Hoon eyed up the airboat like he was considering making his escape, then slowly nodded. "Aye."

"Great! See? We're all good. We're all cool. We're all just chillin' like villains." Tacos' smile was friendly, but he was keeping a careful eye on his partner, whose handgun was still half drawn.

It was only a barked intervention from the older pilot that made Clunge slide the firearm all the way back into his belt. The order was abrupt, and spoken in a voice that belonged in a smoky basement jazz bar.

"Do what he says. Gun away."

"Cheers for that," Hoon said, once Clunge had released his grip on the weapon, but the man in the boat didn't acknowledge him.

"You've got the money?" Tacos asked, his gaze flitting hungrily to the briefcase attached by the length of chain to Hoon's wrist.

Hoon nodded. "You got the gear?"

"Fuck, yeah, we do!" Clunge crowed.

Hoon's nostrils flared. He pointed at the more tanned of the two young men, but kept his gaze on Tacos. "He's fun, isn't he? Bet he doesn't get fucking irritating within two minutes of being in his company."

"The hell did he just say?" Clunge demanded, his hand grasping for his gun again.

"Can we maybe be fucking professionals here?" Hoon snapped. "I don't need you waving your nine-millimetre cock substitute in my face, son. If you try it again, you're liable to wind up fucking chewing on it. Now, here."

He thrust the briefcase into Tacos' arms, the eighteen-inch

chain still tethering him to it. Then, with a stabbing finger, he pointed to the suitcase on the other boat.

"You check this, I'll check that, then we can all fuck off and go our separate ways. How does that grab you all?"

Tacos ran his hand across the top of the case, his eyes blazing with excitement, like he'd uncovered some priceless ancient artefact.

Behind him, the older man picked up the suitcase and slid it onto the platform deck, where Clunge picked it up, then placed it back down beside his partner.

Hoon, meanwhile, patted at his pockets, searching for the key that would unlock the chain securing the briefcase to his wrist.

He had just started to repeat the process for a second time when Tacos flicked the locks that opened the case, and excitedly lifted the lid.

There was silence for a moment, save for the lapping of the swamp water against the boats, and the incessant buzzing of flying bugs.

Then, the spell was broken.

"What the fuck? What the fuck is this?" Tacos demanded.

Hoon felt the fine hairs on the back of his neck prick up. His mind raced both back into the past and forward into the future, already piecing together some possibilities for what might have happened.

And what could be about to.

He'd seen the money with his own eyes. He'd been shown it. He knew it was there in the briefcase.

But he hadn't kept track of the case the whole time.

Tacos spun it towards him, Clunge already drawing his gun.

The satin-white inside lid of the case carried a message written in thick, black marker pen.

'This is what happens when you try and move in on my territory.'

"What the fuck is that?" Tacos hissed.

"Eh, looks like a message," Hoon said. Quite reasonably, he thought, given the circumstances.

"Not that. *That!*"

Hoon followed the younger man's finger to the bottom part of the case. A stash of cut-up old phone book pages had been stuffed in to make the weight feel right.

In the middle of it, fixed to the inside base, a series of numbers counted down on an LED display.

"Oh. Right. That," Hoon said, his heart simultaneously sinking and racing. "I'm pretty sure that's a fucking bomb."

CHAPTER TWELVE

"WHAT THE FUCK? What the fuck? Who the fuck are you?"

Clunge's shouts rolled across the surface of the swamp, scaring the life out of a family of long-necked birds who'd been minding their own business in the reeds by the closest bank. They took to the air, squawking their annoyance as they headed off in search of pastures less populated.

Tacos was still holding onto the case, the lid still open. He stood frozen, as if worried that one wrong move might turn them all into a collective lump of fiery innards.

The guy on the boat—Moominpappa, as Hoon decided right there and then to name him—hadn't shown his hand yet, but Hoon got the impression he was a few seconds away from slamming the throttle into reverse and getting the hell out of the blast radius.

Clunge scurried forward, his Glock handgun fully out and held sideways like he'd no doubt seen people do on the telly. It was pointed very approximately at Hoon's head, but waved around so it covered an area around two or three feet on either side.

"Look, hold your fucking horses," Hoon said. "I can explain."

Tacos risked raising his eyes from the briefcase, but otherwise didn't move a muscle.

Hoon thought for a moment, then shook his head. "Actually, no, I can't think of anything."

"You fucking set us up! You're working with Eisenhower!" Clunge bellowed. He took another lunging step closer, the gun narrowing its target area.

"Right, fine. OK. Aye. I got roped into it," Hoon said. He was still confident that Clunge's shot would go wide, but less so than he'd been a moment before. "You know what the fucking cops are like. I didn't have a choice. But we can fix this."

"Cops!" Clunge snorted. "This isn't about him being a fucking cop. This is about us trying to take some of his territory!"

Hoon looked between the three men. Tacos remained frozen in place, like his personal timeline had ground to a halt. Moomin-pappa had his hands on the controls of the boat, but hadn't yet beat a retreat.

"Wait. What are you saying?" Hoon asked. "He's dodgy? I mean, I suppose that would explain the fucking bomb, right enough."

"Well, *duh*! Hello? Anyone fucking in there?" Clunge cried, rapping his knuckles against the side of his head. It was just as well, for his sake, that he hadn't tried to do that to Hoon. "He and his fucking brothers have got the whole trade sewn up. So guys like us can't even make a start in the business."

"Aw, my fucking heart bleeds, son," Hoon said. "Who knew the drug trade could be so fucking unfair? You should maybe put a complaint in to the Competitions Authority, see what they have to say on the matter."

He pointed to the briefcase that Tacos was holding. "But, in the meantime, there's a fucking bomb we should maybe deal with, eh?"

"Oh, I know how to deal with it," Clunge hissed. He took two big paces forward, brought the gun up until it was level with

Hoon's head, then yelped with surprise when the Glock was wrenched from his grip.

A single gunshot rang out. Clunge teetered for a moment, then looked down at the big red stain in the thigh of his otherwise pristine white suit.

Screaming, he fell onto the deck, frantically trying to stem the blood currently pumping from his leg.

"See, that's why that suit was a bad fucking idea," Hoon told him, waving the confiscated gun at the injury. "Well, one of the reasons, anyway. It also looks fucking ridiculous."

He tucked the Glock into the back of his belt, and started to search his pockets again.

"Now, how long does it say on that timer?" he asked.

Tacos, who still hadn't moved, summoned the courage to divert his gaze downwards. "Three minutes and seven seconds."

"Right. Good. Plenty of fucking time. We'll get this unlocked, horse it into the water, then I'll personally lead the fucking charge back to that sheriff prick, and we can all take turns—"

The bark of machine-gun fire made Hoon duck for cover, just as Tacos' body began to violently spasm. Hot, screaming lead tore through his flesh, as Moominpappa unleashed a volley of fire from an M27 assault rifle in the general direction of the platform.

"Fuck!"

Hoon dived for his airboat, blindly returning fire, the bomb in the briefcase bouncing along the platform behind him.

He was on the boat before Tacos had hit the deck. Some squealed protests and high-pitched pleading from Clunge were cut short by another staccato burst of fire.

The distraction bought Hoon enough time to fire up the airboat and jam the throttle forward. He gripped the seat as the big fan kicked in at top speed, lurching the airboat away from the man-made island.

The assault rifle called after him. Bullets whistled past his head and peppered the swamp on either side, spraying murky water into the air like little volcanic eruptions.

Twisting, Hoon shot the Glock back over his shoulder, but he was in a fast-moving vehicle, aimlessly firing at a target he couldn't see, and all he was doing was wasting bullets.

"Fuck, fuck, fuck," he hissed, ducking as another few rounds of ammunition scorched the air around him.

The boat was still accelerating, but was already skimming across the surface of the swamp. The boat's speed forced the thick and humid Florida air down his throat until he was almost choking on it.

Behind him, the much louder engine of the other boat became a guttural roar, like some hungry predator chasing him down.

Hoon risked a glance over his shoulder, and spat out a curse when he saw the other airboat surging through the swamp behind him, leaving a churning wake of muddy water. Moominpappa was hunched over the controls, his assault rifle still clutched in one hand, an expression of fury etched across his dark features.

Flames spat from the muzzle of the M27. The burst of gunfire ripped through the air, and Hoon ducked instinctively. This time, rather than hitting only water, a few bullets rattled and thunked against the back of Hoon's airboat.

"Fucking quit that!" Hoon hollered, firing another couple of rounds back at his pursuer, trying to scare him off.

No such luck. The chasing boat's engine grew louder. Closer. The hair on the back of Hoon's neck stood up, as if sensing the gun being aimed at him.

He couldn't keep going like this. Not out in the open, with no cover. He needed to find a way to lose his pursuer, and fast.

Scanning the swamp ahead, Hoon's gaze landed on a narrow opening in the wall of cypress trees and Spanish moss, almost hidden from view. It would be tight. It would be a gamble.

But it might just be his only chance.

Yanking hard on the steering stick, Hoon sent the airboat veering towards the opening, the fan's roar rising to a deafening crescendo as he pushed the engine to its limits. The briefcase bounced and clattered on the deck behind him, the bomb's countdown ticking away precious seconds.

The airboat shot into the narrow channel, the dense foliage scraping against the hull on both sides.

Choking on a cloud of insects, Hoon ducked and weaved, trying to avoid the low-hanging branches that whipped past his head. The twisting, turning passage was barely wide enough for the airboat, and he had to fight to keep it from running aground on the muddy banks.

Behind him, he heard the sound of splintering wood and tearing vegetation as Moominpappa's boat ploughed into the channel, the larger vessel struggling to navigate the tight turns.

Hoon's heart pounded in his ears, nearly drowning out the roar of the airboats' engines. He could feel the seconds slipping away, the bomb's timer etched into his mind. How much time did he have left? A minute? Less?

He searched his pockets, still hunting for the key.

"Where are you, you wee prick?!" he hissed, but the key, unsurprisingly, didn't answer.

The channel twisted sharply to the left, and Hoon had to give up his search to wrench on the steering stick, sending the airboat careening around the bend. Bullets smacked into the trees around him, sending splinters of bark flying. Moominpappa was closing in, his gun barking with a throaty, relentless fury.

So much for the narrows slowing him down.

Hoon gritted his teeth, his knuckles white on the controls. He had a number of problems all vying for his attention. The bomb was one. The gun-toting psychopath was another.

He was also careening, mostly out of control, across an alligator-filled swamp.

It was really saying something when that last one was the least of his worries.

Another volley of gunfire ripped through the air, closer this time. Hoon heard a series of worrying clanks, then a *bang*, then watched helplessly as fuel spurted from the boat's motor, and the fan stuttered at his back.

The channel made another sharp turn, and Hoon saw a glimmer of light ahead. A break in the trees.

With a final, desperate heave on the steering, he aimed the airboat towards the opening, praying the engine would hold out long enough for him to get clear of the narrows.

But as he burst out into the open, he realised that he'd made a terrible mistake. The channel hadn't led him to safety, but instead to a dead end, a small, stagnant pond surrounded by a wall of dense, impenetrable foliage.

The airboat's engine coughed, then died. The fan's spinning wound down, and the craft slowed, spinning slightly, just twenty or so feet from shore.

Back around the bend, Moominpappa must've seen the opening ahead. The roaring of his engine grew into a high-pitched whine as he pushed his airboat to its limit.

Any moment now, Hoon would be in his sights.

Bob checked the bomb in the briefcase. A minute left. More than he'd expected.

Not nearly enough.

There was only one thing for it. As Moominpappa's airboat came careening into view at top speed, Hoon took a breath, grabbed the briefcase by the handle, and dived, head first, into the swamp.

CHAPTER THIRTEEN

LUNGS BURSTING, arms burning, Hoon fumbled blindly through the thick, murky darkness. He could feel ground beneath him, a slope rising towards the surface. It was soft and squidgy, though. Impossible to get traction on.

Up on the surface somewhere, close by but muted by the water, he could hear the buzzing of Moominpappa's engine.

He'd stopped shooting, at least. That was something.

The bomb, however, had not stopped counting down. It would be nice to think that a wee dook in the swamp had been enough to disarm it, but that would involve a near-miraculous stroke of luck.

And luck had never been Bob Hoon's strong point.

If it had, he wouldn't be about to drown in a Florida swamp, with a bomb tied to one wrist, and a heavily armed drug dealer readying to blow his head off the moment it rose above the surface.

Lucky people, by and large, didn't tend to find themselves in that sort of situation.

He kicked against the muddy bottom, bending his legs, and

propelling himself up the slope, his every instinct telling him he needed to get out, to get to fresh air, to just *breathe*.

Behind him, unnoticed, but drawn by his frantic thrashing, something large and scaly came gliding towards him through the dark.

Hoon could see his hands, he realised. Until now, he'd been swimming in darkness, but now the Florida sunbeams danced through the shallow water, warming it, and leading the way.

He quickly formulated a plan. It wasn't a great one, and there were an awful lot of things that could go wrong with it, but given the circumstances, any plan that offered even the faintest chance of survival was something of a miracle.

Step one was to get out of the water as quickly as possible.

Step two was to sprint as fast as he could into the forest at the edge of the swamp. There'd be no time to stop and breathe, so his lungs would just have to make the best of it while he ran.

Step three was to find the key to the chain attaching the bomb to his wrist.

Step four was to get the briefcase as far away from him as quickly as humanly possible.

Ideally, he would do all of this without being machine-gunned to death. This was an added complication that he could well have done without, but the airboat sounded more distant now, like Moomin-pappa was doing a wide sweep of the area, trying to find him.

Hoon felt the sun's caress on the top of his head.

He saw the grassy bank at the swamp's edge.

It was now or never.

He scurried up into stifling heat and buzzing mosquitos, and was halfway out of the water when the biggest alligator Hoon had ever seen chose to make its move. It erupted from the swamp behind him, all teeth, and hunger, and primordial fury.

Hoon made a noise that he immediately denied all responsibility for, then fell, twisting, as the jaws of death snapped at him.

"Ooohya fucker!" he ejected, kicking desperately at the animal's snout.

A few hundred yards across the swamp, Moominpappa's boat banked into a turn and started skimming across the waves towards him.

So much for that fucking plan.

The alligator was still mostly in the water, only its head fully above the surface. It opened its mouth wide, showing its ragged rows of teeth, and the vast, gaping maw it was looking to fill with assorted bits of Bob Hoon.

"Fucking chew on this!" Hoon cried.

He shoved the briefcase deep into the alligator's mouth, jamming it open. The monster thrashed, almost wrenching Hoon's arm from its socket.

He realised, all of a sudden, that he was still holding the Glock, but the slide was locked back, the ammo spent, so all hopes of putting a bullet in what he assumed was the alligator's forehead were dashed.

He threw the weapon instead. It landed inside the monster's mouth, right next to the briefcase.

Desperately, Hoon checked his pockets again, searching for the key that would free him from the briefcase, and the ravenous creature trying to swallow him whole.

Moominpappa's boat sped closer, water crashing against the prow, the giant fan a blur of barely visible movement. He was standing upright, braced against the seat, assault rifle ready, like he was waiting to finish off anything the alligator couldn't.

"Fuck, shite, piss, fuck, balls—"

Halfway through a third "fuck," he remembered his shirt pocket, and roared triumphantly as his fingers touched metal.

He hauled the key from the pocket, watched helplessly as it slipped from his grip and tumbled through the air, but then lunged and caught it again before it could be lost to the swamp.

Bracing his feet against the alligator's bottom jaw, he fumbled the tiny key into the swamp-gummed lock.

There could be only seconds left on the timer. Twenty yards across the swamp, Moominpappa realised what was happening, and brought the M27 to his shoulder, squinting down the iron sights.

The lock clicked. The chain went slack. Hoon kicked and hauled his way up the bank, just as the alligator slid back into the water, and the fast-approaching drug dealer tightened his finger on the trigger.

And then, in an eruption of fire and thunder, the alligator exploded.

The shockwave slammed into Hoon's back, a wall of solid heat that resonated in his lungs and hurled him through the air.

Behind him, Moominpappa cried out in panic, as the burst of energy in the water catapulted the back end of the boat into the air, launching him off the deck.

Hoon landed face down in the moss and mud. Sizzling lumps of flash-fried alligator rained down around him, splattering bloodily across the marshy ground.

Breathing animal innards and swamp gas, Hoon rolled onto his back, expecting to see Moominpappa storming towards him.

Instead, he found the dealer impaled on a fallen tree, two jagged branches sticking out of his back, and a third wedged deep in the bloody hole of an eye socket.

"Oof," Hoon remarked.

Moominpappa twitched a few times, his mouth opening and closing pitifully. It was an awful, grisly sight.

But Hoon wouldn't lose any sleep over it.

Instead, he collapsed back into the dirt, taking what little oxygen he could from the thick and humid Florida air.

The dealers' airboat was upside down at the swamp's edge, its big round fan now smaller and more squared-off.

Clearly, Moominpappa had taken the time to retrieve the

suitcase of drugs. It now lay burst open on the bank, dozens of sealed plastic bags scattered on the soft ground around it.

Roughly one-third of an alligator floated in the water. Mostly tail.

While none of it had exactly gone to plan, all things considered, it had worked out pretty well.

Hoon groaned when he heard the *thunk* of a car door somewhere nearby, and the swish of unsteady footsteps through the undergrowth.

The swim and the explosion had taken too much out of him, though. The muddy water in his clothes was weighing him down too much.

If someone was going to stroll up and kill him now, then so be it. He didn't have the energy to do anything about it. Frankly, he couldn't be arsed.

A pair of trainers appeared at the edge of his peripheral vision. With some effort, he turned to see a skinny man in tiny shorts and a knock-off Mickey Mouse T-shirt taking a seat on the grass beside him.

It was a man he knew.

A man whose appearance here made zero sense whatsoever.

"Christ on a bike, Boggle," Iris said, his glass eye jiggling around in its socket as his eyebrows shot up his forehead in surprise. "That was a close one!"

CHAPTER FOURTEEN

"WHERE THE FUCK did you come from?" Hoon demanded.

He continued to lay sprawled on the marshy ground, his muscles, organs, and skeleton all conspiring to insist that he stay as still as possible while they all got their bearings.

He could feel insects biting him, and something wet, squidgy, but very much alive, wriggling about in one of his shoes, but he didn't have the energy to worry too much about any of it.

Iris turned and pointed back the way he'd come.

"Over there."

Hoon sighed. Five seconds in the bastard's company, and Iris was already raising his blood pressure.

"I didn't mean specifically where did you just fucking walk from! I meant more generally than that. How are you even in the fucking country? I thought you didn't have a passport?"

"I don't," Iris said. "That'd be mental."

"So how the fuck did you get here?"

"In the undercarriage. You know, where they keep the luggage?"

"Oh, aye. Because that's far less mental." Hoon raised his

head enough to stare at the one-eyed man beside him. "The fuck are you talking about?"

"I know a guy at the airport in Liverpool. John Lennon. That's the name of the airport, I mean, not the name of the guy. He was one of The Beatles. John Lennon, I mean, not the guy at the airport. Anyway, so's I got the train down there, and he chucked me in a suitcase."

"He chucked you in a fucking...?"

Hoon's rising annoyance levels raised him up so he was leaning on his elbows.

"What the fuck are you saying, Iris? You made the whole fucking flight over here in a suitcase?"

"No! Haha! That'd be mad, like," Iris said. "I got out and stretched my legs for a few hours, then zipped myself back up for landing."

Hoon sat fully upright. "But... How the...? Were you not fucking freezing?"

Iris shook his head. "I had a hat."

"You had a fucking—?!"

Bob was on his feet, all pain and exhaustion forgotten.

"How is that a fucking answer to anything? 'I had a hat.' What does that even fucking mean?"

Iris pointed to his head like he was going to explain, but Hoon slapped his hand away.

"I know what a fucking hat is! But how the fuck did...?"

He pinched the bridge of his nose and did some silent counting, pushing his rising temper back down.

He was closing in on triple figures before he felt able to continue.

"How did you get out at the other end?"

Iris shrugged. "I just waited until I stopped going round the little conveyor belt, then climbed out. My mate in Liverpool's got a mate in Miami, so he sorted it."

"Simple as fucking that, eh?" Hoon cried, throwing his arms

in the air, despite their aches of protest. "Chucked in a fucking suitcase at one end, offloaded at the other. Easy."

"Exactly!" Iris said, smiling like he was glad they'd sorted all that out. "Don't know why more people don't do it, actually. "After that, I just jumped on a bus, then hitchhiked from where they chucked me off. All dead straightforward. Don't know why more people don't fly like that. Saves a fortune, and no messing about with government IDs."

"Oh aye, I can see that fucking catching on, right enough," Hoon retorted. "Mind you, I'm sure if Easyjet thought it could get away with cramming folk in cases in the fucking hold, they'd be all over it. Although, they'd probably charge you extra for no' having other bags piled up on top of you."

"That reference is a bit wasted on me, Boggle," Iris told him, then he held up a hand and Hoon hoisted him to his feet.

The one-eyed man in the knock-off Mickey Mouse T-shirt regarded the scene around them, his gaze lingering momentarily on the remains of the man impaled on the fallen tree.

"That looks nasty," he remarked.

"Aye, well, good e-fucking-nough for him. Arsehole was trying to kill me."

"How come?" Iris asked.

"I had a bomb in a suitcase," Hoon explained.

Upon hearing the word, Iris's eye lit up. Explosives were kind of his whole thing, although it had fairly recently come to light that he thought 'bomb' was a three-letter word.

"Oh. How come?" he asked again.

"Long fucking story," Hoon said. He started to pick his way through the mud and guts, headed for the case of drugs. "Anyway, more fucking pressing issue, how did you even find me?"

"Well, that woman in your kitchen mentioned the town name, so I headed straight here," Iris said.

Hoon continued on and nodded. For a moment, it looked like that might be the end of his questioning on the matter.

But only for a moment.

"Aye, but how the fuck did you find me out here? We're fucking miles away from Muckwater."

"Oh, that? Yeah. Easy. I put a tracking app on your phone."

Hoon stopped and turned. "You what?"

"Your phone. You know that time I borrowed it so I could take a photo of that big spider? Well, there wasn't a big spider," Iris explained. "I just wanted to put a tracking app on it. You know, so I can, like, follow you, and that?"

"So you can follow me and that?" Hoon barked. "And why the fuck would I want you following me?"

Iris looked around them at all the death and destruction, then gestured vaguely like he was bringing it to Hoon's attention.

"Well, I mean, you know," he said. "That."

And, to be fair to him, he had a point.

"Fine. Fuck it. I don't care," Hoon said, continuing towards the drugs. A dozen or so bags of white crystals had spilled out, but they'd remained sealed, and he stuffed them back in before dragging the bag back in Iris's direction.

"Did you have to kill the alligator, Boggle?"

"Yes."

"It was probably more scared of you than you were of it."

"I highly fucking doubt that," Hoon countered. "Or it wouldn't have been trying to fucking eat me, would it? Now come on. Did I hear a car door?"

"What? Oh, yeah! I picked up a rental," Iris said, leading the way through the strip of woodland, apparently oblivious to the tight cloud of mosquitoes buzzing around his head.

"How the fuck did you manage to rent a car?" Hoon asked, following behind. "You've got one eye, no licence, and the demeanour of a fucking madman. I wouldn't let you hire a bike, never mind a fucking..."

Hoon's voice tailed off into silence when he saw the vehicle parked up at the side of a narrow forest track.

It was a black SUV.

A ludicrously, pointlessly large one.

"I didn't actually rent it, like. I pinched it off some lad a few miles down the road from here. Got the jump and ambushed him, like. You'd have been dead proud."

"You fucking..." Hoon tried counting, but gave up before he'd even reached two. "That was me, you witless prick! This is my fucking car!"

Iris looked from Hoon to the SUV, then back again. He shook his head, and his glass eye rolled from side to side like it was trying to catch up.

"Nah, Boggle. I don't think that can be right. Why would I nick your car?"

"That's a very good fucking question, Iris! I was just wondering the same fucking thing myself." He gripped his head, like he was trying to stop it exploding. "But, tell me, were you stark bollock naked at the time?"

"I was, yeah," Iris confirmed, without a moment's hesitation.

"Right, well, we'll put a fucking pin in that part for a later date," Hoon replied. "And get back to the fact that a scrawny wee naked bastard jumped me in the arse end of fucking nowhere and drove off in *this* very monster truck right here, leaving me completely fucking stranded in the middle of the bastard night."

"That does sound quite familiar, actually," Iris admitted.

"I bet it fucking does!"

Iris, once again, considered both Hoon and the vehicle. He rubbed at his chin and the few days of growth that had sprouted there.

"And it's funny, the tracker did seem to think you were somewhere in the area, right enough, but it was being a bit vague, you know? Like it was covering quite a wide—"

"Keys," Hoon instructed. "Give me the fucking keys."

"You sure you should be driving, Boggle?" Iris asked. "I'm not even sure you should be getting in the car. It's got cream seats, and you're covered in swamp water and alligator bits. I'm just thinking about your deposit, like."

"Oh, that's very fucking good of you, Iris. Very fucking considerate. Pity you weren't thinking about that when you hijacked the fucking thing and rubbed your bare arse all over it!" He held out his hand. "Keys. Now."

"Alright, alright. Calm down," Iris said, his Scouse accent briefly becoming a parody of itself. "The keys are in the car."

Muttering to himself, Hoon hobbled around to the back of the SUV and pressed the button that opened the boot.

He lifted the suitcase of drugs to dump it in, then stopped when he saw everything else that was in there.

"Iris?"

"Yeah, Boggle?"

Hoon drew in a breath. All he could taste was swamp water.

"Have you got a load of fucking explosives in the back of my car?"

"Yeah, Boggle," Iris confirmed.

"Right. OK. I've got two questions. How and why? I don't care what fucking order you answer them in."

Iris shuffled up beside him. The Florida sun was already playing havoc with his peely-wally skin, turning his usual stark whiteness into a skelping shade of red.

"Thought it might come in handy, so I packed it in me flight bag."

"On the plane?" Hoon said. "You took a fucking bomb on a plane?"

"God, no. No, I wouldn't do that, Boggle. Crazy dangerous, that," Iris replied. He gestured to the assortment of items in the boot. "I took the *components* of a bomb on a plane. That was all."

"Right. OK. Well, that's all fucking right, then," Hoon spat.

He slammed the boot closed, wasted half a second on shooting Iris the dirtiest look he could muster, then wrestled the case of drugs into the back seat of the SUV.

The climb into the driver's seat proved challenging, given his pain levels, lack of energy, and the additional drag of his wet clothes. He eventually managed, and the engine roared to life when he hit the button to start it up.

"Where to now, Boggle?" Iris asked, clambering into the passenger seat. "You going to go pick your mate up?"

Hoon shook his head. "No."

"Oh. How come?"

"Because I don't fucking know where he is yet!"

Iris looked taken aback by this. He checked the time on the dashboard. "It's not like you, Boggle. What's been keeping you?"

Hoon gritted his teeth, sighed through his nose, then gestured down at himself. "It's been a long fucking couple of days."

"Right. OK. So, what's the plan now, then?"

"We're going to go and kick the living shit out of a crooked fucking sheriff."

Iris pulled on his seatbelt. "I don't know how, but that's exactly what I thought you were going to say. That's spooky, that."

Hoon ignored the one-eyed fuckwit's wittering. The SUV's air conditioning had kicked in, and while it was nice to no longer be choking in the stifling hot air, the chilly blast was already turning his wet clothes cold.

He looked down and saw rivers of dirty water running in the seams of the car's cream-coloured seat.

This, after everything, was the final straw.

His hands tightened on the wheel until the knuckles went white. This was all Eisenhower's fault. The bastard had tried to kill him to send a message. He'd been an unwitting suicide bomber, aimed at the sheriff's competition.

A kicking would be too good for the bastard.

And, enjoyable as it would be, a kicking might not get him the information he needed to help him find Miles.

Or find out what had happened to him.

Hoon turned and looked at the suitcase on the back seat. He had no idea what the street value of all that methamphetamine was, but presumably, it was far more than the quarter of a million dollars Hoon had believed he was carrying.

If Eisenhower was as crooked as that pair of Miami Vice rejects had claimed, then he would surely be interested in getting his hands on that lot.

There was a deal to be made, then.

A trade.

"Actually," Hoon said, turning to meet Iris's good eye. "I think I might have a better idea."

"Nice!" Iris grinned at him, but it eventually faded in the awkward silence that followed. "So, are you going to tell me what it is, like, or...?"

"No, not yet, because you'll only fuck it up," Hoon replied. He sighed, like he knew the next words out of his mouth were going to be a mistake.

He had to know, though. He couldn't keep wondering.

"Why were you naked when you nicked the car?"

"I wanted the swamp people to think I was one of them."

Hoon regarded him in silence for a few moments.

"Who the fuck are the swamp people?"

Iris's brow furrowed, like this was some sort of trick question. "You know. The people what live in the swamp."

Once again, Hoon stared at the man in the passenger seat, saying nothing.

Finally, he shook his head.

"Fuck me," he muttered, facing front. "I'm sorry I asked."

And with that, he slammed his foot down on the gas pedal, and the SUV's tyres spun furiously, before it shot off along the track.

CHAPTER FIFTEEN

MAUDE WATCHED from the front desk of the Sheriff's office, as Hoon squelched his way towards her, leaving wet, bloody footprints on the scuffed and faded floor.

The cell that had previously held the Goggins boy was now empty, and Maude was alone in the station's reception area.

Judging by the look on her face, and the way her eyes kept darting to Eisenhower's door, she hadn't expected to see him again. At least, not in a form that wasn't bobbing up and down across a large expanse of water.

"Alright, easy there, Maudy," Hoon said. He hoisted the suitcase aloft for her to see. "Just bringing back the spoils of fucking war, an' that." He jerked his head in the direction of Eisenhower's office. "Is himself in?"

Maude's gaze flitted anxiously towards the door again, and Hoon gave her a thumbs up.

"I'll take that as a yes. If you're at a fucking loose end, I'll take a coffee," he said, changing direction and heading for the frosted glass door at the back of the room. "Just try and no' poison it, or put a wee fucking snake in it, or anything, eh?"

"You can't go in there!" Maude warned, finally getting over her shock and finding her voice.

"You just fucking watch me, hen," Hoon replied.

Then, dragging the case behind him, he marched over to the door and booted it open with one big, solid kick.

Eisenhower sat with his feet on his desk and a cigar burning away at one side of his mouth. His hat was on the desk in front of him, rather than hanging on the hook, and Hoon immediately surmised the sheriff's sidearm would be tucked beneath it, ready to grab.

Hoon was so focused on the possibility of that gun, that he failed to notice the other one until he heard the *clack* of a hammer being drawn back.

Arthur, the smaller, more sharply drawn of the sheriff's deputies, stood just inside the room, to the right of the door. He was in the same grey uniform as yesterday, with his hat plonked squarely on his head.

With a flick of the gun, he gestured for Hoon to step further into the room, then he closed the door and stood guard over it, the gun aimed at the small of Hoon's back.

"Morning, boys," Hoon said, grinning at the man behind the desk. "I don't know about you two, but I've had quite a fucking day of it so far."

Eisenhower regarded him through the haze of cigar smoke. Gravity had rid him of many of the larger lumps of muck and dead alligator, but he continued to dribble dirty water down his legs, like a man cursed with some terrible and constant incontinence.

Unlike the hard flooring out front, carpet tiles had been laid in Eisenhower's office to give it a touch of luxury. It pleased Hoon immensely to think that he was currently ruining at least three of them.

"Well, well, Mr Hoon. Ain't you a sight for sore eyes? I was starting to get worried."

"Aye? Good fucking instincts there, Bucky-boy. You'll never believe what fucking happened. Mind that briefcase full of cash you showed me? Somehow—and don't fucking ask me how—between here and the drop-off, it magically transformed into a big fucking bomb! You can imagine how that went down. There was egg on my fucking face, let me tell you."

He ran a hand across his forehead, wiping away a smear of mud and gore.

"Among a lot of other things." Hoon shrugged. "So, to cut a long story short, the clueless fucking young team I was sent to meet? They're dead. No' my fault. Their fucking chaperone shot them both.

"And then, and you'll like this, he got impaled on a big fucking tree after an alligator exploded right under his boat. It was quite a fucking sight, let me tell you. As a way to go, I wouldn't be quick to recommend it."

He turned and looked back over his shoulder at Arthur, sizing up the man and the distance between them. "You'll probably be the one that ends up having to clean that up. You'll probably want to bring a power saw and some thick fucking rubber gloves."

Arthur looked to the sheriff like he was seeking guidance on how to respond. When none came, he just tightened his grip on his gun, as if trying to remind Hoon who was in charge here.

Hoon didn't need reminding. He already knew who was in charge here, and it wasn't that gormless prick.

"Right, so, here's the situation as I see it," Bob said, turning back to Eisenhower. "You've got your sticky fucking fingers in a lot of pies around here. You're either the head honcho on the drug production front, or you're their bitch. I don't give a shit either way. I just know that you tried to have me blow up the competition, and myself along the fucking way."

"All's fair in love and business," Eisenhower said, grinning around the stump of his cigar.

"I don't think that's how that phrase goes, but aye, whatever you say. Anyway, point being, everyone you wanted dead is dead."

He gave the suitcase a dunt with the side of his foot, drawing it to the lawman's attention.

"I brought you a peace offering. You said you had information you'd give me if I made the drop, but I don't for one fucking second think you're a man of your word. So, here's the deal, Bucky-boy. You tell me what I want to know, I give you this suitcase full of meth, and we go our separate ways. How the fuck does that grab you?"

Eisenhower chewed on the end of his cigar, then pulled it from his mouth. "Not quite," he said.

Hoon frowned. "Eh? The fuck do you mean?"

The sheriff's chair creaked as he leaned closer to the desk. "You said that everyone I wanted dead is dead. I said, 'not quite.'" He stubbed out the cigar in his ashtray. "You're a loose end, Mr Hoon. And I cannot abide a loose end."

He stood up, collected his hat, and placed it on his head. Sure enough, his Walther handgun had been concealed beneath it. Hoon tensed when he picked it up, then relaxed a little when the sheriff returned it to the holster at his hip.

"Arthur here's gonna take you out back and shoot you. You know, like a dog? Wildlife'll take care of what's left," Eisenhower said.

He approached Hoon and stopped just out of kicking range. Up close, he smelled of stale smoke and cheap cologne. His piercing blue eyes searched the Scotsman's face, like he was memorising it. Capturing the moment to file it away.

"I want to thank you, though, for bringing me such a generous gift. Rest assured, I'll make good use of it. You made me a lot of money today, Mr Hoon. Made me a lot of money, and saved me a lot of trouble. My only disappointment is that I don't have time to kill you myself."

Hoon snorted. "Long day ahead, eh?"

A smile tugged at the corner of the sheriff's mouth. He unhooked his sunglasses from his shirt pocket and slipped them on.

"Every damn one of them."

He turned to give Arthur the nod, but before he could, Hoon interjected.

"Open it."

Eisenhower hesitated. "'Scuse me?"

"The case." Hoon gave it another nudge with his foot. "Open it."

Something about the tone of Hoon's voice, and the slight, smug little smile on his face, made the sheriff take a step back.

"And why would I do that?"

"Because if you don't, everyone in this room is going to die," Hoon said. He raised his voice. "Isn't that right, Iris?"

The lawmen both glanced around, like they expected to find someone else with them in the room.

Nobody spoke.

Hoon muttered something below his breath, then tried again, even louder this time.

"I said, *isn't that right, Iris?*"

This time, after a moment, a small voice spoke from Hoon's sodden shirt pocket. "Sorry, Boggle, I was out having a piss. But, yeah. Absolutely. Everyone in that whole building, I reckon."

"Fuck." Hoon bit his lip in a caricature of concern. "That's worse than I thought. You'd better fucking open it, Bucky-boy. We don't want poor Maude getting fucking vaporised now, do we? Although, she was meant to bring me a fucking coffee, so maybe it's good enough for the lazy bastard."

Eisenhower glared at him through his Aviators, then nodded to his deputy. "Arthur."

"No, no," Hoon said. "Not him. He's got enough to be fucking worrying about. You. I want you to open it. I want you to have that wee moment of realisation like I did, about how you've been fucking stitched up."

They continued to face off for a few moments, neither man backing down.

A tinny Scouse voice interrupted the stalemate.

"Is that a 'go,' to fire, Boggle?"

Hoon stared at his own reflection in Eisenhower's glasses, and watched four tiny eyebrows rising.

"Give it a sec, Iris. I think our man here's about to shit his drawers and buckle."

"You're bluffing," Eisenhower said.

Two identical grins spread across Hoon's twin reflections. "Clearly, you don't fucking know me, pal. I'm a man of many fucking talents, but bluffing's no' one of them. Now, be a good lad, and open the suitcase, before my man on the phone there blows us all to Kingdom fucking Come."

He raised a finger, like he was making an important point.

"And don't even fucking think about making a run for it. He's got the place covered. He'll put a bullet straight through the front of that lovely fucking hat of yours before you've gone two paces. There's a reason we used to call him 'Dead Eye,' back in the army."

This wasn't a lie. There was indeed a reason Hoon's unit used to refer to Iris by that name. It was just nothing to do with his shooting skills.

The sheriff dragged out his silent protest for another few seconds, then turned and picked up the suitcase with a grunt of irritation.

"Open it on the desk, so I can see your face," Hoon instructed. "And you. Randy Eagleflag. Stop embarrassing yourself, and put that fucking gun away before I take it off you."

Arthur, once again, looked to the sheriff for guidance. Eisenhower was too busy hefting the suitcase onto his desk, though, sending stacks of paperwork scattering onto the floor.

Finally, after receiving no instruction to the contrary, the deputy lowered his gun and tried to peer over Hoon's shoulder at what his boss was doing.

What his boss was doing, it transpired, was shiteing himself.

There, nestled in among the bags of drugs, was the most cobbled-together, insane-looking explosive device he'd ever clapped eyes on. A spaghetti of colourful wires ran from a central control unit to two large grey lumps of putty-like material. LED lights suggested that the whole thing was active, and might detonate at any moment.

Although Eisenhower had horsed the case onto the desk without any real care or concern, he now stood perfectly still, like one wrong move might blow the whole thing.

"No' a fucking nice moment, is it, clapping eyes on that fucker? See, told you I wasn't bluffing," Hoon said. "So, here's the score, Bucky-boy. You're going to tell me everything you know about where my pal is, then I'm going to walk out of here and drive away until we're out of radio range. At that point, you'll be a free fucking man and can go about your business. Everybody wins."

The smile, which had been a fixture on Hoon's face for the last full minute, now fell away into a far more serious expression.

"But, if at any point my mate on the other end of the phone thinks you're no' fucking playing ball, or thinks you're trying any funny stuff before I leave, he'll press his wee button, and this whole fucking place implodes around us."

"Explodes, Boggle," Iris corrected. "I can't make it implode. Bombs don't really do that."

Hoon sighed, shut his eyes for a moment, then continued.

"Pardon fucking me. This whole place *explodes* around us. And I don't think you want that, do you, Sheriff?"

"I don't think you do, either," Eisenhower pointed out. "This thing blows, you're dead, too."

"I know. Fucking bold move, isn't it?" Hoon's grin returned.

Madness blazed behind his eyes. "But, like I said, I'm not really one for bluffing. I don't particularly want to die, but fuck it, I'm not wholly against the idea. I've hit that age where everything fucking hurts, anyway, and I have to make a wee noise when I stand up. Better to go out with a fucking bang than a whimper."

He turned and looked at the deputy, standing pale-faced and wide-eyed beside him.

"What do you think, Randy? You ready to go out with a bang?"

Arthur shook his head, his slack jaw flapping loosely back and forth. "N-no. No. I don't want that."

"Oh. Shite. Maybe you'd better tell your boss that, then. Lodge an official fucking note for the record."

"It's fine, Arthur," Eisenhower said. He turned and considered Hoon, looking him up and down like he was seeing him for the first time. "Who the hell are you?"

"I'm the man who's going to make all your toenails explode like jaggy wee bits of shrapnel through your fucking eyeballs, if you don't start talking," Hoon said. "Miles Crabtree. English fella. Go."

"Did you say 'go,' Boggle?" Iris asked from his pocket.

"Fuck! No. I don't mean go go. I was talking to... Take your finger off that fucking button!" Hoon barked, an image of Iris flashing into his mind. "I know what you're fucking like! You'll be fucking hovering over it. Don't you dare blow us up until I fucking tell you to blow us up!"

"Are they making you say this, Boggle? Is this code? Oh, God! What should I do?"

"Nothing! Don't do fucking anything!" Hoon shot back. "Iris, I swear to Christ, if you fucking blow us to bits without being told to, I will haunt you for the rest of your fucking days. I'll be a snidey wee poltergeist constantly nicking your stuff and jamming it up your arse while you're sleeping. Do *not* press that fucking button, alright?!"

There was a moment of thoughtful silence, broken only by a faint, squeaky sound from Arthur. Hoon hoped it was a whimper, but it could well have emerged from the other end.

"Gotcha, Boggle. No worries."

Hoon let out a breath, then looked at Eisenhower and rolled his eyes. "Can't get the fucking help, can you? We'd better be quick about this. He's got no fucking patience, that boy. Miles. Where is he?"

"He, uh, he moved on," the sheriff replied.

Hoon's eyes narrowed. "In what sense? In the leaving town sense, or the shuffling off the mortal fucking coil sense?"

"The former," Eisenhower insisted. "He was here poking round town, asking about some new drug that I been hearing a lot of talk of lately. They call it Elysium. Leezy, for short."

"You making it?"

"Nope. Best I can tell, it's some out-of-town outfit. Mostly rumours, I ain't actually seen the stuff myself. Ain't even sure it exists."

"And that's what Miles was looking for?"

Eisenhower nodded. "It was."

"And did he find it?"

"Nope. Not to my knowledge. And, I'm guessing he gave up, because he thanked me for my time, and moved on."

"Gave up or found something," Hoon said.

"I wouldn't know. Don't much care, neither," Eisenhower said.

"Where did he go?"

"I have no idea."

"Bollocks," Hoon shot back. "A guy coming here asking you about drugs? No fucking way you didn't sit up and pay attention. Where did he go?"

"Like I said, no idea."

"I don't believe you."

Eisenhower shrugged. "I don't much care. That's the truth, and all there is to it."

"Vegas!"

Hoon turned to see Arthur trembling beside him, his eyes like two saucers full of freshly spilled panic.

"Arthur!" the sheriff snapped, but the deputy was too scared of the bomb to pay him any heed.

"I, I heard him talking. On the phone. He was booking a flight from Miami, going to Vegas," Arthur babbled. "But, I think he was going to go there and back. Like a return, or something, I don't know. It was strange."

"What do you mean?" Hoon asked. "What was strange?"

Arthur shot a worried look at Eisenhower, but his eyes didn't linger long enough for the sheriff to scare him off.

"He mentioned a loop. Like, I don't know, doing a loop, or being in the loop. I thought it meant a return trip."

Hoon gritted his teeth. Reference to 'the Loop' might not have made sense to the deputy, but it did to him. Miles must've found something connecting the manufacture of this Elysium stuff to the criminal network.

And then, it seemed, he had vanished.

"Vegas?" Hoon asked, looking from the deputy to the sheriff. "That's where he went?"

"I've always wanted to go to Vegas, Boggle," the voice from Hoon's pocket piped up.

"Shut the fuck up," Hoon told him, then he took a step closer to Arthur, until they were practically nose to nose. "Are you fucking lying to me, Randy? Because I don't appreciate it when people fucking lie to me. It makes me angry. Do you want to see me angry, Randy? Would you like to see what that looks like? Bearing in mind that I'm currently fucking covered in bits of dead alligator? Do you want to see me lose my temper?"

"No. N-no, I don't," Arthur said, hiccuping out the words like he was about to burst into tears. "I'm not lying. Vegas. A loop. That's all I got."

Hoon eyeballed him for a few excruciating seconds, then smiled and straightened his tie for him.

"Right, then. Fair enough. Good lad."

He finished adjusting the deputy's clothing, then patted him on the shoulder.

"I think you're going to fucking go places, son," he told him, then he tilted his head in the sheriff's direction. "But, I'd keep a close watch on Yankee fucking Doodle Dandy over here. He'll blow you up as soon as fucking look at you."

HOON HURRIED AWAY from the sheriff's office, head down, to where they'd parked the SUV.

A few Harley-Davidsons stood in a line outside The Gator's Hole, and though it was still morning, the laughter and loud music coming from inside suggested the place was already jumping.

Iris sat behind the steering wheel, a makeshift detonator in his lap. He called a big, "Alright, Boggle?" to Hoon when he hauled himself up into the passenger seat, and looked amazed when he heard his own voice coming from Bob's shirt pocket.

"Aye. Fine. Go," Hoon urged, reaching for his seat belt.

"Right you are, Boggle."

Hoon was still fiddling with the belt's buckle when the explosion shattered the window beside him, pelting him with a shock-wave of flying glass shards.

The SUV's alarm squealed in fright. Outside The Gator's Hole, half a dozen motorcycles toppled over into one another.

A hundred yards away, a plume of dark smoke rose into the air, as what had, until a moment ago, been a small Everglades police station, became a tangle of collapsing, burning wreckage.

"The fuck?!" Hoon cried, blood flowing from a hundred tiny cuts in the side of his face. "The fuck did you do that for?!"

"You said 'go,' Boggle," Iris explained. "That was the signal to press the button, wasn't it?"

"I meant fucking drive!" Hoon ejected. "Not blow the place up!"

Outside, a gang of leather-clad bikers came stumbling from the bar, whooping and hollering at the sight of the burning sheriff's office.

"Oh. Right. Sorry, Boggle. Bit of miscommunication there."

"Mis-fucking-communication?" Hoon gestured with both hands at the wreckage of the building. Wood and rubble lay scattered in a circle around it. A large metal desk was embedded in the wall of the Muckwater General Store. "I'd say that's a bit fucking more than..."

He pinched the bridge of his nose, and sighed heavily.

"Forget it. Fuck it. Just get us out of here. Go."

Iris blinked in confusion. "Like, d'you mean *drive go*, or—?"

"Yes! Fucking *drive go*! Of course, fucking drive go! You've done the other one. It's too fucking late to do the other one. You've already blown the fucking thing up!"

"Right. Yeah. Gotcha," Iris said. He tossed the detonator into the back seat, and started the engine. "You know, in hindsight, Boggle, do you think maybe we should've come up with a less confusing system...?"

CHAPTER SIXTEEN

ACCORDING TO THE IN-FLIGHT MAGAZINE, the Harry Reid International Airport in Las Vegas boasted an Irish pub, a LEGO store, and one-thousand-eight-hundred slot machines.

The pub was tempting, but Hoon bypassed it and headed outside where a different, but equally unpleasant, heat to the one he'd left in Florida, rushed up to tackle him.

"Fuck sake," he cursed, shooting a dirty look up at the darkening evening sky. The sun barely had its head above the horizon, so how the hell was it still this hot?

Christ, was every part of this country a scorching hellhole?

Still, at least this time the humidity wasn't as intense. At times, back in Florida, he'd felt like he was drowning on dry land. Here, the air was just as hot, but bone dry, like all the moisture had been sandpapered out of it.

He decided not to bother with a hire car this time, given how much of a hassle the other one had turned out to be. Besides, Iris was still driving that one—and would be, for the next thirty-seven or so hours—and Hoon didn't want to trigger any red flags by renting a second vehicle in an entirely different state.

The streets of Las Vegas were also a very different beast than the Florida Everglades. Public transport and taxis were both options here, whereas getting around southern Florida without a car meant relying on the kindness of mad old bastards engaging in questionable relationships with pigs.

Dumping his rucksack into the back seat of the taxi, Hoon slid in alongside it, and nodded to the woman in the driver's seat. "Alright?"

"Just wonderful, dahhling!" the driver replied, turning to shoot him what he assumed was a smile, though could well have been a pained grimace.

She looked to be somewhere between sixty and eighty. He guessed somewhere nearer the upper end, but he had no way of being more accurate than that. Extensive cosmetic surgery had given her a face that didn't just make guessing her age difficult, but also made her look not quite all the way human.

She wore a satiny dress with puffed-up shoulders, and two or three silver rings adorned every one of her fingers. How the fuck she was able to bend them, Hoon had no idea, but he didn't fancy getting a right hook from her.

Or, for that matter, an intimate massage.

"Where might I take you, dahhling?" she asked. Her accent was a sort of generic European aristocrat, and almost certainly fake. He didn't have the energy to call her out on it, though, so instead just nodded towards the road ahead.

"Just take me to a hotel. Somewhere cheap."

"Cheap but nice, or cheap but nasty?" Her eyebrows waggled, but Hoon couldn't tell if this was deliberate or some sort of lingering side effect from all the plastic surgery.

"Lady's choice," he told her, which made her cackle with delight.

She winked at him. "Nasty it is then, dahhling!" she declared.

And then, blasting her horn like she was obliged to warn other vehicles that she was taking to the roads, she kangarooed the car away from the kerb, and lurched, tyres screeching, towards the distant neon light of Las Vegas.

"JESUS CHRIST," Hoon muttered, as the taxi screeched to a halt outside a faded and dilapidated 1960s hotel. "You weren't fucking joking about the nasty bit, were you?"

"The Duchess delivers what the Duchess promises, dahh-ling!" the driver crowed. "Welcome to your new home away from home!"

The exterior of the hotel hinted at a former, long-lost grandeur, which had been weathered and worn by the relentless Nevada sun.

The façade was a mix of classic '60s architecture and whimsical design elements that hinted at a magical theme. The once-bright white stucco walls were now dingy and stained, with patches of exposed concrete spreading through it like an untreated cancer.

A massive marquee sign, shaped like a top hat and adorned with burned-out light bulbs, loomed over the entrance. The faded lettering read 'The Mirage Manor' in a bold, swooping font, while smaller but equally broken neon signs advertised nightly magic shows, bottomless cocktails, and a 'Spellbinding Casino of Wonders.'

The hotel's windows, many of them cracked or boarded up, reflected the setting sun, creating an almost blinding effect. Tattered posters featuring the faces of long-forgotten magicians clung to a few of the panes, their colours as faded as the stars of those they were promoting.

The entrance was flanked by two towering statues of gold-painted lions, their once-regal faces now chipped, weathered, and —in one case—almost completely missing.

A cracked fountain, long since drained of water, sat in the

centre of the circular drive. Its intricate tilework was obscured by years of grime and debris, alongside some graffiti that was fiercely critical of the police, the government, and someone by the name of Tyrone, who apparently had trouble keeping his penis in his trousers.

A few palm trees, their fronds drooping and brown, lined the perimeter of the property, providing a little covered canopy for the line of women who were either sex workers, or waiting for a bus to take them to a sex worker-themed fancy dress party.

Either way, there was a lot of flesh on display. And a fair amount of fishnet and leather, too.

"Isn't it wonderful, dahhling?"

"Are we looking at the same fucking place?" Hoon asked, which drew another cackle of glee from the woman up front.

"This is *old* Vegas, dahhling, from a bygone age! You know, I used to tread the boards here myself, once upon a time? Singing, dancing, acting, the Duchess did it all! What you're looking at here, dahhling, is real, live history!"

"Aye, so were the fucking Highland Clearances, but you don't see us harking back to them like they were the glory days," Hoon said, but the taxi driver just smiled her lopsided, vaguely monstrous smile at him, then held out a hand.

"Sixteen-fifty, dahhling. Tip not included."

Hoon reached for his wallet in his inside pocket, then realised, to his horror, that it wasn't there.

"Fuck," he muttered, patting himself down. "Fuck!"

"Problems, dahhling?"

"My wallet. I've lost my fucking—"

The Duchess grinned, showing her nicotine-stained teeth. She held his wallet out to him and winked. "I was also something of a magician, dahhling. Although, of course, women were generally relegated to being assistants, back then. Knives thrown at us, poked with swords, and so on, and so on."

Hoon snatched the wallet back from her, checked his money

was still there, and handed her a twenty. "Aye, very good. You're lucky I don't have the right fucking change," he told her. "Because I don't tip."

The Duchess laughed, but quickly folded and pocketed the cash in case he asked for it back. "This is America, dahhling. Didn't you hear? Everyone simply *must* tip everyone."

The accent had veered into an upper-class English bray now, like a minor royal trying to move up in the world.

"The fuck are you from, by the way?" Hoon asked.

"Oh, all over, dahhling," the driver replied, with what, on any other face, might have been a knowing smirk, but on hers just looked like bad wind.

She thrust a card out to him that simply said, 'The Driving Duchess,' and a phone number with inexplicable wee dashes between the randomly grouped digits.

"Should you ever care to see the sights behind the sights." She winked theatrically. "*If* you know what I mean?"

"No' really, but cheers," Hoon said, pocketing the card.

"Old Vegas, I mean. The history. All its secrets and forgotten scandals. If you ever want to explore, or hear my tales of a life on the stage, you just call the Duchess, and she'll be right there, dahhling!"

Hoon almost asked why she was talking about herself in third person, but that would've meant spending more time in the mad old bastard's company, so he let it go.

"Right. Maybe don't count on the business, though, eh?" he said.

The taxi jerked forward a couple of times, like the Duchess didn't know how to work the clutch. The fact the vehicle was an automatic just further highlighted her lack of driving ability.

"Fuck sake, I'm no' out of the fucking car yet!" Hoon told her.

The brakes screeched briefly. "Sorry, dahhling! Thought you'd already left."

Hoon opened the door, grabbed his bag, and jumped out

before she had a chance to drive off with him hanging halfway out of the taxi.

"You're a fucking liability," he told her, but she was already speeding off. Horns blared as she swerved across a lane of traffic and down what would be considered a narrow Vegas side street, but in Scotland would be a full-on, four-lane motorway.

"What a mad bastard," he remarked to himself.

Then, ignoring the catcalls of the women waiting at the side of the road, he pushed through the revolving door of the Mirage Manor, and into a lobby that was as vast as it was disappointing.

The Duchess had given him a potted history of the place on the breakneck drive from the airport.

The Mirage Manor, once a dazzling beacon of Las Vegas glamour, now stood as a faded relic of its enchanting past. Built in 1965, the hotel had been the very epitome of elegance and mystery, its walls adorned with ornate posters of the legendary magicians who graced its stage.

The grand lobby, with its crystal chandeliers and plush red carpets, was where the world's elite arrived to witness the impossible.

In its heyday, The Mirage Manor had played host to the world's most famous magicians, not a single one of whom Hoon had ever heard of. The Duchess, though, had whispered their names like they themselves were words of terrifying occult power.

Caspian the Cryptic. Barbaracadabra. Madame Mystique.

"Paul Daniels?" Hoon had guessed, but the Duchess had dismissed the suggestion with a short, slightly confused-sounding cackle.

Apparently, packed-out audiences had gasped in awe as the various magical performers defied logic and cheated death night after night.

That all changed however when, in 1977, the Astonishing Aldrick, renowned for his family-friendly comedy and spectacular, death-defying stunts, had accidentally decapitated himself halfway through a Saturday matinee performance.

The fact that the matinee performance in question had been a special event put on for children with terminal illnesses and their families had not helped with the fallout in the press.

From that fateful night, The Mirage Manor's allure began to fade, Aldrick's untimely—and surprisingly prolonged—death having driven away all but the most morbidly curious of guests.

The once-thriving casino floor now lay dormant, its roulette wheels and slot machines silent and gathering dust. The stage, where magic and mystery had enthralled so many audiences, was now a crumbling and ever so slightly blood-stained reminder of the hotel's macabre history.

These days, the Duchess had gleefully explained, The Mirage Manor barely clung to existence, its once-opulent rooms now rented by the hour to those seeking cheap thrills and fleeting anonymity.

The enchantment that once crackled in the air was long gone, replaced by the stale odour of cigarettes, cheap booze, and desperation.

In hindsight, Hoon thought, the soles of his shoes peeling off the sticky red carpet as he walked across to the reception desk, all that probably should've been a clue for him to go somewhere else.

There was very little magical about the man sitting at reception, beyond the fact that he had managed to get himself dressed that morning.

He looked like someone had shaved an ape, and not with any degree of care or attention. More like an ape had shaved itself, in fact, only without the benefit of shaving foam, a mirror, or anything particularly sharp.

He sat perched on a stool like Humpty Dumpty about to take a header off the wall, his shovel-like hands clamped between his hairy, bare thighs. Given that he essentially lived in the middle of a desert, the legs were oddly pale. Presumably, he didn't get out much. At least, not during daylight hours.

The shorts he was wearing might have been a reasonable length on a normally proportioned human being, but on him, they were about the size of a pair of Speedos, and Hoon was sure he caught a quick flash of a bollock before he was able to tear his eyes away.

"Alright?" Bob asked, stopping a few feet from the reception desk because he knew, without a shadow of a doubt, that the man on the other side of it carried something infectious.

Precisely what *it* was—the flu, nits, the Black Death—he didn't know, but whatever it was, he was keeping his distance.

"You got a room free?"

"They ain't free," the ape-man said, and he scowled like he was trying to scare Hoon away.

"No, I know. It's just a figure of speech," Hoon told him. "I understand how a fucking hotel works."

"How many hours you want?"

The receptionist was a man of few words, it seemed. Although, not quite few enough for Hoon's liking.

"I don't fucking know. Like, twelve? Fifteen?"

The other man's eyes widened a fraction. It wasn't much, but it was the first time his expression had changed from 'surly primate.'

"You want the whole night?"

"Ideally, aye," Hoon said. "Is that a fucking problem, like?"

The ape looked him up and down. Hoon could almost hear his brain whirring away inside his oversized, weirdly shaped skull.

"You a police?" he asked, and though that last word was relatively short, he really managed to mangle it. *Pole-eeess.*

Hoon tutted. "No. I'm no' *a* fucking *police*, son. Nobody's *a police*. That's not a fucking sentence. I'm just a guy, standing in front of... whatever the fuck you are, asking for a room for the night. Whatever else you've got going on. Whoever's shagging who, or doing fuck knows what to whoever, I don't care. As long as it's no' happening in my fucking room, they can poke whatever they want wherever they fucking like."

He slammed fifty dollars down on the counter, and pointed to one of the big iron keys hanging from a rack on the back wall. "Now, give me the best room you've got. Which, looking at the state of this place, will be whichever one has a fucking door."

The hotel gorilla snatched up the money like it was something that shouldn't be left out in public, and hurriedly stuffed it between his bulging belly and the waistband of his shorts.

"Keep the change," Hoon insisted, concerned about where it might come from.

A key was set down on the counter. A plastic-coated Ace of Spades playing card was attached to it by a metal ring, a faded number 11 emblazoned in gold across the card's patterned back. Hoon picked up the key, spun it around on his finger, then pocketed it.

"There. Wasn't so fucking hard, was it?" He started to walk away, then turned back. "Oh. Do you do breakfast here?"

The receptionist shook his big, melon-like head. "No."

"Right." Hoon nodded. He glanced around them at the dirt and decay. "Well, thank fuck for that."

CHAPTER SEVENTEEN

ROOM ELEVEN WAS, inexplicably, on the hotel's third floor, right between rooms six and eighteen.

The walk through the corridors had been a bit like running the gauntlet, the sounds from behind each door assaulting him as he passed.

There had been some standard, fairly vanilla groaning and creaking of bedsprings that had made him snort with amusement the first time he'd heard it, then roll his eyes by the third.

After that, things got weirder. Men cried out in pleasure, and in pain. One of them cried like a baby, before loudly announcing that he'd been a bad boy and soiled himself, and that he really must be punished.

A gruff shout of, "Don't shit in my hair!" had stopped him in his tracks, before the man in the room had apparently had a change of heart, and urged whoever he was with to ignore that instruction and go right ahead.

Hoon had felt compelled at that point to hammer on the door and shout, "You're a dirty bastard!" before continuing through the floors and corridors until he found his room.

Part of him wished he hadn't bothered. The room was large,

and if he'd had a time machine, may well have bordered on the decadent.

The years and the neglect had not been kind to it, though, and he got the sense that everything of value had been stripped from it a long time ago.

There was a big fixing on the high ceiling that suggested a chandelier should have been hanging from it. Instead, the only lights in the room seemed to be a couple of mismatched standing lamps in opposite corners, cobwebs trailing between their shades and the walls beside them.

The carpet looked like it had once been blue, but was now mostly a deathly shade of grey, except for two brown stains, which were almost certainly dried bodily fluids.

It was wrong of him, he knew, but he *really* hoped they were both blood.

The outline of a four-poster bed could be seen on the carpet, and on the torn, faded wallpaper it had presumably once been attached to. The four-poster itself was long gone, though, and in its place was a cheap, metal-framed double bed with bedding that was likely thrown on during the Great Depression, and not changed since.

Two pairs of curtains hung at either end of the back wall. Pulling open the first, Hoon was confronted by a rectangle of brickwork that looked like a relatively recent addition. A snow of plaster dust lay on the skirting down near floor level, suggesting the cleaners hadn't been in since the work was done.

Although, given the state of the place, that didn't exactly tell him much.

The second set of curtains, to both his surprise and delight, actually hid a window. It was small, it was dirty, and it was painted shut, but at least it afforded him a view of the world outside.

Not a great view, granted. Most of it was taken up by the pink neon sign of a neighbouring building that promised 'Live Sex

Shows Nightly.' Further down, the rest of the view was currently given over to a drunk man openly pissing in the street.

At least, Hoon hoped he was drunk.

"This fucking country," he muttered, turning away and letting the curtain fall back into place.

He was sure the whole of America wasn't like this, of course. There were places out there that he'd love.

He'd like nothing more, for example, than being out on a big open plain somewhere, without another human being in sight. That would suit him just fine.

Or, in a wee log cabin in Alaska, maybe, with only the occasional wandering polar bear for company.

Aye, he'd like that, too.

Or perhaps a cave in one of the less explored parts of the Grand Canyon, far from civilisation.

He definitely saw the appeal in that.

Yes, there were a lot of good places in America, he thought. It was just a pity he'd ended up in the shitholes.

The room had an en-suite bathroom, which was a nice surprise. He'd managed to get himself scrubbed up a bit in the airport toilets, but there was only so much you could do standing over a sink, and it was amazing the places that swamp water and dead alligator could find their way into.

A shower, a change of clothes, and maybe an hour or two of sleep would set him up for the night ahead. If he was going to find Miles, he couldn't afford to wait until morning. The sort of people he expected to be dealing with were at their most active during the moonlight hours.

The condition of the bathroom probably shouldn't have shocked him. He'd been so pleased to find out there was one, though, that his natural cynicism had abandoned him for a moment. He really should've known better.

He'd seen active war zones that were less chaotic, and toxic spills that were more sanitary. Flies were holding a big family get-together around the gaping brown mouth of the toilet. Maybe they'd be able to tell him where the seat went, or why whoever had taken it had left the two rusty screws sticking perilously up at the back of the bowl.

Hoon had absolutely no doubt that, if he stepped into the shower, he'd not only emerge dirtier than when he went in, but riddled with Toxoplasmosis.

He had just muttered a customary, "Fuck me," when someone knocked a jaunty rhythm on the door of his room. With a final glance at all the filth, and a shudder that went all the way to his toes, he backed out of the bathroom and went to answer the door.

The woman leaning against the doorframe looked young. Stupidly young.

Nauseatingly, heartbreakingly young.

She was wearing a wig, he thought, the shiny black locks cut into a bob and perfectly straight fringe that half-covered her painted-on eyebrows.

Purple and black makeup circled her furtive, darting eyes. It looked like two big bruises, and may well have been applied that way in order to hide real ones.

She was likely a pretty wee thing, Hoon thought, behind all that war paint. Behind all that false bravado. Behind all that fear he could see in the shadows of her eyes.

She wore a figure-hugging black dress, even though she had very little figure to hug. It clung to her flat chest and stopped high on her thigh, with a series of splits down one side to reveal even more of her flesh.

It took a moment for a smile to spread across her face, like it was a stage performer that had narrowly missed its cue.

"Hey gorgeous," she said. Her accent was New York. Brooklyn or the Bronx. Probably just as put-on as the Duchess's had been. "Harry sent me."

"I don't suppose you're a fucking plumber, are you?" he

asked. Then, when only confusion registered on her face, he sighed. "Who's Harry?"

"The guy on the front desk. Thought you might need some help unwinding. Said you looked uptight."

"Uptight's my middle fucking name, sweetheart," Hoon said. He looked her up and down, appraising her, though probably not in the way she was used to. "How old are you?"

"How old do you want me to be?"

"Sort of early fifties and upwards," Hoon said. He looked past her into the corridor. The sounds of God knew what could still be heard coming from the other room. "What happens if I say no? What do you do then?"

"Why would you say no?" she asked, reaching out to place a hand on his chest. He caught her by the wrist before she had a chance.

"What happens?" he pressed. "If I send you packing, where do you go?"

Her grin was wide and confident. Her eyes told another story. "Wherever I'm wanted."

Hoon met her gaze. She was young enough to be his daughter. Christ, his granddaughter.

"Fuck sake. Right. Come in," he said, stepping aside. "But keep your fucking clothes on, we're no' staying."

She shuffled past him, walking unsteadily on her heels like she didn't have a lot of practice with them. Her fingers fussed with her wig, and he noted the way her hands were lightly shaking.

"Oh? You want to get adventurous somewhere?" She sat on the end of the bed and crossed one leg over another as she patted the spot beside her. "You sure you don't want us to get started here?"

"I wouldn't sit there, sweetheart. The whole thing looks like it's been carved out of fucking diphtheria. There are probably

STDs in here that have gone fucking airborne. The sooner we get out of here, the better."

He took out his wallet, but didn't yet open it.

"How much for a couple of hours?"

"That depends on what you want, honey."

She was aiming for sexy and suggestive, but her attempt at it made Hoon's skin crawl.

He made a mental note to have a word with Harry on the front desk when he was next alone with the bastard.

"I want a tour guide," Hoon told her. "Someone who knows people. I'm looking for someone."

She lay back on the bed, draping her weight onto one elbow. It was a rehearsed move, just not rehearsed enough to be convincing.

"You found someone, gorgeous."

"Aye, I meant a specific someone," Hoon said. "No' just someone in fucking general. Hundred dollars an hour. Three hours, tops. If you help me find who I'm looking for, there'll be a bonus in it."

He opened his wallet, took out a small stack of bills, then nodded towards the door.

"Or, you can go back out there and put fucking crocodile clips on someone's bollocks, or whatever the fuck it is you do with your nights. Totally up to you, sweetheart." He held the money out in front of her. "What's it to be?"

"WHAT'S YOUR NAME?"

The young woman fidgeted beneath the lumberjack-like red checked shirt Hoon had insisted she wear over her dress. "Candy," she said, rolling up the sleeves until they no longer covered her hands.

"Bollocks it is," Hoon said, opening the door onto the hotel stairwell and ushering her through. The place had a lift, but he assumed it would be a piss-reeking metal deathtrap, so he'd rather avoid it. "What's your real name?"

"My name's whatever you want it to be," she told him, and Hoon sighed as he let the door swing closed behind them.

"Fine. I don't care. Candy it is," he said. "Now, watch your fucking step here, there's a couple of junkies lying fucking spangled at the bottom."

The girl didn't seem surprised by this news, or remotely put out when they stepped over the two groaning, dead-eyed men with needles in their arms at the foot of the stairs.

"Harry ain't going to be happy," Candy warned, just before Hoon opened the door that led through to reception. "He don't like us leaving without telling him where we're going."

"That a fact?" Hoon asked. He pulled the door open and gestured, once again, for her to take the lead. "Well, I'm sure I can talk him round."

Sure enough, the moment they appeared in the hotel's foyer, the shaved ape at the front desk knuckled himself up onto his feet.

"Hey, hey, hey. What the hell's this?" he demanded, aiming the question at Hoon, who was already storming towards him. "You don't get to take my girls out of here without my—"

The finer details of the point he was making were lost when his head hit the reception desk. He was a large, imposing figure, which just meant that his forehead had further to travel before it made contact with the wood.

He howled as his teeth cracked and his nose exploded. A hand that could've encased a normal man's head scrambled for the gun tucked into the back of his tiny shorts, but Hoon stretched over, grabbed the thumb, and twisted the arm all the way up past his shoulder.

"You alright there, Harry? You look like you've gone and suffered a wee fucking mishap there," Hoon said, his voice a low growl in the other man's ear. "Anyway, just wanted to let you know that this lassie and me are heading out."

Reaching down, Hoon grabbed the butt of the pistol and yanked it sharply free from Harry's waistband, dragging the metal up his back, scraping a deep red welt along the hairy, spotty skin.

"I'm assuming you don't have a problem with that?" Hoon asked. He slammed the gun down on the counter, making his prisoner yelp in fear. "Do you, Harry?"

"N-no. No problem."

"Good. Glad to fucking hear that." Hoon looked back over his shoulder to where Candy stood, eyes wide, watching on. "Has this tubby bag of fucks got a car?"

"Uh, I don't know," the girl said, but she nodded emphatically, safe in the knowledge that Harry's field of view was currently nothing but wood, blood, and teeth.

"Right. Well, looking at you, Harry, you clearly don't fucking walk anywhere, so I'm going to assume that you do, and I'm also going to assume that you won't mind me taking it for a spin. Nod if you agree."

Harry nodded, his body shuddering like he was suddenly either very cold, or going into shock.

Or maybe just crying uncontrollably.

"Good lad. Where's your keys?"

"P-pocket. In my pocket."

Hoon tutted. "Well, I'm no' fucking reaching in there and getting them, Harry, so chop-fucking-chop, eh?"

The gorilla had to twist his left arm under himself to reach for his right pocket. The belly and the reception desk both conspired against him, but he eventually managed to pull out a set of keys attached to a pink rubber keyring shaped like a pair of disembodied women's breasts.

"The fuck's this?" Hoon asked, dangling the boobs in front of his captive like they were a hypnotist's watch. Harry strained his eyes to look in their direction, only just managing to clock them at the edge of his peripheral vision. "This a fucking stress reliever thing? If you really needed to squeeze a pair of tits, could you no' have just made do with your own?"

With a final twist, Hoon released his grip on the larger man's arm, and Harry stumbled backwards towards his chair. His weight and momentum proved too much for it, though, and it rolled out from beneath him, sending him clattering heavily to the floor.

"Don't wait up, Harry. Candy here's taking the rest of the fucking night off. And, if I find out she's got any grief over that, I'll be a very fucking unhappy man. And that will not work out well for anyone."

Hoon leaned over the counter so he was staring straight down at the man. He smiled. It was all teeth and no humour.

"But, specifically no' for you."

He gave that a second or two to settle, then waved the gun and the keys, one in each hand. "Cheers for these, by the way. Your generosity is greatly fucking appreciated."

Tucking the gun into the back of his waistband, Hoon turned to Candy. "Can you drive?"

The girl, still stunned by what she'd just witnessed, took a moment before she shook her head. "Uh, no. No, I can't."

"Ah well." Hoon tossed her the keys, boobs and all. "Now's as good a night as any to fucking start."

———

HARRY'S CAR, a 1964 Lincoln Continental, was like a mobile version of his hotel, or even of Las Vegas itself—a once impressive and elegant thing now mostly left to go to ruin.

The car's paint job, which would originally have been a glossy, deep black, was now a dull, lifeless grey. Countless scratches and dings marred the surface, telling a story of careless driving and thoughtless neglect.

The once gleaming chrome accents were now pitted and rusted, like the tarnished silver of a family heirloom nobody wanted.

The backward-facing suicide doors, a defining feature of the Continental, hung slightly askew, their hinges loose and worn from years of use and lack of maintenance. The windows, grimy and smudged, seemed to obscure the interior as much as they revealed it, like a veil of filth hiding the car's sordid past.

Inside, the once-plush leather seats were cracked and faded, the rich aroma of new leather long since replaced by the stale stench of cigarette smoke and Harry's sweaty arse. The overhead lining sagged, its fabric stained and torn, while the carpets were threadbare and spotted with mysterious stains that Hoon chose not to dwell on.

The dashboard, a vast expanse of cracked and peeling vinyl, housed a collection of gauges and dials that seemed to function more as a nostalgic decoration than as actual instruments. The steering wheel, its leather wrap worn smooth by Harry's giant, hairy-knuckled hands, had long since lost its once-luxurious feel.

Still, it didn't have a mad old woman with a face like a wasp's nest behind the wheel, so it was a step up from the taxi ride he'd taken to get to the hotel in the first place.

"Harry ain't gonna like what you just did," Candy said. She was sitting in the driver's seat, the keys clutched between her hands, her wide eyes scanning the dusty dashboard like she was trying to decipher some ancient foreign language. "He's gonna be angry."

"I'm sure we'll fucking cope," Hoon said. "Seatbelt."

Candy looked down at her lap in surprise, then shot him an odd, curious sort of look.

"The fuck's the matter with your face?" he asked her. "Come on. Seatbelt."

"Who even are you?" she asked, reaching for her belt like she'd been instructed.

"People keep asking me that," Hoon said. "I'm nobody."

She side-eyed him as she clicked her seatbelt in place. "You don't seem like a nobody."

Hoon sniffed. "Aye, well. You don't seem like a Candy. Now, come on. Keys. Ignition. Let's get a fucking move on."

The girl searched around near the wheel until she found the slot to slide the key into. Once she had, she turned it, and let out a sharp laugh of surprise when the engine rumbled awake.

Her hands gripped the wheel. She stared ahead through the grimy windscreen, like she was seeing a long open road out there, rather than the overflowing bins out the back of a theatre hosting live sex shows.

For a moment, Hoon thought he heard her quietly making engine noises from the side of her mouth, but he couldn't be sure he hadn't imagined it.

"Sarah," she whispered, still looking ahead. All the New York had left her accent, replaced by something altogether less brash. "My name. It's Sarah."

"Nice to meet you, Sarah." Hoon held out a hand for her to shake. "I'm Bob."

It took her a moment, and some internal debate, but she took his hand and shook it, then quickly replaced her grip on the steering wheel like she had to stop the stationary car from careening out of control.

"I'm looking to find some higher-ups in the drug trade, Sarah. Not street level. Bigger boys. Any idea where we'd start?"

The girl in the driver's seat smiled apologetically. The way her eyebrows dipped and her forehead narrowed made her look even younger.

"Um, sorry. I should've really said."

"Said what?" Hoon asked.

"I don't actually know anyone here. Not really. I only really know the other girls and Harry."

"What do you mean?" Hoon asked. "You've no' got, like, connections?"

Sarah shook her head.

"But you must fucking hear stuff. The word on the street, or whatever?"

Sarah winced. "I only really got here about a month ago," she said. "I've not even been to the strip yet. I really want to see the big fountain. At the Bellagio? I'm told it's amazing."

"What?! You've not fucking been to the...? Oh, for fu—"

Hoon saw a look of fear setting up camp behind Sarah's mask of makeup, and cut his exasperated ejection short.

"No. It's fine. It's fine," he said, as much to himself as to the young woman beside him. "We can figure this out. Maybe you can get the other girls to talk to me."

"Maybe," Sarah said, though she didn't seem to fancy their chances. "Although, wait!" She slapped her hands on the steering wheel. "I do know someone who might know about that stuff."

"Aye?" Hoon sat up straighter. "Great! Let's go and fucking see them, then."

"OK!" Sarah cried. Her excitement was short-lived, though, and she sunk down a little, chewing on her lip. "Except, um..."

"What?" Hoon asked, already chastising himself for getting his hopes up. "What's wrong?"

"How do you feel about the police?" Sarah asked.

Hoon considered the events of the past twenty-four hours.

And of the past twenty-odd years.

"That's a complicated fucking question," he told her. "But I'm sure I can be persuaded to give them the benefit of the doubt."

"Right. Cool. OK." She winced again. Another worry. "I'm not sure where he'll be, though."

"Do you have his number?" Hoon asked.

Sarah nodded. "Yeah," she said, then squirmed in the seat.

"But Harry keeps our phones. We have to ask him for them, and tell him why we need them."

Hoon sighed.

Hoon opened the door.

"Give me a minute," he said.

Sarah sat, still gripping the wheel, as Hoon walked away from the car. She watched in the rearview mirror as he entered The Mirage Manor through the front door.

She waited.

She drummed her fingers.

She chewed her lip.

And then, Hoon emerged again, returned to the car, and handed her a mobile phone in a glittery pink case.

"Oh. Wow! He gave you it?"

"Aye," Hoon replied.

Sarah frowned as she turned the phone over in her hand. "Is that... Is that blood?"

"That is a possibility," Hoon told her. "Now, dig out this fucker's number, and let's crack on."

CHAPTER EIGHTEEN

SARAH'S DRIVING wasn't as bad as she'd made out, and Hoon had felt significantly safer with her behind the wheel than he had with the Duchess.

He'd assumed the heaviness of the car, which handled like a tank in treacle, would be a problem, but she let slip that she used to drive around on tractors.

She'd clammed up when he'd asked her about that, and he'd had the good sense not to push it.

Eventually, they'd reached a police station in the northeast of the city, just on the border where it merged into the desert. The area around it was a rough-looking residential street, the road cracked and crumbling, and tangles of electrical wires trailing from house to house.

Most of the houses had high fences. Signs on several of them warned passersby to beware of dogs, while at least one alerted them to the possibility of being shot if they got too close.

The station itself was surprisingly sleek and modern-looking, with a lot of reflective glass and smooth lines. Palm trees lined the approach to it, and it felt more like a holiday resort than somewhere that serious police work took place.

"You sure this is it?" Hoon asked, eyeing up the building's front. A sign declared it was 'Las Vegas Metropolitan Police Department,' but Hoon still wasn't quite buying it.

"This is definitely the place," Sarah told him. She took out her phone and checked the response to the message she'd sent before they'd left the hotel car park. "He's in. We've to go right up."

Hoon sized the place up again, eyeballing it like he was challenging it to a fight.

Then, with a sigh, he opened the door and stepped out. "Fine. I'll take your word for it."

Night had fully fallen now, and the air was cooling to the point that Hoon wished he'd brought a jacket. His thin shirt had helped him avoid heatstroke earlier, but now it was offering little protection from the chill desert breeze.

Sarah got out of the car, too, and hurried to keep up with Hoon as he went striding towards the entrance.

"Wait, wait, hold up, not so fast," she protested, grabbing him by the arm and hauling him to a halt.

"What? What's the fucking matter now?" Hoon demanded.

"I just..." Sarah looked up at the front of the building. "I'm, um. We, people like me, we're not exactly popular in some of these places. You know? Because of what we, like, what we do."

"What you do? Never mind that. I blew up a whole fucking sheriff's office. Sheriff, and all. You're the least of their fucking worries, sweetheart."

He pulled his arm free from her grip.

"And if anyone's got a fucking issue with you, your uncle fucking Bobby'll have a thing or two to say to them."

Turning, he stuck his arm out, inviting her to hook onto it.

"Now, you coming, or what?"

Sarah regarded him curiously for a few moments, then raised her eyebrows and shook her head, like she was no closer to understanding him.

"You're not like other guys I've met in this job," she told him.

"Well," said Hoon, standing just a little taller. "That's about the nicest fucking thing anyone's ever said to me."

Together, with Sarah holding Bob's arm, they entered through the front of the station, and were immediately met by a hatchet-faced older woman who made Hoon think of another police station receptionist based several thousand miles away.

"Can I help you?" she asked. Going by her tone, if the answer was anything but, 'No, thanks,' she was going to be absolutely fucking livid.

"Alright, hen? My friend and I here are looking for a..." Hoon pointed to Sarah, cueing her up.

"Detective Nate Holden."

"Aye. Him. He in?"

The woman behind the counter peered at them through bulletproof glass, sizing them up and finding them very much wanting.

"No."

"No? What d'you mean?"

"I mean, he's not in. I thought that was obvious," the receptionist replied. "You asked if he was in. I said no. Where's the confusion?"

"Fuck sake. Your name's no' fucking Moira by any chance, is it?"

"That language is unacceptable, sir. Please refrain from using it."

"Oh, you think *that* language is unacceptable? I haven't fucking started, ya crusty fucking wasp-minged—"

Sarah elbowed him aside, and flashed a smile that probably dazzled the punters, but did nothing to move the receptionist.

"Sorry, he's got mental health problems," she said.

"The fuck?" Hoon protested, but Sarah talked right over him. "Detective Holden told us to meet him here. He said he'd be in."

"I don't care what he said"—her gaze flitted damningly up and down—"*miss*. Detective Holden isn't—"

"It's fine, Margie! It's OK!"

Sarah spun on the spot, her well-rehearsed fake smile segueing into something more genuine.

A handsome, square-jawed man in his forties, with a deep tan and a muscular build, came trotting across the foyer. He wore a shirt and tie, but the sleeves were rolled up, and the knot was loose.

He was smiling and relaxed, his short but slightly unkempt hair flopping around as he came to meet them.

Were he a teacher, Hoon thought, he'd be the type that insisted pupils all called him by his first name before, inevitably getting fired for making inappropriate comments to the sixth-year girls.

Sarah danced on the spot like she didn't know whether to run to him or run off. Eventually, when he was just a few feet away, she closed the gap and gave him a friendly, but still slightly awkward, hug.

"Hey! You OK?" he asked, searching her face like he was checking for injuries.

He looked at Hoon before the girl could answer, checking him out, sizing him up, trying to work out who he was and where he fit.

It was a copper's look. Hoon knew it only too well.

"I'm fine. I'm OK. This is..." She gestured to Hoon, and winced. "Bob. Sorry, I don't know your last name."

"Because I didn't tell you," Hoon said. "Bob's fine."

"He's a..." Once again, Sarah didn't quite know what to say.

"I'm a friend of hers," Hoon said. "I'm new in town."

"No kidding? The accent was kind of a giveaway," Detective Holden said. "Let me guess. Scotland?"

Hoon nodded. "Aye," he said, and he had a feeling that he already knew where this was going.

"Nice. You know, I'm actually Scottish."

Yep. There it was.

"Well, you don't fucking sound it."

"My mom was originally a MacDonaldson."

Hoon shook his head. "No, she wasn't."

"Excuse me?"

"That's no' a fucking thing, son. It's either MacDonald or Donaldson. It's one or the other. There's no' some fucking mythical hybrid wandering the glens."

Holden lowered one eyebrow and raised the other. "I'm pretty sure she was MacDonaldson."

"Fuck it. I don't care. Good for her," Hoon said. He threw a thumb back over his shoulder. "Now, is there somewhere else we can go where Sedna the fucking She-Cannibal's eyes aren't burning holes in the back of my fucking head?"

"I heard that!" the receptionist cried.

"I know you did, sweetheart." He turned and smiled at her. "That's why I fucking said it out loud."

"HERE. Hot chocolate. Sorry there's no cream and marshmallows."

Sarah took the offered mug and wrapped her hands around it, taking comfort just from the warmth of it against her skin.

"Thank you," she said, blowing away some of the steam that rose from the dark brown liquid. "You got any doughnuts?"

"No. Sorry."

Sarah wrinkled up her nose. "What sort of police station doesn't have doughnuts?"

The detective chuckled. "We do, but you have to get in a lot earlier than this. You sure I can't get you something, Bob?" he asked. "I might be able to find a tea."

"I'm fine," Hoon said. He glanced at Sarah, who was too

engrossed in the swirling steam of her hot chocolate to pay him any attention, then pointed to the door of the small, cluttered kitchen. "Can I have a word?"

Holden's smile remained unchanged, but his eyes narrowed a little. "Sure," he eventually said, then he pointed at Sarah. "You. Stay out of trouble."

Sarah grinned and raised her mug like she was offering up a Viking toast, then went back to blowing on the cocoa.

The detective led the way into an open-plan office that was mostly deserted at this time of night. The few remaining police officers were all dead-eyed, overweight, jowly types, who sat hunched over their desks, their faces illuminated by the glow of their computer screens as they typed up reports or reviewed case files.

Holden's workspace was tucked away in a corner of the office. It offered a suggestion of privacy, even if it didn't fully deliver on that promise.

His desk was cluttered with stacks of papers, case files, and a few empty coffee cups. A corkboard hung on the wall behind an ergonomic back support chair, covered in a web of notes, photographs, and memos he'd left for himself. There was also a photo on there of Holden with a woman and a little girl of around five or six.

Family man, then. Hoon made a note of that.

An old, battered filing cabinet stood beside the desk, its drawers too stuffed with folders and documents to close all the way.

The only sounds in the place were the faint buzzing of fluorescent lights, the sad, slow tap-tapping of keyboards, and a faint but unmistakable hum of disappointment.

"Here. Take a seat," Holden said, wheeling a chair across from an empty desk.

Hoon contemplated remaining standing, but as he was trying to get the man onside, he relented and took a seat.

Holden sat in his own chair and rolled it in closer to the desk. "So, Mr...?" When Hoon didn't reply right away, he grinned, and raised his fists like he was readying to fight. "You're not a McCambell, are you? The McCambells and MacDonaldson rivalry goes way back! Why I outta!"

Hoon sighed. "I'm not even going to go into all the things wrong with what you just said. It's Hoon. Mr Hoon."

"OK, then, Mr Hoon! Now we're getting somewhere." He looked over at the kitchen. Through the open door, he could see Sarah carefully testing that her hot chocolate was cool enough. "How do you know Sarah, if you don't mind me asking?"

"I don't. Just met her tonight."

Holden nodded. "And how did you come to meet her, exactly?" he asked. His smile was still intact—did it ever fade?—but there was a suggestion of something dangerous in the lines of his face surrounding it.

"I'm staying in a shitehole of a hotel, and the gelatinous fucking potato-man behind the front desk sent her up to keep me entertained. Needless to say, he and I had words on the issue, where I made my displeasure abundantly fucking clear." He sniffed, then jerked his head in Sarah's direction. "Why? How do you know her?"

"I'm afraid I can't share that information."

Hoon leaned forward. "Look, son. I know how it all works. I'm a fucking Detective Superintendent with Police Scotland, with oversight of a Major Investigation Team," he said, conveniently neglecting to include the word 'former' anywhere in that sentence. "I'm no' just some randomer off the fucking street."

Detective Holden shrugged. "You are to me," he said, but then he sighed and shot a look in Sarah's direction. "Her mom was looking for her a few months back. She ran away from home when she was seventeen. Farm in Wisconsin."

"How old is she now, like?" Hoon asked.

"Nineteen. She travelled around before she came here," Holden continued. "Anyway, I tracked her down."

"But, what? You didn't bring her back?"

The detective sighed again. This one sounded less impatient and more dejected. "I don't know how it works in Scotland, Mr Hoon, but over here, she's an adult. She can do what she wants."

"Apart from buying fucking alcohol."

Holden gave a little grunt of amusement. "OK, let me rephrase that. I can't make her do anything she doesn't want to do. All I could do was let her mom know that she was alive, and that she was safe."

"Safe?" Hoon spluttered. "In what fucking world is she safe? Have you seen where she's spending her fucking nights?"

Holden raised his hands, conceding the point. "OK. Alive and unhurt, then. I tried to convince her to pack up and head back to the family farm, believe me, but she was having none of it."

He looked past Hoon to the kitchen door again. Sarah was trying another experimental slurp of her hot chocolate.

"Makes you wonder what she ran away from that this is the better alternative." He slapped his hands on his thighs, shook his head, then reapplied his smile. "So, Mr Hoon. Sarah tells me you're looking for some help?"

"Sort of. I'm looking for a mate of mine. Think he might be over here getting himself into trouble."

"Lot of folks getting themselves into trouble in Vegas. You'll need to be more specific."

Hoon sat back in his chair, considering the man on the other side of the desk. Sussing him out, and how much he could be trusted.

Not a lot, he thought. Not enough.

But he didn't exactly have many other options.

Taking out his phone, he opened the Photos app, and presented the detective with a photograph.

"His name's Miles Crabtree. He works for the UK government, but as far as I know, he's not here in an official capacity."

"Vacation?" Holden asked. He pointed to the phone screen. "Can you send me that picture?"

"No," Hoon said, returning the mobile to his pocket. "And no' exactly a holiday. He's sniffing around into some drug thing. Some new designer bollocks. Elysium. They call it Leezy, apparently."

"Who does?"

"Fucked if I know," Hoon said, after a moment's thought. "I hear they're making the stuff out in Florida. Don't know if it's hit the streets yet."

"And your friend from the UK government is over here *not* investigating it in any official capacity?"

Hoon pointed to the detective and mimed pulling a trigger. "Bingo."

"And... what? What do you want me to do with this information?"

"Well, ideally, I want you to tell me you know where the fuck he is, and point me to him, but I'm guessing that's unlikely?"

"I've never seen that man before in my life. Sorry." He turned his chair until he was in front of his ancient, battered PC, and jiggled the corded mouse to wake it up. "Give me his name again."

"Crabtree. Miles," Hoon said, then he watched as Holden pecked, single-fingered, at the keyboard. "Fuck me, even I type faster than that, and I think computers are the work of the fucking Devil."

"Ha! You're not wrong," Holden said. "About the typing, I mean. Not sure about the demonic angle, but you never know. OK. Here we go."

He poked at the Return key. The computer made a series of strained whirring and clunking noises, then concluded its search with the harshest, most negative-sounding electronic *bleep* that Hoon had ever heard.

"I'm guessing that's a no, then?"

"Sorry." Holden shrugged apologetically. "You guys have this same system?" he asked, pointing to the PC.

"No. But the fucking noise it made was a dead giveaway. It sounded like that wee robot bin from Star Wars having an angry wank."

"R2D2?"

Hoon stared blankly back at him, then shrugged. "The fuck does that mean?"

The detective's smile faltered, but rallied quickly. "Doesn't matter. I'm afraid your friend isn't in our system, Mr Hoon. Looking on the positive side, it means he isn't dead. Or, I guess, that we haven't yet identified him, if he is. So, you know, probably best not to rule it out."

"What about Elysium?" Hoon asked. He tapped a finger against the back of the computer monitor. "Anything in there about that?"

Holden turned back to the keyboard. "How are you spelling that?"

"E-L..." Hoon's brow furrowed. His lips moved. "Fucking *eesium*. I don't know."

"E-L-Y-S-I-U-M."

Both men turned to find Sarah sitting on a desk a few feet away, still blowing on her hot chocolate.

"What, have you fucking heard of it?"

"Yeah, course," she said. "It's like Paradise, Las Vegas, and Disneyland all rolled into one."

"Hold on. What are you saying? You've fucking taken it?"

"What?"

Disappointment curved the lines of Holden's face. "Jesus, Sarah. We talked about using. You promised me you were going to stay clean."

"Whoa, whoa, hold on." Sarah looked back at them both, confused. "It's Heaven."

Holden drew a big breath in through his nose. "I know it might feel like that at the time, but—"

"No. In Greek Mythology. It's, like, where heroes and gods go, or whatever."

"Greek Mythology?" Holden asked. He blinked in surprise. "You've studied Greek Mythology?"

Sarah looked offended by the question. "Why is that such a shock?" she asked. "Although, no. I haven't. I got it from Percy Jackson."

"Who the fuck's Percy Jackson?" Hoon asked.

"He's a demigod," the girl explained. "He's the son of Poseidon and a human. He killed a Minotaur."

Hoon looked from Sarah to Holden and back again, his eyebrows furrowing into tight, angular knots.

"Has someone slipped me a fucking acid tab or something? What the fuck are we talking about?"

"It's a book series!" Sarah laughed, and almost seemed surprised by the sound coming out of her. "For kids. Elysium is 'like Paradise, Las Vegas, and Disneyland, all rolled into one.' That's from the books. It's actually one of the reasons I came here."

"Jesus," Hoon muttered. "So Terry Johnson's got a lot to fucking answer for."

"Percy Jackson," Sarah corrected, but Hoon's scowl made it clear how little he cared.

"All things considered, maybe you should've picked Disneyland. I mean, aye, *you'd* be the one paying *them* for the rides, but still a better fucking deal than the one you've got."

Sarah's eyes darted down, but she rallied quickly. "Why are we talking about Elysium, anyway?"

"It's a drug," Hoon said.

"Oh? Sounds fun!"

Sarah winced and held up a hand in apology when both men turned and glowered at her. "Just kidding!"

"You'd better be. Spell it again," Holden prompted, and he typed the letters as Sarah spoke them.

There was another series of whirrs and clunks, then the same unforgiving tone as before.

"Fuck," Hoon muttered. He scratched at his head, then at his chin, then pointed at the computer again. "Try 'the Loop.'"

Holden's fingers, which had been poised above the keyboard, ready to start prodding, remained motionless.

"Fuck sake, you don't need me to spell that out, too, do you?"

"Did you say the Loop?" he asked.

Hoon's eyebrows shot up his forehead. He sat forward, his heart skipping a beat. "Aye. Why? You heard of them?"

"I have," Holden confirmed. "Massive pain in my ass."

"Fuck. OK. So, what? What do you know about them?"

"Nothing. Nothing more than the name." He fixed Hoon with a sceptical look. "What are you saying? Are you saying they're real?"

"Aye."

"Seriously?"

"What do you mean? I thought you said they were a pain in your arse?"

"Not so much them as a guy getting on my case about them. Convinced they're some kinda big bad, I don't know, crime syndicate."

"Aye, well. They are."

"Huh. OK. I'll be damned."

One of the drawers in the detective's desk squeaked as he wrestled it open. After a bit of rummaging, he found what he was looking for.

"Yeah, well, like I say. I don't know anything about them," he said.

He placed a dogeared business card on the desk and slid it

across to Hoon. A simple logo on the front read 'King Investigations.' Below that, in a blocky font, was the motto: 'Taking Care of Business.'

"But," Holden said, eyeing the card up like he was worried what it might be about to do, "I know a man who does."

"Nice one," Hoon said, taking the card and pocketing it.

"I should warn you. He's an... unusual character."

"Course he fucking is. You're all fucking mental over here," Hoon said.

He made a concerted effort not to look at the unlocked computer on Holden's desk. The last thing he wanted to do was draw the detective's attention to it.

"Cheers for this," he said, patting the pocket where he'd stashed the card. "Now, any chance of that cup of tea before we fuck off out of your hair?"

Holden looked a little put out as he glanced in the direction of the kitchen. "I'd, uh, I'd need to go look for it."

"No bother," Hoon said. He reclined in his chair and tucked his hands behind his head, still pretending like the detective's computer and fully searchable police database didn't exist. "You just take your fucking time."

CHAPTER NINETEEN

THE ROUTE to the private detective's office took them partway along the Las Vegas Strip. Hoon drove, giving Sarah a chance to gawp and marvel at all the flashy neon lights.

"Is that the Eiffel Tower?" she asked, pressing a finger against the grubby glass of the borrowed Lincoln. "Is the real one that big?"

"Is it that fucking big? It's about five times that size," Hoon told her. He blasted the horn at a slow-moving driver in front, and gestured for him to get out of the way.

"Really? Whoa. I'd love to see that."

"Aye, it's quite impressive," Hoon conceded. "Be better without all the fucking French folk milling about, but, aye. It's good." He glanced across at her. "You should go. Get out of this fucking place."

Sarah kept looking out at the passing lights. Grand hotels and casinos lined the road. Even at this hour, thousands of late-night revellers roamed the streets, singing, and laughing, and trying their best to stay upright.

"It's not so bad," she said.

"Fuck me. Seriously? Where were you living before this? Guantanamo fucking Bay?"

"Ha," she said, but there was no humour in it. "You're not far wrong."

They drove on, passing spectacular fountains, dazzling lights, and grand, towering casinos. Sarah marvelled at a Pyramid, and gasped with excitement when she saw someone strolling down the strip in an ill-fitting, knock-off Donald Duck outfit.

Hoon wanted to let her enjoy it, but couldn't stop himself from asking the question.

"What happened with your mum?"

Sarah's head whipped around, staring at him in shock, like he'd just stabbed her in the back.

"Your detective pal back there said she'd been looking for you."

"I don't want to talk about it," Sarah said, turning back to the window.

"Tough shit. I'm paying you for this." He shot her another sideways look. In her reflection, her eyes were wide and blurry. "So, spill. What's the fucking story? What did she do?"

Sarah remained tight-lipped, saying nothing.

"Was it a falling out? Abuse? Was she just an arsehole? What?"

"She didn't believe me," Sarah said. Her voice was low, barely audible above the rumble of the Lincoln's huge, bald tyres.

"About what?"

The voice dropped another few decibels, and it took Hoon a bit of figuring out before he realised what she'd said.

"My stepdad."

Hoon flexed his fingers and gripped the wheel. "Right."

"I tried to tell her. She didn't want to know. So, I left."

"Aye. Fair enough," Hoon said, and he closed his eyes, just for a moment. "When did you last speak to her?"

"I'm not doing this," Sarah snapped, anger blazing in her

purple-ringed eyes. "You want me to drive around with you and pretend we're friends? Fine. You want to fuck me? Sure. Why not? But I'm not talking about that stuff. OK? I'm just not."

"Fine. Suit yourself. None of my fucking concern," Hoon said, then he swung the car into a sharp turn, pulling off the Strip and heading for a section of Vegas that Detective Holden had referred to as 'Naked City.'

Just a few hundred yards down the next street, the glitz and glamour of the Strip quickly faded in the rearview mirror, replaced by dilapidated buildings and graffiti-covered walls that stood in stark contrast to the neon-lit casinos and luxury hotels.

The Lincoln rumbled on, Sarah now more interested in her own hands than the sights beyond her window. Hoon couldn't really blame her. It wasn't his cup of tea, but he couldn't deny the Strip had been impressive in its own gaudy, eye-watering kind of way.

There was nothing impressive about Naked City, though. Not unless you were big into cracked roads, and pavements swamped with litter and debris. The buildings lining the street were a mix of run-down apartments and shuttered storefronts, most of their windows and doors barricaded with metal bars and plywood boards.

There were places like this in every city. He'd been in plenty of them. This one, though, so close to all the opulence and grandeur, somehow felt worse than most.

There were no late-night revellers here, just a few zombie-like homeless people, pushing shopping carts piled high with fuck all of value.

A few other figures huddled in doorways or alleys, smoking cigarettes and casting wary glances at the passing car. A group of young men, with expensive trainers and their jeans hanging halfway down their arses, eyed the Lincoln with a mix of suspicion and hostility.

The detective's office was located in a nondescript two-storey building, sandwiched between a heavily barricaded liquor store and a pawn shop advertising 'Cash for Gold' in faded lettering. The building's brick facade was covered in a patchwork of graffiti tags. They were all heavily stylised, and Hoon was disappointed that there wasn't a single classic cock and bollocks to be seen.

Hoon pulled the Lincoln up as close to the front of the building as he could, so he could hopefully keep an eye on it from inside. He couldn't care less what happened to the car, but it would be a pain in the arse to have to wait for a taxi, and there was always a chance he'd end up with the Duchess again.

"Should I stay here?" Sarah asked. It was the first words she'd spoken since her outburst, and they sounded guarded.

Hoon looked at the street around them. "I mean, if you want to be murdered and eaten by crackheads, aye, knock yourself out. Otherwise, you might want to stick with me."

She opened the door and got out before he'd even had a chance to move, and he scrambled to catch up with her.

"Hold your fucking horses, sweetheart," he warned, intercepting her before she could ring the buzzer mounted on the wall next to the reinforced metal door of the detective's office.

The windows were barred, and a set of dust-covered blinds were drawn, but a light was burning inside, and spilled out through the gaps in the metal slats.

"What? You want to talk to him, don't you? We talk to him, you find your friend, and we're done. You give me the bonus you promised, you go, and I get back to work."

Hoon wanted to say something to her. Something clever. Something helpful. Something kind.

But the words wouldn't come. Instead, he just shrugged, muttered, "Aye, fair enough," and then pressed the button beside the door.

They waited.

Along the street on their right, the group of young lads were starting to pay more attention. There were ten or twelve of them, all different sizes, all different colours, but all with the same hungry look about them.

A couple of the more observant ones nudged the others. All eyes turned towards the two out-of-place newcomers.

Hoon took some reassurance from the cold weight of Harry's gun that was still tucked into the back of his trousers, but he didn't for one second think the gang would be unarmed. If it came to a straight firefight, the odds were not in his favour.

He pressed the buzzer again. "Come on, come on," he muttered, holding his finger on the button.

"He might not be in," Sarah said. She'd spotted the group of men starting to drift towards them. The approach looked fairly aimless at the moment, but it could kick into higher gear at any moment.

"Knock on the window," Hoon urged. "And, if I say go back to the car, you fucking run, get in the driver's seat, and go. Alright?"

Sarah caught the keys he tossed to her, stared at them like they were something toxic or explosive, but then nodded.

"Window," Hoon said, and he gave the door a hammering as Sarah slipped her hand between the window bars and rapped her knuckles on the glass.

The gang was fifty yards away now. Less. Hoon could hear them muttering. Goading each other on. Making plans.

Forty yards. They were getting faster. More focused. A school of sharks sensing blood in the water.

"Right. Fuck. OK. Abort," Hoon hissed. "Go. Get to the car before—"

The metal door in front of him opened outwards, forcing him to jump back to avoid being clouted by it.

Hoon caught a glimpse of a dark quiff and a triangle of chest hair, before his attention was drawn to the sawn-off shotgun that was currently being levelled at his head.

"Son, if you're looking for trouble," the man in the doorway drawled in a deep, resonating Memphis accent. "Y'all came to the right place."

CHAPTER TWENTY

"BELIEVE ME, pal, the last thing I'm fucking looking for right now is trouble," Hoon said, holding his hands up.

He'd considered going for the pistol in his waistband, but the guy held the shotgun like he knew how to use it, and Hoon suspected that his brains would be a smouldering pâté on the Lincoln's windscreen before he'd even reached for his weapon.

"Glad to hear it, son. Now, you got ten seconds to get the hell out of here, and I gotta tell you, when I count, I count fast," the man with the sawn-off warned. "So, y'all might want to get going."

Hoon stole a short, sharp look along the street. The gang had slowed a little when the shotgun had come into play. A few had been deterred by it, but several of them continued to creep closer.

"Look. Just hold your fucking horses, alright?" he said, turning back to the man silhouetted in the doorway. "We came here because we were hoping you could help us out. A fucking police guy..." He clicked his fingers at Sarah.

"Detective Holden."

"Aye, him. He gave me your card. Look. Hang on."

Slowly, Hoon reached into his shirt pocket, and held out the business card. "See?"

"That's just a handwritten phone number."

"What? Oh. Fuck. Hang on." Hoon side-eyed Sarah for a fraction of a second, then turned the card over, revealing the same logo that adorned the inside of the barred window beside them. "See? He told me that you might be able to help me find a mate of mine."

"Afraid y'all wasted your time. I don't do that stuff no more."

"Bob," Sarah whispered. Her gaze flitted anxiously along the road. Another few seconds and the gang would be on them. What happened after that was anyone's guess.

"Look, if we can just come in for a minute, we can—"

"You got treacle in them ears, son? Because, I got to counting in my head, and I passed a counta ten up in the ol' grey matter a long time ago."

He raised the gun. His finger hugged the dual triggers.

"Wait, wait! The Loop!" Hoon said, urgently hissing out the words.

There was a moment of heavy, stunned silence.

It was better than the roar of gunfire.

"What the hell did you say, son?"

"My mate. The guy who's gone missing, he was looking into the Loop," Hoon replied. "I know about them. I know they're real. I've fucking dealt with the bastards myself."

Another pause. Another moment of not having his innards painted across the front of the borrowed car.

"Well now. Is that a fact?"

The gun was lowered. The dark-haired silhouette stepped aside.

"In that case, I guess you folks'd better just go right ahead and step inside."

Hoon grabbed Sarah by the hand and pulled her through the

doorway, just as the first few members of the gang broke into a run.

They stopped when the sawn-off was turned in their direction.

"Sorry, fellas," the man wielding it said. "We're closed."

He slammed the metal door shut, then fastened three heavy locks and a couple of thick sliding bolts, ignoring the few half-hearted kicks and bangs from outside.

As he turned to face his guests, he lowered the shotgun to his side, but didn't yet move to put it down.

Now that he was no longer silhouetted by the light behind him, Hoon could get a clearer look at the man he guessed was the proprietor of King Investigations.

He was in his sixties, with a quiff of black hair and thick side-burns that had suggestions of grey at the roots. The height of the hair made him look even taller than the six-foot-odd that he already was. Though age had atrophied him a bit, he still packed the bulk of a man who knew his way around a gym. Or, given the slight flattening of his nose, a boxing ring.

He was dressed in a faded black shirt with a high collar that was unbuttoned to halfway down his sternum, revealing a thick mat of salt and pepper chest hair.

A gold pendant hung from a chain around his neck. It was in the shape of a lightning bolt, with the letters T, C, and B clustered around the top of it. The same logo was repeated on one of the many rings he wore on his fingers.

A shiny silver buckle in the shape of an eagle fastened the leather belt that held up his jeans. They were dark blue, slightly frayed at the bottom, and would've been tight on a man ten pounds lighter.

On his feet, he had on a pair of black cowboy boots, the leather creased and well-worn, carrying the scuffs and scrapes from years of heavy usage and light attention.

"Cheers," Hoon said, giving him a nod of thanks. "It was about to get a bit fucking hairy out there."

"Don't mention it, son, but likewise, don't make me regret it. You caught my interest out there, but that don't buy you a free pass to nothin' or nowhere. So, I suggest you keep talking."

"Hi! I'm Sarah."

Hoon and the P.I. both stared blankly at the teenager as she stepped forward and thrust a hand out to shake.

The shotgun was held in the P.I.'s right hand. He considered his alternatives, then swapped it to his left hand before shaking Sarah's.

"Name's Alvin. Alvin King."

"You've got a lovely office, Alvin," Sarah said.

Hoon stole a glance around at the six-foot by three-foot hallway, with its flaking paint and bare floorboards. He decided to say nothing.

"Well, thank you, little darlin'. Thankyouverymuch," he replied, and he seemed genuinely happy about the compliment. "But this right here ain't even the office. It's like a... a whatchamacallit? A foyer, or some such. The actual office is right through that door."

Sarah managed to look excited by this, and pointed to the door beside her. "What, this door?"

"That's right, honey. The one right there that says 'Office' on it." He held a hand out to her, palm open, pointing upwards. "May I?"

Sarah's smile widened. She placed her hand in his. "You may," she said.

As Alvin led her towards the door, Sarah looked back over her shoulder and pulled a complex series of facial expressions in Hoon's direction.

He had no idea what any of them meant, though, so just shrugged at her and followed them through into the nerve centre of King Investigations.

"It's a shithole." Hoon sighed. "Surprise, sur-fucking-prise."

"Sorry, folks. Can't say I was expecting company. I'd-a tidied up, if I knew you were coming."

The office was a decent size, or would have been, if an office was all it was.

It was like several different rooms were all trying to exist in the same space at the same time, and none of them was the outright victor.

An old oak desk stood in the middle of the room, with a revolving chair beside it that was now more masking tape than leather.

Behind it, against the wall, a sofa bed was unfolded, the blankets knotted and tangled like whoever had been sleeping there had been woken in the middle of a gruelling bout of night terrors.

A sort of mini-kitchen had been cobbled together from wooden crates, a camping stove, and an ancient microwave that probably ran on raw plutonium.

Despite the cooking appliances, around half the surfaces in the room were covered by pizza boxes, Chinese takeaway cartons, and the wrappers of fast food burgers.

Still holding the shotgun in his left hand, Alvin wrestled the squealing fold-out bed back into its original couch form, and gestured for Sarah to take a seat.

"Sorry, it ain't all that comfortable. But it does ol' Alvin just fine."

"Thanks, it's great," Sarah said, still putting on a chirpy front. She gave the seat of the couch a quick wipe with a hand. Which, given the conditions she was used to, Hoon thought, really spoke volumes.

"And how about you, mystery man?" Alvin asked, turning his attention Hoon's way. "You gotta name?"

"His name's Bob," Sarah said, before Hoon had a chance to answer for himself. "He's Scotch."

"Am I fuck. I'm Scott*ish*."

Sarah's eyes narrowed. "Oh. Is that, like, sort of Scotch? Like, you're not fully Scotch, you're *Scotch-ish*."

"What?" Hoon's scowl was so severe it almost turned his whole face inside out. "No! Is it fuck. *Scotch* is a drink. *Scottish* is what you call folk from— Fuck it. Forget it. Explaining that over here's like talking to a fucking brick wall." He pointed at the man with the shotgun. "You. Tribute Act Elvis. Can you help us or not?"

Alvin furrowed his eyebrows. They were either impressively dark for a man of his age, or he dyed them. Hoon suspected the latter.

"Well, now, that depends. Since you ain't actually told me what it is you want, then I'm afraid I can't rightly answer the question." He pointed at Hoon with the index and middle fingers of his right hand. "But, I'm gonna tell you right now, friend, I take offence at being described as some kinda 'Tribute Act Elvis.'"

Hoon sighed. "Aye. Right. Fair enough. It's just, you know, with your whole fucking schtick you've got going on, I'm sure I can be forgiven for seeing a certain fucking similarity between—"

"Ain't nothing 'tribute act' about the King," Alvin continued. He pointed at himself with a thumb. "Ol' Alvin here's the real deal. The current and only physical Earthly vessel for the one-of-a-kind, bona fide, immortal Holy Spirit of the King of Rock and Roll, Elvis Aaron Presley, Hallelujah, Amen, yes sir."

Hoon considered the P.I. for several long, thoughtful moments.

"Fucking hell," he muttered, running a hand down his face.

He looked over at Sarah, but his next question was really aimed at the world in general.

"Is there a single person in this arsehole of a country who isn't completely off their fucking trolley?"

"I was twenty-five years old when Elvis entered me."

"I hope it was fucking consensual."

"September Fourteenth, 1984." Alvin pointed to Hoon with

two fingers. "Eight forty-seven A.M. He's been in here with me ever since, getting things done and taking care of business."

"Course he fucking has." Hoon sighed. He didn't have the time for this, and he certainly didn't have the inclination. "Anyway, glossing the fuck over all that, you're a private detective?"

"That's what the sign on the window says."

"Right. Aye. Fair enough. Like I said, I'm hoping you can help me find a mate of mine. I think he's somewhere in Vegas."

"Vegas is a big ol' place, son, and you ain't giving me a whole heap of information to be working with. Who, what, where, when, why?"

"Well—"

Alvin held up a hand. "But, before we get to that stuff... Y'all mentioned the Loop. That's what made the King's ears prick up and got you through that door. But, I ain't put this gun down yet, which means I don't trust you none. Not yet, anyway. So, how about y'all get to talking, lickety-split?"

Hoon sighed. Again. "Are you going to keep this up the whole fucking time?" he asked. "With the fucking lip-curling and all that?"

"Yes, sir, I am," Alvin said. He raised the shotgun. "Now, y'all going to tell me what you know, or do I gotta throw your asses right back out there on that street?"

CHAPTER TWENTY-ONE

FOR A MAN so keen to hear what his guests had to say, Alvin King wasn't a great listener. He interrupted every few sentences, though never to add anything of any real value.

"Uh-huh."

"Sure thang."

"Keep talkin'."

That sort of thing.

Hoon was one more, "Hoo-mama!" away from killing everyone in the room when the P.I. eventually fell silent.

It was mention of the Loop that did it. Up until then, Hoon had been talking about Miles, and about what had happened on his search so far.

He'd left out the bit about killing a Florida Sheriff and at least two deputies, because that had largely been an accident, and he was putting the blame for it squarely on Iris's shoulders.

Sarah hadn't believed a word about the drug deal and the exploding alligator, but Alvin had just laughed and said, "I'll be damned," throughout the story in a way that suggested it wasn't the craziest thing he'd ever heard.

Then again, the mad bastard claimed to be possessed by the

spirit of a dead musical icon, so when it came to 'crazy,' he clearly wasn't wanting for experience.

Once Hoon had got to talking about his previous run-ins with the Loop, Alvin's lip had uncurled, his shoulders had drooped, and the Presley persona had faded into the background.

Elvis, it seemed, had left the building.

"So, all I really know is that Miles was digging into some new drug."

"Elysium," Sarah said, and she looked pleased that she'd been able to be helpful.

"I think he reckoned the Loop's involved in making the stuff. Whether they are or not, I don't have a fucking clue, but he went digging, and now he's nowhere to be found."

"He might be dead," Sarah suggested. It was the first time she'd heard the full story, and clearly she didn't fancy Crabtree's chances.

Hoon frowned. "I mean, aye. He might be, but I'm hoping he's fucking not."

Sarah winced. "But he probably is."

"Well, thanks for the fucking positive vibes, sweetheart. Jesus fucking Christ! Here's me trying to be fucking upbeat about something for once, and there you come along like a flock of diarrhoetic fucking seagulls and shite all over it."

"Sorry!" Sarah shrugged. "I mean, he might be alive. Somehow."

Hoon tutted and turned back to Alvin. The P.I. had sat the shotgun down on his desk now, and slumped into his chair. From where Hoon was standing, it would be a toss-up as to who could reach the gun first.

Of course, the pistol in Hoon's waistband would tilt the odds in his favour, if it came to it.

But, Alvin didn't seem to be any threat now. If anything, he was shrinking further and further into the chair. He seemed to be getting smaller, while the stressed-out look on his face became more and more intense. Keep that up, Hoon thought, and there was a very good chance he'd collapse in on himself like a black hole.

"Anyway, what's your story?" Bob asked. "Most people I know just stare fucking blankly if the Loop gets a mention. How come you've heard of the bastards?"

Alvin ran a hand through his high pompadour, and seemed momentarily surprised by it.

"Sorry?" he mumbled, like he'd been a million miles away.

"The Loop. The fucking... crime thing. Terrorists. Whatever the fuck they are. Take it you've had a run-in with them at some point?"

Alvin blinked and looked around the room like he was seeing it for the first time. His gaze fell on the shiny silver window blinds, and on his warped and broken reflection in it.

Hoon watched as his lip pulled up and his chest inflated. Alvin rose to his feet, and drew himself up to his full, fairly impressive height.

"Son, that right there ain't none of your business," he drawled, the accent returning with reinforcements. "Now, that was quite a tale you told, and I liked the way you told it, though I didn't much like the cussin'. But, I'm afraid you wasted a trip coming here. I can't help you."

"What? What the fuck do you mean?"

"Can't say it any clearer than I just have. Once upon a time, different place, hell, different man, maybe we coulda helped one another. But that time's long gone, and that man...? Well, that guy's long dead."

"I just need someone who knows their fucking way around, that's all," Hoon shot back. "I'm no' asking you to actually deal with the bastards. Just help me find where the fuck he's got to."

"I said I can't, *alright*?!"

The P.I. barked out the words, flecks of spit flying along

behind them. His hands were shaking, so he leaned on the desk, pressing them against the scratched wood.

"I just can't get involved. Not again. And your friend, if you find him, you outta tell him to leave well enough alone, too. If he makes it outta this alive, he should run from those sons of bitches and never look back."

"Can't see that happening."

"Then he's a damned fool!"

"They killed his fucking family," Hoon said, with a blunt matter-of-factness that made Sarah let out a little gasp of shock. "Wife. Little kiddie. Killed the fucking pair of them. You don't turn the other cheek on that."

Alvin stopped. Stared. Swallowed.

"In that case, I think your pretty young friend here might be onto something," he said, once he'd steadied himself. He drew in a breath. "One way or another, I expect that your friend is already dead."

"Then, help me find who killed him."

"Son, I am sixty-five years old. I got a plastic hip, fading eyesight, and I sometimes have to sit down to take a piss. What you're asking... Well, I don't do that stuff no more. Think your best girl's cheatin' on you? Sure thing. You lost your hound dog? I can help with that."

He inhaled through his long, crooked nose, and shook his head. "But what you're asking...? Getting involved in that whole mess again?"

Alvin looked at his reflection in the blinds. Sitting, it had been broken up and distorted in the metal slats. Standing, there was almost nothing left to see of him at all.

"That, I can't do. I hope your friend's still in the land of the living, and I truly am sorry for all your hardship and loss, son." He picked up the shotgun. Hoon made no move to stop him. "But I'm afraid I'm gonna have to ask you folks to kindly get the hell out of my office."

WHEN THE DOOR slammed closed at Hoon and Sarah's backs, the gang of young lads was nowhere to be seen. That was the good news.

The bad news stood in front of the Lincoln, still looking like a badly shaved ape, though now with the addition of a bloodied bandage taped across his bloated and swollen nose.

"Harry!"

The fear in Sarah's voice made the blood go rushing to Hoon's head. He stepped forward, his fingers already forming fists, a string of barbed obscenities lining up on the tip of his tongue.

Harry didn't move. Didn't flinch. Didn't stop grinning.

Hoon realised, too late, what that meant.

He tried to turn, but something hard hit him across the back of the legs with a hollow, metallic-sounding noise. Hissing, he dropped to his knees, scrabbling for the gun in his waistband.

A punch like a jackhammer was driven into his right kidney. A rough, ragged bag was pulled down over his head. He coughed and choked on the dust, fingers digging into the cord that was pulled tight across his throat, the pistol forgotten.

Another impact rocked him from behind. He felt the world take a sudden, sickening lurch, then pain exploded above his right eye socket as the ground came up to stop his fall.

A foot was driven into his ribcage. He tried grabbing for the gun again, but it was nowhere to be found.

Through the sackcloth material, Hoon caught a glimpse of something close, getting even closer.

The last thing he heard before the foot slammed his head against the sidewalk, was a scream from Sarah, and the low, sickly laugh of her pimp.

CHAPTER TWENTY-TWO

EVERYTHING HURT.

That was good. Pain was good. Pain meant he was alive. Pain meant he was in one piece.

Pain, he could work with.

The spotlight that was currently shining directly in his eyes, on the other hand, he could well do without.

It was blinding. Deliberately, he assumed. It meant he struggled to see where he was, although the smell of the place was a dead giveaway.

He was back at the Mirage Manor hotel.

There was a chair. Hoon was on it. Tied up.

He gave his head a shake, trying to force his jumbled thoughts into some sort of order.

Where was Sarah? She'd been with him. He'd heard her scream, but now...

A couple of large shapes shuffled around in the shadows behind the standing spotlight, like sea creatures drifting through the darkest depths of the ocean.

"The fuck?" Hoon demanded. It wasn't the most nuanced of questions, but it neatly asked for all the pertinent information.

"Oh, look who's awake!"

If voices had knuckles, this one would be dragging them along the floor. Hoon recognised it as Harry's, and immediately strained against the ropes that bound him to the chair.

"I wouldn't bother with that," Harry said. He heaved his weight forward a pace or two until the spill from the light picked out some of his curved edges. "Curly knows a thing or two about knots."

Hoon didn't know who Curly was, but was going to assume he was the cowardly fuck who'd jumped him outside the P.I.'s office.

"Oh aye, why's that? Does he hang around fucking Boy Scouts?" Hoon spat. "And feel free to insert a comma anywhere you like in that fucking sentence, by the way."

Harry's teeth appeared as if from nowhere as the light reflected off his grin.

"Something like that," he said.

With a nod from the ape-man, Curly stepped into the light. Not that it revealed much—his zip-mouthed rubber mask covered his entire head, and even his eyes were cast into pools of deep shadow.

Hoon took in the studded black jumpsuit, the spiked wristbands, and the dog collar around the man's neck, then rolled his eyes and sighed.

"Aye. That makes fucking sense, right enough. Should've seen that one coming. Course he's a fucking weird gimp man on a dog lead. What the fuck else would he be?" He shook his head. "Is there a fucking mental health crisis in the country? Is it no' covered by your insurance, or something? Is your fucking tap water full of lead? What is it with you lot?"

Curly let out a shrill, high-pitched squeal of laughter that faded into the silence of the room. It was a large space, by the sounds of things. The casino section of the hotel, maybe.

No. Spotlight. Wooden floor beneath him.

He was on a stage. This was the hotel's old theatre.

"You stole my property," Harry said.

"You handed me the fucking keys."

More teeth appeared as Harry's grin widened. "I didn't mean the car," he said. "Although, it was the tracker on that what led us straight to you."

"Where is she?" Hoon demanded. "What the fuck have you done with Sarah?"

"I wouldn't worry about her. I'd worry about yourself. You're in a lot of trouble, mister. Ain't that right, Curly?"

On cue, the man in the gimp suit let fly with another shrill burst of laughter that ended as abruptly as it began.

"Christ, his mother must be proud as punch," Hoon said. "'Oh, aye, my Curly's doing awfully well for himself. Some fat prick parades him around on a dog lead, and he's completely fucking wipe-clean these days.'"

He nodded in the gimp's direction.

"Why the fuck do they call him Curly, anyway?"

"On account of his pubes," Harry replied, and the way he said it sounded like some sort of boast. "He's got more pubes than any man, woman, or creature you ever saw."

"Jesus." Hoon's mouth pulled up into a grimace. "I wish I hadn't fucking asked."

He flexed the muscles in his arms, testing the ropes again.

"Where's Sarah?"

"Now, now, Jamal. Don't try and act tough. Your ass is ours."

Hoon scowled into the spotlight. "Jamal?"

Harry looked down, and his jowly, acne-scarred face came further into the light.

"That's you, ain't it? Jamal Mohammed?"

"Fuck. Aye. You've found my passport, then. Good fucking detective work, there. Aye. You got me."

"You're a long way from Sudan, Jamal."

Hoon snorted. "Oh, aye. Like you fucking know where Sudan is. You're all the same, you shower. Anything not on this continent is just fucking 'Here be Dragons' as far as you're concerned."

"You a Muslim?" Harry asked. "You don't look much like a Muslim."

"I'm with the undercover branch," Hoon replied. "Now where the fuck is Sarah? And, fair warning, if I have to ask you that again, I will fucking hurt you."

Harry ignored the threat. "Do you know what this is, Jamal?"

He stepped forward, his bulk partially blocking the light. In his hands, he was holding a magician's prop that Hoon recognised at once.

"It's a guillotine."

"This is a—" Harry realised he'd been beaten to it, and looked a little annoyed when he could only nod in confirmation. "Well done. That's right. I found it through the back a few years ago. There was a little switch on the side that meant when you did *this*" —he pushed down a handle, and the blade sliced through a small circular opening about the width of a wrist—"then nothing bad happened. The sharp bit just folded itself in out of harm's way."

He slowly pulled the back again, drawing the blade all the way to the top.

"I took that switch off. Tossed it in the trash. Now, this thing's razor sharp and rock solid."

"Right, aye. Very fucking good," Hoon said, and there was a note of impatience in his voice, like he wanted them to crack on. "And I'm guessing you're planning on sticking my fingers in there, or something?"

"Your fingers? No. Well, maybe eventually," Harry shook his head, making his jowly cheeks wobble. His gaze flitted to Hoon's crotch. "I thought we'd start somewhere else first."

Curly's shrieking laughter rang out again. Hoon pointed at him with a tilt of his head.

"Can you make him quit doing that? It's like fingernails down a fucking blackboard. I know you've zipped his mouth shut, but it's no' doing much fucking good. It's, honest to God, one of the worst fucking noises I've ever heard."

Suddenly, from somewhere behind the spotlight, came a blast of *Hammer House of Horror*-style pipe organ music. Hoon groaned.

"Wait. No, I stand corrected. That's a worse noise. You might want to answer that. It's going to be my fucking sister. She won't fucking stop phoning if you don't pick up."

"Your sister?" Harry's laugh came slithering out of him. He picked up the ringing phone. "Ha! Do you think she'll want to hear you dying?"

"Knowing her, she'll jump at the fucking chance."

"What's her name?" Harry asked.

"What does it say on the screen?"

Harry held up the phone. "It says 'The Hellbeast.'"

"There we fucking go, then. That's her name."

Harry smirked as he tapped the button to answer. "Well, hi there, Hellbeast."

Even from across the other side of the stage, Hoon heard the response. Harry jerked the phone away from his ear like something had just stabbed him in it.

Curly turned his rubber-clad head to look at the phone, his eyes shifting awkwardly in the shadows of his mask.

"No. Just... Hold on... Wait just a..." Harry took a deep breath. "Shut the hell up!" he roared, holding the handset out so that the caller could hear him, but he couldn't hear them.

Probably for the best, Hoon thought.

"Now, you listen here. We got your brother here with us. We're going to start cutting little pieces off him. And you're going to listen to all of it. You're going to listen, and you ain't going to be able to—"

Berta's tinny voice spat at him through the earpiece. He brought the phone a little closer so he could hear better, but not close enough that she could blow out his eardrum.

After a moment, and some uncomfortable shuffling, he put his hand over the mouthpiece and looked across at Hoon. "She says she wants to talk to you."

"Jesus Christ. Can you no' just tell her I'm busy?"

Harry hesitated like he was considering his options, then he wobbled over to Hoon and placed the phone next to his ear. "Tell her yourself."

"Fucking hell," Hoon muttered. He tilted his head closer to the mobile. "Berta? That you? Listen, I'm kind of fucking tied up here." He looked up at Harry as he listened. "Aye, he is a fucking horrible-sounding bastard, you're not wrong. Aye, he looks even fucking worse, if you can believe that?"

His eyes narrowed as he listened to the voice rasping at him down the line.

"Spooky bastards? What do you mean? What spooky bastards? At the house? What the fuck did they want?"

He listened, growing increasingly irate.

"Well, you could've fucking asked them. So, did you...?"

He fell silent, then shut his eyes and sighed. "Fucking Iris. So, whoever the fuck they are, they know I'm in America?"

Berta's voice barked tinnily from the earpiece, and Hoon's face puckered up in irritation.

"What? For fuck's sake. Seriously? Now? Do you no' think I've got bigger problems to be—"

Even though Harry couldn't make out the words, he got the gist of what the woman was saying from the tone of her response.

"Fine. Fine. Fuck sake." Hoon sighed. "So. Right. Have you pressed the Sky button? No, not on the box. On the remote. Up the top." He gritted his teeth and listened. "What do you mean? It's the one that says fucking 'Sky' on it."

He listened for a moment, then tutted.

"Well, there you fucking go, then! That's why it's not fucking changing the channel. You didn't press the button. I've told you this. We've been fucking through this!"

There was a blast of sound from down the line.

"There. That's you," he said. "No, I know it's fucking Bargain Hunt. I can hear the theme tune. Is it one of the old ones or—? Fuck. Doesn't matter. I don't care. I've got a fucking Sasquatch and a man dressed like a fucking rubber Johnny here, I need to go and—Hello? Hello? Berta." He tutted. "She fucking hung up. Can you believe that?"

Harry was still holding the phone, but was now staring at it like he didn't quite understand what it was, or what he was doing with it.

Quite clearly, the call had not gone as he'd been anticipating.

For Hoon, it was more or less exactly what he'd expected.

"I'd turn the fucking sound off, if I was you," he advised. "She'll only fucking phone back once she realises I've deleted a hundred and seventy episodes of Emmerdale."

Harry shoved the phone in his back pocket, then untucked the guillotine from where he'd been holding it under his arm. It hadn't been a particularly appealing item to start with, and a minute and a half jammed in the ape man's armpit had not improved it any.

"Now, you wobbly bitch. Where's Sarah?" Hoon asked.

Harry shuffled his weight around until he was standing in front of his prisoner. His grin returned, all yellow teeth and caked-on scum.

"Her name is Candy. And, I thought you said that next time you asked, you were gonna hurt—"

Hoon's foot came up quickly, right between the bastard's legs. The guillotine clattered to the floor as Harry clutched his bollocks and staggered backwards, huffing out something that rode the line between a scream and a spray of hot projectile vomit.

"Aye. So I did," Bob said. "Thanks for the fucking reminder."

Over by the light, Curly screeched out another laugh and jumped up and down on the spot, excitedly slapping his rubber-gloved hands together.

Harry swallowed down a mouthful of sick, and hissed, "Hold him down! Get his pants off!" as he retrieved the fallen guillotine from the floor.

"Fucking try it, pal, and we'll see where it gets you," Hoon spat, but it was false bravado. Every word. He knew it, and so did they.

He'd got lucky with that kick, but they wouldn't make the same mistake again. And, weirdo sexual fetishist or not, Curly really did seem to know his way around a clove hitch. Try as he might, struggle as he had, there was no way Hoon was getting free of those ropes.

"You want to know where Candy is?" Harry spat, his blubbery lips twisting into a taunting sneer. "She's upstairs. She's back to work. I gave her one of the rougher ones. A real piece of shit. Violent-like. Maybe stop her from getting any ideas."

Hoon kicked. Spat. Raged. "You fucking arse-eyed donkey's cock! I'll fucking kill you!"

He thrashed against his restraints, face turning purple, veins standing out like electrical cables, coursing his surging anger through his body.

The ropes held. The chair, too. He could do nothing. He couldn't help her. He couldn't even help himself.

Christ. Was this it? Was this really how it was going to end? Cut to pieces, cock-first, by a human blancmange and a deviant in a diver's suit?

After everything he'd been through, was this how Bob Hoon finally met his maker?

He saw the guillotine. Saw the glee on Harry's face, and the dark shadows of Curly's eyes as the gimp rushed towards him, gloved hands clawing at him, grabbing for him, tearing at the belt of his combat trousers, at the buttons, at the waist.

"Get 'em off," Harry said. A purple tongue flicked hungrily across his lips. "Get them pants off." He slammed the blade of the guillotine down. "And let's get to cutting!"

THOOM!

The spotlight died, plunging the stage into darkness.

Harry's voice rang out through the void.

"What the hell? Piece of shit electrics. Curly, get that damn light back on."

The grasping hands left Hoon's waistband. He got a sense of Curly shambling through the dark, then heard the *click-click* of a switch being flicked back and forth.

"Oh, what the hell now?" Harry hissed. "Don't tell me the damn fuses are shot again."

From somewhere in the dark, a voice emerged.

"I wanna start by telling you folks that I'm sixty-five years old," it began, in a low, resonating drawl. "I got a plastic hip, failing eyesight, and I sometimes gotta piss sitting down."

"Who the hell...?"

Harry fumbled in his pocket until he found his phone. He stood staring at it for a few seconds, his slack-jawed expression picked out in the glow of the screen, as he tried to remember how to turn on the torch.

A floorboard creaked. The voice, when it came again, was louder. Closer.

"I ain't telling you any of this to elicit sympathy, or in the hope that it'll make you go easy on me. Quite the opposite. I'm telling you this so you know exactly who it was that waltzed right on in here and kicked your ass."

With a little cry of triumph, Harry found the torch function on his phone. A cone of white light shone onto a broad chest, and was reflected off a thousand golden sequins in the shape of an American eagle.

"Ladies and gentlemen..." Alvin's top lip curled into a playful sneer.

He whipped both hands out into a karate pose, and Hoon could've sworn he heard them whistling as they sliced through the air.

"Elvis has entered the building."

CHAPTER TWENTY-THREE

IT WAS POETRY.

No. Better than that.

It was rock and roll.

The first blow—a fingertip strike that lunged like an attacking cobra—hit Harry between two of his chins, driving deep into his throat.

He stumbled, gagging and choking, letting his phone fall to the floor. The impact switched the torch into strobe mode, and Hoon watched the rest of the fight play out in jerky stop-motion.

From his perspective, it was a fun-packed extravaganza of violence. To those caught up in it, though, it must've been like being in a horror movie. Except, rather than Freddy Krueger or Jason Voorhes being the hunter, it was a vengeful, aging Elvis Presley.

He seemed to flit through the beats of the darkness, there one moment, gone the next, leaving only pain in his wake.

Every pulse of light left Harry more bloodied. More shocked. More scared.

Darkness.

Light.

The gun he'd taken back from Hoon was in his hand.

Darkness.

Light.

He spun on the spot, eyes wide and watery, searching for a target.

Darkness.

Curly let rip with his shrieking laugh.

A burst of flame spat from the pistol. A roar like a rip in the world.

Light.

The gimp clutched at his chest, the laughter becoming a wheeze, blood sliding down the front of his rubber suit.

Darkness.

"Oh, shit! Oh, shit, Curly! Curly, I didn't—!"

Light.

A towering figure, resplendent and majestic in his sequined jumpsuit, emerged from the wall of shadow at Harry's back, arms held wide, cape swaying from his shoulders.

Darkness.

A snap. A scream. The sound of something heavy hitting something hard.

Light.

Harry lay facedown on the floor with one of Alvin's heeled boots pressing down on his shoulder. King held one of the pimp's arms by the wrist, twisting it around like he was trying to pull it clean off. The fact that Harry wasn't howling in pain told Hoon that he was either dead, or very much unconscious.

"And that, ladies and gentlemen," Alvin announced, "is how we do things in Memphis."

With a final twist, he let Harry's arm fall to the floor, then he picked up the phone and peered at the icons on the screen. He was wearing a pair of silver-rimmed, purple-tinted sunglasses, and he leaned his head back as he studied the mobile's controls.

Something about the angle of the head and the scrunching up

of Alvin's eyebrows made Hoon think of DI Ben Forde back in Inverness.

"Hang on. Are them shades you're wearing fucking bifocals?"

"Hush now, son. Unless you know how the hell I stop this damn thing flashing?" he asked.

"Never fucking mind that—"

"Hold on now. Tug on them reins. I think—"

The flashing light became a steady beam. Alvin punched the air like he'd just had an album go double platinum.

"Hoo-mama! Got it first try."

"Aye, good for you," Hoon spat. He thrashed around to indicate his restraints. "Now, get me out of these ropes, turn that fat fucker over..."

He ground his teeth together, chewing through the next few words.

"And pass me that fucking guillotine!"

HARRY'S FIRST INSTINCT, when he regained consciousness, was to scream.

The sound bubbled up in his throat, but then got lodged there when he saw his former prisoner kneeling above him, and realised there was something being held against his face.

"Alright, there, Tubs? I'd stay pretty fucking stock-still, if I was you. Your nose is through the wee fucking hole in what looks to me, a layman, like a very fucking sharp chopping device."

Harry tried to twist away, but Hoon pressed his knee down on his chest, pinning him there, and shushed him gently.

"Easy. Easy. Here's what's going to happen. I'm going to cut your nose off, and I'm going to shove it up your arse. I'm going to cut your fingers off, and shove them up your arse. Basically, I'm going to cut a lot of fucking bits off you, and shove them all, one by one, up your arsehole. And not in any real order of size.

First come, first served. If it doesn't fit, we'll find a fucking way."

He leaned down, forcing the hard wooden frame of the guillotine into the pudgy, scarred flesh of Harry's face. Bob's eyes bulged in their sockets, his lips drawing back into a smile of toothy fury.

"Unless you tell me *right fucking now* where I can find Sarah."

HOON FOUND room twenty-two up on the fourth floor. He heard the stinging crack of flesh being struck. A voice rang out even as he lifted his foot and took aim at where the lock met the frame.

"Fight all you like, you little whore! Fighting only gets Daddy more fired up and—"

The flimsy door flew inwards. Even as he was charging across the room, Hoon took in the scene before him.

He saw Sarah, half-naked, her wrists tied to the bed frame, blood on her lips, lines of purple makeup running down each cheek. Her black wig had been removed, revealing a short crop of reddish-blonde hair that made her look even younger than she had.

He saw a man in his sixties with a head of grey hair and pubes to match standing over her, fully erect and decked out in a leather harness that crisscrossed his toned physique and rode right up into the crack of his arse.

He saw a window. Just the right size.

"Who the fuck are you?" the punter demanded, before a rabbit-punch from Hoon snapped his head back and turned a tap on in his nose.

He let out a sob of shock as blood cascaded from both nostrils, over his trembling lips, and down his chin.

"Wait, wait, wait!" he cried. "I didn't mean it! I didn't mean it!"

Hoon didn't listen. Didn't care. He turned the bastard around so he was facing the window, hoiking him up by the harness like it was a handle.

"D-don't do this! Please! Don't you know who I am?!"

Together, they ran, Hoon driving them forward, racing them towards the tall pane of glass at the end of the peeling, mould-riddled bedroom.

"You c-can't do this!" the punter squealed, but Hoon was an unstoppable force now. The wrath of God Himself. "I'm a United States Senator for the State of Californ—"

Thunk. He hit the window, head first, as if it was a brick wall.

His whole body went limp, and Hoon let the dead weight of him drop like a stone to the floor.

Hoon stood looking down at the slumped, totally spangled senator, with his bare arse sticking up in the air. After a moment, he tutted.

"Fuck. Well, that was disappointing," he remarked, then he shot the window a dirty look, and stepped over the unconscious body.

He untied Sarah from the head of the bed, being careful to avert his gaze until she'd grabbed her dress and hurried her way back into it.

"You alright?" he asked her, once she was fully clothed.

She shook her head, wiped the blood from her lips, then strode over to where the senator lay on the floor.

Though still unconscious, he let out a huff of air as she drove the pointed toe of a shoe into his ribcage.

"Now I am," she told Hoon, and she went sweeping out of the room.

Hoon moved to follow, then had a better idea. Taking out his phone, he used a foot to wrestle the naked man onto his back, and snapped off a few photographs.

"Oh, you're a United States Senator for the State of California, are you, pal?" Hoon grinned as he leaned down and patted the punter on the side of the face. "No' for much fucking longer you're not."

SIX THOUSAND MILES AWAY, Detective Constable Tyler Neish sat surrounded by parents and babies on the floor of Inverness Library's children's section, joining in with an enthusiastic rendition of *Twinkle Twinkle, Little Star*.

He'd just reached his favourite bit—the 'like a diamond in the sky part'—when Bob Hoon's voice barked from his phone.

Hoon had insisted on the ringtone, and that it be set to override any and all of the mobile's *Do Not Disturb* statuses. This was the price Tyler paid in return for Hoon's recent help settling some overdue debts.

Unfortunately, the ringtone he'd set up wasn't exactly ideal for an early afternoon library Bookbub session with his wife and their twins.

"*Answer the fucking phone, Boyband!*" the voice commanded. "*Answer the fucking phone!*"

Tyler was already scrambling in his pocket for it before the ringtone had a chance to repeat, the glares of Sinead and the other mothers making his cheeks burn red.

"Sorry, sorry," he muttered, flashing a smile around at them that was ninety percent wince.

The library assistant, a heavily built Shetlander with an impressive baritone, did his best to keep the song going, but the mothers were all too busy judging Tyler to keep singing, but the babies were all too young to know what the hell was going on.

Tyler shot a sideways look at his wife, Sinead, sitting beside him on the floor. "It's a text. It's from Hoon," he said.

"Is it? I'd never have guessed," Sinead whispered back. She

looked around at the other mums and offered an apologetic smile. "Sorry about that."

"Ooh, fuck!" Tyler yelped, then he slapped a hand over his mouth, glanced around at all the angry faces, and muttered another, "Sorry."

He angled his phone so Sinead could see it. She ejected a "Jesus Christ!" of her own, then picked up their son, Cal, who had been lying on the floor, gazing up at her.

"Excuse us for a moment," she said, rising to her feet. Tyler grabbed their daughter, Lauren, then backed away, bowing his head at all the scowling mums until he reached the non-fiction section.

"Why is there a naked man on your phone?" Sinead asked.

"I don't bloody know!" Tyler replied. It was technically a whisper, but it was so shrill that it carried halfway across the library. "Hoon just sent me a load of photos of some bloodied and naked old guy in bondage gear and said 'Twitter that.'"

Sinead frowned, turning her head to escape the baby's finger that was trying to explore one of her nostrils.

"Well, I mean, no one uses 'Twitter' as a verb, do they? It's 'Tweet.' And, even then, it's all changed. It's not even called Twitter these days."

"Seriously?" Tyler squeaked. "That's what you're focusing on here?"

"Give me the phone. Let me look," Sinead said.

With some effort, she swapped the baby she was holding for Tyler's mobile. The twins seemed delighted to be reunited in their father's arms, and celebrated by slapping him repeatedly on the cheek and forehead.

"Hang on," Sinead said, pressing finger and thumb against the phone screen and splaying them.

"What the hell are you zooming in on?!" Tyler asked.

Sinead tutted. "His face! What else would I be zooming in on?"

"I dread to think!"

He stood, jiggling his children and being slapped by them, while Sinead studied the image.

As she did, she took out her own phone, typed in a quick search, then held both mobiles side by side, her eyes flitting between them.

"Bloody hell, I was right. It is him."

She turned the phones for Tyler to see. Both showed the same man. In one image, he was bloodied, unconscious, and naked. In the other, he wore a crisp blue suit and red tie, and stood at a podium in front of a fluttering American flag.

"Oh, shite," Tyler said. "What the hell kind of trouble has Hoon got himself into this time?"

CHAPTER TWENTY-FOUR

IT WAS lunchtime before the police cleared out. Hoon had called Detective Holden directly, suspecting he may be more understanding of the situation than the average Vegas copper.

Also, he couldn't remember the American number for 999.

Holden had rocked up with a squad of gum-chewing, gun-wielding, uniformed cops. They'd arranged an ambulance for Curly, who was miraculously still breathing. And, after all the explanations had been given and cross-checked, Harry had been placed under arrest and led away.

His gun, it turned out, wasn't registered in his name. Nor, in fact, was the Mirage Manor hotel, where he'd been squatting for just shy of the five years that would've allowed him to legally claim the place for himself. A stay in prison was going to put paid to that plan.

Despite some pretty stern questioning, there was no talk of Hoon or Alvin facing prosecution, even when a dazed, mostly naked US Senator was carried down the stairs by two policemen and a member of the Secret Service.

He was hurried out to a waiting black Sedan, but not before

Hoon snapped off a couple more photos and sent them whooshing off through the electronic ether.

Eventually, after some moderate-to-heavy interrogation in the hotel's dilapidated restaurant, Holden sent the Uniforms away, looked around at Hoon, Sarah, and Alvin King in his full Elvis Presley regalia, and shook his head.

"I'm going to tell you what I don't want," he announced. "I don't want to see the three of you again anytime soon. I don't want you causing trouble. Or, if you do, then I don't want to hear about it. I think that's fair, isn't it? I think that's a reasonable request."

Hoon shrugged. "Can't promise anything, but I'll do my best."

Holden's laugh was dry, but genuine. "I'm sure you will." He handed Hoon the fake passport he'd found on the theatre floor. "You might want to get rid of that. A better cop than me would have questions."

Hoon took the passport, gave him a little wave of thanks with it, then slipped it into his back pocket. Beside him, Sarah yawned so hard she almost split her whole head in half, and he had to fight to stop himself following suit.

"And get some rest," Holden said, though his concern seemed to be mostly aimed in Sarah's direction. "You look like you're ready to drop."

Sarah tapped her forehead in salute, then covered her mouth to hide a second yawn.

The detective looked around at them all again, gave another shake of his head, and set off for the door.

He had almost reached it when he stopped and turned back. "Oh! I meant to say, Mr Hoon. I looked you up."

"Oh, aye?"

"Yeah. Public knowledge stuff, mostly. But you've had a very interesting career."

"It's had its fucking moments," Hoon confirmed. He tried not to look pleased about the comment, but there was a suggestion of pride in the angle of his head and the lines of his shoulders.

"I especially liked the piece they did on TV about your experience in that shopping mall," Holden continued. He frowned. "What was the show called? Loose Women?"

Hoon's nostrils flared, and his lips drew up in distaste. "I wouldn't know," he said. "If it was a choice between watching those braying, hatchet-faced harpies utter a single fucking syllable, or eating my own bollocks, I'd be asking you to pass the fucking salt."

"Oh? I thought the ladies on it seemed like a lot of fun!"

Hoon groaned. "Ah, shite," he said. "And here, I was just starting to fucking like you, too."

Holden smiled, then pointed back at the trio. "Looking forward to not seeing you around," he said, then he pulled on a pair of Aviator sunglasses, and headed out into the midday Las Vegas sun.

"Well, folks, that sure was quite a night," Alvin said. He pulled a chair out from under one of the restaurant's tables, spun it around so the back was facing the others, then straddled it.

"Aye, you can fucking say that again," Hoon agreed.

Sarah nudged him with an elbow, and waggled her eyebrows in Alvin's direction. Hoon tutted, but took the hint.

"And, eh, cheers for that, by the way."

"Sorry, son? What am I cheering for?"

"No. I mean, like, thanks."

"For what?"

"For..." Hoon tilted his head at the space behind him, like he was pointing back through time. "All that."

"Riding to your rescue, you mean?"

Hoon pulled a deeply sceptical face. "I mean, 'rescue' is a strong fucking word. I had that under control."

"Not from where I was standing. Looked to me like they were about to chop your pecker off." He held his hands up, all ten digits adorned with chunky, gaudy rings. "I mean, listen, man, maybe that's what y'all are into back in Scotland. And, if so, then I'm sorry if I ruined your night. That was not the King's intention, no sir."

Hoon sighed. "Right. Fine, fine. Don't keep doing the fucking voice. Thank you for the rescue. There." He glanced from Alvin to Sarah. "We all fucking happy now? Or do we need to fucking hold hands and sing Kumbayah?"

Alvin closed his eyes and curled his lip. "Kumbayah, my Lord. Kumbayah," he sang, and he seemed to drift away to some other time and place.

It was, though Hoon hated to admit it, quite impressive. Maybe it was because he still had some ringing in his ears from that gun being fired in quite close proximity to him, but Alvin didn't sound half bad.

"That was beautiful," Sarah said, once he'd finished the song. "Is that one of yours?"

"Wait, wait, hold the fucking bus here," Hoon said, cutting in.

"What's wrong?" Sarah asked.

"What's wrong? I've got a few fucking issues with that question, that's what's wrong. One—no, Kumbayah's no' one of Elvis's. And two"—he pointed to the geriatric in the sparkly jumpsuit—"he's no' actually fucking Elvis."

Sarah frowned. "How do you know?"

"Because— The fuck do you mean, how do I know? Because Elvis has been dead for about fifty fucking years!"

Sarah looked doubtfully across the table at him.

"What's that face? Don't do fucking cynical face at that!" Hoon shot back. "That's the fucking problem with you lot, you're all gullible bastards. He's like, 'Aye, I'm possessed by the spirit of Elvis,' and you're like, 'Oh, aye? That's a very real possibility, right enough.' No, it's fucking not!"

He pointed to Alvin, who still straddled his chair. Amusement sparkled in his eyes, even through the purple haze of his bifocal shades.

"He's no' Elvis. He's some fucking mad old geezer. And I don't mean that in a fucking bad way. Each to their own, I say. You want to pretend to be Elvis, fine. Fire on. More fucking power to you. But you're *not* Elvis, because that would be fucking impossible."

"You really have to cuss so much?" Alvin asked.

"Aye, I fucking do!"

Sarah blinked, a little taken aback by the outburst. "So, what? You don't believe in an eternal soul?"

"For fu—" Hoon shook his head. "No. In the same way that I don't believe in the Bigfoot, or the fucking Tooth Fairy, or trickle-down economics."

"Oh." Sarah looked saddened by this. Like she pitied him, even. "I'm really sorry."

"Save your fucking sympathy, sweetheart. I'll be grand."

He grunted as he stood up. Pain had settled into his legs and his chest, taking root there. Holden had recommended getting checked out at one of the local hospitals, but Hoon had dismissed the idea out of hand. He was fine, he'd insisted. Just a few scrapes and bruises.

Also, he'd heard some real fucking horror stories about US medical bills, and would rather not have to put his insurance coverage to the test.

He looked down at Alvin. "Right. So, is that you in then, or what? You going to fucking help me find my mate?"

Alvin drummed his fingers on the back of the chair, the metal rings clack-clacking against the wood.

Finally, he stood up. "The King can't make no promises, but I got a few places I can hit up. A few folks I can shake down. You give me a name, a photograph, and eight-to-ten hours, and I'll see what I can do."

"Ten hours? Fuck sake, and what the fuck am I meant to do in the meantime?"

Alvin shrugged. "You seem like a creative kinda thinker, son, and this is a big ol' vibrant city. Sure you can find plenty of ways of getting yourself into trouble."

He looked both Hoon and Sarah up and down, then laid a hand on Bob's shoulder.

"But, you want my advice. It's the same as that there detective who just left. Get some rest. Both of you." He gave the shoulder a squeeze, then patted Hoon on the cheek. "Y'all look like the turd that killed the King."

"THE FUCK?"

Hoon stared in wonder at the lavishly decorated hotel suite he now found himself in. Unlike the rest of the Mirage Manor, it was immaculate, the decor pristine, the furnishings still grand and impressive.

Sure, the pink-dyed tiger skin rug spread on the floor in front of the fireplace was a bit gaudy, and the framed paintings on the walls of long-dead stage magicians weren't really to his taste, but there was no denying that the room was a lavish slice of luxury.

"How the fuck has this stayed in this nick?" Hoon demanded. "Have you seen the state of the room I was given? It looks like it's been used to throw orgies for the fucking Wombles."

"The who?"

Hoon tutted. "They're, I don't know, wee fucking dancing mole things. They wear hats. They pick up litter. Doesn't matter. It was a striking image, just take my fucking word for it."

"Harry made sure his suite was looked after. He got a couple of the girls to clean it every day," Sarah said. Her gaze was drawn to a set of double doors at the far end of the living room area, before she quickly looked away again. "That's, uh, that's his bedroom back there."

One of Hoon's eyes twitched. His fingers spasmed into fists.

He should've killed that bastard when he had the chance.

"Right. And what's that one?" he asked, distracting her by pointing to another door.

"Just another bedroom, I think. Like a spare one." She shrugged. "I've never been in there, though."

Hoon strode across to the door, his feet sinking into the thick, lush carpet. Pulling it open, he revealed a dated but clean bedroom with a large double bed and a '60s-style dressing table that was all gloss and curves.

The whole room, in fact, felt like it was from another time and place.

The walls were adorned with a vibrant, patterned wallpaper designed in psychedelic shades of orange, green, and yellow. The curtains, a heavy velvet material that matched the wallpaper's bold colour scheme, were pulled across the window, so the whole room felt a bit like an enclosed cocoon.

The bed was the centrepiece of the room, both literally and figuratively. Its headboard was upholstered in a plush, tufted fabric that really embraced the overall retro aesthetic. The bedspread, a rich, deep green, was embroidered with intricate gold patterns that reminded Hoon of the sequins on Alvin's jumpsuit.

On the dressing table, a large, ornate mirror with Hollywood-style bulbs around its edges hinted at the hotel's history as a haven for performers and entertainers. A plush, velvet-covered stool sat in front of the table, inviting the room's occupant to sit and prepare for their moment in the spotlight.

In the far corner, a vintage record player stood atop a small cabinet, its polished wood surface reflecting the soft glow of the table lamps. The lamps themselves were ornate works of art, their bases crafted from colourful glass in abstract shapes that seemed to dance and shimmer in the light.

"Fuck me," Hoon remarked, as he took in all the details of the room. "It's like Liberace shat out a fucking time machine."

He clocked Sarah yawning, and watched her eyeing up the bed.

"Right," he said, checking his watch. "Might as well get some shuteye while we wait for charity shop Elvis to do some digging. I haven't slept since..." He tried to calculate how long it had been since his last proper sleep, but the various time zones made it too complicated. "Fuck knows. Days."

"Didn't you get knocked out?" Sarah asked.

Hoon tutted. "Aye, but I'm no' counting that! Getting your head kicked into the pavement's no' exactly a restful fucking experience."

Sarah wrinkled her nose. "No. I guess not," she conceded, then she took a breath and turned herself so she was fully facing him. "So, um, do you need anything from me?"

Hoon looked down at her, his confusion clear. "Like what?"

"Like, you know... anything?"

The penny dropped. He really wished that it hadn't.

"No," he assured her, and all his usual gruffness and bluster was notable by its absence. "I don't need anything. You get some sleep."

This was the permission she needed. Her shoulders crept down as the worst of the tension left her body. She smiled and gripped his forearm, her eyes saying all the things her words couldn't.

And then, with another yawn, she plodded over to the bed, and Hoon slipped quietly out of the room.

CHAPTER TWENTY-FIVE

HARRY'S BEDROOM WAS FINE, provided you didn't look too closely, or think too much about who had spent his nights here.

Or the things he'd done.

This room, unlike the generic '60-style one that Sarah was almost certainly already fast asleep in, really leaned into the Mirage Manor's magical theming.

The slightly faded wallpaper was a regular pattern of top hats, playing cards, strings of handkerchiefs, and doves in muted shades of burgundy and gold.

A grand, king-sized bed commanded the centre of the room, directly below a ceiling-mounted mirror that gave Hoon the heebie-jeebies.

The bed's headboard was upholstered in rich red velvet with a subtle silver starburst motif running the length of it, like whatever that glittery stuff was that tumbled out of Tinkerbell's arse in the cartoons.

Hoon wouldn't have pegged Harry as the type of guy to be into cushions in a big way, but a scattering of plump throw pillows lay up near the head of the bed. There were half a dozen of them, each one embroidered with classic magical symbols—linking rings, a magic wand, and a startled-looking rabbit popping out of a top hat, like it was wondering how the hell it had ended up there.

Before Hoon flopped onto the bed, he checked the drawers of the bedside table, hoping to find a gun there. Instead, all he found were condoms, lubricants, and something that he at first thought was a torch, but which turned out to be some sort of severed vagina in a plastic tube.

Despite everything he'd been through in the past few days, he reckoned that was the thing that was most likely to give him nightmares.

He returned it to the drawer, went to the en suite bathroom, and spent a full three minutes washing his hands.

Then, when that was done, he stripped down to his boxer shorts and vest, cleaned and checked out all his various injuries and concluded that they were all survivable, then got into bed.

The mattress was like a cloud. It hugged his aches, and eased his pains, and assured him that he was safe now, could rest now, and that everything would be OK.

He bought into it fully. As soon as his head hit the pillow, he was asleep.

A moment later, he was awake again, roused by a gentle tapping on the door.

"Eh... hello? Aye?"

He rolled onto his back and watched as Sarah inched the door open. She hung back by the entrance to the room, one hand on the handle, the other clutching the frame.

"Um, sorry. Did I wake you up?"

"No," Hoon lied. "What's the matter?"

Sarah shook her head. "Nothing."

"Right." Hoon waited for more, but it wasn't forthcoming. "So, why the fuck are you here, then?"

"Can I sleep with you?" Sarah asked, then her eyes widened

and she quickly rushed to correct herself. "In here, I mean. Not *with you* with you. Just, like, on the floor, or something?"

She picked at her thumbnail, scraping at the thick layer of red polish.

"I just... I usually sleep in with one of the other girls, but the cops sent them all away, so—"

Hoon ran a hand down his face. "Eh, aye. Fine. But I snore like a fucking band saw."

Sarah smiled. "That's fine. So do most of the girls."

She opened the door a little further, as if to enter, but the threshold was an invisible barrier, blocking her entrance. Hoon watched her shrinking back from the room, and the memories it dredged up.

Hoon allowed himself just another moment in the embrace of the mattress, then forced his aching body to move.

"Tell you what," he said, grabbing a pillow and dragging the duvet off the bed. "Why don't I come through to you?"

"YOU AWAKE?"

Hoon lay on his back on the floor, gazing up at the ceiling. A strip of daylight spilled in through gaps at the edges of the curtains, but they were doing a pretty decent job of keeping the room in near-darkness.

The carpet, he was saddened to discover, was not nearly as comfortable as its thickness implied. He'd formed a sleeping bag type arrangement with the quilt, which helped a bit. It would've been fine, had it not been for the lingering memory of those few moments in the tender caress of that luxury mattress.

"No," he said, hoping that would be the end of it.

Up on the bed, Sarah smiled. "I can't sleep."

"Nor can I," Hoon replied. "Some bastard keeps talking to me."

"Sorry!"

She fell silent.

It lasted all of five seconds.

"What a crazy day."

"I've had crazier," Hoon told her.

The bed creaked as Sarah propped herself up on an elbow. "Really? The gimp man? Elvis?"

Hoon gave this some thought. "I mean, aye. I suppose it was up there, right enough," he admitted. "But he isn't Elvis."

"He's pretty close," Sarah said. "It's like that saying."

"What fucking saying?"

"If it walks like a chicken, and it talks like a chicken, it's probably a chicken."

"Duck," Hoon said.

There was a sharp, sudden movement from the bed.

Sarah's reply sounded faint and muffled. "What? Why?"

Hoon raised his head and squinted through the half-dark. He could make out the vague shape of her under the bedclothes, but her head was nowhere to be seen.

"I didn't mean that *you* should fucking duck!" Hoon said. Despite himself, he laughed. "You're a fucking— The saying. 'If it walks like a duck,' no' a fucking chicken."

Sarah emerged, grinning sheepishly, from beneath the covers. "I knew that. It was a joke."

"Your arse it was," Hoon said, then he lay back on his pillow, one arm tucked behind his head.

Silence fell again. Hoon's eyelids grew heavier, his breathing more shallow and—

"You still awake?"

He sighed. "Surprisingly enough, aye."

"Sorry," Sarah said again. "I just wanted to ask. Your friend. The one you're looking for. You must be really close to risk your life for him."

Hoon shrugged. "Not really."

"No? Oh. Then why are you doing all this?"

"Fuck knows," Hoon said. "Habit, I suppose." He kept his eyes closed, making the most of at least this half-sleep. "And he's a good guy."

"Like you."

Hoon snorted. "Very fucking much not like me."

"You are," Sarah insisted. "I meet a lot of... people. Most of them aren't good. Most of them are pretty bad, actually. But you're different."

"I'm really not."

Sarah sniffed. "Well, I think you are."

Hoon chose not to argue. There was a whole catalogue of things he could rattle off to the girl to change her mind. A litany of past sins he could list.

But, for now, he was happy to leave her with her delusions.

"What's the story with your mum?" he asked, changing the subject. The atmosphere in the room took a turn, too.

"No story," Sarah said, and Hoon heard her turning over to face the other way.

"Sounded like there was a story," Hoon persisted. "You told her about your stepdad. She didn't believe you. So you left. That's what you said."

"There we go. That's all of it."

"When was this?"

Sarah sighed. "Doesn't matter."

"Maybe not, but indulge me."

"I want to go to sleep."

"Aye, well, so did I, but someone wouldn't shut the fuck up," Hoon reminded her. "When was this?"

"About three years ago."

"Jesus. And you haven't spoken to her since?"

There was silence, then a slightly croaky, "No."

"You know she was looking for you, aye?"

"Yeah. Nate told me. That's how I got to know him."

"Right. Aye." Hoon yawned. "He said you didn't want to talk to her, though?"

Another pause, longer this time. "No."

"Fair enough. I get it. I'd be pretty fucking raging, too," Hoon said. "But I'd want to fucking tell her that. Face to face. Eye to eye. Make her fucking squirm."

"Yeah, well, I'm not like you."

"Good. Try and fucking stay that way," Hoon suggested. He took a breath, blew out his cheeks, then tried again. "But, you know, what? People are fucking idiots. All of us. We make mistakes. We sometimes react badly to things in the heat of the fucking moment. Believe it or not, I've occasionally been known to be guilty of that myself."

The silence was shorter this time. "No kidding?"

Hoon smiled. "Aye, I'm full of fucking surprises, me. Then again, lots of people are, if you give them a chance."

His nostrils flared, and he shook his head in disgust.

"Fuck me, I sound like a fucking Hallmark card. Do me a favour, and never tell anyone I fucking said that."

There was no reply from the bed. Hoon sat up and peered through the gloom, but could only see the back of Sarah's head.

"You awake?" he asked.

Nothing. Just the soft, slow in-and-out of the girl's breathing.

"Oh well."

Hoon punched up his pillow, jammed an arm beneath it, and lay down.

"Thank fuck for that."

He yawned and closed his eyes, and the welcoming arms of sleep at last reached up and wrapped themselves around him.

HOON'S EYES FLICKED OPEN. The fog of sleep dissipated immediately, and he realised he was holding his breath.

Something had woken him, then. Something that shouldn't have.

The curtains were still pulled, keeping the room wrapped in a thick blanket of darkness. Hoon could still hear the slow, regular rhythm of Sarah's breathing from up on the bed, but adrenaline was already surging through him, making his heart beat faster.

Something had woken him. Something that shouldn't.

But what?

The duvet had become a cocoon around him, forcing him to wrestle his way free until he was standing in the dark in his faded boxer shorts and grey vest.

The crack of daylight he'd seen through the curtains earlier had now vanished. It was night, then. They'd been asleep for hours.

Was that all it was? Had some internal alarm just kicked in to get him up and moving again?

The answer came in the form of a sound from somewhere beyond the bedroom door. A shuffling of a foot on thick carpet. The creaking of a floorboard as weight was applied.

Someone was through there. Someone was there with them in Harry's suite.

Hoon scanned the darkened room for something he could use as a weapon, and settled on one of the ornate lamps. It had a decent weight to it, and the attached cable added a certain degree of versatility to its damage-doing potential.

He was creeping back to the door with it when Sarah's breathing changed, and she shifted around under the covers.

"Hey, what's—?" she began, before Hoon shushed her with a look and a finger to his lips. He pointed to the door of the en suite bathroom, and she followed the order without question.

Hoon waited until he heard the soft clicking of the bathroom's lock, before turning his attention back to the bedroom door, and whoever was sneaking around on the other side.

His options were limited. He could go big, throw open the

door, and try for the shock and awe approach. That might work, assuming there weren't half a dozen armed men waiting out there.

Or, he could go small. Try the stealth approach. Inch the door open and try and get a feel for what was going on out there. Size up the situation before rushing in like a bull in a—

"Ah, fuck it," he muttered, then he pulled the door open and raced out, roaring like a wild animal and swinging the lamp around by its cable.

"Right, ya fucker!" he cried, locking sights on a solitary figure sneaking around the room with a small pocket torch lighting his way. "Eat lamp!"

Hoon broke into a run, the lamp *whumming* as it looped in the air around his head.

The intruder turned. Panicked. Screamed. His torchlight spilled across his face. As Hoon barrelled closer, he saw the fear in the other man's eyes.

Or, in one of them, anyway.

"Jesus Christ, Boggle, it's me, it's me!"

Hoon ejected a strangled, "Oof, fuck!" It was too late to fully abort the attack, so he released his grip a half-second earlier than planned, and the ornate light fixture sailed wide of the intended target, and smashed against a portrait of the late Mungo the Mesmerising.

"Fuck sake, Iris!" Hoon cried. "I nearly fucking lamped your head off there! What the fuck are you doing, you creepy bastard?"

"I was looking for you, Boggle," Iris replied.

Hoon flicked on the light, and Iris flinched like a vampire as the gaudy chandelier sparked into life. His good eye was so blood-shot it was almost entirely red, and the puffy black bags beneath both of them carried the weight of his recent journey.

"How the fuck are you even here?" Hoon asked.

"I'm still tracking your mobile, like. Snuck in because I thought you might be in trouble."

"And you couldn't have fucking phoned me first?"

"Phoned you? No way, Boggle. You know I don't trust technology. They can use it to find you, you know?"

"I'm sure I don't need to point out the fucking irony in that sentence," Hoon said. He checked his watch, but still couldn't figure out the time difference. "But I meant, how the fuck did you get here so quick? Did you drive for thirty-seven straight hours?"

"What? No!" Iris laughed and shook his head. There was something almost delirious about both actions. "It was only, like, thirty-five and a half."

"Jesus fuck, Iris. How long have you been awake?"

Iris winced, like he was bracing himself for the upcoming mental arithmetic. "What day is it?"

"Wednesday."

"The?"

"Third."

"Of?"

"For fu—" Hoon tutted. "July."

Iris's good eye looked up at the ceiling, like the answer might be written there somewhere. The glass eye, for once, was looking straight at Hoon. The effect was a little disconcerting.

"Don't know, Boggle. But it's fine. I took a load of pills."

Hoon's brow furrowed. "What kind of pills?"

Iris shrugged. "Just pills. Blue ones. I got them off a guy at a petrol station. Or—" He grinned, looking very pleased with himself—"a *gas* station! That's what they call them over here, Boggle."

"Aye, I know."

"Even though petrol's a liquid, so it doesn't make sense. They don't like it if you tell them that, though." He rummaged in the pockets of his heavily creased camo jacket. "You want to try the pills? I think I've got some left."

"No, I don't want to try your pills, Iris. Knowing you, they're either fucking horse laxatives or blue Smarties. Either way, I'm grand."

Hoon realised that Iris was no longer listening to him. The glass eye still gave the impression that he was paying attention, but the real one had now swivelled to look at the door at Hoon's back.

"There's a lady there," Iris said. He swallowed, and doffed an imaginary cap. "Hello, Miss," he said, then both eyes teamed up to point in Bob's direction. "There's a lady in your bedroom."

"That's no' my bedroom, it's hers."

"You were in a lady's bedroom," Iris corrected.

Hoon sighed. Already, he could feel the urge to start counting. "I was just keeping her company."

Iris waggled his eyebrows so high and so fast he had to grab for his glass eye to stop it falling out.

"Like, sexy company?" he asked.

"What? No! Nothing like that, Jesus. I'm old enough to be her—"

"Grandfather," Iris said.

"Father," Hoon shot back.

"How old are you, miss?" Iris asked, leaning past Hoon to get a better look at her.

"Uh, nineteen."

"Bloody hell, Boggle. So, maybe even great-granddaughter." He started to count on his fingers. "If you had a baby at sixteen, and then that baby had a baby at sixteen, and then—"

Hoon slapped the Scouser's hand away. "I get the fucking point. But it was nothing like that. I'm just... looking out for her."

Iris folded his arms and grinned. "Aha! She's one of them, is she?"

"One of what?"

"Berta said that you're always doing this."

"Doing what?"

"Taking in waifs and strays. That's what she says. You're a

sucker for a sob story and a lost cause, she says. Always saddling yourself with the lost and the hopeless." He shrugged. "I mean, personally, I've never seen it."

Hoon looked back at him, waiting to see if the realisation would hit.

It didn't.

"Iris, you live in my fucking loft," he pointed out.

"Exactly, Boggle! So, if anyone was going to see anything like that happening, it'd be me. I'm right there on the scene." He glanced around, then leaned closer and dropped his voice to a whisper. "Personally, I think your sister's a bit of a head case. But you didn't hear that from me."

Hoon couldn't really argue there. Instead, he yawned, gave his arse a scratch through his boxers, then pointed between the other two people in the room. "Sarah, Iris. Try and no' listen to anything he says, if you can avoid it. It's probably shite."

"Yeah, he's not wrong," Iris confirmed. "I sometimes think I'm totally losing it. I mean, on the way in here, like, I could've sworn I saw Elvis Presley kicking around out front!"

Hoon's eyebrows rose. He turned and pointed at Sarah. "Right, get dressed and organised. Five minutes."

Sarah gave him a thumbs up, then disappeared back into the room. Hoon looked down at himself as if considering whether he could go out in his current state, then concluded that no, of course he couldn't.

"I need to chuck some clothes on," he told the Liverpudlian. "You want to stay here and get some sleep?"

"Sleep? Nah, Boggle!" Iris tossed a circular blue pill into his mouth, swallowed it, then grinned. "I'll be wide awake for hours yet!"

Hoon shook his head, and set off for the room where he'd dumped his clothes. "Fine. But if you shit yourself inside out, or grow a pair of tits, then don't come fucking crying to me!"

CHAPTER TWENTY-SIX

"SO?" Alvin asked, gesturing around at the diner he had taken the group to. "What do you think?"

For perhaps the first time in his life, Bob Hoon had no words.

He'd had a fair few of them when, following Alvin's directions, he'd turned a corner in the rental car and seen the illuminated sign—*McHaggis's Highland Diner*—casting its red and blue glow across the half-empty car park.

Most of them had been variations on one specific word. A few of them were entirely new and had never been heard before.

He'd had a couple of things to add when they'd been met at the door by a camp thirty-something man wearing a thigh-length kilt, a Tam o' Shanter hat, and an outrageous ginger wig.

When the guy had ejected a high-pitched, "Och aye, the noo!" it was only a rare display of quick thinking from Iris that had held Hoon back and prevented an ugly incident.

Now, though, sitting at a booth, with its plastic tartan tablecloth, single artificial thistle in a vase, and clumsily painted portrait of Mel Gibson in *Braveheart* daubed onto the wall beside him, he had finally reached the point of speechlessness.

Or, he was simply too enraged to get the words out.

"It's Scottish," the P.I. explained, in case all the Saltires and screeching bagpipe music had somehow gone over Hoon's head. "I thought I'd give y'all a little taste of home."

Alvin was smirking, but Hoon couldn't tell if he was just happy about having done a nice thing, or was on the full-on wind-up. He suspected the latter. Nobody, surely, could think this was an accurate representation of any country that existed in the real world.

"Where the fuck do you think I live?" Hoon asked him. "In a tin of fucking shortbread?"

An artist—and Hoon used that term very loosely—had painted a dozen or so Scottish 'icons' on the walls around the place, each one looming over one of the diner's tightly packed booths.

They'd actually got off quite lightly with Mel Gibson's William Wallace. They could've had the pasty, shivering face of Ewan McGregor's heroin-addicted character, Renton, from the movie *Trainspotting* gawping down at them.

Or, worse still, John Barrowman.

Nobody was currently sitting in the Wee Jimmy Krankie booth, and had it not been that the table was covered in the debris left by the last customers, Hoon would've considered swapping. At least Wee Jimmy Krankie was actually Scottish, even if 'he' was really a seventy-six-year-old woman named Jeanette, wearing a cap and short trousers.

It was still more convincing an act than Mel Gibson in *Braveheart*.

Or John Barrowman in anything.

"What is this noise?" Sarah asked, pointing to the ceiling, where the bagpipes were blaring from several mounted speakers. "Is that... Is that music?"

"No. Is it fuck," Hoon said. "That's the fucking mistake

people make, thinking it's music. It's not. It's a fucking declaration of war. Bagpipes aren't a musical instrument, they're a fucking weapon. They're meant to be used on a battlefield to bring abject fucking terror to all the English bastards lying in wait over the next hill. They're all hiding out with their guns and their fucking horses, and here we come marching in sounding like we're giving the Incredible Hulk a fucking colonoscopy."

He gestured with a thumb in the direction the sound was coming from.

"It's meant to invoke fucking fear, that, no' to be danced to."

Iris's head was bobbing from side to side, making his glass eye swivel in the socket. "I don't know, Boggle. I think it's quite catchy."

"Hoots!"

That single word, chirped by a woman in a ginger wig and tartan apron, was enough to let Hoon know that he was about to be subjected to the most mangled attempt at a Scottish accent he'd ever heard in his life.

He gripped the edge of the table in preparation, and tried to ignore the swelling bloodlust that the bagpipes were bringing to the fore.

"Och aye! Welcome tae McHaggis's Highland Diner!" the woman proclaimed.

The accent was incredible. It was from every corner of Scotland all at the same time, yet had simultaneously never set foot in the place. There was a bit of Welsh in there, some Irish, and something that might conceivably have been early nineteenth-century Dutch.

"We bring only the freshest fare aw the way fae waw up high in the *moontains* o' the homeland of oor founder, Archie McHaggis," the woman continued in the same, fascinatingly awful, style.

She was, to her credit, giving it laldy, delivering her lines like she was auditioning for the London stage. Hoon wasn't sure, however, if that made it all better or worse.

Archie McHaggis was the diner's cartoon mascot. From what Hoon could gather, he was a sentient, kilt-wearing haggis with a big bushy grey moustache and a tartan bonnet.

He was playing the bagpipes with one arm, and thrusting a claymore towards the sky with the other, like he was summoning the Power of Grayskull. All he needed was to be tossing a caber and eating a Deep Fried Mars Bar, and he'd have been the single most offensive stereotype ever immortalised on a laminated restaurant menu.

Which, given some of the Mexican places Hoon had been in over the years, was really saying something.

"Just coffee," Hoon said, without so much as a glance at the food on offer. He couldn't do that to himself. He refused to.

"Aw, c'mon, man," Alvin said, tilting his head so he could peer through the reading part of his varifocal sunglasses. He scanned the list of offerings. "You ain't gonna try the McHaggis Burger? Says here it's as tall as Ben Nevis."

"Well, clearly that's bollocks, because Ben Nevis is a fucking huge mountain," Hoon said. "So making a burger that size isn't fucking possible."

"You couldn't get a bun big enough," Iris said, as if this was the only issue with the whole thing.

"What's a square sausage?" Sarah asked, peering down at the menu. "Is that, like, a cube?"

"Och, noo, lassie! It isnae a cube, so it's naw. Although, a lot of pipple mak' that same mistak', so's they doo."

"Wait, what? What are you on about?" Hoon asked, snatching the menu from Sarah's hands. "Do they fuck do square sausage."

He searched the menu, then did a double-take when he saw it.

Square sausage roll. Brown sauce. Tattie scone optional.

"Fuck me!" Hoon ejected. "I'll have that, then. As long as it's a fucking proper one, and no' just fucking blended up chlorine and sawdust. I know what you're like over here. I've tasted that monstrosity you've got the fucking cheek to call chocolate."

The waitress's face rotated through a few different expressions, but found it impossible to commit to any of them. Instead, she just wrote down the order, and looked around at the others while she waited for them to make up their minds.

"Fuck it. Make that four," Hoon said, his impatience getting the better of him. "Trust me, you'll all thank me for it."

He waited for the waitress to murder her way through a farewell, then looked across the table to where Alvin was sitting next to Iris.

He realised then that introductions were yet to be made, and hurried to remedy this so they could crack on.

"Right. Iris. This is Alvin King. He's a private detective who thinks he's Elvis."

"Not true," Alvin said, raising the index and pinkie finger of one hand and offering a correction. "I ain't Elvis."

"Good. Well, I'm glad you're finally seeing fucking sense."

"I am a vessel within which resides the eternal spirit of Elvis. That's a whole different thing."

Iris nodded in agreement. "That *is* a very different thing, Boggle," he said, with a slight air of reproach.

"It doesn't fucking matter. It's all bollocks," Hoon shot back. "Anyway. Alvin, this is Iris. He's a..."

Hoon looked across the table at the Scouser, trying to find the right words to sum him up.

"Guy I know," was what he settled on. When he decided that this wasn't quite enough, he followed up with, "He likes to blow stuff up."

"I do like that," Iris said. "I like that a lot."

Alvin offered his hand to shake, but Iris eyed it warily. "Did you not work for the CIA? Like, the Elvis you, I mean?"

Panic flashed across his face, and he turned with some urgency to Hoon.

"Aw, shit. You shouldn't have told him my real name, Boggle!"

Hoon sighed. "I didn't."

"Yeah, you did, Boggle. You told him my name was Iris."

"That's no' your fucking real name!" Hoon practically shrieked at him.

The Scouser relaxed. "Oh, yeah. Right. Phew. That was a close one."

He shook Alvin's hand, his fears apparently assuaged.

Hoon muttered below his breath. It wasn't anything specific —not actual words, as such—more just some general, low-level grumbling.

Then, when that was done, he turned his attention to the man in the Elvis jumpsuit. It was, he noted, a different jumpsuit than the one he'd worn earlier. The sequins on this one weren't in any discernible pattern, and it didn't have a cape.

Unlike the last one, the front was open almost all the way down to the slight curve of Alvin's pot belly. At least if he dropped any of his square sausage roll, his forest of chest hair would trap it as a tasty snack for later.

"Right. Did you find anything?" Hoon prompted. "About Miles, I mean?"

"Not exactly."

"What does that mean?"

"It means that his name and description ain't seeded through the grapevine. Nobody I spoke to has heard a thing about him."

"Fuck. Great. So, we just wasted half a fucking day for nothing, then?"

"Well, not exactly," Alvin drawled. He sat forward, interlocking his fingers as much as his multitude of garish rings would allow. "Tell me, son, you ever heard of a place called the Skyliner Lounge?"

"Have I fuck."

"It's a hotel and casino, just off the Strip. Dates back to the tail end of the fifties." Alvin glanced around at the scattering of other diners to make sure they weren't listening in. "Maybe the name Frank 'Crazy Legs' Caruso means something?"

"Nope." Hoon shook his head. "Not a fucking clue."

Alvin's eyebrows rose, like this came as a surprise. "Seriously?"

"Never heard of him," Hoon insisted. "Who is he? He sounds like a cartoon frog with a gammy foot."

Alvin shook his head, like this was actually a possibility he felt the need to refute. "No, sir. More like one of the most feared Vegas mob bosses of his time."

"Right. So, has he got Miles?"

"Huh? No. Crazy Legs died back in the seventies."

"For fu—" Hoon ran a hand down his face. "So, why are you fucking mentioning him, then?"

"I just thought you might enjoy hearing the history of the Skyliner Lounge."

"No. Of course not. I've got no fucking interest whatsoever."

"Quite a history it is, too," Alvin continued. "See, Caruso liked to throw his cash around, and spared no expense in—"

Hoon tossed a sachet of ketchup at him, which bounced off his shoulder and landed on the padded bench between him and Iris.

"I don't fucking care! What's this got to do with Miles?"

Alvin sighed, sensing his big moment slipping away. "Fine. But I recommend you look it up on your own time. It's a fascinating insight into old Las Vegas, back before the corporations all moved in and—"

He held his hands up when Hoon unwrapped his paper napkin to reveal a knife and fork.

"OK, OK. Point I was trying to make is, the Skyliner's always been a front for some kinda criminal activity. First Crazy Legs, then his son, Frank Jr—better known as 'The Chiropractor.'"

"Is that because he had to fix his dad's legs?" Iris asked.

"No, it's because he liked to remove people's bones and keep them, pride of place, on his mantle."

"Jesus," Iris muttered. He stared blankly ahead like he was either picturing this, or trying very hard not to. "I didn't know that's what chiropractors did. How's that a job? Who pays for that?"

"I don't think he was exactly certified in a traditional sense," Alvin said. "Anyhow, Frank Jr eventually lost the Skyliner in a takeover by Mickey 'The Mortician' O'Shea, who sold up a few years later to Salvatore Santorini. 'The Sausage Maker.'"

"He doesn't sound too bad," Sarah said.

Alvin's gaze shifted to her from behind his purple lenses. "Guess that depends on who or what went into them sausages."

Sarah's mouth became a little circle of surprise as she realised what the P.I. was getting at.

"Oh."

"Anyway, when he died, Benny 'The Blender' Bernstein, Helga 'The Castrator' Ramanov, and 'Tiny Toes' Tony Mullins, stepped up and ran the place for a while."

"Are you fucking making these names up?" Hoon demanded.

"Wish I was, son," Alvin shot back. "As, I'm sure, do a lot of folks currently weighed down at the bottom of the Lake Mead reservoir."

"I wish I had a fun nickname," Iris said.

"Jesus fuck. You do, Iris."

The one-eyed Scouser's face lit up. "Oh yeah? What is it?"

Hoon picked up his knife and fork and gripped them, one in each hand. "It's Iris."

"Oh. Yeah. Right." It took a moment, but then Iris grinned. "Nice one."

Hoon bit his tongue and counted to ten, then forced his fingers to release their grasp on the cutlery.

"Right. Tiny Tears and Bobby the fucking Blender, or whoever," he said, turning to Alvin. "Where the fuck are you going with this?"

For a moment, it looked like Alvin might be about to correct him on the names, but he saw sense and continued with the history lesson, instead.

"Uh, so, yeah. Those three took over the Skyliner back at the turn of the century, and ran it for a decade and a half before the current owners made them an offer they couldn't refuse."

"They killed them?" Sarah asked.

Alvin shook his head. "No, ma'am. Full buyout. Hard cash. Sixty million dollars, from what I heard, give or take the spare change."

"Is this fucking getting us anywhere?" Hoon asked.

"It is now, son," Alvin assured him. "See, the current owner ain't some old school gang boss with a fun gimmick and a name to match. It's a corporate entity, name of TFLS."

Iris frowned. "What does that stand for?"

"Best I can tell, not a thing," Alvin said.

"The fuck do you mean?"

"TFLS's business interests are both sizeable and diverse. Foreign investment. Arms trade. Import, export. Overseas manufacturing. And that's just the legitimate side. They're a lot of things to a lot of folks. The name, far as I been able to find out, don't mean a thing. If them there letters are an acronym or whatnot, then your guess is as good as mine as to what it stands for."

"Tooth fairies lick shit," Iris suggested.

"I take that back," Alvin said, not missing a beat. "But the point still stands. The letters don't stand for nothing, and the company? Well, all evidence I can find points to it standing for nothing but trouble. It's a front for a whole heap of criminal activity, just like it's always been. 'Cept now, it ain't some Vegas gangster running the joint, it's those sonsa-bitches in the Loop."

He sat back and fell silent as four rolls and square sausage, three coffees, and a mug of hot water for Iris, were all placed on the table.

Once the waitress had *och ayed* her last *the noo*, the P.I. continued.

"You're of a mind that your friend was caught in a trap by those guys?" he asked. He looked quite pleased with the song lyric reference as he tore open the top of a sugar packet and tipped it into his mug. "Then the Skyliner Lounge is just about the best and only chance you got of finding him."

CHAPTER TWENTY-SEVEN

THE ROLL and square sausage was surprisingly adequate. It wasn't a patch on the stuff Hoon could get back home, of course. Not even close. But, for a Brigadoon hellscape thousands of miles from Scotland, it wasn't terrible. Everyone seemed to quite enjoy it, even Sarah, who'd spent the first minute or so just poking at the flat sausage patty with a fork, like she was waiting for it to get up off the plate and make a dash for the door.

Now the plates had been cleared away, and all eyes were on a photograph that Alvin had placed on the table. It was a glossy 5x8 headshot that showed a serious-looking woman in her mid-to-late forties with golden blonde hair and piercing green eyes.

The background was a blur of out-of-focus grey, giving the impression that the picture was taken as part of a professional shoot.

She looked like a Hollywood actress, though probably not one who could open a tentpole movie solely on her name alone. She'd be a romantic foil to Tom Cruise in some high-concept action caper, or the caring-but-burned-out daughter of Anthony Hopkins in something she hoped might finally bag her an Oscar.

Although, as it turned out, she was none of these things.

"Scarlett Fontaine. Founder and CEO of TFLS," Alvin said.

"She's beautiful," Sarah remarked.

"And deadly. Real Devil in Disguise. Rumour has it, she's sent a whole heapa folks to their deaths over the years, and that ain't even counting all the lives she's taken and ruined through her part in the North American drug trade."

"She's got nice hair," Iris observed. He put a hand across the lower half of her face. "If you cover the bottom bit, it looks like a hat."

Hoon slapped his hand away, then nodded for Alvin to continue. He didn't even object this time when the P.I. launched into a history lesson.

"Born into wealth in New York's Upper West Side back in the early eighties. Smart as a whip, and twice as cutting. Graduated top of her year at Harvard. Twice. Simultaneous degrees. Chemistry and Business."

"Wow." Sarah looked impressed, and perhaps slightly jealous. "She must be really smart."

"That ain't the half of it, honey. Speaks six different languages, and got herself a PhD in something the King can't even understand or pronounce the name of."

Sarah pursed her lips a little.

Yep, definitely jealous.

"Started her working life on Wall Street. Quickly made a name for herself. And, rumour has it, attracted the attention of some seriously wealthy folks with an agenda of their own."

Hoon looked up from the photo. "The Loop?"

"Bingo. With her talent for finance and her family's connections, she got herself involved in laundering the Loop's cash, and growing their investments. But, I guess that weren't enough for someone with all her ambition. So, Scarlett, she starts to work her way up through the ranks of the organisation. Bit by bit, piece by piece, one step at a time."

He paused to take a sip of his coffee, then winced at the taste and poured in two more sachets of sugar.

"Eventually, back in twenty-fifteen, she founded TFLS, and hit it right outta the park on her first swing. It's now got offices in ten different states and half a dozen countries, and while there's a whole heap of talk about it being a front for all kinds of illegitimate business, ain't nobody been able to make nothing stick. And, those who came close, pretty much just upped and disappeared off the face of the earth."

"What about drugs?" Hoon asked. "She got a hand in that?"

"A hand, a foot, a head, and a torso. Shake the grapevine hard enough, and you'll hear talk of her either manufacturing, refining, or distributing everything from cannabis to crystal meth. You ask me, that right there's the whole reason TFLS exists in the first place."

"You heard about anything called Elysium?"

Iris perked up at the mention of the name. "What, the song by Ultrabeat? They're from Liverpool, you know?"

"No. No' the fucking..." Hoon caught himself in time and lowered his voice. "I heard it's a new drug being made in Florida," he said, addressing this to Alvin. "I think it's what Miles was looking into."

Alvin gave a single shake of his head. "It's a new one on me, son, but that don't mean a whole heap of nothing to no one. The King ain't exactly had his ear to the ground lately."

There was a note of something in his voice. Sadness. Weariness, maybe. Possibly regret.

Sarah wasn't the only one to pick up on it, but she was the only one to do anything about it.

"This is really good," she told him, resting a hand on top of his. "Everything you've found out here. It's awesome." She turned to Hoon, seeking his support. "Isn't it?"

"Eh, aye. Pretty decent," Hoon said, which was about as gushing as he was physically capable of being.

"Well, thank you," Alvin said. "Thankyouverymuch."

Hoon fought the urge to let his internal sigh and eye roll manifest physically, and instead stabbed a finger down on the photo of the woman.

"So, she's our best lead, then?"

"Seems like it," Alvin confirmed.

"Right. Good. So, where the fuck do I find her?"

"She ain't an easy woman to pin down. Travels all over the world, visiting all her different offices, doing who knows what."

"Well, that's just fucking great," Hoon grumbled.

"But she has a base of operations right here in Vegas."

"The Skyliner Lounge," Sarah said.

Alvin clapped his hands together, then pointed across the table at her with two fingers. "Right on, little darlin'. She got herself a big ol' fancy corner office right up there on the penthouse floor."

"Right. Perfect. So, we fucking start there, then," Hoon said. "We break in."

Alvin laughed. "Whoa there, son, ain't gonna be that easy. This here's a Las Vegas casino we're talking about, not a Scottish... whatever you guys have over there. All I know are castles and the Loch Ness Monster, and I'm guessing both are pretty damn secure.

"But, my point is, the Skyliner Lounge'll be way more so. We're talking thousands of cameras and dozens of highly trained security guards, and plenty of them armed, into the bargain. And that's just standard Vegas casino stuff. If Miss Fontaine's office holds half the secrets we think it does, it's gonna be more locked up and locked down than Fort Knox."

"What if we blew it up?" Iris suggested. He looked around the table to see if he had any takers. "The casino, or hotel, or whatever it is. I wasn't really listening to that bit. But, what if we, like, blew it to smithereens?"

Hoon glowered at him across the table. "How the fuck would that help us?"

Iris's good eye stared back at him, the brow angled downwards in confusion.

"Just, you know, sort of..." he began in a faltering voice, then he interlocked all his fingers, and pulled them apart while making the sound of a bomb going off.

"Miming a fucking explosion doesn't answer the question," Hoon pointed out. "If we want to get access to her office, how the fuck will blowing up the building help us to do that?"

Iris considered this in silence.

"You could poke around in the rubble," he eventually suggested.

"I'll poke around in your fucking rubble," Hoon replied. Nobody at the table, himself included, knew exactly what this meant, but they all understood that it was almost certainly nothing good.

"So, sorry, just so I know I'm following properly," Sarah said. "We think this woman might know where your friend is, and have that information, what? Written down on a sticky note in her office?" She sat back, wrinkling up her nose. "Seems like a bit of a stretch to me."

"If y'all have a better idea, I'm all ears," Alvin said.

"No. I don't," Sarah admitted. "I'm just saying, it doesn't sound very likely."

"Miles was going after the drugs," Hoon said. "That's what we're looking for. Find them, we find him. Or whatever's fucking left of him, at least."

"I mean, I suppose that makes sense," Sarah conceded.

"What about leverage?" Hoon asked. He tapped the photo. "She got family? Husband? Kids?"

Sarah gasped. "What? You wouldn't!"

"No, sir," Alvin said. "Never married, no children, no

siblings, even her parents are dead. Under mysterious circumstances, I feel obliged to add."

Hoon muttered his annoyance. Beside him, Sarah breathed a sigh of relief.

"Make no mistake, Scarlett Fontaine's a cold-blooded killer. We cross this woman, we all paint big ol' targets on our heads for the rest of our days."

"There is no *we* here," Hoon told him. "This is on me. No one else needs to get involved."

"Ain't no way you can do this on your own, son," Alvin told him. "Me and the Loop got our own history, anyhow. And your friend?" He thumbed the middle of his sunglasses, nudging them up the bridge of his flat, crooked nose. "Well, let's just say that story of his you told me hit kinda close to home." He nodded. "If you'll have me, the King's all the way in. Been a long time since I made a difference. High time I got back to it."

"Me too," Iris said. He looked around at the others, while his glass eye completely avoided them. "I mean, I'm not completely sure what's happening, like. Or, you know, why. But I've got your back, Boggle. All the way. Always have."

Hoon gave a grunt. It was quite an appreciative-sounding one, even if it didn't involve any actual expression of gratitude.

"Well, if they're in—"

Hoon cut Sarah off before she could continue.

"No. No way. Get that idea right out of your fucking head. It's one thing dragging these two into it. They're both clearly two sausage rolls short of a fucking picnic, and the world might well be safer without them in it, but no fucking chance am I letting you get involved."

"Hey! I get to decide," Sarah said.

"Do you fuck. *I* get to decide, and I'm deciding you're fucking staying well out of it."

Alvin cleared his throat, inserting himself into their argument.

"Well, that's great, an' all. Your concern there sure does you credit. Only problem is, we're gonna need her."

"Need her?" Hoon scowled. "The fuck do you mean?"

"Ah, come on, man," Alvin said, and his grin was pure, raw, rock 'n' roll legend. "Y'all don't think the King hauled himself all the way over here without a plan up his sleeve, did ya?"

THE CAMERAS WERE the first problem. The first of many.

The Skyliner Lounge wasn't the largest casino in Vegas, not by a long shot, but it still boasted over a thousand high-definition, 360-degree cameras with infrared capabilities and facial tracking software built in.

And that was just on the casino floor itself. There were dozens more around the hotel, bar, and restaurant, plus an unknown quantity of them up on the penthouse floor.

Taking care of those wasn't going to be easy. Luckily, Alvin had it all figured out.

"Me?" Iris pointed to himself, then looked around the booth, like he was expecting to see someone else by the same name lurking nearby. "You want me to take out the cameras?"

"That's right, son," Alvin replied. "Ain't nothing to worry about. All it'll take is a distraction, a uniform, a fake ID, and a little bit of improvisational skill on your side."

Hoon scrunched up his napkin and tossed it onto the table.

"Right. Well, that's that plan fucked, then," he announced. "He can barely have a normal fucking conversation on a topic he understands, never mind one he's making up as he goes along."

"It'll be fine," Alvin insisted. "I have total faith."

"So do I," Sarah said, adding her support.

"I wish I did," Iris mumbled.

"We'll get you inside, get you access to the security room,

then all you gotta do is plug in one itty-bitty device, and you're done."

Sarah flashed Iris a smile of encouragement. "See? That doesn't sound so hard!"

"That's where you come in, little darlin'," Alvin said, turning Sarah's way. "See, that there device is gonna act as a relay, taking them camera feeds and firing them out into the ether. You're gonna be stationed nearby on the receiving end."

"Oh, great. So she can watch us getting fucking murdered?"

"The signal works both ways. When we give the signal, you'll be able to turn them cameras off with the flick of a switch."

"I think they might notice all their fucking cameras powering down," Hoon pointed out.

"We can be specific. Flick 'em on and off one by one, clearing you a route up to the penthouse. Once the distraction's in full swing, that should keep security busy enough for you to make your move unnoticed."

"What distraction?" Hoon asked.

A lop-sided grin tugged up one corner of Alvin's mouth. "That's where the King comes in. Y'all just leave that part to me. But, before you head up to that penthouse, we got another problem to deal with."

"Course we fucking do."

"I got a man on the inside. He tells me that to access the penthouse, we're gonna need a keycard. Top-level clearance. Head of Security only."

"Wait, hang on. You've got a fucking man on the inside? Can he no' just break into the office for us, then?"

Alvin shook his head. "I said he was on the inside. I didn't say he was on a suicide mission. He's given us intel, that's all he can do. Hell, he's put a lot on the line just doing that much."

Hoon grunted. "Aye. Fine. Fair enough."

"You get to that penthouse, and y'all are gonna have an armed guard to contend with. How you deal with that, that's on you, but I suggest you make it quick and keep it quiet."

"Hoots!"

Hoon, being the one in the direct firing line of the waitress's enthusiastic, corporately sanctioned casual racism, jumped a little and ejected a sharp, "Fuck!" at the sound of her voice.

He turned to find her standing nearby, grinning at him. Behind her, looming like some sort of 1950s monster movie villain, was a seven-foot-tall anthropomorphic haggis dressed in full Highland attire.

A giant pair of googly eyes wobbled around as the mascot danced from foot to foot, slapping his big hands against his grinning mouth like he was trying to look excited. Or maybe bashful. His facial expression was fixed in place, so it was quite hard to read.

Also, he was a haggis.

They hadn't gone for the whole 'hairy haggis' mythical creature thing, either. Archie McHaggis had been designed to look like a literal sheep's stomach filled to bursting point with pureed entrails and oatmeal. It was a bold enough choice on paper, but translate that into a full-sized adult mascot costume, and it veered headlong into the unhinged.

"Mr McHaggis wanted to say hello," the waitress said.

She'd dropped her attempt at a Scottish accent now, and just sounded generically midwestern. Presumably, Archie's mere presence was already fulfilling their offensive stereotype quota for the day.

"Mr McHaggis likes to meet other Scottish people, like himself."

Hoon had no response to offer to any of this. None that didn't involve explosive and spectacular acts of violence, at least.

Something about the 'Mr McHaggis' thing made the whole situation seem even more absurd, like it was more than the woman's job was worth not to pay the googly-eyed haggis man the proper respect.

Hoon could only imagine that disciplinary meeting. The waitress, sobbing and profusely apologising for accidentally addressing the mascot by his first name, while, across the desk, a sentient sheep's stomach in a tartan hat drew up her letter of termination.

"Mr McHaggis would love you to get your picture taken with him for William Wall-Face," the woman continued.

"What the fuck is—?" Hoon began to ask, but Archie gestured excitedly with his big gloves at a section of wall with a different but equally awful painting of a kilt-wearing Mel Gibson on it.

Beside Mel's outstretched claymore were rows and rows of photographs of Archie McHaggis hugging random people who, Hoon assumed, were on holiday from Scotland. There were children in a few of the photos. Every single one of them looked in fear for their life.

"Who's Mr McHaggis?" Iris asked. He pointed to the enormous lumbering character next to their booth. "Is that Mr McHaggis?"

"The fuck do you mean? Of course he's Mr Mc-fucking—" Hoon held his hands up and sat back, annoyed at himself for being drawn in. "I'm no' fucking getting involved in this. Sorry, sweetheart, we're in the fucking middle of something here. So, tell your big tit-eyed mate there that he can fucking do one."

Upon hearing this, Archie McHaggis put his hands over his eyes and shook his whole body, like he was sobbing. The fact his mouth remained fixed in that terrifying big grin just made him look all the more demented.

"Aww, you've made him sad," Sarah said.

"He does look quite upset, Boggle," Iris agreed. "You overstepped the mark a bit there. I think you've hurt his feelings."

"What? He's no' a fucking real thing! He's no' got fucking

feelings! He's a guy in a suit! A fucking horrifying suit, I should add. Look at him! He's like fucking nightmare fuel. If I saw that bastard out in the street, I'd hit it with my fucking car. And I'd be doing it a favour. It'd be an act of fucking kindness."

Archie had stopped pretending to cry now, and just stood with his arms by his side, looking just about as awkward as an enormous sentient haggis could look.

The waitress, too, seemed to have fallen off her stride a little. She looked around at the smattering of other diners, who had been beaten into stunned silence by Hoon's outburst, then turned her attention back to the occupants of the booth.

"So, am I right in thinking that's a 'no' to the photograph?"

Hoon didn't need to answer that out loud. The look on his face was enough.

Without another word, the waitress took Mr McHaggis by one of his big hands, and led him clumsily between the other tables until they disappeared through the back.

A few moments later, the sound of cutlery on plates, and the low murmur of conversation returned.

"Still think that was a bit harsh of you, Boggle," Iris said.

"Was it fuck," Hoon said, necking the rest of his now luke-warm coffee.

"The guy's a successful businessman," the Scouser continued. "That's no mean feat."

Not for the first time during the course of their relationship, Hoon found himself wondering if Iris was joking, or if he actually believed what he was saying.

Surely it had to have been said in jest? Surely he didn't actually believe that a humanoid haggis creature was the proprietor of the establishment they were eating in?

And yet, there was nothing in Iris's expression that said otherwise.

Hoon opened his mouth to ask what the fuck he was talking

about, but then decided it might be best for his blood pressure if he didn't know.

"Maybe you were a little hasty there, son," Alvin said.

"Don't you fucking start," Hoon warned.

"I ain't saying you shoulda got your picture taken, or nothin'. I'm saying that, for my plan to work, we're one short."

"One what?" Hoon asked.

"One person. Someone to help sell the story that's gonna get you inside. A wife, maybe." He nodded slowly, rubbing at his square chin. "Yeah. That works. A wife. I like that. Older, maybe. Real ornery, argumentative type. Bossing you around, getting under your skin, making you act all erratic, like. Really help to sell the scene."

"And what, you think Archie Mc-fucking-Haggis was the right man for the role? Because, I think even in Vegas, that relationship might raise a few fucking eyebrows."

"I ain't suggesting they bring the suit, but maybe there's a sweet sixty-something actress in there that coulda stepped in."

The door through which Archie had lumbered opened. The waitress emerged, followed by a red-faced young Asian man who shot Hoon's table a wary look as he headed for the kitchen area.

"Or maybe not," the private detective conceded. He sucked in his bottom lip, and looked across the table to where Sarah was nursing her coffee cup. "Don't suppose you know any thespians, do you?"

"What? Like... who'll do girl-on-girl stuff, you mean?" Sarah asked, then she smirked at the look of shock on Alvin's face. "Sorry, obvious joke." She slurped her coffee, deep in thought. "I mean, some of the girls are pretty good performers, and I'm pretty sure some of them have played wives, but I'm not sure how convincing they'd be. Generally speaking, they aren't being paid for their acting talent."

"What about you?" Iris asked the P.I. "Don't you know

someone who can do it? You're from here, aren't you? You must have contacts, or that."

"Not as many as I used to," Alvin replied, and there was something a little cagey about the way he said it. "Ain't a lot of people who'd be willing to put their lives on the line for the King these days. Anyone who knows what the Loop is and what it's capable of has enough sense to stay out of its way."

Hoon let out a long, slow sigh, like he'd just suffered a puncture.

He knew where this was going. In a way, this had been destined ever since he'd set foot in this state. He really should have seen it coming.

"It's fine," he said, with the weary resignation of a condemned man finding out they'd run out of the chips he'd ordered alongside his last meal. "If we really need me to have a wife for this, then, much as I fucking hate to say it, I know someone we can call."

CHAPTER TWENTY-EIGHT

"DAHHLING! How wonderfully sweet of you to call!" The Duchess grabbed for Hoon's arm, possibly as a sort of greeting, but more likely to steady herself given that she appeared to be quite heavily intoxicated. "Tell me, how was the Mirage Manor? Is it wonderful, dahhling? Is it everything you could hope for, and more?"

"Is it fuck," Hoon told her. "It's a shitehole brothel, where I nearly got my cock cut off with a magician's guillotine."

The Duchess threw back her head and cackled, like this was the funniest thing she'd ever heard. "Oh, yes! That sounds like the old Mirage, alright! Never a dull moment, what?"

Her accent had been all over the place back when Hoon had taken a ride in her taxi. Now, it was all over several different places, and often during the course of the same word.

Even though it was shortly after midnight, the Duchess had agreed to meet Hoon and the others at Alvin's office in Naked City. She'd been hesitant at first—she was about to hit a winning streak at the slots in Caesars Palace any minute—but at mention of a possible acting role, she'd gathered up her tub of quarters, necked her eighth free drink of the evening, and hopped in a cab.

Unfortunately, the cab had been her own, and it was now partially wrapped around a lamppost twenty feet from the office's front door. Luckily, she'd been too drunk and loose-limbed to be badly hurt in the impact.

Or, for that matter, to notice it.

When they'd all arrived at Alvin's place, Hoon had been quick to notice a change. The place still looked like an office, a bedroom, and some basic living quarters were all trying to exist at the same point in space and time, but at least they no longer looked like they were at war.

The office still had a sofa bed in it, yes, but it was folded away and pushed against a back wall, not unfurled in front of the TV and half-buried beneath greasy food wrappers.

There was still a microwave in the corner, but it no longer had stacks of paperwork piled up on top of it, or a congealing bowl of chilli visible through a gap in the half-open door.

In between searching for information on Miles, Alvin had clearly taken the time to tidy the place up.

"Oh, Alvin, dahhling! Is that a Chesterfield?" the Duchess cried, pointing to the flimsy, slouching sofa bed.

"Uh, no, Duchess. It ain't," Alvin replied, but this didn't seem to put the old woman up or down.

She let out a little cheep of joy, cried, "Wonderful!" and then went striding around to the other side of the recently decluttered desk.

"Wait, do you two fucking know each other?" Hoon asked.

"Oh yes, dahhling! Alvin and I go way back," the Duchess replied, with a wave of a hand that suggested this should be common knowledge.

"We crossed paths a couple times," Alvin confirmed, in a way that suggested he had no more to say on the matter.

"Do you have any drinkies in here?" she asked, pulling open a drawer.

"Hey now, d'you mind?" Alvin said, moving to intercept her.

"Come on, my boy! Alcohol? Booze?"

She shunted open a second drawer, before the P.I. could stop her, cried, "Oh, what a lovely family!" at a framed photograph, then almost had her fingers chopped off when the drawer was slammed shut again.

The *bang* it made rang around the room, making Sarah and Iris both jump. Alvin stared, red-faced and visibly distressed, at the mad old woman in the purple hair and costume jewellery.

"Sorry, Duchess. Now ain't the time for drinking," he told her, catching his breath. "And, well, the stuff there in that desk? That stuff's private."

The Duchess rolled her eyes, but grinned as she reached into the folds of her long, vintage dress. "Oh, fine, boy! Don't get your knickers in a twist."

From somewhere about her person, she produced a small glass flask containing an ominously dark brown liquid. In an ideal world, it would've been a strong slug of hot coffee, but the smell— old paint stripper with a hint of operating theatre—soon put paid to that hope.

"The Duchess never leaves home without her own supply!"

Hoon took the flask from her before she had a chance to bring it all the way to her lips.

"Right. You need to go fucking canny," he told her. "We've got an important job for you. We can't have you rocking up pished."

The Duchess's gleeful expression hardened into something altogether less amused. "I never had you down as a spoilsport, Gary!" she declared. She hiccuped, burped, then swallowed it all back down. "Not after all these years!"

"We only just met yesterday. And who the fuck's Gary?" Hoon muttered.

He sniffed at the open flask, recoiled both in shock and in an attempt to preserve the lining of his nose, then screwed the lid back on.

The Duchess, meanwhile, sat heavily down on the couch, then ran a hand across the thin, bobbled fabric of the cushions.

"I say, this *is* lovely. Is it a Chesterfield?" she asked, directing the question at Iris. "Look at me when I'm talking to you, young man!"

"I am looking at you," Iris replied, which brought an exaggerated frown of confusion to the old woman's face.

"*Are* you? I say!"

Hoon sighed. "This isn't going to fucking work," he told Alvin. "There's no way. I mean, look at the fucking state of her. There's no chance she's going to be able to help us. I mean, will they even let her set foot in a fucking casino in that state?"

Alvin chuckled, his earlier discomfort at the old woman searching in his desk apparently now passed.

"There's a reason they give out free drinks in those places. Don't matter what they say, or how they talk about a duty of care, the Duchess there is pretty much their ideal guest. They'll welcome her with open arms."

"Aye. I mean, I suppose," Hoon conceded. He gestured to the mad old cow, who was now searching her dress for the flask Hoon still held in his hand. "But she's no fucking use to us in this state. We need a new plan."

The P.I.'s lopsided smile made his eyes sparkle behind his shades. "The King's gonna have to disagree with you there," he said, as they both stood watching the Duchess becoming increasingly irate at her inability to find her booze. "This little lady right here is the real deal. She's got the whole damn package, and you can take that to the bank."

Hoon tutted. "Can you no' just talk fucking normal?"

He was wasting his breath, though. Alvin was in full swing as he turned and took in all four other occupants of the mishmashed room. His hips thrust forward, and his hands whipped out like he was karate-chopping some invisible assailant.

"Seems to me like we're just about ready to hit the road," he declared. "So, what say we shake, rattle, and roll, get our asses out there, and go take care of business?"

"Don't get me wrong, I want to get cracking on this, too," Hoon replied. "But we need to go over the plan a few more times so everyone understands what the fuck they're doing. Especially Iris."

Iris nodded. "Especially me."

Alvin clapped Hoon on the shoulder and kept his hand there. He grinned like he'd just won a Grammy.

"No need, man. Best if we just shake it down and keep it loose. You think the King ever rehearsed for his big shows?"

"Yes. Of course he fucking did."

This only made the P.I.'s smile widen. "Y'all gotta trust me on this. Right here, right now, this is our best chance of getting in there. We gotta strike while the iron's hot, make our move while we can." He gave Hoon's shoulder a squeeze. "It's now or never, daddy-o. What do you say?"

There was no logical reason why the pep talk from a man who was so clearly unhinged should move Hoon in any way. If anything, the little speech should've had the opposite effect.

And yet.

"What are we meant to do? Just all rock up together in my fucking hire car?" Hoon asked. "I mean, don't get me fucking wrong, it's big enough for us all to live in, but it's going to look a bit suspicious if we all pull up together like one big happy, but highly fucking dysfunctional, family."

He gestured to the Duchess, who appeared to have dozed off on Alvin's couch.

"We can't take her taxi, because she's mangled it around a fucking lamppost, and I'm sure it'll have been stripped for parts and the rest fucking melted down by this point. So, how are we getting there?"

"Son," Alvin said. He winked behind the purple-lensed shades. "It's funny you should ask."

HER NAME WAS LISA-MARIE. She was, though Hoon would never admit it out loud, one of the most stunningly beautiful things he had ever set eyes on.

He rarely felt more than one or two very specific emotions at the best of times. Rarely had he felt anything quite like the one he was experiencing now.

And never once about a car.

"She's a 1959 Cadillac Eldorado Biarritz convertible," Alvin explained, trailing his fingertips across the smooth, almost sensual curves of the bonnet. "A true embodiment of American automotive genius, painstakingly restored and rebuilt over the best part of twenty years."

Iris, who had let out an audible gasp when Alvin had pulled back the dust sheet to reveal the car's hot pink bodywork, sidled up to Hoon and spoke in a worried whisper.

"Is it wrong that I sort of want to make love to it, Boggle?"

Hoon ignored him. It was the only way he was going to learn.

The convertible's white soft top was lowered, affording a clear view of the Eldorado's interior. It was, if anything, even more impressive than the outside.

The supple white leather seats, with their intricate gold stitching, were so large and imposing that they looked almost like thrones. The dashboard was a mesmerising blend of chrome and gold accents, and housed a set of big, chunky gauges with domed glass covers that made them look like precious gems.

At the back of the garage, Sarah was marvelling at the Cadillac's iconic tailfins. They seemed to want to stretch to the heavens, like the car was longing not just to drive out of its cramped, drab enclosure, but to take flight and soar through the skies high above.

"She's quite a sight, ain't she?" Alvin continued. "And she ain't just a looker, either. This little lady right here's got it where it counts, too. Under the hood, she's packing a remodelled, good as new, 390 cubic inch V8 engine."

"Is that good?" Sarah asked.

Alvin smiled at her. "It's better than good, darlin'. It's fit for a King."

"Oh!" The Duchess, who had been standing there trying not to fall back asleep the whole time they'd been in Alvin's lockup, suddenly reacted to the car like she'd just been powered on. "That's rather nice, isn't it? I love the colour, dahhling! And how shiny! One can see their face in it."

She waved at her curved reflection in one of the car's doors, like she was greeting an old friend she hadn't seen in a while, then she hiccupped, closed one eye, and looked around the garage like she was wondering where she was and how the hell she'd got there.

"Is this for me?" she asked, turning her attention back to the Cadillac. "Is this my car?"

"Afraid not, Duchess," Alvin told her, shuffling protectively in front of his pride and joy. "These here wheels are mine. When the King arrives, he's gonna be arriving in style. You and Mr Hoon'll go in his car. Or, better yet, we'll hire you a limo. Help sell the thing. Sarah, Iris, you'll take the van."

Iris's face fell. "Aw. Do I have to take the van?" He lightly touched a finger against a shiny chrome part of the Cadillac's trim, then whipped it away again like he daren't risk doing any damage. "I want to come in that."

"Aye, you made that very fucking clear," Hoon muttered. He pointed past the one-eyed man to where, just a few feet away, a much newer, but far less well-kept, vehicle stood in a drying puddle of old engine oil. "For this fucking plan to work, you need to be in that thing."

The van was about the size of a Ford Transit and, unlike the Cadillac, was probably ten-a-penny on the street of every town and city in the US. Hoon was fairly sure he'd passed a few dozen of them during his first drive over to Alvin's place, but they were all so nondescript, it was impossible to be sure.

This one had been painted in a bog-standard shade of white, though there was some rust around the wheel arches and some of the metal seams.

A simple logo had been stencilled on the side in a crisp shade of navy blue. It featured a stylised eagle's head with piercing eyes that either suggested vigilance and sharp observational skills, or that something small and fast-moving was about to be carried off and eaten.

Below the logo, the company name 'Eagle Eye Security Solutions' was written in peeling lettering the same navy blue colour. A phone number and website address were also listed beneath it, though whether they connected or led to anywhere was another matter entirely.

"And you've just got this fucking knocking about, have you?" Hoon asked.

"Sure do. Comes in handy if I have to go undercover, or whatnot."

Hoon couldn't imagine Alvin ever being undercover. If life was a book, he'd pop off the page, regardless of what he was dressed in, or what he was driving.

"It's a bit on the fucking nose, isn't it?" Bob asked.

He pointed to the motto that sat between the logo and the contact details, which read, 'We spy with our eagle eye.'

"I mean, do people no' get a bit fucking suspicious when they see that lurking outside the hotel where they're banging their mistress, or whatever?"

"You'd be surprised how little attention people pay to most things," Alvin countered. "I ain't saying they're dumb, or nothing, just... distracted. People see what they care to see. One more white van in a city chock-full of them? That don't amount to a hill of beans."

The Duchess snored so loudly that she jumped awake, having

apparently fallen asleep standing upright. She blinked a few times, then smiled graciously at Hoon.

"Well, thank you for asking, dahhling," she said. "I'll have a gin and tonic."

Hoon let out a long, slow, weary-sounding sigh.

"Oh, God," he mumbled. "We're all going to fucking die."

CHAPTER TWENTY-NINE

"RIGHT, we're nearly there. You all set for this?" Hoon asked, gazing out through a tinted window of the rented Limo at the approaching blaze of blue neon.

He hauled at the tightly restrictive crotch of his borrowed trousers, trying to give his goolies a bit of breathing room.

"You remember who the fuck you are and what you're doing?"

Beside him, the Duchess sat in a tipsy, happy little silence, before eventually concluding that Hoon was talking to her.

"Hmm? Sorry, dahhling, I was miles away," she said. "This is a nice car. Is it for me?"

"What? No. Is it fuck," Hoon whispered.

The glass barricade between the front and back of the car was raised so, theoretically, the driver couldn't hear them. He wasn't about to take any chances, though.

"You remember what we're doing?"

"Of course I do, dahhling! You know what they say. Duchesses never forget!"

"Elephants."

The old woman squinted at him through one half-open eye. "Sorry, dahhling? You say something?"

"It's fucking elephants. Elephants never forget," Hoon explained.

"Forget what?"

"For fu—" Hoon pinched the bridge of his nose, counted for as long as he dared, then stopped when the Limo began to slow.

He could see a man in what looked like a pilot's uniform already lining up his approach, getting ready to open the car door and welcome them.

This was it, then. Everything rested on this. Miles's life depended on them getting this right.

From beside him, there was a hollow *thonk* as the Duchess's head hit the window. She jumped awake again, grabbed for her pearl necklace like she was worried someone might have stolen it, then smiled at Hoon like she was being introduced to him for the first time.

"This *is* a lovely car," she said, then the door was opened beside her and she tumbled, perfectly sideways, onto the pavement.

"Aw, Jesus Christ," Hoon whispered, then he gave a quick thumbs up to the driver through the glass, and slid out of the Limo in time to see the profusely apologising man in the pilot's uniform helping the Duchess back to her feet.

"I am *so* sorry, madame!" the doorman said, supporting her by the arm. "Are you OK?"

"I don't know, dahhling. Am I?" she cried, the sharp nasal braying of her voice cutting through the hubbub of the Vegas night time scene.

"Does she look OK?" Hoon demanded, putting a protective arm around her shoulders.

"Hello!" the Duchess said, offering Hoon a hand to shake, or possibly to kiss. "Who are you?"

Hoon fixed the young, worried-looking doorman with a glare that could've shattered rocks. "Great. She's hit her head. You've made her forget me. Well done, son."

"Sorry! I didn't... I don't think she hit her head."

"Are you a doctor, son? Have you been to medical school?"

"What? I mean, no, but—"

"No, because clearly she hit her head." He turned the Duchess towards him and stared into her eyes as he spoke, very slowly and emphatically. "Because, otherwise, she'd remember that she is my wife and I am her husband."

He watched, gripping her shoulders, and waited to see if a light might turn on. If the words might cut through her drunken haze until they found whichever part of her brain had actually been paying attention when they'd relayed the plan to her four separate times.

She frowned, her wrinkled face becoming rubbery with confusion.

This was all a mistake. Hoon should never have agreed to it. He was about to reach for the handle of the Limo's door and abort the whole thing, when something changed in her eyes. Something flickered. Sparked. Came to life.

"Sorry, dahhling, I don't know what on Earth came over me," she trilled, tossing her long, red feather boa around her neck. "I think you're right. I must have hit my head in the fall."

The doorman cleared his throat. "I really don't think—"

"Oh, hush now, young man. No harm done! We mustn't worry, what? Dahhling, tip this young man." She pinched the doorman's cheek and gave it a wobble. "And generously. I like the cut of his jib."

Hoon stared blankly at her. A moment ago, she hadn't recognised him. Now, the shoe was on the other foot.

"Come on, Jamal. Chop, chop! Pay the nice man, then get our bag!"

Hoon continued to look nonplussed. They'd agreed to use the name on his fake passport, in case anyone decided to run a background check. He was here posing as a high roller, and the fictitious Jamal Mohammed's backstory would lend far more weight to that than Hoon's own.

He was amazed that the Duchess could remember her own name, let alone the name of the character in his cover story.

"Eh, aye. OK," he said, fishing in his wallet.

"I am *so* sorry about him, dahhling," the Duchess said, turning back to the doorman. "He's my fourth husband, and—between you and I—my least favourite of them all. At least the others, God rest their souls, knew how to treat a lady." She winked theatrically and tapped the side of her nose. "*If* you know what one means?"

"Um. Haha. Yes!" the young man in the pilot's uniform said.

He glanced over to a couple of much stockier looking men in black suits and matching ties, but while they'd taken a bit of interest to begin with, their attention was waning. He was on his own with this mad old bastard, he realised.

He perked up a bit when her husband stuffed a hundred dollars in his top pocket. It pained Hoon immensely to do so, but Alvin had said the key to selling the high-roller story was to go big and tip generously. He hadn't specified what exact level of generosity to go for, but a hundred bucks for standing around doing fuck all felt plenty generous enough, as far as Bob was concerned.

He caught sight of himself reflected in one of the smokey glass windows of the Skyliner Lounge, and suddenly felt an urge to tug at his crotch again.

When Alvin had presented him with the suit, Hoon had told him in no uncertain terms where he could shove it, and had even provided quite detailed step-by-step instructions as to how he might go about this.

The P.I. had insisted, though. Maintaining the illusion that Hoon was some flash bastard moneybags from out of town was the only way the plan was going to succeed, and no one with significant cash ever rocked up at a Las Vegas casino in dirty combat trousers and a faded T-shirt. Not if they expected to be taken seriously.

Hoon had been quick to point out that no fucker was going to take him seriously dressed in a shimmering electric blue suit with lapels large enough to go hang gliding on, and trousers so tight you could gauge the temperature in the room with just a glance.

Alvin had disagreed, though. This, he insisted, was precisely the sort of thing a visiting high roller would wear, from which Hoon had concluded that 'visiting high roller' was clearly some sort of code for 'insufferable arsehole.'

Beneath the suit, he wore a crisp white shirt with the top three buttons undone, showing off a gold chain thick enough to anchor a ship. He was sliding around in a pair of white alligator skin slip-ons that were a size or two too large for his bare, sockless feet.

The only silver lining was that no bastard knew him here. If Jack Logan—or, God forbid, Berta—could see him now, he'd never live it down.

"Jamal!"

Hoon realised that the Duchess was speaking to him, and he tore his gaze away from his garishly dressed reflection.

"Eh?" he asked, then he hurried to pull himself together. "Oh. Sorry. Aye."

There was one other tip Alvin had given him for selling the high roller persona. It was the one part he actually felt comfortable with, and essentially boiled down to being an obnoxious, loudmouthed bastard.

He forced a big, boorish smile onto his face, then thrust both hands into the air, two fingers of each raised in a V-for-victory salute.

"Right, then, darling," he boomed. "Let's you and me get our arses in there and go take these fuckers for every penny they've got!"

––––––––––

SARAH SAT in the passenger seat of the van, her gaze flitting between the road ahead, and Iris sitting behind the steering wheel.

They were currently at a standstill, stopped at a road crossing just a few hundred yards away from the Skyliner Lounge's side entrance.

"Uh, you OK?" Sarah asked.

Iris nodded, his good eye searching the darkened road ahead of them.

"It's just that you seem to have stopped the van for no reason."

"It's the crossing thing," Iris said, indicating the white-striped crosswalk that ran across both lanes of the road ahead of them.

"What about it?"

"I don't understand them," he said.

"It's a marked crosswalk. What's not to understand?"

"Is it like a zebra crossing?"

Sarah frowned. "A what?"

"A zebra crossing. You stop at them," Iris explained. "I think because, like, if you saw a zebra, you'd stop, so that's..."

"You can just drive," Sarah told him. "There's nobody waiting."

"Oh. Is that how it works?" Iris asked. "Right. That makes sense."

He continued to sit there, not moving, the van's engine chugging away.

"Is there something else wrong?" Sarah asked.

Iris turned to look at her for the first time since they'd left Alvin's lockup.

"Can I tell you a secret?" he asked.

Sarah nodded. "Sure," she said.

There were many circumstances in which this would have been a mistake. Fortunately, the particular secret Iris wanted to share was one unlikely to do any lasting psychological damage to those who heard it.

"I'm a bit scared," he told her. "About doing all this. What if I mess it up?"

"You won't mess it up," Sarah assured him. "Alvin said his guy on the inside is going to have your name on the list. You just have to go in, plug in that USB stick, and you're done."

She rubbed the palms of her hands on her thighs and looked through a gap in the curtain that separated the back of the van from the cab. Two ancient monitors and some dusty computer equipment were all set up and ready to go.

"I've got the tricky part," she said. It was meant to reassure Iris, but all it did was chip away at her own confidence. "I'm the one who has to actually do all the camera controlling stuff and make sure none of the others get caught by security."

Iris considered this for a few moments, then perked right up. "That's a good point," he said. "If anyone's going to fuck it up and get everyone killed, it'll be you!" He smiled at her. "Cheers for that, love. That's really helped set my mind at ease, that has."

He pressed down on the accelerator and the van lurched forward, headed for the Skyliner Lounge.

"Um, yeah. Happy to have helped," Sarah said, settling back and chewing on her thumbnail, as Iris guided them around the final bend, and onwards towards their destination.

THE BRILLIANT BLUE of the Skyliner Lounge's towering signage reflected off the polished pink paintwork of the Cadillac as it screeched to a stop by the casino's main entrance.

The sign, featuring a stylised plane motif, stood out like a beacon against the inky black darkness. The building's sleek, Art Deco-inspired architecture evoked a sense of timeless elegance. The gentle curve of the facade, adorned with intricate geometric patterns and soaring vertical lines, drew the eye upward, as if inviting onlookers to embark on a journey to the stars.

Out on the Strip, it would've been lost among a sea of neon. But here, away from Vegas's main artery, but still within easy reach, allowed it to maintain an air of exclusivity and allure.

It was close enough to the action to attract high rollers and thrill-seekers, yet far enough removed to offer a tantalising sense of escape and privacy.

Plus, while not intentional, the casino's proximity to all the smaller side streets and darkened alleyways hinted at the hidden depths and secrets that lay within its walls.

"Hey there, son," Alvin said, getting out of the car and tossing the keys to a parking attendant. "Treat her nice, y'hear? She comes back with so much as a scratch, and the King's gonna have your head."

He pressed a couple of folded twenties into the attendant's hand, waited for his half of the ticket, then tapped a finger to his forehead in salute.

"Not a scratch, remember?"

He went striding towards the casino's front door, the neon glinting off his shiny black leather jacket and trousers.

Tonight, he was '68 Comeback Special Elvis. It had felt like the most appropriate choice of outfit.

"Well, hey there, fellas," he declared, pointing to the two suited and booted security guards looming by the door. "How about y'all make yourselves useful and point me in the direction of Larry Junior."

One of the bouncers looked at the other. They were both heavy-set bald men in matching suits, so it was a bit like one man looking at his own reflection.

"Who?" he asked in a surprisingly thick English accent. Specifically Essex, though Alvin had no idea about that.

The P.I. stopped. "Larry Junior? Larry 'Laughalong' Junior?"

The other bouncer's meaty forehead furrowed into lines of confusion. "Who's Larry 'Laughalong' Junior?" he asked, in more familiar midwestern tones.

"Well, I'm gonna go out on a limb and guess he's the son of Larry 'Laughalong' Senior," Alvin said. He took an envelope from inside his jacket and held it up. "More importantly, he's also my named contact on this here booking form, which I'm guessing makes him your entertainment coordinator, or some such?"

"Oh. Him," the bouncer with the English accent said. "Little guy? Weird hair? Bit gay?"

"I wouldn't know, son. I ain't the man's biographer. All I know is, I'm supposed to be up there on stage doing my thing in less than thirty-five minutes. So, unless y'all want a whole heap of trouble coming your way, I suggest one of you fine gentlemen helps me find him."

The bouncers both continued to stare at him, their hulking bodies angled towards each other so they looked even more like a single individual and his reflection.

Eventually, the first of the security men took a step towards Alvin, breaking the illusion. He held a hand out for the letter, and Alvin stood impatiently tapping his foot while the guard slowly read the deliberately wordy legal terminology.

From the wrinkling of his forehead and the movement of his lips, it was evident that he was finding it all a bit of a struggle.

"Fine," the bouncer said, tiring of the effort. He handed the letter back to Alvin, then looked him up and down. "What is it you do?"

Alvin glanced down as his iconic black leather outfit, TCB

pendant, and multitude of rings. It was all slightly purple tinted, thanks to his chunky EP-branded sunglasses.

"What the hell d'you think I do, son?"

The bouncer shrugged. "I don't know. Magic, or something?"

Alvin couldn't hold back his smile. He patted the man on the shoulder. It was like patting the flank of a bull.

"You know something, son?" he drawled. "Maybe this is all gonna be a whole heap easier than I thought."

CHAPTER THIRTY

GETTING the Duchess through the casino to the hotel check-in desk proved more challenging than Hoon had expected. The allure of the slot machines had dragged her in like an invisible tractor beam, and, after losing sight of her at one point, he'd eventually found her pumping quarters into a freestanding machine with a big handle on the side, and a galaxy of lights all flashing in her eyes.

Eventually, they'd reached the check-in desk, where a young woman they'd never met before welcomed them like long-lost friends.

She was dressed like a 1950s air hostess, with a straight skirt that stopped just below the knee, a fitted suit jacket, and a little pillbox hat pinned atop her head at a slightly jaunty angle.

"Welcome aboard the Skyliner Lounge, new passengers," she said. "It's so wonderful to have you flying with us today!"

The way she said 'wonderful' almost convinced even Hoon that she meant it, and wasn't just rehashing the same tired script she'd trotted out a thousand times before.

"Do you have a reservation, or are you looking to book your flight with us this evening?"

She smiled at that last part, like it was some sort of witty, off-the-cuff remark, despite it being neither of those things.

Hoon sat down the small suitcase Alvin had given them and forced a smile. Time to find out if the P.I.'s inside man was all he'd been made out to be.

"We should have a reservation already. Mr and Mrs Mohammed."

Her smile flickered. A suggestion of uncertainty clouded her eyes.

Hoon placed his fake passport on the counter, open to the details page.

The receptionist picked it up, studied the name and the photograph, then looked back at Hoon.

"Jamal Mohammed?"

"Aye," Hoon said. "Why? Is there a problem?"

The Duchess tugged on his arm. "Oh, come on, hurry up, dahhling! I'm desperate to get out there to start spending your money!"

The receptionist checked the passport again, then snapped it closed. Her smile found its footing again, and she handed the passport back.

"Thank you for that," she said, turning her attention to the computer in front of her. The keys murmured appreciatively as her fingers danced across them. "Let me just check if we... Aha! Yes. I see a booking was made earlier this evening, Mr and Mrs Mohammed. Room 8047. That's a great room. It's one of our executive suites up on the eighth floor."

"Is that the penthouse?" Hoon asked.

"I'm afraid not, sir. Our penthouse is on ninth, but it's off-limits to guests. *But*, I can see that the cost of the room is being covered by us with..." Her fingers flitted across the keys and her smile broadened. "Breakfast and a drinks package included."

"Drinks package?" Hoon and the Duchess both asked at the same time.

The receptionist placed two black plastic keycards down on the counter. Each one had 'VIP' printed on them in white.

"These are your room keys. Just present these at any bar here aboard the Skyliner, or show them to any server, and your drinks will be taken care of."

"Well, I like the sound of that!" the Duchess cried, snatching up one of the keycards.

Hoon took the other one and nodded his appreciation to the woman behind the counter.

"Cheers for that," he said, then he hooked an arm around the Duchess before she had a chance to make a dash for the bar, and guided her towards the elevator.

Once inside the lift, Hoon had a quick scan of the buttons. He tried pressing the one with a number nine on it, but nothing happened.

Then again, nothing happened when he pressed the one with an eight on it, either.

The Duchess tutted, scanned her room key, then pressed the eighth floor button again. It illuminated in a cool shade of blue.

"Come on, dahhling. Don't you know anything?" she trilled, then the doors closed, and the lift began to climb.

Hoon scanned his card on the reader, and pressed the number nine. Once again, it didn't respond. It seemed that Alvin was right about it being locked down. Shame, but not unexpected.

They reached the room a minute or so later, and Hoon bundled the Duchess inside. He took a moment just to come to terms with the size and sheer opulence of the place, then shut the door and took out his phone, while the Duchess went in search of the minibar.

He punched in a number, waited for the call to connect, then spoke before Sarah even had a chance to finish her, "Hello."

"Right," he said, crossing to the window and looking out at the shimmering lights and baubles of Las Vegas. "We're in."

IRIS LURKED AROUND the corner from the Skyliner's side entrance, taking a series of long, slow breaths. The disguise he'd been given by Alvin—a pair of grey slacks and a blue shirt with the fake security company logo on the breast pocket—were too large, but some hasty tucking in and pinning had made them passable.

Along the alleyway behind him, the van's headlights flashed twice. His breathing became faster and deeper. That was it, then. That was the signal.

He was up.

Picking up his tool bag, he made his way around to the door, keeping one hand on the wall like it was the only thing grounding him to reality.

There was a buzzer and an intercom. The beady eye of a camera stared down at him from above the secure metal door.

He didn't like cameras at the best of times. Anyone could be watching him right now. And not just in the casino, either. The government. The people behind the government. The people behind the people behind the government.

Aliens.

The list went on.

He pulled his cap down a little so it hid some of his face, then pressed the buzzer, and tried not to choke on his own racing heart.

A voice hissed from the wall-mounted speaker almost immediately.

"Yup?"

"Um, hello," Iris said.

He had considered doing an American accent, but had already become too panicked to be able to remember what Americans even sounded like. It was probably safest, he decided, to stick to his own.

"I'm here about the cameras, an' that."

"The what?"

"The cameras. You know. For the update?"

"Update? What do you mean?"

Iris swallowed. One eye darted up to the camera, while the other gazed glassily at an unremarkable patch of wall.

"It's just on my job sheet, mate. Should be on yours, too. Eagle Eye Security Solutions. Camera system update. Won't take long."

Iris bit his lip, stopping himself saying anything more. Hoon had stressed that part to him. Say too much, and he'd sound like he was lying. Say too much, and he could blow the whole thing.

"It's half-one in the morning," the voice on the other end of the intercom pointed out.

Iris had been prepared for this question.

"Tell me about it, mate. I've been on the go since three this afternoon. You're my last job for the day, then I can get home to my kids. John, Paul, George, and Ringo. Great boys, they are."

He realised he was veering wildly off-script. There had been no mention of his character having children, much less his having named them after all four members of The Beatles.

"It should be on your job sheet," he said, then he held his breath, waiting to find out if Alvin's contact had done their part.

"Hold on," came the reply.

Iris looked up and down the alleyway. From here, he could see the main street, where cars passed, and drunken pedestrians laughed and sang. It all felt like an impossibly long way away.

"OK. Eagle Eye. Yeah. I got you on here."

"Great!" Iris said. He looked at the door. "Can you—?"

There was a loud buzzing sound, and the door opened just a crack.

"Up the stairs. First door on the right. You can't miss me," the voice on the intercom said.

"Nice one," Iris said. "See you in a sec, mate."

He pushed the door all the way open. A cold, sterile corridor was revealed as motion sensors activated the fluorescent strip lighting. At the far end, a set of metal stairs led up to the floor above.

"Here we go, then," Iris whispered. Checking his shirt pocket for the USB transmitter, he shuffled onwards into the belly of the beast.

"THAT'S HIM," the English bouncer said. He pointed to a raised stage where a man with the proportions of a ten-year-old boy danced in front of three women dressed almost exclusively in feathers.

He wore a yellow unitard that reminded Alvin of a baby's romper suit, albeit much, *much* tighter around the groin area.

The man's movements were sharp and precise, like he'd been rehearsing them his whole life. The look on his face made it clear that he hadn't enjoyed a single moment of it.

"You see? It's not *difficult*. Heel, toe, heel, heel, toe, *sashay*, shake the moneymakers, shake the moneymakers, sashay, sashay, spin, heel, heel, kick, back, aaaand toe. But this time *smile*, for Christ's sake. Sasha, you especially. You looked like you'd just heard your mother had been raped in that last run through. Come on! Tits and teeth, remember? You don't have much of the first, but you've got a full set of the second, so *use* them. Janet, sweetheart, I know that's just your face, but if you could try and do *something* with it? OK, people? Energy. Here we go. Come on. Energy, energy, energy!"

He clapped his hands like he was trying to scare off a wild animal, then rushed down the steps at the side of the stage and stood watching from the floor.

"Manuel, lights and music, please. If you'd be kind enough to at least *try* to get both running in synchronisation this time, I'm sure we'd all *very* much appreciate it. Alright, ladies? Sasha, teeth. And a-one, and a-two, and a—"

"Hey there, man," Alvin said, turning his back on the bouncer and striding over to the entertainment coordinator. "Are you Larry?"

The smaller man turned and lowered his head like he was peering at the new arrival over the top of a pair of imaginary spectacles. For a man with 'Junior' in his name, he was anything but. He had to be pushing seventy, but his vest-style T-shirt showed off his remarkably toned and muscular arms.

"Yes, yes. Who are you?" Larry demanded.

Alvin stopped a few paces from the older man, frowning behind his oversized shades. "I'm sorry?"

Up on stage, the feathery women quietly ran through their steps, making the most of the extra time the interruption had afforded them.

Larry sighed. "Look, whoever you are, I am *trying* to rehearse for the breakfast cabaret here. Open mic night is Wednesday." He caught the eye of the security guard. "So, if you could be so good as to run along?"

"What the hell are you talking about, Larry?" Alvin gestured around them at the grand, but notably empty theatre. "You got me booked to perform here tonight. Where is everyone?"

"Booked? *Perform?*" Larry's nostrils flared. "I'm afraid you've made a mistake."

Alvin took the contract from his pocket and thrust it in the entertainment coordinator's direction. "Larry, I'm gonna ask you something. Is that there a performance contract written on Skyliner Lounge headed paper?"

"It is," Larry agreed, after giving the sheet the most cursory of glances.

"Right on. And is that the name of my act? 'The Elwood Preston Elvis Entertainment Experience,' with me, Elwood Preston?"

"I have *absolutely* no idea."

"OK. I'm gonna go ahead and give you a pass on that one. Just know that it's correct," Alvin said. "Now, look down at the bottom there. Is that, or is that not, your signature on that agreement?"

"No."

Alvin blinked. "I'm sorry?" he asked, after a moment's hesitation.

"That's not my signature. It's nothing *like* my signature."

"But it's your name, right?"

"It's my name, but it's not my signature." Larry folded the letter neatly in two, then used it to wave over the bouncer. "Where did you get this?"

Alvin scratched his head. "Well, from you. It was sent through by you to my agent."

"Who is?"

"Kathy Ross."

One of Larry's thin, landscaped eyebrows rose. "Kathy Ross?"

"Yes, sir."

"With the office on East Sahara Avenue."

"The very same," Alvin confirmed.

"The Kathy Ross who passed away in 2022?"

Alvin swallowed. He raked fingers across his cleanly shaved jawline like he was looking for stubble.

"Wait, did I say *Kathy* Ross?"

Larry turned to the hulking bald bouncer in the black suit. "Get Victor." He pointed at Alvin with the folded contract. "Watch him. Don't let him leave."

"Aw, hey, man. Clearly, there's just been some kinda admin mix-up or some such," Alvin said, holding his hands up in a gesture of surrender. "How about I just take this one on the chin and leave you fine fellas to it? No harm done."

"This? This isn't an admin error," Larry said, holding up the contract. "This is forgery. This is attempted fraud. Clearly, you weren't *actually* expecting to perform, so I have to ask myself, *why*?"

He moved closer, stretching up and up on his tiptoes, every word he spoke bringing him closer to Alvin's face.

"Why are you here? What do you want? What *exactly* were you hoping to *achieve*?"

"I just want to do my act, man. That's all."

Larry fired a look at the stage, where the dancers were now watching on with interest. His glare was enough to make them jump right back into rehearsals.

"This is the Skyliner Lounge, sir," he said, turning back to Alvin. "It is *not* a karaoke bar. It is *not* a place for tribute acts."

For the first time during their conversation, Larry smiled. Something about the curve of it, about the teeth, made Alvin really wish that he hadn't.

"And it is *not* a place that tolerates whatever sort of shit it is that you're trying to pull."

One of the theatre's side doors flew inwards, striking the wall beside it with a *bang* that recoiled like a gunshot. Alvin jumped. The bouncer jumped. All three women on stage did the same.

Larry's smile just widened as he rubbed his hands together.

"Uh-oh," he said, in a sing-song whisper. "Here comes Victor!"

CHAPTER THIRTY-ONE

IRIS HAD NEVER SEEN anyone quite like the man in the security room. He was wedged so tightly into his chair that it looked like it was part of him. His bulk spilled over the top of it, and through the gaps in the arms, like he was made of some sort of putty.

If so, they'd gone overboard with it.

He had to be four times Iris's weight. Even his hands were enormous. They looked like hand-shaped balloons that had been over-inflated almost to the point of bursting.

His head went straight into chest, with no sign of a neck in between. His shirt size must've had more X's than Elizabeth Taylor, but was still straining at the buttons. A slittering of food stains ran down the front of it, their heritage traceable to the dried debris that clogged his moustache.

The guard raised a takeaway soda cup that could've rehydrated an entire African plain in greeting, then nodded towards the door. Both movements took audible and visible effort.

"Come on in. Shut the door. You're letting the cold out."

His voice was slurred and slack-sounding, like the muscles in his throat couldn't be arsed working hard enough to shape the words properly.

Iris was assaulted by a rolling wave of chilled air as he entered the room that took his breath away and turned his nipples to bullets beneath the thin nylon of his borrowed shirt.

"Um, alright, mate?" he asked, his breath forming clouds as he slipped in and closed the door behind him.

"What the hell's wrong with your eye? It glass, or something?"

"What? Oh. Yeah." He tapped it with a fingernail, which made the security guard both recoil and laugh at the same time.

"Holy shit, that's the craziest thing I ever saw," he claimed, then he shook his head. "No, that's not true. I seen crazier shit than that. One time, I saw this chick having sex with a horse. You ever seen anything like that? Chick and a horse going at it?"

Iris was forced to admit that he had not.

"Wild." The guard stared into the abyss as he took a sip through the straw of his soda. The liquid inside burbled noisily. "Real wild."

He snapped out of his mini-trance, then pointed at himself with a close-to-popping thumb. "I'm Lyle. Didn't catch your name."

Name.

Name.

They hadn't come up with a name for him as part of his cover story.

Shit. *Shit.* Ten seconds in, and his cover was about to be blown.

"Kevin Keegan," he announced.

Quite why the name of the former Liverpool footballer and England manager had popped into his head, Iris had no idea, but if Lyle recognised it, he wasn't letting on.

"Nice to meet you, Kevin. Always good to catch up with a fellow night owl. Twinkie?"

Iris, who was still recovering from the mental strain of thinking of a name that a real human male might have, just stared back at him, blinking slowly.

With a grunt and a straining of fabric, Lyle picked up a half-empty box of *Hostess Twinkies* and offered it to the newcomer.

"The sugar'll put a bit of pep in your step. It does for me, anyhow."

"I'm fine. Thanks," Iris said.

He had already switched the USB transmitter from his shirt pocket to his left hand while standing outside the room. Now, he just had to figure out where to stick it.

The room wasn't very large, despite the size of the man who inhabited it. It gave the sense, in fact, that he'd been there first, and the walls had been built around him to provide shelter from the harsh desert climate.

The part of the room that wasn't taken up by him was taken up by a bank of monitors, each one no more than eight inches wide. There were thirty of them, laid out in a six-by-five grid on the wall.

Iris tried not to stare at the one near the bottom that showed a man dressed like Elvis being manhandled along a corridor.

Or at the one on the far left that showed Hoon and the Duchess stepping out of a lift onto the casino floor.

Instead, he looked down at the control desk that the monitors were mounted above. It was the sort of thing he had only ever seen on reruns of old *Star Trek* episodes.

There were hundreds of buttons, dozens of little dials, and a few small levers that presumably controlled what level of warp speed the Skyliner Lounge was travelling through space at.

The controls nearest the front of the desk were well-used, many of their markings having been rubbed off over the years. Those at the back looked untouched, though, and Iris realised that the guard's proportions—particularly those of his stomach— would prevent him from reaching those.

Nowhere on the control panel, as far as he could, was a slot to insert a USB device.

"Shite," he said, then he grimaced when he realised he'd spoken out loud.

"Sorry, Kevin?"

Iris frowned. "Who? Oh! What? Sorry. Just admiring your, um, your..."

"Desk? She's a beauty, ain't she?" Lyle crowed, with a note of pride like he'd built the whole rig himself by hand. "Cyclical feeds from the cameras as standard, but controllable with a flick of a switch. Give me a number between one and six hundred."

Iris thought for a moment. "One."

Without looking, Lyle pointed at the top left screen. "Too easy. Give me another one."

"Two," Iris said.

Lyle tutted. "A higher number. In the hundred."

Another panicky pause.

"Two hundred."

Lyle tried to maintain confident eye contact as he fumbled around on the desk, trying to feel for the right controls. Eventually, he had no choice but to shoot a sideways look at the desk until he found the buttons he was looking for.

He hit two-zero-zero, and Iris watched as all thirty screens changed to show a top-down view of a Blackjack table.

"Pretty neat, huh?" Lyle said.

"Yeah. Great. Very cool," Iris agreed.

"This baby here's like my guitar, and I finger her until she wails."

It was, for a man of Iris's limited cognitive ability, a difficult image to grapple with. Rather than dwell on it, he just nodded, and had another look around for somewhere to insert the USB device.

At the back of the room, sandwiching the security guard

between it and the monitors, was a rack of what Iris could only describe as 'computer stuff.'

A spaghetti of colourful wires connected pieces of equipment together, apparently at random. Thousands of little LED lights blinked, or flickered, or pulsed, or just stayed resolutely, defiantly lit. They were red, orange, and green, and Iris's mind wandered off for a moment, imagining how small cars would have to be to use those LEDs as traffic lights.

"Properly tiny," he said out loud, which drew a slightly offended look from Lyle.

"OK, it might not be the biggest server rack in the world, but it packs a punch."

He started to list off some more details about the technology powering the servers, but it almost immediately became clear that he didn't have a clue what he was talking about.

"It's got gigs of RAM. Gigabytes, that is. It's got hard drives. Big ones, too. They can hold, like, all the books in the world, or whatever. Music, too, if you wanted."

Iris had already stopped listening to him. His attention, instead, was laser focused on the rectangular slot he'd just spotted on the front of one of the bits of computer equipment. It was surrounded by six solid green lights which, though he had no idea why, he decided was a good sign.

He adjusted the USB stick in his sweaty palm. All he had to do now was plug it in, and it was mission accomplished.

Unfortunately, Lyle was still staring straight at him, talking about how many miles all the wires would stretch if they were laid end to end—almost one mile, he reckoned, though he'd obviously never tested that.

Iris rolled the USB device between finger and thumb. He swallowed. The room's excessively cold air conditioning turned the sweat on his back into an ice rink.

"Bloody hell! Is that allowed?" he asked, pointing to the bank of screens, which still all showed the same shot of the Blackjack table.

Wheezing with the effort, Lyle turned his chair to face the screens.

"What? What's happening?"

Iris made his move. He took a short, quick step towards the servers, loosened his grip on the USB stick, and then felt a jolt of horror as it slipped from his hand, hit the floor, and landed directly in front of his still-moving foot.

There was a crunch.

Iris froze.

Oh, no.

Oh, God.

"What? What did you see? Did someone do something?" Lyle cried. He took a slurp of his soda to settle his nerves. "Shit, shit, did something happen when I wasn't looking?"

"Um, no," Iris said. He still hadn't moved his foot. He didn't dare. "False alarm, sorry."

Lyle's chair creaked as he relaxed his weight back down in it.

"Jesus, don't do that to me! You almost gave me a heart attack. You have any idea what Victor would do if I missed something?"

Iris didn't really care. His only concern at the moment was the broken device currently pinned beneath the sole of his shoe.

At least, it *might* be broken. Until he actually looked at it, though, there was still a chance that it might not be. There was still hope that he might not have completely screwed this whole thing up.

Steeling himself, he twisted his foot on the heel, considered the plastic and metal debris on the floor, then twisted it back.

Nope. It was definitely fucked, then.

"Where's your accent from, Kevin?" Lyle asked. "You ain't from round here, I can tell that much."

"Liverpool," Iris said on autopilot.

"Liverpool, New York, or Liverpool, Texas?"

Iris looked back over his shoulder. "Liverpool, England."

"Huh!" Lyle pulled a 'well, I never' sort of face. "I did not know they had one over there. You're pretty far from home, Kevin."

"Yeah." Iris swallowed, his brain still desperately trying to figure out a solution to his current predicament. Or, at least, one that didn't involve turning around and running away. "Tell me about it."

"You must travel around a lot, huh? Doing this, I mean."

"Oh, yeah. All over the world. Right around the globe."

Lyle's snort of laughter was like a pig choking on a smaller, angrier pig.

"Ha! Oh, yeah. *Sure.*"

Iris's heart stopped dead in his chest. Lyle had laughed, but he didn't sound amused. There was a note of outrage in his voice. Anger, even.

He knew. Somehow, Iris thought, the security guard had seen through his whole deception.

"*Globe,*" Lyle said, sniggering at the absurdity of it. "Oh, because the world's round, right? Because the world is"—he made quote marks in the air, but because he didn't want to put down his soda cup, they were one-sided—"a sphere."

He let out a little bemused sounding sigh and shook his head. The soda in his cup burbled up the straw again as he took another sook.

"It's true what they say," he announced, after smacking his rubbery lips together. "There are none so blind as those that cannot see."

Even to Iris, even in his current state of near-full panic melt-down, this didn't sound quite right.

"Who else would be more blind than that?" he asked, pivoting on the spot in order to turn around while keeping the USB stick hidden.

"*Clearly,* nobody," Lyle said, with a smug, self-satisfied air that suggested he'd won some argument only he had been aware of.

"No. But, I mean... If they can't see, then of course they're the most blind ones," Iris reasoned. "I mean, who else would be more blind than them? You wouldn't say, 'There are none so blind as those who cannot hear,' would you? You're basically saying, no one is as blind as a blind person."

Lyle, now very much on the back foot, tried to disguise his discomfort by taking a Twinkie from the box and unwrapping it.

"It's true, though."

"I think you meant *will not* see," Iris told him. "People who, like, refuse to see the truth, even if it's obvious. Like, you know, government mind control, and chemtrails."

"Yes!" Lyle ejected the word through and around the entire Twinkie he'd stuffed in his mouth. "That's what I'm talking about!"

He grimaced as he forced the whole cake down in one painful swallow, then wiped his hands on the bulging thighs of his trousers.

"You know the Earth is flat, right? You know about the Firmament?"

Iris shook his head. He'd encountered such theories before, but had never delved too deeply into them. Even to him, a man who had, until very recently, lived like a hermit in a bunker in the forest, they'd always seemed a bit far-fetched.

"Jesus! Seriously? You don't know about the dome?" Lyle fished a bit of Twinkie out from between his teeth and gums with a pinkie finger, then swallowed the sugary mush. "You know the moon's a hologram, right?"

The widening of Iris's eyes, both real and artificial, told the security guard that this was news to him.

"Wow. *Wow.* Don't tell me you've bought into their bullshit?"

"Whose bullshit?" Iris asked. "You mean *Them.*"

"Exactly! *Them. They.* The Ones Who Watch. The Global Elite. The Shadow Government."

"The Shadow Government?" Iris whispered, all thoughts of the mission, and the shattered USB stick leaking from the broken plumbing of his mind.

"You said it, brother," Lyle confirmed. "Those reptilian bastards have got eight-tenths of the world buying into their bullshit. But me? My eyes are open. I see the truth."

"The world's flat?" Iris said. It was meant as a question, but Lyle either chose to ignore the note of skepticism or, more likely, missed it completely.

"Amen, Kevin. A-fucking-men!"

His breathing had become louder, like he'd just been exerting himself. He popped the top of the drinking straw back in his mouth, but rather than sucking on it, he chewed it, crushing and deforming the plastic tube between his teeth.

Eventually, with a solemn nod, he reached a decision.

"You want to see something cool?"

Some part of Iris knew that he should be worrying about something else, but the rest of him really did want to see something cool.

"Yeah. Go on," he urged.

Lyle put a finger to his smiling lips, urging for silence, or maybe secrecy.

His chair squeaked out a protest as he turned back to the bank of monitors, and stabbed three sixes on the control desk's number pad.

As one, the displays changed. The bird's-eye view of the Blackjack table vanished, replaced by something else entirely.

Something that made the breath catch at the back of Iris's throat.

Something worse than he could have ever imagined.

There was a rustling sound as Lyle reached for another

Twinkie. His saggy jowls pulled upwards into a wide, monstrous grin.

"So, Kevin," he said, his bloodshot eyes sparkling with delight. "What do you think of *that*?"

SARAH SAT in the back of the van, huddled under an 'Eagle Eye Security' branded jacket to fend off the cold. The days were stiflingly warm in Vegas, but after the sun had been down for a few hours, the lack of cloud cover let most of the heat escape.

The van's engine was switched off, so there was no power to the heating. The little bank of monitoring equipment ran off their own power supply, Alvin had explained, although the screens were currently displaying nothing but squares of solid blue.

"Come on, Iris," Sarah whispered, and the words echoed strangely around the confined space.

She checked her mobile in case there were any missed messages from anyone.

Nope.

She prodded at the power button on the front of one of the monitors, gave it a few seconds, then turned it back on again.

Still blue.

Still nothing.

"Come on, Iris," she said again, a little louder this time, like he might be able to hear her through the walls and the distance.

If he did, the screens did nothing to show it.

She had no idea what she would do if he didn't plug in the USB device, and the connection wasn't made. She knew what Hoon had told her she should do—leave, as quickly as possible, and don't look back—but she couldn't just abandon them like that, could she? She couldn't just sneak off and leave them to their fates?

A little nagging voice in her head asked her why not? She barely knew these people. She didn't owe them anything.

Yes, Hoon had saved her back in the hotel, but it was all thanks to him that she'd been in that situation in the first place. He'd dragged her into all this. She'd only gone up to his room to keep him company, in whatever form that might have taken.

And now, here she was, sitting alone in someone else's van, pretending to be some sort of spy or secret agent. And for what? What did she possibly stand to gain from any of this?

That's what the nagging voice kept asking her.

But Sarah had put up with the whinging bitch for a few years now, and had long ago learned to tune her out.

She gave the second monitor a little slap, like she might be able to jolt it into action.

It remained resolutely blue.

"Come *on*, Iris," she groaned. "How difficult can it be to plug in one—?"

A hammering on the back doors of the van cut the sentence short. The handle rattled as someone tried to open it.

Sarah listened, breath held, to the scuffing of footsteps making their way around to the front of the parked vehicle.

The driver's door handle was tried. Through a tiny slit in the curtains, she saw the beam of a torch cutting through the cab.

"Hey! Open up!"

The voice was male. Stern. Commanding.

A fist thumped on the side of the van just a foot away from her. The *boom* it made echoed all around her like she was caught inside a thunderclap.

"If anyone's in there, they'd better open up and come on out," the voice warned. "Or, so help me God, I'm going to start cutting my way inside."

CHAPTER THIRTY-TWO

ALVIN STUMBLED into Victor's office, yelping a, "Hey, man, no need to shove!" as he fought to keep his balance.

The office was larger than almost the entire floor space of Alvin's building. Unlike that clutter of furniture and old junk, though, this room was mostly empty.

There was a desk with a chair, a blue leather couch with space for two people to sit, and three large TV screens mounted on the wall in place of windows. Each screen was divided into two-dozen images, each showing different feeds from the casino and hotel.

And, Alvin noted, the alleyway outside, where a man in a security guard outfit was currently prowling around his van.

He watched it for as long as he dared, then turned to face the two men who had brought him here via a network of corridors and off-limits hallways.

The bouncer he'd met outside had done most of the pushing and shoving, like he'd been trying to show off to the other man. He hung back by the door now, looking nervous, like he wasn't quite sure what to do with himself.

Victor, however, knew exactly what he should do.

"Leave us," he instructed. "Wait outside."

The Englishman cleared his throat. "You, eh, you sure you don't need a hand, sir?"

Victor turned to look at him. Alvin couldn't see the face he pulled, but it was enough to send the bouncer scarpering out the door without another word.

"Look, man, this is all just some kinda crazy misunderstanding," Alvin said. "I'm sure, if you'll just let me go talk to my agent, we can get this whole thing all worked out before—"

"Stop talking," Victor instructed.

He was as tall as the private detective, but had so much hard-packed muscle distributed around his upper body that he appeared almost malformed.

A few years back, Alvin had seen an artist's impression of what a human being would look like if they'd specifically evolved to survive high-speed car accidents. It had been a hell of a thing. He had basically been a giant head on a sort of flesh cylinder body.

Victor wasn't quite that extreme, but he was about as close to it as Alvin had ever seen in real life.

He moved like a tiger in a pinstripe suit that had to have been tailor made. And, even then, the tailor probably had to ask for a second opinion.

Padding across the floor on expensive Italian loafers, Victor placed the contract Alvin had brought with him, along with the P.I.'s confiscated phone, slap bang in the centre of his desk.

"Could you, uh, could you at least turn the cellphone back on?" Alvin asked, stealing a glance at the darkened screen. "I'm waiting for my agent to call back and sort this whole mess out."

"No," the head of security said.

He took off his suit jacket, and hung it over the back of his chair. Very slowly, very deliberately, he rolled up the sleeves of his pale blue shirt, then unfastened the bottom button of his waistcoat.

"Tell me why you're here," he urged.

He was in his fifties, Alvin thought, but age hadn't diminished him. Or, if it had, he must've been an actual, bona fide monster back in his prime. A bald Bigfoot, maybe, or a shaven Yeti.

There were tattoos on the backs of his hands, intricate patterns that Alvin didn't recognise. As he'd rolled up his sleeves, he'd revealed more of them, and Alvin wondered if his whole body was covered in the same series of secretive swirls and symbols.

"Like I said, man, I thought I had a booking here tonight. Turns out I was wrong. No harm, no foul."

A huff of air through Victor's nostrils made it clear that he didn't agree.

He opened a drawer in his desk, and took out a pair of brass knuckles. Alvin watched as he wriggled his fingers into them.

"Let's try that again. Tell me why you're here."

Alvin swallowed, then held his hands up. "Alright, alright, you got me. I was chancing my arm. Hoping I could either get a gig, or maybe have you guys pay me compensation, if I could convince you that someone'd messed up. I see now, that was wrong of me. Reckless move, lesson learned, won't happen again."

Victor looked up at the ceiling above him, stretching his neck until the tendons creaked. He sighed, but there was a suggestion of pleasure in it, like he was relieved, not disappointed, that his prisoner continued to lie to him.

"That was two chances," Victor said. He flexed his fingers in and out, clearly enjoying the feeling of the brass knuckles around them. "I'm in a generous mood. I'm going to give you a third." He met Alvin's eye again. "But that's as far as my generosity goes. Three chances. There will not be a fourth. Do we understand each other?"

Alvin nodded. "Uh, yeah. Sure, man. I hear you," he said.

"Good." Victor's expression remained utterly neutral. Chillingly so. "Then, let's try that again."

HOON CHECKED his phone for the third time in as many minutes and grimaced at the lack of update.

"I can't track him," he said.

The Duchess fed another quarter into the slot machine she was standing in front of, and responded with a, "Hmm?"

"Iris set up the fucking tracking app thing on his phone, but I can't see him," Hoon whispered. "They must've turned his phone off. Fuck."

"Whose phone, dahhling?" Another coin was swallowed by the machine. "What on Earth are you talking about?"

"For fu—Alvin."

The Duchess glanced at him, a puzzled look on her wrinkled, rouge-caked face. "Who?"

Hoon stared back at her. "What do you mean, 'who?'" Alvin. The fucking... the guy whose fucking office we were just in. The guy with the bright fucking pink car."

"Oh! Elvis?"

"He's no' Elvis."

"He looks like Elvis."

"I mean, a bit, aye, but—"

"Sounds like Elvis."

"He isn't fucking Elvis!" Hoon hissed, then he plastered on a smile when the woman at the next slot machine along scowled in his direction, and stepped in closer to the woman pretending to be his wife. "We need to find him."

"He's a big boy, dahhling. He can look after himself. He's been doing it for a long time."

Hoon gritted his teeth. "But we need to find him for the

fucking plan to work. He's drawing out the head of security, we're interrupting, you're nicking the keycard."

"Ready when you are, dahhling," the old woman said, yanking down on the slot machine's handle again. Her eyes seemed to roll in time with the tumblers.

"You're no' fucking listening!" Hoon growled. "We can't carry on with the plan because we're meant to be fucking tracking him on his phone. But his phone must be off, so we've got no fucking idea where to even start looking for the delusional mad weirdo bas—"

A slap from the old woman stopped him mid-sentence. It came out of nowhere, a swinging open palm strike that rushed up on his left and snapped his head a full ninety degrees to his right.

Hoon touched his fingers to his stinging cheek, eyes widening. He was shocked by the slap, but even more by the speed at which the mad old bastard had moved.

"An *affair*?" the Duchess shrieked.

Hoon blinked. "Eh?"

"With my own *sister*?!"

She slapped him again. He was half-expecting it this time, and was able to roll with it. It still stung, all the same.

"How *could* you, Jamal? You rotten, awful man!"

Hoon glanced around. A dozen or so gamblers had started to look their way. The Duchess raised her eyebrows at him, urging him to join in.

"Um, aye. Aye, I did. And I don't fucking regret it, either!"

"You revolting, pathetic little man! I mean, *why*, for God's sake? How could you even hope to satisfy her, with that shrivelled, limp, impotent, little micro-penis?"

"Here, fucking steady on," Hoon muttered, but she lashed out at him again, hands flying, her wrinkles all puckered up in fury.

"My mother was right about you! I should have listened to her! She always knew you were a worthless, wretched, wicked waste of skin!"

Hoon felt the mother thing might be stretching credibility a little bit. If the Duchess's mum was still alive, she'd either be in the record books, or sleeping in a coffin all day, then terrorising the villagers come nightfall.

"Aye, well, no' fucking wonder your other husbands all left you, you bat-eyed old arsehole," Hoon shouted back, getting into the spirit of the thing.

The Duchess gasped. She moved to slap him again, then, when he blocked it, she booted him in the shin with a force that felt all too intentional.

"You know full well they didn't leave! They *died!*"

"Aye, that's what they wanted *you* to fucking think, at least! They're all probably living it up together in Acapulco, celebrating no' having to look at your fucking face."

That did it. The Duchess snatched up the handbag of the woman at the machine beside her, swung it around her head like Thor's hammer, then launched it at Hoon.

He karate-chopped it out of the air, sending the contents spilling across the floor, much to the distress of the bag's owner.

"What the hell?!" she rasped, in a voice that sounded like Marge Simpson gargling thumbtacks. "That's my purse!"

"Oh, *fuck off!*" the Duchess shot back, shoving the woman hard in the chest.

The extensive surgical enhancements that strained the front of the woman's dress cushioned the blow somewhat, but she staggered backwards into another gambler, sending her tub of coins crashing onto the carpet.

Hoon stole a quick glance at the ceiling, checking for cameras. Two were already pointing their way.

Perfect.

"Now look what you've fucking done!" he bellowed, picking up the purse. He hurled it, but aimed just to the right of the Duchess so it hit its owner square in the face as she turned away from the woman she'd crashed into.

The impact snapped her head back, and she fell again, arms windmilling wildly. Her momentum was too great for her to stop this time, and when she collided with the woman who was bending to pick up all her spilled quarters, they both went down hard.

"Hey, what the hell?" a gruff male voice demanded. A hand was placed on Hoon's shoulder, spinning him around. "That's my wife!"

The man was a lot younger than Hoon, a little taller, and considerably more orange. His teeth were so white they cast a shadow, and his suit was even more distressingly awful than the outfit Hoon was wearing.

A fist was swung, big and telegraphed, because this bastard was all about showing off. Hoon leaned back, easily avoiding the punch, then responded by shoving the off-balance assailant with the sole of his alligator slip-on.

The man yelped as he landed on top of some of his wife's scattered belongings, including quite a sharp-looking hairbrush.

From the corner of his eye, Hoon saw some men in black suits come hurrying towards them. Behind him, the Duchess stood watching her two fellow slot-machine junkies, who were now trying to pull each other's hair out on the floor.

Before him, the downed fake-tan aficionado scrambled to his feet, puffing himself up like he had a point to prove and some dignity to regain.

He was, Hoon knew, not going to do either.

"Right then, you fucking Tango-slapped, porcelain-toothed, piñata full of liquid shit!" Hoon rolled up his sleeves and smiled for the camera. "Let's make some fucking noise!"

IRIS STARED AT THE SCREENS. At all of them, and all the horrors they showed.

"Pretty crazy, huh?" Lyle asked. The light of the monitors reflected in his eyes, his mouth curved up into a shallow, sickening little smile. "It's down in the basement. Never been myself. Not even supposed to know about it, I don't reckon. Found it by accident one day."

He turned his head, and exhaled with the effort of it.

Iris didn't notice. How could he? How could he pay attention to anything except those screens?

"What do you think?" Lyle asked. "Pretty fucking cool, huh?"

Iris swallowed. For once, both his eyes were pointing in the same direction, such was the significance of what he was looking at.

"Are those...?" He chewed on his bottom lip for a moment, like he was reconsidering the question. "Are those people?"

Lyle snorted. "I mean, barely. I think they're transients, mostly. You know?"

"Bums?" Iris muttered, like he was hearing the word for the first time.

"Mole people."

Iris's look of confusion continued. Lyle chuckled.

"New around here, huh? They live in the tunnels. Thousands of them. Underground." He gestured at the screen again. "I guess it's some kind of, I don't know, lab, or something? Like, a meth lab, or whatever."

Iris nodded slowly as he continued to stare at the screens. They all showed the same high-angle view of something that may well have been a laboratory. Although, Iris didn't think that many labs had naked people secured in cages in them.

Real people.

Human people.

Suffering people.

"They pump 'em full of the stuff," Lyle explained. "I've watched 'em do it. Guys in white coats. They come in, hook 'em up, and see what happens. Most of them don't last long. Some of them go crazy on it. Some of them just sort of lay down and stay there. After a while, they drag 'em out, and bring in new ones."

He sucked on his straw, but nothing came up it. After giving the cup a sad little shake to check that it was indeed empty, he placed it on the desk.

His tongue flicked across his lips, like some sort of snake searching for sustenance.

"I like it when they bring in the women. They've had some real beauties. Really hot." He leaned forward, stretching for some of the further away controls. "I took screenshots, if you want to take a look at their—"

His head hit the desk with a *thunk* that split his nose open and painted the controls with a slick of snot and blood.

It was his yelp of pain that finally made Iris tear his eye from the screen. He noted, quite absentmindedly, that he was gripping the security guard by the hair on the back of his head.

Before Lyle could cry out again, Iris pulled his head back, drove it hard into the metal frame of the control panel, and stepped back as the man's bulk pulled him forward and downward, until he lay folded, upside-down, on the floor.

On-screen, four people sat, or lay, or paced in four different plexiglass enclosures, their eyes sunken, their bodies exposed.

"Um. OK. Shit." Iris gripped his head, holding it steady. "Not good, not good, not good."

What should he do? What could he do? He'd knocked out one security guard, but Lyle had hardly been a physical threat to anyone. Not unless he'd fallen on them from a height, at least. There was no way Iris could infiltrate a lab and free a bunch of hostages. It wasn't really in his skillset.

But he knew a man who could.

He opened his toolbag and took out the phone he had stashed in there. He was fumbling for the button to turn it on when his gaze fell on the broken USB stick on the floor.

The plastic casing had been obliterated, revealing a small green circuit board inside.

A green circuit board that still appeared attached to the device's metal plug part.

He knelt beside the USB stick, and carefully picked it up between finger and thumb. Sharp shards of plastic fell away, but the circuit board remained attached.

Slowly, one eye fixed on the socket on the front of the computer, the other too afraid to look, Iris inserted the USB device, held his breath, and waited.

"I MEAN IT! You've got five seconds to come out of there, or I will rip this whole damn vehicle apart!"

Sarah crouched on the floor of the van, swaddled in electric blue darkness, as the fist hammered again, and the thunder rumbled around her.

She had no idea who he was. Security guard? Police? Axe murderer? Short of climbing into the front and looking out, there was no way of her seeing who was pacing around the van.

On the other hand, that meant he had no way of seeing her, either. That was something. That was good.

If she kept still, kept quiet, maybe he'd give up and wander off. Maybe she could wait him out.

All she had to do was remain perfectly still, and not make a—

There was a loud crackle of static from the mixing desk. Sarah made a dive for the volume dial, but froze with her hand on it when an image appeared on one of the monitors.

People. Cages. Closed eyes and open wounds.

"Oh. Oh, God!" she gasped.

The hammering came again. Louder. Angrier. More urgent.

"I heard you! I knew it! I knew someone was in there!"

Something hit the handle of the rear doors, a sharp, solid smash, like it had been struck with a club, or the butt of a rifle.

"Open up! Open up right fucking now!"

Hands shaking, Sarah took out her phone, turned on the video camera, and began to record the monitors.

Two seconds.

Five seconds.

Another jolting impact. The *creak* of bending metal.

Eight seconds.

Ten.

It would have to do.

She stopped recording and stabbed a finger against the screen, searching for the share button.

A final *clang* rocked the van. One of the back doors was torn open.

The last thing Sarah saw was the blinding beam of a torch, and then hands grabbed at her, tearing at her, pulling her out into the chill night air of Las Vegas.

CHAPTER THIRTY-THREE

VICTOR ENJOYED THESE LITTLE MOMENTS. The calm before the storm. The anticipation of what was to come.

Of the things he was about to do.

He was a simple man of simple pleasures. He enjoyed good food, nice wine, the company of women with low self esteem and plenty to prove.

And the inflicting of pain. That, he enjoyed most of all.

But before the pain, came the fear. In some regards, he preferred that part. *The Night Before Christmas* of it all—before the disappointment of empty stockings, and screaming parents, and a warning to *stop fucking crying!*

He could sense the fear now in the old man in the Elvis suit. He could feel it radiating off him, and taste it in the air.

Victor wasn't a spiritual man. He didn't believe in God. But moments like these were about as close to religious experiences as he got.

"Look, man. I made a mistake. I did. I know that, I see that, and I take full responsibility for it.

Victor flexed his fingers in and out, drawing the old guy's attention to the brass knuckles. They'd once belonged to Victor's father, and Victor knew from experience just how badly they hurt.

He didn't need them, of course. Not for this clown. Not for anyone, in fact. But it added to the effect. To the fear.

It was all part of the ritual.

An old sock hung from the end of his bed.

A half bottle of *Jack Daniels* left out for Santa Claus.

Where would people be without their little traditions? What would be the point of it all?

He advanced on the idiot in the Elvis get-up, letting the fist with the brass knuckles drop to his side, ready to swing.

The guy could deny it all he liked, but Victor had seen enough scammers and shysters in his time to spot one at fifty paces, and Elvis here was up to something.

The forged documents themselves were unimportant. He didn't give a shit about some attempt at light fraud.

But they were good. The headed paper was right. The details were all accurate. He'd gone to a lot of trouble for what appeared to be an utterly pointless exercise.

And that meant there was something bigger going on.

Or maybe it didn't. Maybe the guy really was just an entertainer, desperate to get a gig.

It was going to be fun finding out.

"OK, here we go. Third and final time," Victor said, still advancing. "Tell me why you're here."

The other man's eyes darted to the right behind his purple shades, looking over Victor's shoulder, just for a moment. Half a second, maybe less.

The glance was telling, but it was the intense eye contact that followed that was the real giveaway. Rock solid, unwavering.

Far too deliberate.

Victor looked back over his shoulder. There, on the centre TV screen, one of the feeds was showing a commotion on the casino floor.

No. More than a commotion.

A riot.

A dozen or more casino guests were laying into each other, while some of his security team tried to pull them apart. A couple of women in sparkly dresses seemed to be ganging up on a geriatric, while a grey-haired guy in a blue suit was being set upon by a group of younger lads who really should have known better.

Victor watched the chaos for a few moments, then turned slowly back to the guy in the Elvis suit. "Is this you?" he demanded. "Is this part of your... whatever it is?"

"No, sir. I ain't no part of whatever's going on out there. Looks to me like some kinda general ruckus is all."

"A general ruckus?" Victor ran a hand across his chin. The cool brass of the knuckles was soothing against his skin.

Elvis was staring too intently at him again. Trying too hard not to look at the screen. To not give the game away any more than he already had.

Victor pointed, right up close in Alvin's face, warning him without uttering a word to stay right where he was. Then he headed for the door, stopping only to address the guard on duty outside it.

"Get in there. Watch him," he warned, stabbing a finger at the man in the leather outfit. "If he tries to leave, or tries anything clever, you have my full permission to kill him."

"Uh, cool. Yes, sir," the guard replied. "I won't let him out of my sight."

Then, Victor went storming off towards the heart of the chaos, and the door closed behind him with a *bang*.

LEFT behind in Victor's office, Alvin took a moment to watch the violence spreading across onto another couple of camera feeds, then searched the screens for any sign of himself. He didn't find any, or any footage showing the rest of the office, either.

And yet, a quick glance at the ceiling when he'd been led in had revealed a 360 camera fixed up there, watching everything going on below. Victor's office was monitored, but the feed must be private, probably for his own eyes only.

It meant that anything Alvin did in this room would be on record. He rolled his tongue around inside his mouth for a moment, then shrugged.

He could live with that.

"Son, how about ya do me a favour and let me just walk out of here, no hard feelings?"

The bouncer with the English accent frowned, like he didn't quite understand the question, then shook his head. "Nice try, pal. You're not going anywhere."

Alvin sighed heavily, making it clear that he didn't want to do this next part, but had been left with no choice.

"You know, man," he began, turning to face the guard. "I am sixty-five years old."

He stretched his neck from side to side, and cracked his knuckles beneath his rows of rings.

"I got a plastic hip, failing eyesight, and I sometimes gotta piss sitting down."

"What the fuck are you on about?"

Alvin jogged lightly on the spot, like a sportsman limbering up.

"I ain't telling you this to elicit any sympathy, or to make you go easy on me," he drawled. "Quite the opposite. I'm telling you so that you know, in your darkest moments and longest nights, exactly who it was that kicked your ass."

He rested his weight on his back leg and whipped his hands out in front of him, adopting a karate stance.

With one hand, he made a beckoning motion, inviting the hulking security guard to try his luck.

"Come get some, daddy-o," he urged. "And see just how the King takes care of business."

HOON DUCKED a punch that might have done damage, then let one land that was clearly destined to do fuck all. He made a show of it, though, stumbling backwards and clutching at his jaw like he was worried it had been punched clean off.

The Duchess, he couldn't help but notice, was back pumping money into a slot machine. The women she'd bumped into were wrestling on the floor, pulling at one another's hair and tearing at their clothes.

A gaggle of spectators had gathered around to watch, and were actively cheering them on until another man—a husband or boyfriend, presumably—went windmilling into the crowd, arms swinging, fists flying.

Someone screamed.

A chair was hurled.

Security men expended a lot of energy achieving very little.

Hoon took a punch to the stomach from a balding man who apparently had the physical strength of a five-year-old.

"That the best you can fucking do?" he asked, and then he saw him, cutting through the crowds like a shark through the waves, making a beeline towards them.

That was the head of security. It had to be. His very presence belied his seniority.

That was good news. They'd wanted to draw him out, and now they had.

What was less good news was that Hoon recognised him. Not fully. Not all the way. Not at first.

But he'd seen that man before, he was sure of it.

Another punch from the bald guy caught him off guard. There was some force behind this one, and Hoon almost actually felt it. It hit him on the shoulder, which felt like a weird place to be aiming, but he grabbed at it like he'd been shot, and half-spun around, hiding his face from the approaching security man.

"Oh, God. Oh, I'm sorry," baldy gushed. "I didn't mean to hurt you that badly!"

Hoon held a hand up, like he was pleading for his life. "Please. I've had enough. No more. You win."

The man looked shocked for a moment, then a smug, satisfied little smile settled on his face, and he drew himself up an inch or two in height, straightening his stooped shoulders.

"Yes. I did. You're damn right." He wagged a finger in Hoon's direction. "And don't you forget it, buddy boy!"

Hoon shrank back again as the head of security arrived on the scene. As he snapped to a sudden stop, something itched in the darkened corners of Hoon's memory banks.

"Does someone mind telling me what the hell is going on here?" he demanded.

He didn't shout. He didn't need to. The other security guards all came to a panicky sort of attention at the sound of his voice, and the three younger men looked at the slightly older of the group.

"Um, Victor. Yeah. We were just going to call you."

Hoon didn't hear the rest of the sentence, or the reply, over the sound of the blood rushing through his head.

Victor.

Oh, fuck.

"Who started it?" Victor asked, looking around at the group.

Hoon rubbed at his face like he was trying to ease a wound. It was the only way he could think to hide.

The plan was collapsing. All it would take was for the head of security to recognise him, and the whole thing was fucked.

"They did, dahhling," the Duchess said, indicating the women on the floor with a wave of a cocktail glass she had procured from somewhere. She moved to stand by Victor's side, and looked ridiculously small by comparison. "I don't know what came over them, but I found it all very upsetting. Perhaps some sort of compensation would ease the stress of it all? Hmm?"

"Get them up," Victor barked, pointing to the women.

The guards were not gentle as they hauled them, still pulling and scratching, to their feet. Their partners protested the rough treatment, but Victor rounded on them, his stare alone enough to shut their mouths and fix their feet to the floor.

While the head of security was engaged with all that, the Duchess swanned over to Hoon, and gave his arse a thoroughly good groping.

It took him a moment to realise the keycard was now in his back pocket. The Duchess winked at him above the rim of her glass, but Hoon was in no mood to celebrate.

"I know him," he whispered.

The Duchess leaned in closer. Close enough that Hoon could smell the full spectrum of alcohol on her breath. "Who?"

"Him. The fuck do you think? Victor."

"Oh. Friend of yours?"

Hoon shook his head. "No' exactly. Gulf war. Military coalition in Kuwait. He was a Marine, I think. Green Beret, maybe. Can't remember. Nutter, either way."

He looked back over his shoulder in the direction of the lift. Victor was still busy. The security men weren't looking. It might be the only chance he got.

"Keep him busy," he urged, then he turned and skulked off, headed for the ring of onlookers who were now starting to wander back to the gambling tables.

"Hey! Where do you think you're going, buddy boy?" the baldy bastard cried. "You get back here, if you know what's good for you!"

Hoon winced, but kept walking, ignoring him.

He couldn't ignore the instruction that followed, though.

"You. Stop."

Fuck.

He turned to see Victor striding towards him. The head of security had looked straight-down-the-middle furious since arriving on the scene, but as he got closer to Hoon, it was tempered by something else. Confusion, maybe, or curiosity. Not recognition, though. Not yet, at least.

"Where are you going, sir?" Victor asked.

Hoon didn't meet his eye. He daren't risk it. "Just to get a drink," he said, in a diluted, toned-down version of his usual voice. "Looks like all the excitement's over."

"Were you involved in this? In the fighting?"

"What? Me? No."

"Yes he was!" the man with the bald head cried. "I punched him. Almost knocked him clean out!"

Hoon nearly rose to that. The words, 'You couldn't knock out a crafty wank in a porn star's dressing room,' were right there on his lips, but he managed not to say them out loud.

"Who are you?" Victor asked. "What's your name?"

His name.

Fuck. What was his name?

"Oh, come on, Jamal! Don't be shy. You've done nothing wrong!" the Duchess told him.

Hoon nodded, both agreeing with her and acknowledging her help.

"Jamal Mohammed," he said, and he tried to sell it with confidence.

Victor, though, wasn't buying. "Bullshit. What's your real name?"

"That is my real name," Hoon insisted. He managed to pull together an offended look. "What are you trying to say, exactly?"

"I'm saying you're lying," Victor shot back.

He was taller than Hoon. Younger, too. If this kicked off, Hoon genuinely had no idea how it would end. Just the two of them? He fancied his chances. With a small army of security men in Victor's corner? That changed things.

"You can check the booking," Hoon said. He held up his VIP lanyard. "And my passport's upstairs in the room, if you want me to get it."

Victor continued to stare down at him, searching his face, either committing it to memory, or trying to dredge it up from there.

Finally, the head of security turned and stabbed a finger at one of his security men. "You. Go with him. Keep him in sight. Weapon ready. Get the passport, get all his stuff, and bring him to my office."

He motioned around at everyone else who'd been involved in the fighting. "Keep them all here. Nobody leaves until I say so."

The Duchess raised her empty glass and waved it at him. "Can we at least get another drink, dahhling? Where *is* that waitress?"

Victor stared at Hoon again. His eyebrows pulled down and together, still trying to place the face.

And then, turning on his heel, he marched away, taking out his phone and thumbing through his contacts.

A hand was placed on Hoon's shoulder. A gun was pressed against his lower back.

"This way, sir, if you'd be so kind," a voice instructed, and Hoon was led off in the direction of the elevator.

Thirty feet away, over by where the poker tables started, Victor issued an order into his phone.

"Jamal Mohammed. One of the VIPs." He shot a look back over his shoulder, but could no longer see Hoon in the crowd. "You've got five minutes to find out everything there is to know about him." He checked his watch, noting the second hand. "Starting now."

CHAPTER THIRTY-FOUR

"SO, your boss seems likes a right barrel of fucking laughs," Hoon said. He looked back over his shoulder to where the security guard stood behind him in the lift. "That was sarcasm, by the way. I know you don't really fucking understand that over here. Or is it irony that you don't get?"

"Shut up," the guard warned. He poked his gun into the small of Hoon's back. "Eyes front."

"Alright, alright, keep your fucking hair on." He flicked his gaze up at the bigger man's shaved head. "Oh, hang on, too fucking late for that."

The gun was pressed hard into his kidney. Hoon grimaced and faced the doors. Beside them, the lights moved up through the buttons, marking their journey towards the eighth floor.

"It's no fucking way to treat VIPs, this," Hoon grumbled. "I bet they don't pull this shite at the fucking Bellagio. Is that the one with the fountain?"

"Stop fucking talking."

Hoon sighed. "Fine. Suit yourself. Just trying to be fucking friendly. Sorry I bothered my arse."

The lift stopped, and the door opened. A prod in Hoon's back urged him onwards along the corridor.

"Lot of fucking cameras in this place," he remarked, pointing up to one mounted on the ceiling as they passed it. "Must be a nightmare trying to find somewhere to go and skive off. That's why I always loved having my own office. No one could see what I was up to in there."

He shrugged as they trudged past a door to a neighbouring suite.

"Mind you, I suppose you could always just nip into one of the empty rooms. No cameras in them. No bugger would know what you were doing in there."

Hoon could feel the guard's irritation through the gun pressing against his back. It became harder still when he reached for his pocket.

"Wait!" the guard barked, and they both stopped dead in the corridor. "What the fuck are you doing?"

Hoon very slowly withdrew his room's keycard, holding it between the tips of his thumb and index finger.

"Easy, pal. Just getting my fucking key out. No need to shite your kecks."

Hoon waited for permission to continue. It came in the form of another jab in the kidneys.

"No fucking apology or nothing?" Hoon muttered. He stopped outside the door to his suite. "I thought this country fucking prided itself on customer service? You'll be getting a shite Tripadvisor review from me, I'll tell you that much. 'Carpets are sticky, banter is shite, and they hold you at fucking gunpoint. One star.'"

He swiped the key, and the door's lock gave a mechanical whirr. Pushing down the handle, he led the way inside, and waited for the door to close again behind them.

"Passport," the guard said, in case Hoon had forgotten why they were there.

"Aye, aye, give me a sec to remember where I put the fucking thing," Hoon said. "I was right, though, wasn't I? About the rooms. No fucking cameras."

He spun around, pivoting on a foot so the gun was now pointing at thin air. His hand clamped around the guard's wrist, a grin already spreading across his face.

"No bastard can see what you're up to."

He twisted the arm and lunged with his forehead at the same time, angling the gun away, and pulling the larger man towards him, nose first.

Hoon felt the impact jarring through his skull, but not half as much as the other poor bastard. The guard gargled on a gush of backward-flowing blood. His finger tightened on a trigger that was no longer there. He blinked through his haze of tears just in time to see the butt of his own pistol racing towards him.

It connected with the side of his head with a hard, heavy *clank*, and his legs gave way beneath him like the strings that held him up had all been sliced in one go.

Hoon searched the downed man's pockets for his phone, then opened the window and tossed it out into the darkness.

With some difficulty, and quite a lot of swearing, he stripped the unconscious guard of his shoes, suit jacket, trousers, and under-arm holster, and hurriedly changed into them.

That done, Hoon opened the small suitcase Alvin had given them, took out a pair of handcuffs, a length of rope, and a disturbingly well-chewed ball gag, and set to work securing the half-naked guard so that, should he wake up at an inopportune moment, there'd be fuck all he could do about it.

He put the blue trousers, waistcoat, and white alligator skin shoes he'd been wearing in the case, and was about to shut the lid when he remembered the stolen keycard was still in the pocket. After retrieving it, and slotting the guard's gun into the holster beneath his arm, he checked himself out in the mirror.

Anyone remotely familiar with the Skyliner's staff would see through it right away. In fact, anyone paying the slightest bit of attention would note that the suit's arms were a couple of inches too long, and the trousers were rolled up at the bottom.

But if he kept his head down and avoided looking straight at them, he could hopefully fool the cameras.

Of course, if the rest of the plan had gone smoothly, that wouldn't be a problem.

He went to the door, peeked out through the spy hole, then opened it a crack and looked along the corridor.

Empty.

Stepping out, he took out his phone and called Sarah, listening to the ringing as he made his way back towards the lift.

Each ring made him more and more uneasy. Of everyone, she should be the quickest to pick up. She was supposed to be the one on standby.

"Fuck," he hissed, when the call went to voicemail.

He hung up just as he arrived at the elevator. With a prod of the button, the doors opened. He was already calling Iris's number by the time he'd stepped inside.

Of course, getting an answer from that cycloptic fuckwit was unlikely, but he had to try. He had to know if the cameras had been disabled up on the floor above.

To his surprise, the phone was answered before he could even swipe Victor's stolen keycard on the pad.

"Boggle. Thank God."

Hoon's whole body tensed from the arse upwards. 'Thank God,' was rarely a positive start to a conversation, especially one involving Iris.

"What's the matter? What's happened? Is it Sarah? Fuck! I knew we shouldn't have got her fucking mixed up in this."

"No, Boggle. It's not that. There's people."

Hoon pressed a finger against the button that held the door open, so nobody could summon the lift. "The fuck do you mean?"

"There's, like, a drugs lab in the basement. They've got people there. In cages."

Hoon's eyes crept past his finger to the button marked B. Text beside it revealed it was where guests would find the gym and pool.

"You sure?" he asked. "Because according to this... Hang on."

There was another button below it, he realised. A plain silver square set into the metal, so it looked like decorative trim. He pushed it all the way in, but the controls didn't respond.

"I'm looking at them, Boggle," Iris insisted. "They've been pumping them full of their shit. It's horrible, Boggle. We need to help them. We need to do something. They kill them, Boggle. They pump them full of their shit, and then they die, and then they get new ones."

Hoon looked at the button for the penthouse, sitting there, one floor above. Scarlett Fontaine's office was right there, within reach. Possibly his only hope of finding Miles.

The plan should be relatively easy from here. Get up there, get what he needed from the office, take the stairs back down to this floor and hide out in the room until Iris sounded the fire alarm, and they all escaped in the chaos that followed.

But, though Hoon couldn't see it for himself, the wobble in Iris's voice told him just how awful the situation in the basement must be. Iris had seen almost as much as Bob had over the years. Seen the same friends killed on the same battlefields. Seen the same innocents caught in unnecessary crossfires.

Whatever was down there, it had to be bad.

Besides, if they were looking for info on a narcotics shipment, an underground drug lab felt like a pretty good place to start.

He scanned Victor's card against the reader.

He pressed the unremarkable square button.

The doors closed. The floor moved beneath him. The lift descended down, down, down through the storeys.

"Alright," Hoon said, feeling the weight of the gun beneath his arm. "I'm on my fucking way."

VICTOR STALKED THROUGH THE CROWDS, headed for his office, his phone pressed to his ear. The look on his face made it clear that the news he had just received was not good.

"What do you mean 'inconsistencies?'" he demanded, pushing a man in a Hawaiian shirt aside and shooting him a look that made his protest dry up in his throat. "What kind of fucking inconsistencies?"

His face, which had already been a shadow mask of rage, darkened even further.

"So, what are you telling me? He doesn't fucking exist?"

It wasn't a shock. Not really. He knew the bastard, he was sure of it. He'd seen him before, in another time. Another life.

He arrived at his office and threw the door open with enough force that it swung all the way until it hit the wall with a *bang*.

The voice in his ear replied to the question, but Victor barely heard it.

The first thing he noticed when he opened the door was the black-clad security man lying facedown on the floor.

The second thing he noticed was the absence of a man in an Elvis costume.

He gritted his teeth. The fingers of his free hand balled into a tight, furious fist.

"Oh," he hissed. "*Fuck.*"

He stormed across the room, swung a foot back, and drove a kick into the ribs of the man lying on the floor. The guard wheezed as the air was driven from his body, coughing until phlegm and bile dribbled onto the carpet beneath his head.

Spinning, Victor held the phone in front of his face and

bellowed into it, the veins on his forehead bulging, the tendons in his neck standing out like knots.

"Find them!" he roared. "Find them all, now!"

There was a moment of silence from the other end of the line. It was a heavy, pregnant pause, like the person on the other end was wary of what might be about to happen.

When they did speak, some of the angry furrows on Victor's face transitioned swiftly into worry lines.

"He's where? How the hell did—?"

He choked on the end of the question. His free hand flew to the inside pocket of his jacket, then to the hip pocket of his tailored trousers.

His keycard.

They'd taken his keycard.

For the first time in as far back as he could remember, Victor felt something stirring deep in his gut.

Fear.

"I'm on my way," he barked, racing out of the office and slamming the door behind him. "And if one word of this gets back to the boss, I'll cut your fucking children's faces off in front of you."

SARAH STUMBLED ON, the fingers of the hand gripping her, digging deep into the soft flesh of her upper arm.

The cop was in his thirties, she thought, with a close-shaved haircut and a moustache that could've insulated the bottom of a door.

He hadn't identified himself as police, but the tan uniform with the gold Las Vegas Metropolitan Police Department badges and the black utility belt that would've put Batman's to shame, had somewhat given the game away.

"What are you doing?" she demanded, trying to wrench her arm free of his grip.

He held his nightstick in the other hand like he was ready to swing with it. She'd seen the damage it had done to the van's door handle, and eyed it warily as he led her along the alleyway.

"Am I under arrest? I didn't do anything! I was just sitting in the van!"

"I ran those plates, ma'am," the cop told her. His voice was flat. Robotic, almost. "Do you know who's the registered owner of that vehicle?"

Sarah hesitated, but only for a moment. "Uh, the company I work for. Eagle Eye Security."

He looked at her. It was the first time he'd made deliberate eye contact since he'd grabbed her.

Something about it made her hope it would be the last.

"There is no Eagle Eye Security, ma'am, and you know it."

He hauled her on, forcing her bottom half to hurry to keep up with the top. She could feel the bruises forming where his fingers dug into her arm, and yelped in pain when he pulled her around a corner and towards the side entrance that Iris had used to gain access to the casino.

"Why are we going in there?" she asked, watching in confusion as the cop took out a keycard and scanned himself in. "Where are you taking me?"

He opened the door, then shoved her hard, sending her staggering inside.

"Just shut the hell up and get walking," he barked.

She thought about running, but the corridor was too long, too open. She was a fast runner—she'd learned to be—but he had a gun. She'd be an easy target.

Sarah did as she was told and walked along the long, narrow corridor, to where a set of stairs rose up at the far end.

This didn't make sense. If she was being arrested, why wasn't she being taken to his car? Why hadn't she been read her rights, or handcuffed?

He hadn't called for backup to secure the van.

He hadn't even identified himself as a cop. Weren't they supposed to do that? Didn't they have to?

A cold, clammy feeling of dread prickled the skin on the back of her neck.

"What is this?" she asked, and her voice was a breathless, croaky whisper. "What are you going to do to me?"

"That ain't up to me, ma'am. That's up to Victor," the cop replied. His moustache twitched. "But, if experience is anything to go by, anything he damn well pleases."

CHAPTER THIRTY-FIVE

THE LIFT DOOR opened into a hallway not much bigger than the elevator itself. A single door took up most of the wall directly across from the lift entrance, a security scanner mounted beside it.

There was a 360 camera on the ceiling, because of course there was. No time to worry about that now.

He scanned Victor's keycard. A red light illuminated on the pad, then turned green with the faintest of *beeps*.

And, like that, he was in.

The sprawling subbasement was a concrete box with a few cinderblock passageways junctioning off from different places. A number of cubicles had been formed from plexiglass and metal poles, creating tiny rooms filled with chemistry equipment.

Here, in what Hoon assumed was the main section, rows of stainless steel tables held an assortment of beakers, test tubes, bunsen burners, and centrifuges, all crusted with the residue of whatever had been brewed-up here.

In the shadows, large metal vats gurgled and hissed, distilling the liquids within. The sickly sweet smell of precursor chemicals hung heavy in the damp air. Plastic tubing snaked from the vats to smaller mixing tanks, and from there to pill presses that looked capable of stamping out thousands of doses of tablets.

Harsh fluorescent lamps flickered and buzzed overhead, casting shadows that moved like they were alive, albeit only barely.

Unfinished cinderblock walls were discoloured with chemical stains and thick with cobwebs in the corners. Puddles of dark, unidentifiable liquid pooled on the cracked concrete floor. The distant hum and clank of hidden generators and ventilation fans echoed through the chilly underground chambers.

Crates of unmarked vials and gallon drums of toxic raw materials were stacked haphazardly along the passageways that led off from the main area.

Lines had been painted on the floor to create walkways that wound through the clutter.

The door to an adjacent room hung slightly ajar. Hoon caught a glimpse of a hospital gurney and some small, rusty cages that conjured up thoughts of animals being pumped full of experimental toxins.

It was a lab, alright. He could see that.

What he couldn't see were any people.

He took out his phone and hit the button to call Iris back. It went silent for a few seconds, then notified him with a chime and an on-screen message that he had no signal.

Great.

He drew the gun from the underarm holster and very carefully and quietly closed the door behind him, so as not to draw the attention of anyone who might be lurking along one of the passageways or in the side rooms.

He wouldn't object if someone was. A scientist would be good. The project leader, ideally, or another high-up. Someone who could provide him with useful information, but who would crumble the moment a pistol was pointed in their face.

He headed for the room with the gurney in it first, keeping

low and sticking to the flickering, shifting shadows where he could.

The room was mostly in darkness, aside from the light spilling in through the partly open door. As Hoon inched it inwards and poked his head and the gun around the frame, fluorescent strip lights, like those in the main chamber, automatically burst into life.

This room, mercifully, had nobody in it. What it did have were cages, and hospital beds, and deep, burgundy stains dried into the concrete floor.

The sweet chemical smell from the other room had infiltrated this place, too, where it mingled with something richer. Thicker.

Meatier.

Hoon backed out, keeping the gun low, but ready. As he turned away from the door, his gaze fell on a computer standing on a desk against the far corner of a wall.

He skirted through the shadows until he reached the desk, and gave the keyboard's space bar an experimental prod.

A hard drive stuttered into life. The monitor illuminated. He'd expected, at best, to find a password prompt, but instead was taken straight to a desktop crammed with dozens of icons and files.

One file—a spreadsheet—was highlighted, like someone had got halfway through double-clicking it, but didn't have the energy to finish the job. Hoon checked the file name and felt a little surge of hope.

ElysiumWall.xls

He reached for the mouse to complete the double click. As his head lowered, the monitor exploded in a shower of sparks and hot flying plastic.

"Fuck!"

Hoon hissed. Dropped low. The sound of the gunshot reverberated around the cavernous lab. He scrambled into cover behind one of the metal lab tables, the gun clutched in both hands, his captured breath already burning holes in his lungs.

"There's no point in hiding, Mr Mohammed." Victor's voice was flat and direct, but the acoustics of the room added a vague sort of sing-song quality to it that somehow made it all the more threatening. "Or can I call you Bob?"

Hoon grimaced, but kept his mouth shut. He was pinned down. Victor knew exactly where he was.

He searched the area around him for options. The mouth of a passageway was maybe ten feet away on his left. If he could get there, he might be able to put some distance between them, and get himself into a position to fight back.

But Victor would have his gun raised and ready. He'd been anticipating the move. Ten feet may as well have been ten miles.

"It took me a while," the head of security announced. "Man, you've gotten old, Bobby. You're not the man you used to be."

"Bit fucking rich," Hoon replied, then he bit his lip, annoyed at himself for replying.

"Haha. You're right, I am. I'm *very* fucking rich," Victor said. His voice was on the move. He hadn't come closer yet, but he was winding his way between the tables, Hoon thought. "A few of the guys from back then are, in fact. Decided that a handshake and scrabbling around for a veteran's pension wasn't enough."

A footstep sounded further over on the left as Victor continued to move. Hoon adjusted his grip on the gun, and glanced at the entrance to the passageway.

Ten feet.

Two seconds, if he got off to a good start.

"Looks like that wasn't enough for you, either," Victor continued. "Otherwise, why would you be here, rooting around in my shit? You're clearly a man on some sort of mission, Bobby. Stand up, let's talk about it. Maybe there's a place for you here. I'm guessing the Brits don't give two shits about their old soldiers, either. Well, fuck them. Fuck all of them. Men like us, Bobby, like you and me, we don't have to ask for anything from anyone. Men like us? We take what we want."

He was getting closer now. He wasn't rushing in, though. He must know that Hoon was armed.

Either that, or he was enjoying the build-up.

"You were always one of the most resourceful ones, Bobby. A lot of us looked up to you. You'd do well here. Not just in Vegas. You could be part of something much, much bigger. I am. I could loop you in."

Hoon slowly breathed out, steadying himself, and his arm, and his aim. Was he fast enough? Could he pivot, straighten, line up the shot and fire before Victor pulled the trigger?

Once, maybe. But, like the bastard said, he'd gotten old.

He checked his pockets, but all he had was his mobile phone. It was useless down here, anyway, and they already knew his real identity.

Fuck it. It would do.

With a flick of his wrist, he tossed the mobile so it clattered against a cabinet way over on the left of the room.

He heard the rustle of expensive fabric. Another gunshot erupted, filling the room with noise and a flash of fire.

Hoon stood, raised his gun, and squeezed the trigger three times.

It felt wrong. It felt all wrong. The kick was off. He could tell straight away.

Halfway down the room, Victor smiled back at him, unharmed.

"Come on, Bobby. You really think I'm going to let a grunt use live rounds in a crowded casino? Imagine the lawsuits if some rich bastard got shot."

He shuddered like the very thought of it horrified him. Hoon dived even before Victor raised his gun, throwing himself into the passageway and stumbling along it, head down.

Shots fired. Bullets ricocheted. Chunks of cinderblock

5

became clouds of flying dust that rained down on Hoon as he raced for the relative safety of the next room.

More fluorescent lights clunked on at his arrival.

The sight of the vast stone walled room, with all its dirty glass boxes, made him hesitate, his legs stumbling like his brain was too in shock to keep them functioning properly.

Iris had been right about the captives, but only to an extent. He hadn't known the half of it.

There were fifteen or so, Hoon thought. He didn't have time to count. Fifteen cages. Fifteen people. Some of them living, some of them dead, some of them hovering somewhere in the space between.

Prisoners.

No, worse than that.

Guinea pigs.

Naked, shivering, dead-eyed Guinea pigs.

There were wheeled metal cabinets beside each glass cage, with banks of medical equipment stacked on top. Video cameras on tripods stood in front of each cell, flashing red lights indicating that every moment of their suffering had been recorded for posterity.

The sound of running footsteps in the corridor behind him turned everything else into a problem for later. Hoon made a sprint to his right, to the closest cell, where a woman lay in a puddle of her bodily fluids, her eyes open but empty, her throat and mouth clogged by a plug of thick, yellow vomit.

Hiding behind the cell was pointless. While the glass was dirty, it was still transparent enough to see through. Hoon ducked behind the cabinet instead, the gun still held in one hand.

It wasn't the weapon he'd thought it was, but it was the heaviest thing he had, and could still do damage if he got close enough.

Of course, it was the getting close enough bit that was going to be a challenge. For all of his talk of job offers, Victor had opened fire as soon as he'd heard movement. The head of security wasn't on a recruitment drive. He was on the hunt.

Which suited Hoon just fine. He'd have told him to stick his job up his arse, anyway.

The footsteps slowed as they neared the end of the passageway. Hoon had gone to the first available hiding place, but that was where Victor would go, too. He took perhaps the biggest gamble the Skyliner Lounge had ever seen, and made a mad dash along the back of the next two cages, ducking into cover behind the medical equipment just as Victor popped his head around the corner.

If he ducked, he'd be able to see Hoon's feet through the four-inch gap created by the cabinet's wheels. Hoon could do nothing about that, except hope that he didn't.

"I don't advise you to touch anything in here, Bobby."

The voice echoed, bouncing off the glass and the high ceiling.

"There's a lot of dangerous shit in here that you *really* don't want swirling around in your system. Just ask these guys."

Hoon watched through a gap in the desk as Victor banged a fist against one of the cells. A man inside it, who Hoon had presumed had been dead for weeks, thrashed fitfully, his stick-thin arms and legs slapping against the angled gurney he was strapped to across the legs, waist, and chest.

His face was all eyes and teeth, the meat of it having shrunken away, leaving little more than a parchment-covered skull behind. When he opened his mouth to scream, there was a chewed-off stump where his tongue should have been.

If Hoon's gun had been loaded with live ammo, he honestly didn't know who he'd shoot first, the man trapped in hell, or the sick bastard who'd sent him there.

The squealing of the zombie-man covered the sound of Hoon's movements as he scurried across to the next cabinet of medical equipment. Several syringes lay on a metal tray. A scalpel rested atop a notebook beside them, its blade dotted with blood.

Hoon grabbed it, then ducked back into cover a split second before Victor turned his way. The man in the cell fell silent, save for the hiss of his breath rasping in and out of his ravaged lungs.

"There's nowhere else to run, Bobby!" Victor warned, as he advanced between the glass cages. "So, I'm going to make you a deal. For old time's sake. Come out, and we can talk. Come out, and maybe we can settle all this."

He continued on for a few more slow, sideways steps, one foot crossing over the other, the gun held ready in both hands.

"Don't come out, though? Then you and I, we have a problem. Don't come out, and I will personally see to it that you and your friends wind up in one of these cases, being pumped so full of poison that your organs fall out of your ass."

He was close. Close enough that Hoon could hear the little metallic *clinks* of the gun, and the creaking of his handmade leather shoes.

Victor had been a killer back in the day. One of the best. And that was before he'd become this monster.

None of this was going to be easy.

But fuck it. Worth a go.

As Victor passed his hiding place, Hoon ran at him, pushing the metal cabinet in front of him like a battering ram, the castor wheels squeaking in surprise, like they'd been caught off guard by the move.

Victor turned. The gun raised.

And the world, and everything in it, wound down into slow motion.

CHAPTER THIRTY-SIX

SARAH'S SHOES clanked on the corrugated metal steps as she made her way up them. The cop was a couple of feet behind her, his gun still in his hand, the look on his face daring her to try something stupid.

She had considered it. If she ran, there was a chance she could get around the bend in the stairs before he could take aim. From there, if she was quick enough, she could reach the top of the steps and then...

And then...

That was where the plan fell apart. She had no idea what she was walking into up there. If it happened to be a twisting maze of short, right-angled corridors, then she had a chance.

Anything else, and it was only a matter of time before he put a bullet in her back.

And so, she did what she'd done through her entire time in Las Vegas.

She did what she had to do to survive.

"Right at the top," the cop barked. "First door."

Sarah's heart was thrumming in her chest as she reached the

top step, each beat of it rolling directly into the next. Her hand shook on the metal railing.

He was three steps behind her. His head was almost level with her foot.

She could kick him. She could knock him back down the stairs.

She could. She should.

But her body refused to react, and then he was in the corridor beside her, his moustache twitching with irritation.

"You fucking deaf?" He waved the gun past her. "Door on the right. Get inside."

Sarah swallowed back a sob of fear. The momentary hesitation enraged the cop, who grabbed her by the hair, his face twisting into a knot of rage.

She cried out as he dragged her towards the door, grabbing at his wrist, trying to free herself from his iron grip.

"I gave you a fucking chance, but you didn't take it!" he barked.

He pushed the door open and shoved her inside.

Sarah's fear was replaced, at least partly, by confusion. A semi-naked man with the proportions of a bull walrus lay face-down on the floor while Iris attempted to pull off his trousers at the ankles.

Iris himself was wearing the man's shirt. It was so large on him that he looked like his head was poking up through a hole in the top of a tent. He turned to look at Sarah as she entered, then continued craning his neck around until he was eye to eyes with the gun-toting police officer.

"Honestly," Iris began. He flashed a nervous smile. "This isn't what it looks like."

THE IMPACT WAS HARD. Metal on flesh. Sudden. Brutal. Pain burst from Victor's lips, and Hoon felt a surge of something like elation, even as the sudden stop sent all three of them—him, Victor, and the wheeled metal cabinet—crashing to the concrete floor.

The sound was like the tolling of a broken bell. It rang around the room, bringing squeals of terror from the few test subjects still alive enough to react.

The gun was the target. Hoon clocked it still in Victor's hand, and swung the scalpel down, blade aimed at the exposed veins on the inside of the bastard's wrist.

Victor saw it coming. Dodged. The blade buckled against the floor, and Hoon barely had time to block an elbow-strike that came up on his left. Hard. Fast. Too fast.

He deflected the worst of it, but not all. His balance went, so he dropped onto the gun arm, keeping it pinned, swinging a wild left that clipped Victor's chin, but only barely.

A twist. A knee. The air was forced out of one of Hoon's lungs. He grabbed for Victor's face, fingers like claws, thumb searching for an eye, even as their legs wrestled and locked together, each preventing the other from sticking the boot in.

Hoon was still holding the gun with the blanks in it, but he couldn't get any leverage with it. Couldn't swing it, or use its weight.

He pulled the trigger, instead, and the blank roared just inches from Victor's ear, the sound deafening him, the burst of fire forcing him to turn his head away.

Around them, the human wreckage that Victor had helped create howled, and screeched, and thrashed like wild animals.

Hoon lunged with a finger strike that found the softest, fleshiest part of the bastard's throat. Victor's eyes snapped open all the way, then a bit beyond, bulging in their sockets as he choked on his own lack of breath.

Rolling, clambering, Hoon swung himself up so he was on top

of the other man, straddling him and pinning him down. Victor still clung to the gun, but Hoon kept a hold of his arm, pointing the weapon away, so the Marine couldn't get a shot in.

He didn't see the second scalpel. He felt it pierce the skin and muscle of his thigh. Felt it wrenching around, gouging the wound wider.

Roaring in pain, he grabbed for Victor's free arm, digging his thumb into the joint where the hand met the wrist. Pressing down. Twisting.

The scalpel slipped out and clattered to the floor, a pump of blood not far behind it.

Fighting through the pain to keep both the bastard's arms pinned, Hoon brought his head down, aiming straight for the bridge of Victor's nose. He saw it coming, though, and angled himself to minimise the damage. Instead of Hoon splattering the Marine's nose across his face, their foreheads met with a solid, dizzying *thunk*.

That, and the pain, and the cramp in Hoon's lung made the room lurch around him, revolving it, spinning it, like he was Dorothy, fucking off to Oz.

He managed to kick the scalpel out of reach, but the effort of it made more blood spurt from the wound in his thigh, which did his head no favours whatsoever.

Victor seemed to surge beneath him, like he'd been possessed by some supernatural strength that launched Hoon sideways, hands grasping at thin air as he fought to slow his fall.

His head only started to clear after he'd hit the ground. It took him a couple of seconds to work out what had happened and to get his bearings.

A couple of seconds that he didn't have to waste.

The squealing of the prisoners had ebbed away into silence, Hoon noticed. That was good. That was something.

He grimaced with every pained breath as he turned to Victor, who was now up on his knees, the gun still in his hand.

The Marine's bottom lip was split from some lucky strike that Hoon couldn't quite remember. His voice, when he spoke, was a rasp through his swelling throat.

"Always knew you English were pussies," he said, and he grinned to reveal blood on his teeth.

Hoon spat a wad of the stuff onto the floor between them. "How many fucking times do I have to tell you fudd-brained, flag-shagging, eagle-bothering, hotdog-munching, circus of star-spangled fucks? Do *not* fucking call me English."

Victor's laugh was a low, sinister hiss. "Or what, Bobby? You going to kill me?"

Hoon shook his head. "Regretfully not," he said. His eyes flicked past the Marine. "But he is."

Victor snorted. "Oh. Jesus. Seriously? 'He's behind you!' That's fucking desperate!"

A gun was pressed against the back of Victor's head in a way that left no doubt whatsoever as to what it was.

"Well, hey there, daddy-o," Alvin drawled. "Y'all miss me?"

"Thank fuck," Hoon wheezed, slumping down onto the floor while he tried to catch his breath, and stem the blood flowing from the hole in his upper leg.

"Come on, man. Y'all didn't think the King would just up and leave you, did you? That just ain't the way he rolls." He pressed the pistol harder against Victor's head. "I'd drop the gun, son, 'less you want everything within a five-yard radius painted with the contents of your skull."

"You don't have the guts!" Victor spat.

A hammer was drawn back. "Son, you have no damn idea who I am, or what I am capable of. You won't be the first one of you Loop bastards I put an end to, and I pray to God that you won't be the last. Gun. On the floor. Right now."

For a moment, it looked like Victor might continue to resist, but then he growled in frustration and let the gun clatter onto the concrete. Alvin slid it away with a foot, putting it beyond the Marine's reach.

"How the fuck did you get down here?" Hoon asked, using the scalpel to cut a strip from the bottom of his shirt.

"Turns out he's got a whole drawer full of them keycards just sitting right there in his office," Alvin said.

"Fuck sake." Hoon gave a grunt as he tied the makeshift bandage around his leg. "If we'd known that, it'd have made life a lot fucking easier."

"From there, I just took out one of them security guards, stole this here gun from him, and made my way down here."

Hoon's eyes met Victor's. They both looked at the weapon lying on the ground.

"Fuck!" Hoon hissed. He dived, but the Marine had moved first, throwing himself to the floor, arm stretching for the weapon.

Alvin pivoted to follow him and pulled the trigger. There was fire, and noise, but that was where it ended.

"The hell?"

Victor's hand found his pistol. He rolled onto his back, the gun clutched in both hands.

"Don't!" he warned, aiming at the centre of Hoon's chest. "Back up."

Hoon winced in pain as he shuffled back on his knees, his hands raising beside his head.

Alvin was still pointing the gun at the man on the floor, but the puzzled look on his face was now shifting into one of realisation.

"Blanks?" he asked.

Hoon sighed. "Aye. You couldn't have just kept your fucking mouth shut, could you?"

"How the hell was I supposed to know?" Alvin protested. He let the gun fall to the floor, then raised his hands like Hoon had.

Victor waved the gun at him as he stood up. "On the floor. Beside him."

"Aw, c'mon, man. I'm sixty-five years old, and that's a concrete floor. My knees ain't what they used to be. How about I just stand here, and—"

"*On the fucking floor!*"

The shout echoed as loudly as any gunshot. The half-dead people in the cells screeched and wailed like howler monkeys.

Alvin nodded, his knee joints cracking as he hurriedly complied. "Alright, man, alright. Take it easy, now. Ain't no need for this to end badly."

"End badly?" Victor sniggered and pressed the gun against Alvin's forehead. "End fucking badly? You have no idea how badly this is going to end for you two. You can't fucking grasp how much you're going to suffer. But first..."

He cracked Alvin on the side of the head with the butt of the Glock, sending him spilling sideways onto the floor, and his purple bifocal sunglasses skidding across the concrete.

The gun took aim at one of his knees. Victor turned to look at the kneeling Hoon.

"Tell me what the fuck you're doing here, or we'll see how well Elvis can dance without the use of his fucking legs."

———

IT WAS Sarah who made the move, as the cop swung his sidearm in Iris's direction. She drove her elbow back. Her weight with it. She felt bone crunching, and screamed at the visceral horror of it, even as the cop was lashing out at her, pushing her away, turning the gun on her.

With a roar, Iris launched himself towards the door, his stolen security guard shirt billowing around him like the body of a jellyfish.

Sarah tried to duck, but a hand grabbed her by the hair, and she was wrenched backwards until all three of them slammed into the wall with enough force to make the monitors in the security room flicker.

The floor lurched beneath her, like it was a rising wave. It was only as it was about to hit her that she realised she was the one moving, the cop having shoved her to the ground.

The sudden impact rattled through her, jarring her bones and jolting her organs.

She tried to get up, but her breath was short, and her head was light, and the floor was soft, mushy quicksand beneath her feet.

All she could do was watch as the cop unhooked his nightstick from his belt, and swung at Iris as they wrestled with the gun.

The impact, just above Iris's knee, made him lurch forward. His forehead connected with the bloodied, rapidly swelling mess of the cop's nose.

And that, Sarah would later recount, was when the chaos began.

CHAPTER THIRTY-SEVEN

HOON HELD his hands up higher, like he could somehow surrender even more than he already had. He glanced down at the fallen Alvin, and at the gun still trained on his knee.

"Alright, alright, cool your fucking jets. I'll tell you what you want to know," Hoon said. He indicated the lab around them with a glance. "I heard about the drugs in Florida. Seemed like a good product. I want in."

The gun fired. A bullet ricocheted off the concrete right beside Alvin's legs, sending a puff of white dust into the air, and setting the captives off howling and wailing again.

"Hey, careful where you point that thing, man!" Alvin yelped.

"Wrong answer," Victor said, still eyeballing Hoon. He adjusted his aim a fraction. "Second one won't miss. Why are you here? The truth?"

"Alright, alright, alright. Fuck!" Hoon hissed. He shot Alvin a dirty look, like this was all his fault, then came clean. "I'm looking for a mate of mine. Miles Crabtree. Think your fucking Loop buddies might have done something to him."

Victor didn't fire this time. Instead, his eyes narrowed as he looked at them both in turn.

"What do you know about the Loop?"

"I know I've had a fucking high time killing the pricks that are in it," Hoon said. He clenched one of his hands into a fist, then raised the fingers one-by-one. "I've shot them, blown them up, set them on fucking fire, stuck a funnel up their arse, drowned them —you name it, son, I've fucking done it."

He grinned up at the towering Marine, then stabbed a finger in his direction.

"And trust me, I'm going to do far fucking worse to you. You'll be *begging* for me to jam a big funnel up your bahookie and set you alight. Burning to death with a piece of plastic kitchenware up your arsehole will be a fucking pipe dream that you'll one day hope to aspire to by the time I'm fucking done with you."

"Oh, yeah, Bobby? And just how the fuck are you going to do that?"

"I'll   work   something   out.   I'm   surprisingly   fucking resourceful."

Victor smiled. There was still blood on his teeth. It made him look even more demented and dangerous.

"You know what? I just realised something," he said. "I don't need both of you. One of you will do. And I reckon Elvis here is more likely to be the talkative type."

He turned the gun on Hoon. His smile widened until his face was all bloodied teeth and gums.

"To the Victor go the spoils."

Hoon tutted. "You've been fucking desperate to say that your whole fucking life, haven't you, you sad fucking—"

The sound of gunfire rang out, sharp and sudden, like reality itself had cracked open. A spray of hot blood covered Hoon's face, and then Victor went spinning past him, eyes wide with shock, a ragged hole in his shoulder.

Hoon was grabbing for Victor's pistol almost as soon as the

bastard hit the floor, wrenching it from his fingers and taking aim at the skinhead in the black suit advancing across the floor.

"Hey, whoa, whoa!" the security man said, and Hoon was caught off guard by his Essex accent. The guard slowly put his weapon down on the floor and held his hands up. "It's OK. We're cool. I'm with Mr King."

"High time you turned up, son," Alvin wheezed. He picked up his sunglasses, grimaced at the state of the lenses, then put them on. "Robert Hoon, Terry Radcliffe. And vice versa. Terry here's my inside man."

He panted heavily, getting his breath back, then gestured down to where Victor was writhing on the ground, his right arm completely limp and pinned beneath him.

"He and I been playing this guy like a sweet old six string all night long." He shook hands with the bouncer, and then hugged him. "I owe you one, baby."

"No. Not by a long shot, Mr King," Terry told him.

Hoon wasn't paying them any attention, and had instead turned his attention to Victor, who was trying to drag himself away with his good arm. His progress was slow, though, and even if he'd been able to sneak off without them noticing, the shiny trail of blood would've been a dead giveaway.

Hoon picked up the gun, considered his options for a moment, then retrieved a syringe full of dark green liquid that had been knocked over along with all the other medical equipment.

He removed the plastic covering from the needle, gave the pointed tip an experimental sniff, then stood over Victor with it.

"I'm guessing you know what this shite is," he said. His eyes raised and looked around at the cells, where the skin-and-bone zombie people had fallen back into a rasping, breathless silence. "And I've got a pretty fucking good idea what it does to people."

He squatted down until he was sitting on Victor's chest,

pinning him in place. The syringe was clutched in his hand like a dagger, the needle pointing down.

"So, here's what's going to happen, Vic. I'm going to show you a photo of the guy I'm looking for. You're going to fucking tell me where he is. If you don't, I'm going to ram this fucking needle through your eye, press the plunger, and spurt its whole fucking load into your brain. Do we understand each other?"

Victor spat a wad of blood up at him. "Fuck you!"

He tried to struggle when Hoon's hand pressed down on his face, grinding the back of his head against the concrete. The needle was moved into position just an inch above his eye. Close enough that he wouldn't be able to focus on it, but would know it was there.

"How long does it take to start working, this shite?" Hoon asked. "Elysium. That's meant to be fucking paradise, I hear. These poor shrivelled fucks would probably disagree with that assessment, mind you."

"Hey, steady on there, man," Alvin urged. "We don't know what that stuff does."

"Aye, well, we'll soon fucking find out," Hoon spat.

He moved his hand from Victor's mouth to his forehead, and pinched an eye wide open with finger and thumb.

"Get my phone out of my pocket," he told Alvin.

Despite his reservations about Hoon's current course of action, the P.I. did as he was told. Hoon talked him through opening it up and bringing up the photograph of Miles.

"Right, show it to him," he instructed, nodding down at Victor. "Let him fucking see."

Alvin held the phone above the head of security, the screen angled down at him.

"Just tell him what he needs to know, man. Don't be a damn fool."

Victor, whose gaze had been wavering between Hoon and the

out-of-focus needle, ignored the instruction for as long as he could, before curiosity got the better of him.

His eyes flitted to the phone screen and stayed there.

Hoon and Alvin both watched what little colour was left in his face drain away.

A tear ran sideways from the eye Hoon was pinning open, rolling down his temple and onto the concrete floor.

"Oh," Victor whispered. He gulped down a few unsteady breaths. "Oh, fuck."

And then, with a howl and a Herculean effort, he wrenched an arm free, caught the syringe, and pulled it down until the needle was buried deep in his eye socket.

Roaring in pain, he fumbled for the plunger and pressed it down, emptying the syringe's entire contents.

"Fucking hell!" Hoon yelped, leaping to his feet as Victor began to thrash and buck beneath him. "That wasn't fucking me! You two fucking saw that, right? He fucking did that to himself!"

Victor's whole body convulsed and spasmed, white foam bubbling from between his lips, blood streaming from his nose.

"What do we do?" Terry yelped, backing up like he was worried whatever the hell was happening to his boss might somehow be contagious. "Should we do something?"

Hoon stood and watched as Victor's convulsions became more violent. They folded him in the middle, his upper and lower halves being flung together like he was in a malfunctioning hospital bed.

"I mean..." Bob put his hands on his hips. "I'm open to fucking ideas, but this is a new one on me."

An inhuman screech exploded from deep inside the Marine. He vomited up something black and slimy that coated his face and pooled on his chest.

And then, with a final gargle, his head fell backwards with a *crack*, and his open eye stared glassily up at the ceiling.

There was a moment of shocked silence, and then Alvin gave the Marine a nudge with the pointed toe of a boot.

"Hey, man. You OK?"

"What the fuck are you on about? Of course he's no' fucking OK!" Hoon spat, gesturing down at the very obviously dead man. "He's got a dirty great needle rammed through his eyeball, and I'm pretty sure he's just fucking shat himself inside out."

He turned on Terry, the bouncer. Despite the gun in the Englishman's hand, Hoon ran at him, grabbing him by the lapels of his suit, and hissing in his face.

"Did you fucking know about all this?" he demanded. "This shite? These people?"

"No. No, I had no idea," Terry insisted. He glanced around, but the horror of it all was too much for him to bear, and he focused his attention on Hoon again. "Honest. I didn't know. I swear, mate."

"I'm no' your fucking mate, pal!"

"Yeah, well I am," Alvin said, stepping in. "Terry's a good guy. Take your hands off him. Weren't for him, least one of us'd be a stain on the floor right now."

Hoon relented and released his grip, but clearly wasn't happy about it. He shoved the security guard back a step, then pointed to the corpse on the floor. "Get his phone. Maybe that'll fucking tell us something," he said. "There's a computer next door, too. You'll know the one, because the fucking monitor's on fire. Get that. Bring it upstairs. Meet us outside. You!" He stabbed a finger at Alvin. "With me."

The P.I. limped along behind Hoon as he went racing back towards the main room, and the elevator.

"Right behind you, man. But where are we going?"

"We're going to find Sarah," Hoon said, breaking into a jog. "And if anything's fucking happened to her, I'm going to burn this whole fucking place to the ground."

CHAPTER THIRTY-EIGHT

RAGE. Fear. Dread.

But mostly rage.

"No, no, no, no, fuck, fuck, no!"

Hoon slammed the broken door of the empty van, and rounded on the man in black leather hobbling up behind him.

"She's gone! She's fucking gone!" he roared. He flew at Alvin, grabbing him by the leather jacket just as he'd done with Terry down in the subbasement. "This is your fucking fault! I didn't want her involved, but you and your stupid fucking plan made me!"

"Hey, now. Easy, man," Alvin protested. "Don't you fret none. The King's gonna find her."

"You're no' the fucking King!" Hoon roared, the heat of his anger steaming up the P.I.'s shades. "You're not fucking Elvis! You're a mad old bastard with a fucking personality disorder!"

"Like I said, man, ever since September Fourteenth, 1984, eight forty-seven A.M., old Alvin's been the Earthly vessel of the one-and-only—"

"No! Bollocks! Are you fuck!" Hoon shook him. "You're fucking delusional, that's all you are! You're a nutter in fancy dress. You're no' Elvis. I don't care what wee fucking *Viva Las Vegas* fantasy you've got going on between them fucking sideburns, you are *not* Elvis fucking Presley!"

"*Then what the hell am I?*" Alvin roared back. His eyes widened, and he took a sharp, sudden breath, as if the outburst had caught him by surprise.

The accent had fallen away a little, like it was offering a glimpse of the man beneath the persona. His eyes flitted back and forth behind his bifocal sunglasses, searching Hoon's for an answer.

Somewhere in the distance, police sirens wailed.

"If I don't have the King, what the hell do I have?" he asked, and there was a note of panic in his voice, like he was in danger of losing something. Everything, maybe.

"The fuck's that meant to mean?" Hoon asked, after a moment's hesitation. It was less aggressive than his previous statements, though he continued to hold Alvin by the lapels.

The clearing of a throat beside them made them both turns their heads.

"Alright, Boggle?"

Hoon and Alvin both stared at Iris and Sarah. They stood side by side, Sarah lightly shivering in the cold night air, Iris wearing the tan-coloured uniform of the Las Vegas Metropolitan Police Department.

Alvin's leather jacket creaked as Hoon released his grip.

"You're OK?" Bob muttered. He tilted his head towards the van. "I saw that broken, and I thought—"

"It was a close one," Sarah said. "But me and Iris sorted it." Her eyes narrowed, like she wasn't entirely sure what had just happened. "Just don't ask me how."

"The fuck are you wearing?" Hoon asked, turning his attention to the one-eyed man beside her.

"It's a policeman's uniform, Boggle."

"No, I can see that, right enough," Hoon said. "Sorry,

should've phrased that better. Why the fuck are you wearing a policeman's uniform?"

"Security guard's was too big," Iris replied.

"OK." Hoon nodded like he was trying to convince himself he was satisfied with this answer, but his furrowing brow said otherwise. "I feel that just opens up a whole load of other questions, but I don't have the fucking energy. The cops are coming."

"That was me," Sarah said, straightening up like she was preparing to accept a medal. "I sent Detective Holden a video of what was going on down in the basement." She shuddered. "Those poor people."

"Aye, right. Very good," Hoon said, though he had no idea if it had been the right move or not. No point worrying about it now. "You two get in the van and get the fuck out of here. We'll meet back at—"

He turned to Alvin, but the P.I. was already walking away. Hoon scratched at the back of his head, cursing himself for his outburst.

"Fuck. Here, listen, Alvin..." he began, but a wave of a hand silenced him.

"I'm going to get the Duchess and get the car," Alvin said, in an uncharacteristically flat monotone. "I'll see you all back at the office."

Hoon winced, and they all watched, listening to the growing scream of the approaching sirens, until the detective disappeared around the corner and out of sight.

"That was a bit mean of you, Boggle," Iris said.

"It really was," Sarah agreed.

Hoon sighed. "Fine. Aye. I'll fucking apologise," he said. "But he's still no' fucking Elvis!"

"What harm is he doing?" Sarah asked.

"What fucking harm?!" Hoon spluttered. "I thought you'd been fucking killed!"

Sarah shrugged, her arms wrapped around herself to fend off

the cold. "And why would him thinking he's Elvis have caused that?"

Hoon opened his mouth to offer some clever barbed reply, but couldn't think of one, so just pointed to the van again. "Right. In. The pair of you. I'll fucking drive. We're just waiting on—"

He turned to find Terry standing behind him, and reacted with a hiss and a, "Jesus Christ!"

"Sorry." The bouncer flashed an apologetic smile, as Iris and Sarah clambered into the van. "I didn't mean to give you a fright."

"Don't you worry about that. You didn't give me a fucking fright, son, you surprised me, that's all. There's a big difference. You couldn't give me a fright if you popped out of my cornflakes holding a fucking severed head and dressed as my sister." He pointed to a backpack Terry was holding in front of him. "Is that the stuff?"

"Uh, yeah. Phone and computer. There was some paperwork knocking around, too, so I chucked that in."

Hoon took the offered bag with a grunt of acknowledgement. "Right. Aye. Cheers." He looked over his shoulder in the direction the sirens were coming from. "If I was you, I'd fucking scarper. Sounds like this place is about to be crawling with the fucking polis."

Terry nodded slowly. "Yeah, maybe. Or maybe I'll stay and try to help. Give them a keycard for the lab, or whatever the hell that place is." He shuddered at the thought of it, then glanced up at the livery on the side of the van. "Is Mr King OK?"

Hoon scowled. "I'd say he's pretty fucking far from OK." The look of worry on the younger man's face made him sigh. "He's fine. He's off to get the car."

Terry relaxed at that, a smile of relief breaking out across his broad, square-jawed face. "Good. That's good. He's, uh, he's a really good guy. He found my daughter."

"What?"

"Yeah. Some guy grabbed her off the street. Pushed my wife

over and just bundled our little girl into a van. The police were useless. Mr King got wind of it, though, and he went looking. We didn't have a lot of money, but he didn't want any. Just wanted to help."

The bouncer's voice cracked. There was something quite striking about a man of his size letting the rawness of his emotion break through like that. Striking enough to make even Hoon shut up and listen.

"He found her. And the guy. He'd been keeping her in the basement of his mum's house." Terry rubbed at his forehead, like he was trying to keep the memory from coming out. "He'd, eh, he'd hurt her. But Mr King found her, and brought her back to us, when no one else could."

Hoon looked back over his shoulder in the direction the P.I. had gone storming off in.

"He wouldn't take payment. I tried to give him what we could, but he wouldn't have it," Terry continued, sniffing and pulling himself together. "I found out later what had happened to him. I looked it up, and it all made sense."

"What do you mean?" Hoon asked. "What happened to him?"

Terry flinched at that, like he'd said something he shouldn't. "He didn't tell you?"

"Tell me what?"

"Shit." The bouncer looked down for a moment, then met Hoon's eye again. "About what happened to his family? Back in the eighties? Some crime boss, or gangster, or something. He killed them. Shot Alvin, too, but he survived."

"Aw, fuck."

Hoon closed his eyes and rubbed at them. One by one, the pieces clicked into place.

"September Fourteenth, 1984, by any chance?"

Terry blinked. "Oh. Yeah. So, he did tell you, then?"

"No' exactly," Hoon admitted. "But I should've fucking seen

it coming." He patted the bag. "Cheers for this. And, you know, for stepping in down there."

"Anything for Mr King," Terry said, then he nodded, turned away, and headed back in the direction of the Skyliner Lounge.

Hoon watched him go, quietly processing the information he'd given. Then, the sound of the sirens became too loud to ignore, and he hurried around to the driver's side of the van.

And then he continued around to the other side, when he remembered the fucking steering wheel was on the wrong side.

Christ, he hated this country.

"OK, Boggle?" asked Iris from the passenger seat.

Hoon dumped the bag in Iris's lap, then fired up the engine. "Be better when we're far away from this fucking place," he said.

And, in a cloud of exhaust fumes and a screeching of tyres, he powered the van out of the alleyway and into the cold neon lights of Las Vegas.

CHAPTER THIRTY-NINE

THE ATMOSPHERE back at Alvin's office was heavy and thick with the absence of words that needed to be said.

They'd hooked up the computer they'd stolen from the lab to Alvin's monitor. Iris was working his way through it, while Sarah tried, without much success, to unlock Victor's phone.

The Duchess reclined on the couch like an old film star on a chaise longue, reading through the documents that had been bundled into Terry's bag, while sipping on a margarita that she'd insisted she bring with her from the casino.

Hoon wasn't quite sure what she was still doing here. He'd paid her a not-inconsiderable sum of money to pretend to be his wife for a while, but had assumed that would be the end of it.

She seemed content to hang around, though, and while she was clearly a full-blown fruitcake, he was happy to take all the help he could get.

In terms of good done for the world, everything that happened back at the Skyliner Lounge was not to be sneezed at, but he was no closer to finding Miles.

Victor's reaction to Crabtree's photograph had been... interesting. The secret service man wasn't the best-looking guy in the world, but the Marine's response to seeing him felt a bit extreme.

The only thing Hoon could think of was that Victor had preferred to face an agonising death rather than admit to what he and his cohorts had done to Miles. Which, given all the other shit he'd clearly been happy to take credit for, didn't exactly bode well.

Alvin sat by the office window, nursing the same glass of Scotch he'd poured himself when he'd returned with the Duchess half an hour ago. He'd taken off his sunglasses, and his eyes seemed out of focus as he peered out through a gap in the blinds.

There were still a couple of hours until the sun would be fully up, but suggestions of pink and yellow had started to paint themselves across the darkness to the east.

Everyone else was busy. Everyone was hard at work.

It was, to quote the man himself, now or never.

"You alright?" Hoon asked, pulling up a chair across from the detective.

Alvin raised his glass, but said nothing.

Hoon drew in a breath that became a groan. "Look, I'm no' very good at this sort of fucking thing," he began. "But, that stuff I said—"

"You were right."

Alvin's voice was still lacking its usual Memphis drawl. It was still in there somewhere, Hoon thought, but buried deep.

"I don't like it. But, you're right." Alvin shrugged. "I'm not Elvis. Of course I'm not. I am..."

He brought his glass to his mouth and wet his lips with the liquid, while staring blankly into space.

Finally, after concluding that the rest of the sentence wasn't going to occur to him, he shrugged.

"Damned if I know." He went back to holding his drink between the fingers and thumbs of both hands. "I'm sorry we couldn't find your friend. I can't imagine how worried you must be."

Hoon rubbed at the back of his head. There were words he could say, he was sure of it. The right combination of letters and syllables existed that could fix this. They had to.

But he was fucked if he knew what they were.

"Um, aye. Cheers." He looked over at the rest of the group. "Maybe they'll find something."

"I hope so," Alvin said. He cleared his throat. "If they do. If they find where he is. If you'll still have me, I'd like to help."

"Of course. Fuck. Aye. Definitely," Hoon said. "I'd like that."

Alvin nodded. "Thank you."

Hoon waited for the 'very much.' For the curling sneer of his top lip.

Neither came.

"You were right. I shouldn't have got Sarah involved," the P.I. continued. "It was far too risky. Anything could've happened."

"Aye, well. It didn't. She's fine. Seems like she can handle herself."

"Seems like it," Alvin agreed. They both watched her working away at the phone, her frustration clear from the way she stabbed her finger against its screen. "She looks up to you. She likes you."

Hoon checked his watch. "Probably not for long," he said.

Alvin raised a questioning eyebrow.

"Long story," Hoon said. "But I'm thinking any minute now, she won't be able to stand the sight of me." He offered Alvin a smile that, on any other face, might have been construed as an apology. "I can be a right fucking annoying prick sometimes."

Alvin raised his glass again, but didn't pass comment either way.

"Who's the Viper?"

All eyes went to the Duchess, still lounging on the sofa, swirling the dregs of her cocktail around in the glass. She looked up from the paperwork she'd been studying, her powdered face creased into lines of confusion.

"Anyone? Any ideas?"

"What the fuck are you on about?" Hoon asked. "What fucking viper?"

"It's in here, dahhling. This woman, Scarlett Fontaine, I think she's making some sort of deal or whatnot. Either with, or on behalf of, or assisted by someone called 'the Viper.'"

She pursed her lips and shoogled them from side to side, like she was trying to keep an angry bee trapped in her mouth, for reasons best known to herself.

"I mean, I'm assuming it's not an actual snake. But then... I mean, it doesn't specifically say otherwise, dahhling, so I don't know what to make of it."

Hoon strode across the room and snatched the paperwork from her hands.

"Here, give me a fucking look at that."

He scanned the page. It seemed to be a computer transcript of a conversation, and had been laid out on the paper in tiny print with no punctuation whatsoever.

It took about three seconds to give him a headache. Two more, and he'd lost the will to live.

Halfway down, his eyes stopped on the word 'Viper,' and rested there, like it was an island in an ocean teeming with hungry Great White sharks.

He risked a quick scan of the sentences on either side, but was as immediately confused by them as the Duchess had been. Someone called the Viper was involved in either the buying or selling of Elysium, but it would take some work to figure out which.

"Don't know. Codename for Victor, maybe. Pretty similar. Keep reading," he said, passing the paperwork back to the Duchess, who looked crestfallen to have it back in her possession again.

"As you wish, dahhling," she said with a sigh. "No rest for the wicked, what?"

She necked the last of her margarita, then shook the glass at him, encouraging him to fill it up again. He took it off her, looked around for a moment, then headed to the drinks cabinet and poured her a gin and tonic.

He had just handed it back, and was idly wondering when the fuck he'd become a waiter, when Iris stood straight up out of chair, making it topple backwards onto the floor.

"Boggle!"

He was still, for reasons yet to be explained, but which Hoon had no intention of questioning, wearing the cop's uniform. An unbuttoned sleeve flapped around as he pointed at the computer screen in front of him.

"I think you're going to want to see this!"

ALL OF THEM, with the exception of the Duchess, who seemed content to lie on the couch, stood watching the grainy grey footage playing on Alvin's monitor.

It was from a security camera down in the lab. The same one that Iris had been shown by the guard.

This time, as well as the people trapped inside the perspex prisons, Victor stood talking to a tall, glamorous woman that Alvin was the first to recognise.

"That's Scarlett Fontaine," he said, the Elvis accent still notably absent. "That's the head of the whole thing"

"Is there sound? What are they saying?" Hoon asked.

Iris cranked up the volume on one of the dusty speakers beside the monitor. The hissing of the background noise made it hard to hear exactly what was being said, but Hoon could pretty much piece it together.

"They're talking about a deal. Offloading their whole stock of Elysium in one go."

"She said something about the Mexican cartels," Alvin said. He squinted and cocked an ear towards the speakers, trying to work it out. "Something about the border?"

"Sam Diego," Iris said. He looked at Hoon. "Who's that?"

"It's no' a fucking who, it's a where. *San* Diego," Hoon said. "Now, shut the fuck up."

"Hold up, rewind," Alvin said, but he pushed past Iris and scrubbed the video timeline back a few seconds himself.

The hiss from the speakers grew louder as the P.I. cranked the volume up all the way.

They listened to the broken voices, piecing together the snippets they could make out.

"Did she just say they're giving it away?" Hoon asked. "The fuck would they do that for?"

"Doesn't make any sense," Alvin agreed.

"Why would they spend all that time and money making a big load of drugs, and then just give them away to the Mexicans?" Iris asked. "Don't Americans hate Mexicans? Weren't they trying to build a wall, or something, at some point? Or did I dream that?"

Hoon blinked.

Wall.

Wall.

Elbowing his way to the computer, he minimised the window, and scoured the crowded desktop until he found the icon he was looking for.

ElysiumWall.xls.

He double-clicked. The computer's hard drive toiled away for a moment, and then the spreadsheet opened, filling the screen.

Rows and rows of dates and numbers ran down the length of the document, crammed into narrow columns with headings that didn't seem to mean much of anything.

"What the hell are we looking at?" Sarah asked. She was still holding the phone, but had pretty much given up on getting it unlocked now.

"Beats me, honey," Alvin said, then he shook his head, annoyed at himself. "I don't know."

"What's that? A hundred percent?" Hoon asked, pointing to one of the spreadsheet's cells.

"It's like the full thing, Boggle," Iris helpfully explained. "A hundred percent of a thing is all the thing."

"I know what it fucking means! I mean, what does it fucking mean, though?" Hoon winced. That sentence hadn't gone nearly as well as it could've. "A hundred percent of what?"

"It's marked in green, which must be good," Sarah reasoned.

Alvin pointed to the heading at the top of the column. It was just two letters, marked in bold. "FR," he said, then he sucked in his bottom lip and spat it out again. "French?" he guessed. "Could stand for France, I suppose. Though, unlikely."

"For Realsies," Iris said.

Hoon turned to look at him. "Eh?"

"FR." Iris pointed to the screen. "For Realsies."

"I'm no' even going to fucking dignify that with a response."

"Fatality Rate."

It was the Duchess who had spoken, her accent-of-no-specific-origin bringing silence to the room.

Hoon looked at the percentage, then at the heading, then over at the mad old cow.

"What?"

"It's in here, dahhling." She waved one of the documents she'd been reading. "Fatality Rate. Hundred percent, apparently. I get the impression they were really rather pleased with that."

Despite all the awfulness and horror Hoon had already witnessed in the last few hours, this revelation somehow managed to tie yet another knot in his stomach.

"It's not drugs. It's poison," he muttered. "Or, fuck, I don't know. It's drugs *and* poison. They're no' giving it away out of the goodness of their fucking hearts, they're wiping out the competition. Shipping the whole fucking lot to Mexico."

"But...that could kill hundreds," Sarah gasped.

"Thousands," Alvin said.

Hoon shook his head. "Millions."

"Billions!" added Iris, who didn't want to be left out.

"Let's no' go fucking overboard," Hoon told him.

"We have to tell someone! We have to stop them!" Sarah cried. "We have to stop this."

"We will," Hoon assured her.

"And just how the hell are we supposed to do that?" Alvin asked, and the note of defeat in his voice made Hoon miss his previous hip-thrusting, lip-curling persona.

"San Diego," Hoon said. "That's where they're going, right? We go there and try and find them."

"It's a big place," Alvin countered.

"They'll be near the border."

The P.I. shrugged. "Still a big place."

"And for all we know, Boggle, it's already happened. Maybe everyone in Mexico's dead."

"I'm sure someone would have fucking mentioned that, if that'd happened," Hoon snapped. "And I don't fucking know how we find them, but we'll work something out!"

"Fourth of July," the Duchess said.

She squinted at the document she was holding, and brought it close to her face, her nostrils flaring and her eyes widening as she struggled to read the tiny text.

"What about it?" Alvin asked.

"It's today!" Sarah realised, and she seemed pleased about this fact, if only for a brief, all-too-fleeting moment.

"It's in here. That's when they're doing the doodah, doodah, blah, blah, blah, whatever it is, with the Mexicans."

Hoon didn't have the energy or the inclination to listen to her any longer. He snatched the paperwork from her for a second time, and this time forced himself to pay closer attention to the densely packed text.

"Fuck. It says here they're making the drop at noon. Fourth of July. We can still make it." He glanced at his watch, then over at Alvin. "Can we still make it? This stupid fucking country's so big and got so many fucking time zones, I've got no idea."

"San Diego's in the same time zone as Vegas," Alvin said. He looked at a clock on the wall. It was in the shape of early-years-Elvis, with pendulums shaped like his legs swaying back and forth below. "Gonna be tight, though. We got just under six hours. If we left now and drove straight through? We could maybe make it, but given that we don't even know where we're going, I can't say I like our chances."

"Fuck!"

Alvin rubbed at his chin, deep in thought. "I might have a way. I know a couple of guys with helicopters."

"Course you fucking do," Hoon said. "Right, well, get onto them and—"

A phone rang, cutting Hoon off before he could finish barking out the instruction.

They all looked at the landline on Alvin's desk, then at the P.I. himself. He shook his head, denying all knowledge.

Only then did Sarah realise the ringing was coming from her hand.

"Oh. Oh!" she yelped, tossing Victor's phone to Hoon like it was suddenly too hot for her to hold.

He fumbled with it, then caught it, and whistled through his teeth when he saw the initials on the screen.

"S.F."

Iris clicked his fingers and pointed. "San Francisco!"

"Scarlett Fontaine," Alvin said. He gave Hoon a nod, then crossed his arms and clamped a hand over his mouth, like he was bracing himself for whatever came next.

Hoon took a moment to scribble down the number displayed under the initials, then tapped the icon that answered the call.

He didn't speak. He didn't dare.

By the sounds of it, the person on the other end of the line was in a car, or maybe even a plane. There was the rumbling of an engine, anyway. It was the only sound for several seconds, and then a woman spoke in clipped, irritated tones.

"Victor? Are you there?"

Hoon looked around at the others, then grimaced and quietly cleared his throat.

"Yes," he said, in what he hoped was a passable attempt at the now-late Marine's voice.

There was silence, save for the rumbling of the engine in the background.

And then, without another word being spoken, the call was terminated.

"Ah, shit," Iris groaned. "Why didn't you do his voice, Boggle?"

"I was doing his fucking voice!"

Iris frowned. It made his glass eye take a sharp left turn. "Was that you doing his voice? I thought you said he was American?"

"He was American! That's why I did a fucking American accent!"

Alvin and Sarah joined Iris in looking doubtful.

"Kind of sounded a bit Australian to me, Boggle."

"Personally? I thought South African," Alvin said.

"Does it fucking matter?!" Hoon barked.

Iris shrugged. "I mean, I suppose it doesn't now that you've already blown it, Boggle, no."

"I've no' fucking blown it! I've got her number," Hoon said, waving the scrap of paper he'd scribbled it down on.

"Oh, nice one," Iris said. "Maybe you can phone her up and ask her where she is."

For a moment, it looked like Hoon might be about to ram the

scrap of paper down Iris's throat, but instead he slammed it onto the desk in front of Alvin.

"Can we run a trace on it, or something?" he demanded.

Alvin raised an eyebrow. "Who, me?"

"Aye! You're a fucking detective, aren't you?"

"Not this level," Alvin said. He nudged the number back towards Hoon like he didn't want to get too involved with it. "Like I told you before, I find missing dogs and cheating husbands."

"And infiltrate casinos and underground fucking murder labs," Hoon reminded him.

"Don't mean a thing," Alvin said. "Way above anything I can do. Maybe if you knew someone high up in Californian law enforcement. Or, hell, I don't know, the government. Maybe then they could pull some strings, but even then—"

"Whoa, whoa, hold on!" Sarah said.

Hoon was a step ahead of her. "No. Fuck off. No chance."

Sarah crossed her arms in defiance and glared at him. "It's our best bet."

Hoon spat out a string of obscenities, but none of them constituted an actual argument. He was already taking out his phone, in fact, and muttered below his breath as he tapped on one of the contacts.

He stood, still mumbling and sighing, as he listened to it ring.

The moment it clicked, he started speaking before the person on the other end had a chance to.

"Boyband. Shut the fuck up. Them photos I sent you of that naked bastard with all the fucking leather straps..." He looked over at Sarah, who nodded, giving him her permission. "Please tell me you've done what you usually do, and failed to follow a simple fucking instruction."

CHAPTER FORTY

SENATOR ETHAN HOLBROOK was midway through his morning workout when the phone rang. It was far away, elsewhere in the family mansion, and not his primary concern.

His primary concern was his arse. Specifically, in sculpting away the little wobbly bulge of fat where the bottom of his buttocks met the tops of his thighs.

It was a stubborn spot to shift. It was also, he thought, the thing about himself he hated the most, not counting his big toes, which pointed sharply in opposite directions like they were old enemies who couldn't stand the sight of each other. He hated those the most.

Well, them and his elbows. Wrinkly bastards that they were.

This morning, though, was all about what he'd come to think of as his 'ass pockets.' A few months back, when he'd first noticed them in a video he'd shot of himself going to town on a couple of local girls, the pockets had looked full.

Now, through careful, diligent exercise, an assortment of creams, and the application of heat, he'd describe them as half-empty. Maybe a third empty, in the case of the one on the left, which was proving to be more stubborn.

The phone stopped ringing. Ethan lowered himself into a low squat and held it, held it, held it, feeling the warmth of the heating pad on the floor working its magic on the ass pockets, and on his bare, exposed anus.

He admired himself in the floor-to-ceiling mirror that he liked to exercise naked in front of. Usually, he'd practise facial expressions while he was mid-workout, figuring that if he could look 'sombre but hopeful' or 'dynamic but caring' while engaged in a full reverse lunge, doing it when he made his eventual run for the White House would be a walk in the park.

Today, though, he didn't want to look at his face. The bruising from yesterday had only continued to grow, to the point where he now looked like the Elephant Man doing blackface. Or black-and-blue-face, at least.

He focused instead on his abs, tensing them so the muscles reached their full, impressive definition. The effort made his penis twitch, like it was waving at him.

Despite the pain it brought, he smiled and waved back.

From along the corridor, he heard the *clopping* of his wife's footsteps. He hoped, for her sake, that she wasn't about to interrupt his workout. She knew how he felt about that, and it would be unlike her to test him. Especially after she'd dared to question him about his injuries last night.

Surely, she'd have learned her lesson from that?

To his immense frustration, it seemed not.

She didn't even bother to knock, which wasn't like her at all.

"For Christ's sake, Diane, can't you see that I'm—"

The phone hit him between the eyes, opening the wound in his nose and drawing a scream of pain from his swollen lips. He raised a hand to shield his face, but neglected to first drop the dumbbell he'd been holding.

His scream became an animal squeal. Some very expensive dentistry made a deeply concerning cracking sound.

By the time the blinding flash of white light and the accompanying tears had started to clear, his wife had left the room, slamming the door behind her.

"What the fuck?!" he sobbed, blood cascading down his naked body, and staining his wispy grey pubes. A few drops sizzled as they hit the heating pad below him.

The phone lay on the floor. From it, even over the ringing in his ears, the senator could hear a tinny, but angry-sounding male voice.

Hand shaking, head throbbing, anus slowly cooling, Ethan picked up the phone.

"H-hello?" he said. The words burbled wetly and lightly whistled through a newly-created gap in his teeth. "W-who the hell is this?"

His face, which he would've considered already to be at rock bottom, found a way to fall further.

He swallowed.

He whimpered.

"OK," he whispered, and the man who looked back at him from the mirror had far more pressing problems than his ass pockets. "I'm listening."

"ARE WE DONE?" Sarah asked.

She'd paced back and forth during Hoon's call. Now that he'd hung up, she stood chewing her thumbnail, waiting for the verdict.

"Is he going to do it?"

Hoon nodded. "He's going to do it."

Sarah let out a little yelp of excitement and threw her arms around Bob's neck, hugging him. He stood there, awkward and rigid, then relented and gave her a pat on the back.

"We're still putting them fucking photos out as soon as all this is done," he said.

"Totally, yeah!" Sarah agreed. She released her grip on him, but continued to grin from ear to ear.

"How long until we hear?" Alvin asked.

"He's going to get back to us within the hour," Hoon said.

He glanced at the window, and felt an uncomfortable pressure at the back of his eyes. The sun was up now, and was already too bright and too hot for his liking.

"Cutting it kinda fine," Alvin said.

"Aye," Hoon conceded. "You get that chopper sorted?"

"He's fuelling up. Reckon we can head over there in around thirty minutes."

"I've never been in a helicopter before!" Sarah said, and the prospect seemed to both excite and terrify her.

Hoon took a breath. This was it, then.

"Aye. Well, you're no' going in one now, either."

Sarah's smile stayed fixed in place, but she wasn't selling it as well as she had been a moment before.

"What? What do you mean?"

"It's too dangerous. You're not coming."

Sarah shook her head. "You're not leaving me here. Not after everything we've already done."

"Everything we already did nearly got you hurt. Or killed. Or whatever the fuck they'd have done to you," Hoon reasoned. "I can't bring you. I won't."

"I can look after myself."

"Can you fuck," Hoon said, and it sounded harsher than he'd intended.

Sarah's smile fell away. She wrapped her arms around herself, suddenly defensive.

"I've been surviving fine."

Hoon shook his head. When he spoke, his voice had softened. "This isn't surviving. What you've been doing, Sarah, what you've had to do, that's not right. It's not fair."

Sarah clenched her jaw and looked away from him, her eyes moistening, her weight shifting from one foot to the other.

"Fine. Go. Fuck off, then. I'll be fine on my own."

"You're not going to be on your own," Hoon said.

Sarah snorted and flicked her gaze over to where the Duchess lay snoring on the couch, her glass still held in one hand, the paperwork scattered on the floor beside her.

"Yeah, I don't think she's going to be much of a babysitter."

"That's not what I mean," Hoon said.

He raised a hand and gave a wave out of the window.

Outside, a car door opened.

"I called your mum, Sarah," he told her. "I got her number from your detective pal's computer when he wasn't looking, and I called her up."

Throughout this explanation, Sarah's eyes had grown wider and wider, her lower jaw slowly dropping until her mouth hung open.

"You did *what*?" she whispered.

"I talked to her. She kicked your stepdad out the day you left. Called the police on him. Warned him that she'd cut his bollocks off if she ever saw him again. They're divorced. She's been looking for you since you left."

A tear ran down the girl's cheek. She was hugging herself more tightly, like she might be able to quell the full-body shakes that had started.

"You *called* her?"

"I'm not saying you have to go with her," Hoon said. "I'm not even saying you should. I'm just saying... people are fuck-ups. We really are. We do things that will fucking haunt us for the rest of our lives." He gestured around at Iris, Alvin, and the sleeping Duchess. "All of us. We've all made mistakes."

"Especially me, Boggle," Iris helpfully added.

"Especially him, aye," Hoon agreed. "But the rest of us, too. I mean, fuck, if I started making a list of my fucking regrets, I'd never reach the bottom.

"And, aye, you know what? Maybe me calling your mum'll end up on there one day. But I really fucking hope not. And I don't think it will."

The buzzing of Alvin's doorbell was like a punctuation mark that ended his speech.

Sarah stood there in silence, her eyes and mouth still open, like she was in a state of shock. She slowly turned her head to look at Alvin, who offered her a supportive smile.

"It's your call, darlin'," he said, slipping partway back into his Elvis persona. "I can let her in, or I can tell her to go."

She just looked at him, like she couldn't understand what he was saying. Or, perhaps, didn't even recognise it as language.

Then, she turned back to Hoon, and slapped him hard across the face.

He didn't react to it, but she did. She drew back in fright, her hands covering her mouth for a moment, before she threw herself at him and wrapped her arms around him again.

This time, rather than *squeeing* with excitement, she just sobbed against his shoulder, her full weight leaning on him, a child in a woman's body.

He hugged her back this time, both arms supporting her, holding her up, giving her strength.

"He's right," Hoon told her. "We can let her in, or we can send her away. But I think you should at least talk to her."

Sarah stepped back. Sniffed. Nodded. Alvin moved to go answer the door, but she blocked his way.

"I'll do it," she said, but the words came out as a croak. She cleared her throat, and tried again. "I'll go."

The three men watched as she headed into the hallway. Listened as she opened the door.

Heard the gasp of a woman, and the raw emotion behind it.

"Sarah?"

"Mom?"

Her voice cracked, then became muffled as she buried her face against her mother's shoulder.

"*Mom!*"

"Oh, baby! Oh, my baby, my baby, my precious girl! I'm sorry, I'm so sorry! I'm so sorry!"

Hoon quietly closed the inner office door to give the women their privacy, then plucked a handkerchief from a box on Alvin's desk and handed it to Iris, who blew his nose so hard his eye changed direction.

"Cheers, Boggle." He waved a hand in front of his chest like he was trying to feed himself air. "I just get a bit emotional sometimes."

"Aye. I know," Hoon said, and there was no judgment in it.

He turned to Alvin. The P.I. had pulled his sunglasses on, but the purple lenses couldn't quite hide the reddening of the older man's eyes.

"Right, so we've got a chopper. All being well, we should be able to track that bitch shortly," Hoon said, laying out the plan. "We find her, fuck up her day, stop the whole drug thing, find out where Miles is, rescue him, have a fucking taco and some Mexican beer, and consider it a job well done."

"That sounds like a plan to me," Alvin said.

"Only one thing missing," Hoon said. He clapped his hands and rubbed them together. "We're going to need a *proper fuck-load* of guns."

CHAPTER FORTY-ONE

THE HELICOPTER DROPPED them behind a ridge, a half-mile trek from where Scarlett Fontaine's phone had last pinged the network. The senator had come through, just as Hoon knew he would, the threat of exposure as a sadistic wee pervert having proven too big an incentive to resist.

At Hoon's insistence, they had taken time to source desert camo outfits before leaving Vegas. This, it turned out, wasn't difficult, given the obsession a certain demographic of the American public had with all things military-related.

Despite the realisation that, when standing together, the three of them resembled "an ill-advised Dad's Army remake on UK fucking Gold," they were grateful for the camo when they clambered up the rough desert ridge and peered in the direction of the border.

"See anything, Boggle?" Iris asked, his voice barely audible above the desert breeze.

"You don't need to fucking whisper," Hoon told him. "They've no' got fucking super hearing."

He lay on the rocky outcrop, watching events through a set of binoculars.

"And aye," he confirmed. "Three SUVs, four big trucks. I'm guessing that's where they've got the drugs stored."

"The SUVs?" Iris asked.

Hoon pulled his eyes away from the binoculars just long enough to flick him a dirty look. "The trucks."

"Oh. Yeah. Right."

Hoon passed the binoculars to Alvin, who lay on the rocks beside him.

"No sign of the cartel. Looks kinda one-sided right now," he said.

He passed the binoculars to Iris, who didn't bother to look through them before passing them back to Hoon.

"You think your friend's down there?" Alvin asked.

"Doubt it," Hoon replied. "But I reckon someone down there will be able to point us in the right fucking direction."

He folded the binoculars closed, then tucked them into a trouser pocket of his camo gear.

"Listen. Alvin. You don't need to do this. There's no fucking saying what might happen if we go down there. It could all go tits up. This isn't your fight."

Alvin narrowed his eyes, like he was considering this.

It didn't take him long.

"It's been my fight for a long damn time. I guess I just kinda forgot that for a while. I want to thank you for reminding me."

"Aye, but—"

"I'm coming. I'm in. That's final."

Hoon considered arguing, but it was clear from the older man's face that he wasn't going to be dissuaded.

"Fine. Right. Well. Thanks," Hoon said. He ran a hand down his face. "But, listen, that shite I said before. About how you're not—"

"We don't have time for this," Alvin said. "It's in the past."

Keeping low, he backtracked down the ridge a little, then

squatted down next to the large holdall they'd brought with them in the helicopter.

Unzipping it, he took out a couple of handguns, tucked one into the back of his trousers, and handed the other to Hoon. He offered a third to Iris, who shook his head.

"No. Boggle says I'm a liability with them."

"He's hanging back up here," Hoon explained. "He's our eyes. Or eye, I suppose."

He nodded to Iris, who produced an extendable telescope from his pocket, and pulled it out to its full length. He held it to his good eye and squinted at the vehicles parked up half a mile away. All he needed, Hoon thought, was a peg leg and a parrot, and he'd have checked off the full pirate tick sheet.

"Right, you fit?" Hoon asked.

Alvin produced a couple of SMGs from the bag and handed one to Bob.

"I'm sixty-five years old. I got a plastic hip, failing eyesight, and I sometimes gotta piss sitting down." He straightened his sunglasses and nodded. "And I sure as hell ain't getting any fitter."

HOON CRAWLED down the slope towards the vehicles, pulling himself along on his elbows and driving himself on with his toes. Sharp rocks scraped down his front. Dust blew up and lodged itself in his airways. The blazing midday sun blinded him and burned at the top of his head.

There was still a good third of a mile to go until they reached the rearmost vehicle—a black SUV that had been parked a little back from the others.

A third of a mile. His knees were already killing him, and he was pretty sure his forearms were bleeding.

"I'm too old for this shit," Alvin hissed from behind him.

Hoon heard the clatter of the P.I.'s feet as he stopped crawling and broke into a crouching run.

"Fuck it," Hoon concurred, and they both raced, keeping low, in a wide arc that kept them as out of sight of the people in the vehicles as possible, until they closed in on the rearmost car.

There were two people in it, one behind the steering wheel, the other in the back. Hoon gestured for Alvin to take the driver, and the older man nodded his understanding.

They moved in unison, approaching the car from opposite sides.

The driver's window was open, and the sound of Alvin's running footsteps made him turn, but just a half-second too late to avoid the butt of a submachine gun bludgeoning him into unconsciousness.

Even as the passenger in the back seat reacted, Hoon pulled the door open and pointed the SMG in his face.

"Make a fucking sound, and..."

He stopped.

He stared.

"Miles?"

The man sitting in the back seat let out a gasp. "Bob?! What are you doing?!" he hissed.

"The fuck are *you* doing?" Hoon demanded. "I'm here to fucking rescue you!"

Miles stared back at him, his jaw slack. "But...why?"

"Because I thought you were in fucking trouble!" Hoon looked the MI5 man up and down, taking in his tailored suit and polka-dotted pocket square. "But, I can see that... Actually, I don't fucking know what I'm seeing."

He pointed to a length of colourful fabric that Miles wore loosely around neck.

"Is that a fucking cravat you're wearing?" he demanded. It wasn't the most pertinent issue, but he felt it worth mentioning, all the same. "Who the fuck do you think you are, Fred out of Scooby Doo?"

"Shh. Shut up," Miles hissed, peering anxiously ahead through the windscreen.

"What the hell's happening?" Alvin asked, adjusting his grip on his gun. "You know this guy? This is your friend?"

"Who the hell's he?" Miles asked.

"Never fucking mind who he is," Hoon said, indicating a shiny silver badge pinned to Miles's lapel. It was in the shape of a coiled snake. "Who the fuck are you, more importantly? Don't tell me you're the fucking Viper!"

"Shh!" Miles urged again. "I'm undercover. You shouldn't be here, Bob! I've got this in hand."

Hoon picked up a bottle of champagne that was chilling in an ice bucket on the seat next to Miles. "So I fucking see! Looks like you're having a fucking high old time to yourself."

Up front, the driver began to stir. Alvin sent him back to sleep with another wallop from the gun.

"You know they're doing a fucking deal with the cartel, aye?" Hoon said. "You know this place is going to be fucking teeming with mad Mexican bastards any minute?"

Miles shook his head. "They're not cartel," he whispered.

Hoon blinked. "Eh?"

"They're not the cartel! They're DEA! I've been setting this up for weeks!" He gasped. "Wait! It was you that hit the casino last night! You killed Victor, didn't you?"

Hoon shook his head. "No' really. He killed himself. Jammed a fucking syringe full of that Elysium shite straight through his fucking eye socket when I showed him your picture."

"You showed him my picture?!" Miles squealed. "Are you out of your mind?!"

"Well I didn't fucking know what you were up to! Gabriella came to my house and said you were in fucking trouble, so there I go, dropping fucking everything, and here you are living the fucking high life!"

"He must've realised," Miles muttered, not really listening. "He ran my background checks. He bought the story. He must've realised what Scarlett would do to him if she ever found out."

He glanced ahead again, and all his features almost fell right off his face. He began speaking very low, very quickly.

"Shit. OK. Listen, Bob. You need to trust me, OK? They're coming. You need to put the guns down, or they will kill you. They'll kill you both."

"Hands on your fucking head!"

The voice was gruff. No nonsense. The voice of a killer.

Hoon held Miles's eye, and couldn't miss the flames of fear burning away behind them.

"Fuck," he muttered, then he looked over at Alvin, lowered his gun, and nodded.

"Aw...shit," the P.I. grunted, then he, too, lowered his weapon.

He and Hoon both turned from the car to find four armed men surrounding them, guns raised and trained.

"Don't shoot them," Miles instructed. His accent was American now. Perfectly, generically so.

He slid from the car, drew himself up to his full height, and eyeballed Hoon like a boxer squaring up to his opponent before a press conference.

Hoon glared back. In that moment, he wasn't quite sure if he was playing along, or if he really did want to punch the MI5 man's teeth down his throat, but the effect was the same, either way.

"We'll bring them to Miss Fontaine," Miles said, and the smile that crept across his face seemed all too real. "And she can decide what she wants to do with them."

IRIS PEERED THROUGH HIS TELESCOPE, his weight shifting anxiously from one foot to the other.

This wasn't good.

This was all the way bad, in fact.

He'd watched Hoon and Alvin all the way to the car, just like he was supposed to.

Yes, there was a *chance* that he'd become a little distracted by what he'd thought was a ghost, but had actually turned out to be just a plastic carrier bag being carried along on the breeze, but that was only for a few seconds. A minute, tops.

And now, Hoon and Alvin were surrounded by men with guns, and Iris hadn't been paying enough attention to warn them.

He lowered the telescope, then looked through it again, as if this might somehow reset the situation. A sort of cosmic turning it off and back on again.

It didn't.

"Shit," he whispered.

What should he do?

What *could* he do?

Boggle would know what to do, but he could hardly ask him.

He was on his own. He couldn't ask anyone else for help, because the only someone there was him.

Some deep-rooted childish instinct made him turn his back on the scene, as if him not being able to see it meant it didn't exist and wasn't happening.

As he stood alone on the ridge, Iris's good eye spotted the duffel bag Alvin had left behind.

There, tucked away inside the bag, metal glinted in the harsh light of the desert sun.

CHAPTER FORTY-TWO

THEY WERE, to their credit, very good at tying knots. Hoon wasn't happy about that fact, but he couldn't fault them on their work. He couldn't see what knot they'd used—his hands were behind his back, after all—but it felt secure. Annoyingly so.

He and Alvin stood with the sun blazing directly in their eyes, and a number of guns pointed directly at their heads.

Eight burly, armed men in black suits stood haphazardly around them, like a firing squad on a fag break. They all had matching haircuts, buzzed in close to the bone, and had apparently studied facial expression—or the lack thereof—at the same school.

If there was anything going on inside their heads or behind their eyes, they were playing their cards very close to their chest.

Miles stood off to the side, his hands clasped behind his back like he was tied up, too. He was still in character, but Hoon could feel the waves of panic radiating off him, and reckoned it was only a matter of time before someone else did, too.

Not the gunmen, of course. They wouldn't sense an earthquake going on beneath their feet. But someone.

Most likely, the woman in the crimson trouser suit who stood listening to one of the men who'd caught Hoon and Alvin at the car. He was tall, but she was taller, although the squared-off heels of her knee-length leather boots no doubt added an inch or two.

"Do you have a plan?" Alvin whispered.

"I've always got a fucking plan," Hoon muttered.

"Thank God."

Hoon sniffed. "Just hasn't quite fully come to me yet. But it will."

Alvin groaned. "We're dead men."

"Haw! You alright there, sweetheart?" Hoon called. He whistled and raised his eyebrows, in case shouting hadn't already been enough to get the woman's attention. "Are you the one Victor told us about?"

The woman turned and regarded him with cold disinterest while the grunt in formalwear finished filling her in. She dismissed him with a snap of her fingers and a wave of a leather gloved hand, then came striding over to Hoon and Alvin. Despite the heels, she seemed unbothered by the rough terrain.

"Who are you?" she asked, searching Hoon's face like she might find something she recognised there.

She leaned in a little closer, and for a moment he thought she might be trying to sniff out his identity, and all his secrets.

Scarlett Fontaine was even more beautiful than her picture had suggested, although money and makeup were doing some of the heavy lifting. Even her skin looked rich, and her teeth probably had a better credit rating than anyone Hoon knew.

"Him, I recognise," she said, pointing to Alvin. "King, isn't it? The private detective? I'd heard you'd retired." She shrugged. "Or died. I wasn't really listening."

She spoke rapidly, like all this was an unwelcome formality to be rattled through as quickly as possible. It made Hoon think of the voice he'd heard at the end of adverts for prescription drugs on radio stations over here. Any minute now, she'd gloss over a warning about how he might develop diabetes and erectile dysfunction, and have all his hair fall out.

In the distance, over her shoulder, Hoon saw a trail of dust rising into the sky. If he strained his hearing, he could just make out the sound of approaching engines.

He wanted to glance over at Miles to gauge how relieved he looked, but didn't dare, in case it gave the game away.

"You were at my casino last night. Weren't you? That was you, yes?" Scarlett asked, her focus firmly back on Hoon. "I hear Victor's dead."

"Very fucking much so," Hoon confirmed.

She searched his face, though Hoon couldn't even guess what she was hoping to see there. "Shame. He was useful. Not irreplaceable, of course. Very few people truly are. Why were you there?"

The question was tacked on so close to the statement before it that Hoon missed it. Fortunately, another one came around a moment later.

"Hmm? What were you looking for? Who sent you?" She tilted her head left and right as she spoke, like she was a dog trying to understand human language. "Who are you? What... Who sent you?"

"I'm the wrath of fucking God, sweetheart," Hoon told her.

"Ha." Scarlett looked him up and down again, then glanced to the sky. "He is slipping, isn't He? If you're the best He has."

She turned away and saw the approaching line of vehicles. The heat haze from the sand made them wobble, but they were close enough now to make out four, possibly five vehicles.

"Should we kill them?" asked one of the grunts. "Before the Mexicans get here?"

Scarlett's perfectly straight teeth chewed on a ruby red lip as she considered her options.

She was about to answer when Miles cleared his throat and

stepped forward. "I'd say shoot both of them," he began, in his borrowed accent. "But we should find out what they know. Maybe it's nothing, but maybe they know more than we think. This could be our only chance to figure that out."

He shot both captives a look of contempt. If Hoon hadn't known better, he'd have sworn it was genuine.

"Then, if they don't know shit, or if we think they've told us everything, we shoot them and leave them to be eaten by the vultures."

"Bit fucking harsh," Hoon muttered.

Scarlett's eyes narrowed. She pointed to one of the gunmen, then brought her hand to her mouth like she was having second thoughts.

"Fine. But gag them. I don't want them interrupting. If they do, just, I don't know, shoot them."

She walked over to Miles, while a couple of rags were tied roughly across Hoon and Alvin's mouths, tight enough to silence them both. They exchanged glances, but whatever each was trying to communicate was lost on the other.

"Is everything ready?" Scarlett asked.

Miles nodded. "Should be."

"And your cartel contacts. They can be trusted?"

"Hundred percent," Miles confirmed. "But, uh, maybe let me do the talking. At least to begin with."

Scarlett didn't look happy about this, but relented with a nod.

"If this all goes smoothly, you're going to be an extremely wealthy man."

She placed a hand on his chest and slid it inside his jacket, her fingers trailing up and down his shirt.

Miles tried very hard not to swallow. "I'm looking forward to that," he said, then he adjusted his cravat, ran a hand through his hair, and stepped away from her, like he was preparing to meet the approaching vehicles.

"Guns away, but be ready," Scarlett told her men. "And,

again, if either of those two utters so much as a sound, shoot them both."

"What about the Mexicans?" one of the grunts asked. "Won't that freak them out?"

Scarlett's laugh was a nasal, high-pitched thing. "Come on. This is the cartel we're talking about. Knowing them, they'll get a real kick out of it!"

A nervous silence fell as five tank-like SUVs pulled up a short distance away from where Miles and Scarlett stood.

Tyres crunched on loose gravel. Doors opened. Twenty men emerged, and Hoon could practically hear Scarlett's goons bristling with discomfort.

They were mostly dressed in dark colours—blacks, navy blues, and dark greens—with a few wearing heavy leather jackets, despite the blazing sun.

Several of them—presumably the less deranged—wore plain T-shirts stretched over muscular frames, or shirts with the sleeves rolled up, revealing their tattooed forearms.

They were all wearing sunglasses with polished mirror lenses, which helped make them look even more intimidating.

Their skin was weathered by both sun exposure and their violent pasts, many of them sporting scars old and new. They all had facial hair, and while it was in near uniform shades of black and dark brown, it was trimmed into a variety of shapes and styles.

They were all armed, of course, with handguns holstered at their hips or tucked into the waistbands of their jeans. A few of them had assault rifles slung over their shoulders, and they carried themselves with a sense of barely restrained aggression, like coiled snakes ready to strike at the slightest provocation.

Miles didn't appear to be put off by any of this, however. Instead, he strode confidently up to them, and offered a hand to their leader.

He was the smallest and oldest of the group, with a bit of a paunch and a brighter coloured shirt than his companions. He regarded Miles's outstretched hand like it was some strange alien object.

"Uh, good timing," Miles said, letting his arm fall back by his side. He turned and pointed to the trucks. "The drugs are in there." He folded his arms and smiled triumphantly. "You've caught them red handed!"

Behind his gag, Hoon attempted to mutter a, "For fuck sake," but the fabric was too tight across his mouth.

All he could do was watch, helplessly, as Miles's carefully laid plan went to shite.

"Who the fuck is this?" asked the cartel leader, who was very clearly not, by any stretch of the imagination, an undercover DEA agent.

Scarlett smiled. Under certain lighting conditions, it might've been a nice smile.

These were not it.

"Sorry, *Viper*," she said. "Turns out your contact in the Drug Enforcement Agency is also *my* contact in the Drug Enforcement Agency. Bit awkward. But, needless to say, they won't be coming."

She pointed past him to the small army of cartel men.

"These? I arranged this. I thought about killing you when I found out, but then thought it'd be funnier to see your face." She grinned. "And I was right! It's hysterical. I don't think I've ever seen anyone look quite so shocked!"

Her hand moved like a striking cobra. Hoon didn't even have time to move when he saw the gun. When he heard the bang. When he saw the blood.

Miles collapsed, howling in pain, a ragged hole where a fully intact left shin had been just a moment before.

The cartel men all whipped out their guns. Scarlett's grunts did the same, though they were hopelessly outnumbered.

"Easy, boys, easy!" Scarlett cried, holding her gun up in the air, the finger well clear of the trigger. "No need for a gunfight. This man is my gift to you," she said, smiling at the cartel boss who was now being shielded by two younger, larger men. "His name is Miles Crabtree. He's with the British Intelligence service. Sort of. He's not really meant to be here, and nobody actually knows where he is."

She shrugged, and slowly tucked her gun back into the waist-band of her dark red trousers.

"I thought it might be fun for you to play with him. Given that he was hoping to sell us all out to the DEA."

That wasn't quite true, of course. Miles had no interest in the cartel. He hadn't expected them to be there.

Still, that didn't stop half a dozen pairs of sunglasses turning in his direction, and a dozen bushy eyebrows twitching in contempt.

The cartel boss dismissed his two bodyguards with a jerk of his head. They stepped apart, then regrouped behind him.

On both sides, weapons were very slowly, very carefully pointed towards the ground.

"You have the drugs?"

"We do indeed," Scarlett confirmed. She turned and gestured to the trucks. "And, there are plenty more where this came from."

She turned back to the old man, all smiles and positivity.

"In fact, we'd be delighted to—"

She stopped talking when the old man toppled backwards. His two guards tried their best to catch him, but they'd been so busy scowling at the men standing across from them that they hadn't seen him start to fall.

They both looked down at him. At his open eyes. At his shocked expression. At the bloody hole just off centre of his forehead.

Had they possessed super hearing, they might just have made out a distant cry of, "Bullseye!" in a thick Liverpudlian accent.

The cartel men looked at Scarlett's grunts.
Scarlett's grunts looked at the cartel men.
"Mmmf 'uck," Hoon mumbled beneath his gag.
And then, the world erupted into gunfire.

CHAPTER FORTY-THREE

HOON THREW himself to the ground next to Miles, while Alvin high-tailed it into cover behind one of the trucks. The air was thick with smoke and flying lead. Voices cried out, and were silenced in sprays of warm blood and cold vengeance.

Hoon angled himself so that his hands were next to Miles, and the MI5 man released his grip on his injured leg long enough to hurriedly untie the ropes.

Tearing off his gag, Hoon grabbed Miles under the arms and pulled him towards the truck that Alvin had taken cover behind. Bullets whistled past them, shattering the windows of the SUVs, and filling the air with the high-pitched wailing of their alarms.

"Grab them fucking guns!" Hoon hissed, as he dragged Miles past the downed corpses of two of Scarlett's men.

Crabtree scrambled for the handguns, snatching them up just as Hoon hauled him around the side of the truck.

"She shot me! The bitch shot me!" he yelped, once they were out of the firing line.

Hoon dropped him, then quickly untied Alvin's hands, freeing the P.I. to remove his own gag.

"I would've fucking shot you myself, if I'd had the chance,"

Hoon said, ducking low and peering around the edge of the truck. "I mean, how the fuck did you think they were DEA? Did you even fucking look at them?"

"I just thought they were really good at being undercover!" Miles protested.

Hoon took both guns from him, and handed one to Alvin.

"Unlike you, you mean?" Hoon spat. He shook his head and flared his nostrils. "The fucking Viper. Why no' just fucking call yourself Sneaky McPolis and be done with it?"

"I was undercover!" Miles protested.

"What as, a fucking Bond villain? And no' one of the fucking good ones, either. A guy that Roger Moore kills in the opening credits, then fucks his girlfriend on a boat."

Bullets slammed into the side of the truck, making Hoon pull back.

"Maybe we can save this for another time?" Alvin suggested.

He ejected the clip from his Sig Sauer, and counted the bullets. "Eight shots. You?"

"Nine," Hoon said, slamming his magazine back into place.

"Want to swap?" Alvin asked.

"Do I fuck," Hoon replied.

Down on the ground, Miles hissed with pain as he dragged himself into a sitting position. "The one at the back," he said, pointing to the furthest away truck. "There's weapons in there. They brought them in case it all went to shit."

"Fucking hell, and they've no' gone for them yet?" Hoon asked. A few feet away, one of Scarlett's men landed, choking and gargling, on the ground. "Are they expecting it to get fucking worse than this, like?"

"We could try and make a run over there," Alvin suggested, though he didn't sound keen on the idea. "Be out in the open for longer than I'd like."

"I'll go," Hoon said. "Cover me and keep an eye on the fucking Viper here. I'll be..."

He realised that something had changed. Something that either bode very well, or very badly.

The shooting had stopped.

It was entirely possible, he thought, that everyone was dead. That would work out nicely.

But then, Scarlett's voice rang out, ruining everything.

"*Thank* you!" she hollered. "Now, as I was trying to say, that wasn't us. We didn't shoot. It was *them*."

The way she spat that last word told Hoon there was a bitter look and some first class angry pointing going on.

"So, before we go ahead and just all kill each other for no reason, how about we put our heads together, and find the ones who are *actually* responsible?"

Hoon and Alvin both held their breath. Some disagreement would be lovely. A bit of angry shouting and some more shooting would go down a treat.

But, of course, it wasn't to be.

"OK. Let's do it," a gruff, Spanish accent replied. "Let's find those pieces of shit, and chainsaw their fucking balls off."

IRIS'S first shot with the sniper rifle had gone wide of the target. The next shot had missed, also. And the one after that.

The fourth had been a direct hit, albeit not on the person he was actually aiming at. Still, it had done the job, and he'd watched Hoon and Alvin drag some other fella out of the firing line.

After that, he'd gone through every bullet he had trying to hit someone else, but they'd all been moving around, which didn't really seem fair.

Out of ammo, he'd taken off down the hill, running as fast as he could to go help Boggle. He'd just arrived by one of the trucks when all the shooting had stopped, and all the remaining men had fanned out, guns raised, clearly on the hunt.

Iris had clambered into the back of the truck, where he now lay flat on the floor, wedged in behind a wooden crate, covered by a blanket of shadow.

He could hear footsteps crunching away outside, and the rattling of a rifle shifting in a grip. Holding his breath, he waited, listening as the heavy curtains at the back of the truck were pulled open, feeling the floor shifting just a fraction beneath him as someone climbed aboard.

Feet shuffled. A man muttered something in a language Iris didn't understand.

And then, the floor shifted again, and a pair of feet *thacked* down onto the gravel, then continued their search.

Iris exhaled, but didn't move. Not yet. Not until he was sure they were gone.

As he lay there, his eye began to adjust to the dark.

Something on the box beside him caught his attention.

A notice.

A warning sign.

'Danger,' it read. 'Explosives.'

"Well, well," Iris whispered. He ran a hand across the side of the crate. There was something almost sensual about it. "What do we have here?"

HOON AND ALVIN sat with their backs to the rear of the truck, their guns ready. Alvin's rattled in his grip. His tongue flitted anxiously across his dry lips.

"Oh, man," he whispered. "My hands are shaking."

Hoon looked across at him. "And your knees are weak?"

Alvin chuckled drily, recognising the lyric.

"Something like that, yeah."

Hoon lowered his head to look under the truck. The number of pairs of feet he could see gave him cause for concern.

"Right, listen, I need to fucking say something," he whispered. "I was wrong. What I said. I had no fucking business flying off the handle like that. You fucking be whoever you fucking want to be. Don't let a miserable prick like me have a fucking say in it."

Alvin shook his head. "You were right."

"Was I fuck." Hoon nodded at the older man's trembling hands. "This isn't you. No' really. The real you's the guy who swooped in and saved me from having my fucking nuts cut off. The real you's a fucking karate kicking, no-shit taking, bona fide rock and roll fucking legend, and anyone who thinks otherwise needs their fucking head examined."

The footsteps were getting closer. Voices muttered in both Spanish and English.

"If we're about to be fucking shot to ribbons here, and it looks very much like that's the fucking case, then I say we go out in fucking style," Hoon said. He tapped the barrel of his gun to his forehead in salute. "Long live the King."

Alvin looked back at him, the sunlight reflecting off his purple shades.

Slowly, like it was waking from some long hibernation, his top lip curled upwards into a sneer.

"Long live the fucking King!" he replied.

And then, he was up. He was moving.

Hoon could've sworn that he heard it as the P.I. launched himself to his feet. The music.

The opening chords of *The Wonder of You*. The middle-eight of *Suspicious Minds*. The final, joyous chorus of *Viva, Las Vegas*. Every fucking chord. Every glorious note.

He leaped up and went right as Alvin went left. They both brought up their guns and fired, spilling blood and brains onto the sand.

They ran, weapons spitting lead and fire. Cartel and Loop grunts dropping like flies.

"Two o'clock!" Hoon barked, and Alvin spun, already squeezing the trigger before he'd fully processed the warning.

A moustachioed man in a muscle T-shirt was thrown backwards, his life spurting from his chest as a gush of wet crimson.

There were maybe ten of them left, but the ferocity of the surprise attack had scattered them, sending them running for cover.

Hoon put a bullet between the shoulder blades of a man in a black suit. Another in the crotch of a pair of stonewashed jeans.

Eight left. Thereabouts.

Alvin emptied the rest of a clip at a running cartel man. The bullets punched a line of holes in the metal of one of the SUVs, until the last one found a fleshier target.

He dropped the gun, wrenched one from the hand of one of the dead men, and was about to open fire again when Scarlett shrieked out a warning.

"That is *enough!*" She emerged from behind the truck holding Miles in front of her, her gun jammed against the side of his head as he hobbled along on his injured leg. "Lower the guns. Now. Or, I swear to God I will paint every inch of you both with his fucking brains!"

CHAPTER FORTY-FOUR

HOON AND ALVIN both lowered their weapons, but neither man could quite bring themselves to drop them. Dropping them was surrender.

Dropping them was suicide.

There was only one chance left now, he knew. Over here, they called it a Hail Mary. Back home, he'd say he was on a hiding to nothing.

Either way, it was a long shot.

"I'd try and call your fucking bluff, love," Hoon said. "But I've got no doubt you're telling the truth. You'd kill him in a fucking heartbeat, wouldn't you?"

"You'd better believe it," Scarlett said, still tucked behind Miles's back. "So, put the guns down. Now."

Hoon looked around him at the remaining cartel men. They outnumbered Scarlett and her guys two to one. Or, six to three, to be more precise.

"She fucking will, too. She's a cold-blooded bastard, this one," Hoon said. He nodded to the closest truck. "Your fucking drugs there? Totally fucking toxic. Lethal. Hundred percent fatality rate."

This, apparently, was news to Miles. "What?!" he whimpered.

"He's lying," Scarlett said.

"Nope. Am I fuck," Hoon said. "It's all in the lab notes. Which, hold on..." He slowly raised a hand and very deliberately opened a Velcro pocket on the front of his camo jacket, revealing a folded bundle of paper. "I just so happen to have brought with me."

"Shut up. He's lying. Don't listen to him!" Scarlett hissed. "This is a trick."

Hoon pulled the paperwork from his pocket and held it out to the closest of the Mexicans. With a nod of encouragement from one of his compatriots, the cartel man took the notes, unfolded them, and squinted at the top page through his mirrored shades.

"The writing's fucking tiny," Hoon said. "Don't fucking ask me why, it's no' like they can't afford another few sheets of paper. But, the gist of it is, this Elysium shite is poison. They might've wrapped it up like a fucking present, but anyone who takes that stuff... Well, let's just say, I've seen what happens to them, and it's no' fucking pretty."

"You're lying!" Scarlett shrieked.

"He ain't," Alvin said, and he was back in full-blown Memphis drawl mode. "Saw it with my own two eyes. Damn stuff turns people into zombies. Kills 'em dead. We can even send you video, shows you the whole thing."

"You know my theory?" Hoon said. "About why she's fucking doing it?"

"I'm all ears, daddy-o," Alvin said.

And, from the looks on their faces, the cartel men were, too.

Hoon pointed at Scarlett, still hiding behind her human shield. Her two remaining henchmen still had their guns trained on Hoon and Alvin, but were shuffling away from their boss, like they could sense a turning of the tide.

To everyone's surprise, Scarlett burst out with an explanation before Hoon could voice his theory.

"OK, fine!" she cried. "You know how many immigrants come swarming across the border every day? Every week? Every year? Millions. *Literal millions* of them! Pushing in, taking over, fucking the place up for the rest of us!"

Hoon decided it was best not to reply. There was no need to. He'd clearly touched a nerve that had triggered some self-destruct sequence she'd programmed into herself.

He wondered, though, when she was was going to realise that she'd started the countdown.

"Oh, of course, people will say it's racist, but is it racist not to want crime rates to keep going through the roof? Is it racist to want to put our own people first?"

"Not necessarily," Hoon said, throwing her another coil of rope.

"No! Exactly!" Scarlett gestured out into the desert with her gun. "We were supposed to build a wall. We were meant to keep them out. But, oh no. Once again, it was all just politicians and their empty promises saying whatever they could to win votes.

"Well, *I'm* building a wall. No bricks. No barbed wire. No empty promises."

"Just, what? Genocide?" Hoon asked.

"Ha! If only!" Scarlett replied, and her eyes blazed with some dark form of madness. "But, no. Not quite. Not all the way. Just a thinning of the herd. That's all. It's not perfect, but it's enough. It's a start."

"Aye, very good," Hoon said. He shook his head. "But, I'm not buying it."

"I beg your pardon?"

"Good doggy, though. Protecting the hand that feeds you, and all that. But, your lot? You don't give a fuck about immigration. That's just more people to fucking sell to. And, I mean, it's no' like the fucking cartel's going to exclusively sell to people south of the fucking border, is it? They punt it up here. So, your plan makes no fucking sense."

"Shut up," Scarlett warned.

Hoon shrugged. "It's impressive the fucking loyalty you have to your bosses, stitching yourself up like this. Trying to take the fall as a random fucking nutter, but that's no' the truth, is it, Scarlett?" he asked. "See, I know you fuckers. I know you well enough to know that you're all about the bigger fucking picture. There is no value in killing off your customers."

He pointed to the remaining cartel men, who were all listening intently.

"But there's a lot of fucking value in killing off *their* customers, especially if you can make it look like it's their gear that's doing it," Hoon continued. "Suddenly, the cartel's a fucking dodgy source, and there's a big fucking gap opened up in the market. It's not a genocide you're doing, it's a fucking expansion plan."

He nodded over at the cartel men. The one who'd been holding the notes had now folded them up and put them in his jacket pocket. "Only problem is, they all now know about it, and I'm going to go out on a fucking limb and say that they don't look happy."

Scarlett seethed, her hand trembling, bumping the gun against Miles's temple over and over again. "You think you're smart?" she asked.

"Pretty much, aye," Hoon confirmed.

The gun was pointed in his direction. "Let's see if you're smart enough to—"

An exploding truck stopped her from going any further. It exploded with enough force to launch the whole thing a clear five or six feet in the air, and sent a red and black mushroom cloud billowing up towards the sky.

Miles instinctively ducked, which conveniently left Scarlett standing open and exposed.

Alvin and Hoon both raised their guns and fired at almost exactly the same time. Scarlett's head snapped back and she fell, arms flailing limply, until she hit the ground.

By the time she had fallen, both her remaining men were on the way down, too, riddled with bullets fired by six angry Mexican men with a righteous sense of betrayal.

"Right, whoa, whoa, whoa!" Hoon said, dropping his gun and holding his hands up.

Alvin, against his better judgement, did the same. The cartel men's weapons remained trained on them, but nobody had opened fire. Not yet, anyway.

"No need to shoot us, we were on your fucking side," Hoon reminded them. "We came here to fucking warn you about the drugs, and what that milk bottle of fucking Mad Cow Disease was planning. We've just fucking saved millions of lives between us. We should be fucking high-fiving and bumping chests. Getting oiled up and playing volleyball. No' pointing guns at each other."

"When he's right, he's right," Alvin said. "A lot of bad shit went down here today, and there ain't no good in making it worse. You want to get revenge? This little lady was only the tip of the iceberg. She's got a whole organisation she's part of."

Eyes narrowed and guns pointed as he unzipped his camo jacket to reveal a sequinned white and gold jumpsuit below. He produced a business card from the inside pocket, and presented it to the closest of the Mexicans.

"Y'all want help tracking them down, and getting your own back? Just go ahead and give the King a call."

The cartel men swapped looks among themselves. Nods were exchanged. Complaints were offered, then shut down.

One by one, they lowered their weapons. Two of them picked up the body of the old man who'd been first to die, and laid him in the back of one of their cars.

Then, leaving the rest behind, they piled into a couple of

vehicles, spun their tyres, and went racing back in the direction of the border.

Hoon and Alvin both exhaled. Down on the ground, Miles quietly vomited, then looked up at the other men.

"It's poison?"

"Aye. Or something. Fucking awful stuff, anyway," Hoon said. "You didn't know?"

"No! I had no idea! I thought it was just a drug deal!"

Alvin smirked. "Some undercover agent you are, son."

"Bloody hell," Miles said, as Hoon hoisted him to his feet. "I don't know if it's just the blood loss, but your pal *really* reminds me of Elvis."

"Fuck me," Hoon said, looking the P.I. up and down. "Now you fucking mention it, he actually sort of does."

"Alright, Boggle!" Iris emerged from behind one of the abandoned cars, stripped to the waist, and waving frantically like he was sending his children away on a train during wartime. "Did you see that truck blowing up?"

"I'd have been hard pressed to fucking miss it," Hoon said.

Iris grinned and pointed to himself. "That was me!"

"No fucking kidding?" Hoon shouted back. "I'd never have guessed."

Alvin chuckled and gave Hoon a slap on the back. It was quite a nice moment of levity, despite the almost twenty fresh corpses lying around the place with holes where many of their vital organs were meant to be.

Birds were circling overhead, word of the all-you-can-peck buffet clearly already starting to spread.

"Well, I guess all's well that ends well," Alvin drawled. "We beat the bad guys, rescued your friend, saved the lives of a whole heapa folks, and even rekindled something deep in this old heart of mine." He drew in a breath and nodded. "As days go, it ain't too bad."

"Aye. I've had worse," Hoon admitted. "But, we're no' quite done yet."

He, Alvin, and Miles all looked over at the remaining trucks.

"Iris," Hoon said.

"Yeah, Boggle?"

"I don't suppose you've got any of them explosives left?"

THE HELICOPTERS CAME in low and fast, rotor blades sending dust clouds spiralling into the air, and blowing away some of the smoke from the burning trucks.

Hoon and Alvin reached for their guns, but Miles intervened, urging them to keep them lowered.

"Wait, wait, I think this lot might be for me," he said.

All four men watched as the choppers landed, and six men in suits climbed out. They walked over to Hoon's group, all but one of them lowering their heads like they were worried the blades might decapitate them.

"Oh, bollocks," Miles muttered, then he plastered on a smile as the only man who wasn't ducking made a beeline straight for him. "Agent Fotheringham! I was going to call you."

"I'm sure you were, Agent Crabtree," Fotheringham said. He was wearing mirrored sunglasses, but his glare almost burned clean through them.

He left it lingering on Miles for a while, before turning it on Hoon, where it had considerably less effect.

"The fuck are you meant to be?" Hoon asked.

Fotheringham let out a mirthless little laugh. "I see you and your sister have plenty in common, then," he said.

"You're the spooky wee bastard!" Hoon realised. "She mentioned you on the phone. I don't think she likes you. In fact, I fucking know she doesn't."

"Because she doesn't like anyone," Iris added.

Hoon grimaced. "I mean, true. Aye." He stabbed a finger against Fotheringham's chest. "But she *really* fucking doesn't like you."

The agent's smile was as joyless as his laugh. "I get that a lot." He turned his attention to the scattering of corpses on the ground around them. "Someone's been busy, I see."

"Here, Boggle," Iris said, but Hoon scowled him into silence.

"I can explain," Miles said, even though he wasn't *entirely* sure that was true. He could have a pretty good stab at it, he thought, but might have to defer to Hoon for some of the finer details.

Fotheringham pinned him in place with another look. It was a look that said he would absolutely be called on to explain, but in a more formal setting, and at a later date.

"Are you here to fucking arrest us, or something?" Hoon asked.

"Boggle!"

"No' now, Iris!"

"I don't much recommend trying to take us downtown, son," Alvin said, squaring up to the agents. "I can't see that working out well for any of you folks."

Fotheringham frowned behind his sunglasses, gave Alvin a cursory look, then shook his head. "What an odd man. But, no. We're not here to 'arrest' anyone. We merely shared your concern for the whereabouts of Agent Crabtree. I had thought that we could pool our resources."

He looked around at all the dead bodies, then turned back to Hoon.

"But, I can see we made something of a wasted trip." He bit down on his bottom lip and sucked air in through his teeth, then nodded. "So, I suppose the best thing we can do is all just pretend that none of us were here, and that none of this happened, and hope the US government allows themselves to believe that."

"Boggle!"

Hoon sighed. "Fuck sake. What is it, Iris?"

Iris pointed to the burning trucks just thirty or so feet behind them. "Is that stuff not poisonous?"

Hoon frowned, then his eyes shot open to their full, impressive stretch.

"Fuck, so it is!" he cried. Then, burying his nose and mouth in the crook of his arm, he grabbed hold of Miles, and they all high-tailed it to the waiting choppers.

Together.

CHAPTER FORTY-FIVE

THE BELLAGIO FOUNTAINS, Alvin informed them, spanned over a thousand feet, and featured over one thousand, two hundred jets that could shoot water up to four hundred and sixty feet in the air.

It cost over seventy-five million dollars to build, had a yearly maintenance bill of five million, and the water show was accompanied by a range of songs including 'Time to Say Goodbye' by Andrea Bocelli, and 'My Heart Will Go On' by Celine Dion.

This evening, though, the musical backing track was something far more appropriate.

"Viva Las Vegas, baby!" Alvin hollered, as the Elvis track kicked into high gear, and the water soared towards the Heavens. "What do you think, Mr Hoon? Quite a show, huh?"

Hoon shrugged. "No' really my cup of tea. Just a load of fucking water being pissed around. Give me a couple of beers and I can do that myself."

Alvin laughed and patted him on the back, then returned to watching and singing along with the music. Behind it, Fourth of July fireworks exploded against the sky, painting the already colourful Vegas night in a whole new host of vibrant shades.

The P.I. wasn't the only one enjoying the spectacle. Sarah stood by the fence, gripping the metal bars, gazing in wonder at how the light played off the jumping jets of water. Her eyes sparkled with it, her whole face alive with the wonder of it.

Maybe it wasn't *that* bad, Hoon thought. As fountains went.

When it was over, and the throngs of tourists had started to drift away, Hoon led the others over to where Miles and Iris sat on a low wall that bordered the Bellagio property.

Miles's leg had been patched up, but even with his crutches, he didn't fancy standing to watch the show. Iris had hung back because he didn't want to get trapped in the middle of a crowd, and also because he didn't trust water that could dance.

"There you go. You saw it," Hoon told Sarah. "Was it as impressive as you thought?"

"Yes!" Sarah gushed, then she wrinkled her nose up. "Sort of. A bit. I mean, it was cool! Thanks for taking me! It's just..." She looked around them, at the hordes of half-drunk revellers, and the lights of the Las Vegas Strip.

"Aye. I know what you mean," Hoon agreed. He danced around the subject for a moment, then went for it. "So, are you...? You and your mum, I mean?"

Sarah nodded. "I think so. For a while. Just to see."

"Good. That's great," Hoon said.

"Best damn news I heard all day," Alvin agreed.

"You can come and visit me," Sarah told them. "Both of you. Anytime."

"You never know," Alvin said. "I might just take you up on that someday. But for now, the King's gotta hit the road. There's a whole lotta people out there with a whole lotta problems. I think maybe I'd like to try doing a thing or two to help with that again."

He leaned closer, lowered his voice, and winked. There was a swagger to all of it.

"And besides, I got me a date with a Duchess!"

"Christ. Good luck with that. Just don't let her fucking drive."

Hoon offered his hand for the other man to shake.

"And, listen, if you ever happen to find yourself in Scotland—"

Alvin hugged him. A proper, full-on, arms-locked, bear hug that lifted Hoon clean off the ground.

"Thank you," the P.I. whispered. "Thankyouverymuch."

He set Hoon back down again, patted him on the shoulder, then turned and strode off like he owned the whole damn city.

He turned just before he could be swallowed by the crowd, and flashed them a big, toothy grin.

"Ladies and gentlemen," he announced. "Elvis has left the building."

And with the dipping of a quiff, and a spin on a cuban heel, he was gone.

"I, uh, I'd better go, too," Sarah said. She smiled, but there was a sadness there. Worry, too.

"It'll be fine," Hoon said. "And if it isn't, you fucking phone me, alright? You phone me, and I'll sort it. Assuming they let me back in the fucking country. Which, you know, is fifty-fifty."

Sarah laughed at that. Then, she leaned in, kissed him on the cheek, and did the same to Iris. She smiled a quick goodbye at Miles, then turned and walked away as quickly as she could, not once daring to look back.

Iris sidled up to Hoon as they watched Sarah leaving, wiping at her eyes with the back of a hand.

"Waifs and strays, Boggle. Waifs and strays."

Hoon didn't have the energy to argue.

Or, more likely, didn't have an argument to offer.

"I'll be glad to see the fucking back of this country," he said, turning away as Sarah was lost to the crowd.

"Oh, I don't know," Miles said. He looked along the Strip, just as more fireworks burst in the air, and took in the lights and the spectacle of it all. "It's got its moments."

He reached into his pocket and took out a small, thin black book with gold embossing on the cover.

"Here, Iris. I managed to sort this for you."

Iris eyed the offer item warily. "What is it?"

"It's a passport," Miles said. "It'll get you home."

"A passport?" Iris swallowed. "Like, an ID? With a photo, and that?"

Miles smiled. "Uh, well, yes. That's sort of the idea. Bob told me how you'd got into the country, and well, I thought it'd be safer if you— Where's he going?"

He and Hoon both watched as Iris jumped the fence of the Bellagio and went running into the water, putting as much distance between himself and the passport as possible.

"Best just to let him make his own way back," Hoon said. "He'll turn up sooner or fucking later."

Miles returned the passport to his pocket. "You've got interesting friends, Bob," he said.

Hoon gave this some thought.

"Aye," he conceded. "You can fucking say that again."

Miles laughed. He checked his watch. "Pub?"

Hoon held out a hand to help the MI5 man up. "D'you know?" he said. "I thought you were never going to fucking ask."

JOIN THE JD KIRK VIP CLUB

Want access to an exclusive image gallery showing locations from the books? Join the free JD Kirk VIP Club today, and as well as the photo gallery you'll get regular emails containing free short stories, members-only video content, and all the latest news about the world of DCI Jack Logan.

JDKirk.com/VIP

(Did we mention that it's free...?)

HAVE YOU READ...?

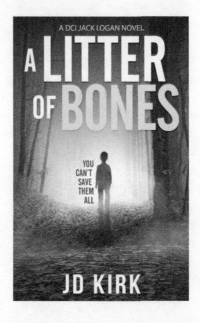

Discover Hoon's previous life in the multi-million selling DCI Jack Logan series.

Made in the USA
Las Vegas, NV
09 July 2024

92067900R00225